REVELATION

Also by Brad Mathews

The Venom Storm
The Satyr of Fulton Manor
Tomb of the Phoenix

Era Sinistra Trilogy
Era Sinistra
Era Sinistra-The Shadow
Era Sinistra-Skyglow

Decay
The Girl from South Track
Revelation Trilogy
Revelation (Book 1)
Reflection (Book 2)

REVELATION

Book 1

BRAD MATHEWS

Fear Not...

Unity Star Books

Published by Unity Star Books

ISBN: 978-1-962577-10-6 (Softcover)

ISBN: 978-1-088162-59-0 (Hardcover)

Re-release Second Edition 2024

For Elena, Makaiah, and Kristy

Courage is knowing what not to fear.

Plato

1

Nocturnal Sun

The rain is blurring my vision, icy shards of pain ripping through my abdomen and shredding the essence of my lone existence. I flail in the dark, besieged by visions of flaming arrows piercing the sky. Agony is a sweet, carnal feeling. I thrive on it, even as it poisons me. Thick black smoke appears over the western horizon to signal darker times. Huge wings beat in the distance, whipping in the strong wind like large canvas sails on a ship, followed by screams that range from terror to bloodthirsty zeal.

When the monsters begin to march, their roars grow darker, even as the smoke thickens and billows overhead like a cloud of volcanic ash. One hellacious squeal signals the beginning of the attack, a volley of arrows loosed. Hundreds perish; bodies are mown down by the arrows, some flaming and some impregnated with snake venom. The villagers cannot withstand the assault, so they retreat into their homes.

Then it truly begins. Ignited by torches and the advancing beasts, the houses burst into flames and the citizens flee in panic. Yet they are not alone in the fight.

Six warriors have assembled to assist in the battle. They carefully slice the flaming arrows in half as they fly, successfully evade the barrage of projectiles, and wield sleek swords to defend the terrified villagers.

The moonlight peeks from behind the tide of black smoke, offering a false sense of peace in the midst of panic. But the townspeople are being slain en masse, and even the six warriors cannot escape.

One by one they fall, until only one woman remains standing. The ravaging monsters howl at her, belch fire, and charge, while a thousand arrows arc towards her.

Flames have stained the landscape in hues of orange and red, accompanied by the scent of angry smoke. I inhale it and scream when an arrow punctures my calf. Somehow I am the woman warrior, and I'm going to lose.

I fall painfully to the scarred, blackened earth when a poisoned arrow pierces my chest. My agony makes the stars flicker like erratic supernovae, and the mud flows like lava over the ruined hellscape. The cloud of oil-black smoke closes in to swallow me whole.

The villagers succumb to defeat, and before I can survey the surrounding ruins, the scene swirls before me like the dark insides of a hurricane. In the eye of the storm, I vanish. A mere second later, I sit bolt upright in bed, sweating profusely and gasping.

What the hell kind of nightmare was that, and how did it seem so real? My mind trembles hopelessly as I attempt to make sense of it all. How long was I asleep? And who was that woman?

My phone pulses to remind me of unread messages. The act of clumsily reaching for it drains away some of my agony. I lie down, using my elbow to prop up my abdomen, dig into my messages, and browse through social media between bouts of rubbing my eyes and picking the little crusty bits from their corners.

By the time I've climbed into the shower, the images from my nightmare have completely dissolved, leaving behind only the pain and negative emotions as vestiges of the horror I witnessed.

Today doesn't promise to be a good day—in less than six months, I have grown weary of the tasks in my job description. My mind is filled with regret that after years of hard work I have still not achieved something more enjoyable than delivering plans and cleaning up the foreman's mess.

If only I could focus on what energizes me, I could ice away the shame, but as the months wear on, it becomes more and more difficult. I once had ambitions of making it in the construction industry, but time has stretched my ideas into little more than amorphous shapes in a dark void.

Though my plans have never been particularly well-conceived, I knew the basic steps by heart: I would spend six months in an apprenticeship, taking measurements, fetching tools, and gradually work my way up to more rewarding tasks. After six months I would be welding, drilling, and wrapping, and in six more months, the foreman would show me how to use the Total Station, and I'd be shooting points for slab penetrations. I would be so good at it that they would have to promote me to journeyman, and in another year, I would be the one calling the shots on a project of my own.

After two years of this, I would graduate to the office, sitting in a high-backed leather chair and punching data into astonishingly well-crafted charts, and creating schedules for the construction teams as the project manager feeds me the data sheets for procurement, which I would diligently file and then place the orders for the field workers.

A few years of that, I figured, would lead me to the top of the food chain: the project manager. I would be the one pushing papers, directing coordinators, running meetings, poring over specifications, and finding data on available supplies.

It would be the greatest career story ever written, if I could only get out of my own way and stop sabotaging myself. But life teaches different lessons. I'm still alone, living day-to-day in an apartment I can scarcely afford. Relief comes with each paycheck, but it is short-lived, often not lasting long enough to polish off the most delicious burger in the greater Philadelphia area before panic sets in again.

As if the years are working against me faster than usual, women are beginning to look younger, more voluptuous, and entirely unattainable. If only they could get to know the real me, I imagine, they would reach a point of desire they could not ignore.

And yet they still ignore me. I'm out of practice, I'm getting older, and the bills are piling up. Damnit if life must be this cruel. Had I known, I would never have volunteered to face it.

The very last message is from my friend Joaquin, a guy I met and hated in high school. He stands about five-foot-eight, which is shorter than me, but he can bench press more than I can and run faster. Yet neither of us is particularly active; in his time off he plays video games, creates elaborate characters, and dreams up impossible storylines. Our other friend, Kel, whom we hang out with once a month or so, dwells even deeper inside of the realm of fantasy. He is known to organize live-action roleplaying games from time to time, by donning a ridiculous costume and arranging battle sequences written by guys like Quin. He's good at it, and the biggest nerd I've ever known. The punk even has a girlfriend who carefully observes his LARPing parties to make sure everything goes according to plan.

Quin isn't totally irredeemable, though; he mostly dedicates his time to work and videogames, but every weekend he finds time for football and socializing over a beer if he's up for it. He works in an investment office, doing what he describes as normal office duties. I can imagine him sending faxes, answering phones, typing out official-sounding emails, and informing customers that their premiums are past due. He makes good money at it because he is smarter and better educated than I am.

I finish up my morning by dressing for work: a pair of carpenter jeans and a T-shirt usually suffice. For instances when I need to go inside the fence, I keep my hard hat, personal protective equipment, and reflective yellow vest in a small compartment in the job trailer. If I'm lucky, the snowfall forecast for today will not yet have begun to pile up. I peer out the window in dismay when I see frost covering all the car windows.

It is more than an hour before dawn as far as I can tell, yet the night is filled with an almost blinding blue light. If I wanted to go outside and read a book, I figure I could do it without the aid of artificial light.

Is there something special about the lunar cycle today, or is this simply a phenomenon of a clear night with a nearly full moon? I don't pay attention to the lunar cycles, the sky maps, or astronomy in general, yet the subject still fascinates me. In high school I grew somewhat well-versed in ancient Western mythology. When I learned how many constellations in the night sky are named after mythological figures, I grew even more interested. If I had enough money or time, I would invest in a telescope just for the fun of it.

I check my phone again and search the lunar cycle. There is nothing interesting happening on this date. I shrug and put the phone away, before cramming a large bite of granola bar into my mouth and sipping on an instant coffee.

If it successfully wakes me up, I'll go into work early and hope it will impress my foreman, Jamal. Jamal is a bulky guy with tattoos all the way up one arm; he smokes casually and sports a booming voice. In our little trailer it is easy to imagine him at a bar chasing women, yet Jamal has a beautiful wife. What does she see in him? I often wonder.

Charming as he may be in his time off, Jamal is all business when he's on site. He carefully enforces OSHA rules and adheres to the Bones Holdings safety code, by making sure all visitors that go inside the fence are wearing the proper safety equipment.

I think he's a hard ass, but when he wants to be, he is a great boss. If it were in my personality to be like him, perhaps I would find more success, but that just isn't my way. I'm just me—lost, inadequate, and socially adrift. If I can find comfort in this life and personality, then maybe my later years will reward me handsomely. But in my present situation, all I can do is live in the present.

I gulp and try to prepare for the biting cold. A major storm is expected to impact travel later today, and the forecasts are calling for a few inches of snow. The weekend promises a slight thaw before another clipper comes down out of Canada, bringing more snow and cold.

I hate winter, and climate change sounds like great news to me, despite all the warnings from scientists and politicians.

When I step outside, I look straight up into the sky. I can hardly tell whether it's cloudy or clear. In the city, it can be difficult to differentiate clear from cloudy around dawn, particularly in the winter. Searching for clouds or the moon, I scan the horizon. In the absence of the moon, I chalk it up to light pollution. The city is not a great environment for casual observers of the sky.

I could have easily been fooled into thinking it was dawn. The streetlamps are shining, but from the sidewalk I can barely tell. There are no yellowish circles of light on the concrete, just a general gray. My watch confirms the time as 6:05 a.m. Six-oh-five yesterday was as dark as midnight. What the hell is going on?

Some religions foretell the second coming of a deity, where light persists for three days, following three days of darkness—though astronomically this is an impossible phenomenon at Philadelphia's latitude. Above the Arctic Circle, days can stretch for weeks, and dawn can last many hours.

If I were truly interested, I could do some more searching on the internet, go to the library, read through farmers' almanacs, and gain a better understanding of why this is happening. But I don't care that much.

The trauma from my nightmare lingers like a dull haze. I squint in the unusual light, get in my car, and turn the key in hopes that something remotely interesting will happen today—anything to shake off this feeling of perpetual dread. In that regard, perhaps the woman from my nightmare was lucky, as much as I can remember her.

Why do I remember her? Is she real? Or is she a product of Joaquin's imagination—or mine? By now the dream has totally dissolved, save for the lingering emotions, which are set to shroud yet another day in a murky, inescapable distress.

2

Arc of the Pleiades

S logging across the muddy staging area while carrying a heavy set of plans in the biting wind is not a pleasure, but it is part of the job. Every night after Jamal has left me alone in the trailer, he goes home to a warm bed and a loving wife, while I dutifully stay to organize loose paperwork, set aside hand-drawn sketches, and return the mechanical prints to the sprawling trailer complex of Bones Holdings—the overbearing and sometimes snooty general contractor under which we all work.

When I started this job, I was neither experienced enough in trade work nor smart enough in the technical sense to land one of the sought-after jobs with a high salary and world-class benefits, so I settled for an internship. One of these days I'm going to leave this all behind and play in the big leagues, but for now I must earn my lumps by sweeping floors and acting as a courier.

Delivering the plans is a burden I could do without. The staging area is a large dirt lot behind the fences off Washington Avenue, which darts through a network of midrise apartment buildings downtown. They offer stunning vistas of glass high rises, their offices displaying a spectacular checkerboard pattern of yellow light and dark blue shadow at night. Within the gates, the subcontractor trailers are arranged in a horseshoe shape opposite the field offices of Bones Holdings; our trailer is situated three hundred yards from the main complex. To navigate the staging area successfully, one must zigzag through a maze of metal studs, piles of rebar, chunks of rejected concrete, and hefty stacks of various types of pipes and fittings.

These supplies usually arrive early on Monday mornings by truck, and I help catalogue and keep inventory on vendor items while our bookkeeper tracks orders and stamps bills of lading to note reception.

The trip is a bore and I hate it. I curse as the wind slaps my face with a coarse shower of snow, which has been whipped off the roof of the nearest trailer. My hands go numb as I cling to the metal binding rod. If I were smart enough, I might have rolled them print-side out and bundled them under my armpit, but I have a history of doing things the hard way.

I look up and gaze across the pipes, which have started to collect sticky snow. Beyond the job trailers, the parking area is mostly empty, but I spy her car and smile. The only positive aspect of visiting the general's complex is the radiant Sarah Bryson-Carter, whose flowing red locks flutter behind her and frame her pale slightly freckled face with silky curtains of amber. Her lips sparkle when she smiles, and those sapphire eyes glitter like pulsing stars. By six in the evening she is usually gone, as is almost everyone else including the receptionist.

In the distance, loose plastic tarping flaps in the gusts across the rising framework of iron columns and beams, which seems to be engaged in a perfect square dance around the shaft of concrete that will soon house the elevators and the hidden mechanical and plumbing stacks that must rise to each of the thirty-six floors. The billboards affixed to the fences fronting Washington Avenue promise grand views in five hundred vertical feet of prime office real estate amid the city's best business district, with ground floor restaurants and floor-to-ceiling windows.

The architecture seems like a ludicrous choice in this climate, but the developer has recently announced a plan to achieve the highest level of certified energy efficiency. But by my guess, the generous glass surfaces will lead to a certain amount of energy loss, in the winter months especially.

Sarah's car is sitting caked in snow beneath the cone of light from the nearest streetlamp, occupying one of several rows amidst the hundreds of parking stalls. I stop to eye her vehicle just long enough to gather my senses and steel my nerves, and then that damned wind pelts my face with millions of ice crystals. I frown in reaction and try to put my best foot forward.

The first time I'd ever seen Sarah was on an evening in the late summer, before the crane was erected. My task was to deliver a set of redline prints to the main office for approval, in relation to a complex Request for Information that would be adopted on subsequent Supplemental Releases to alert the trades of the desired changes. Keeping track of all this paperwork always proves to be an overwhelming nightmare, and the project engineers seemingly make life as difficult as possible for lowly serfs like me. If I were daring, I'd grasp the rungs of that career ladder and race for the top, but it's a one-man ladder and dozens of people are attempting to climb all at the same time, resulting in complete chaos.

I want to see her pretty face again. In my wildest dreams I think I could someday ask her out. In a previous encounter I uttered a sheepish, nasal 'hello' and scurried back to the sub trailer feeling smaller than a strut washer. A month later, I managed an equally embarrassing "Good weekend?" And then giggled like a teenage girl. After eventually graduating to "How's the dog?" I at last summoned the nerve to ask her directly what her plans were for the holidays.

Was she being suggestive in smiling and saying, "Nothing at all"? I'm notoriously bad at all this, and probably look like a raging lunatic to boot. If I'm half as charming as I imagine myself to be, I'd consider it an accomplishment. Women have always been dangled in front of me like the proverbial carrot, and yet I am clumsy and have been blessed with relatively short arms.

On our last meeting, something about Sarah seemed shrouded in mystery. Her usual joyful demeanor had been replaced by traces of sadness, evident by her looking down when our eyes met and speaking quietly. What was it? I was too clumsy to ask, so I could only offer a silly grin, which led her to simply raise her eyes and give me a questioning glance.

Maybe today will be better. But perhaps I will crash and burn yet again, leaving behind a pile of smoldering ruins.

I pause twenty feet from the steel diamond-plate ramp to the elevated front doors, gather my senses, and exhale. A whirlwind of blowing snow crosses my path, and an eerie chill turns the blood in my veins to ice.

I'm prepared to utter an observation on the ridiculousness of these SRs and how they are haphazardly assembled, even if it offends her. Instead, I put it on the back burner and attempt to piece together a conversation in my mind.

You're still here, Sarah? I'd ask.

And her predisposed reply would go something like, *Unfortunately. We're buried in paperwork over here. How's life treating you?*

Same old, same old. Hey, what are you doing this Friday?

Larry, you know I'm always free, but we're friends and I'm good with that.

The venerated friend zone. The lair of clumsy goofballs and swash-buckling morons alike, and I'm about to meet its newest occupant: me. And my name is Kerry, but of course she wouldn't know that, because I've never bothered to inform her of my real name. Maybe some time in the future, I will change my name to Larry just to appease her, and only then will she realize she's been misnaming me all along. It sounds about right.

I shake my head and pretend to cough, though I'm certain no one is around to hear me. I clear my throat and proceed after the whirlwind has abated, leaving behind ... a pair of footprints in the freshly fallen snow? And they don't seem to have originated from anywhere. From the shape of the prints, the mysterious figure is a woman, but I look around and cannot see her anywhere. Is there a set of tire tracks that would indicate she had just gotten out of a car only moments ago? I frown as I scan the vicinity. There are no tire tracks, and behind me there are only my own erratic footprints disturbing the snow.

In addition to being clumsy, I must be going crazy. That will make for some light-hearted conversation.

When did you get so unique?

Unique? My friends call it delusion. *I don't know. I guess I've always seen the world a little differently. Would you be down for dinner with a friend this week?*

She would give me that curious 'nice try' smile, at which I'd chuckle in humiliated defeat.

Then again, tonight seems different. A newfound energy courses through me, though I cannot ascertain its origin. What kind of paranoia could offer the fresh shot of adrenaline that now seems to be pulsing through my veins?

I clutch the plan set's binding rod more tightly and feel the whole set flop against my body. I react by trying to roll it with my numb fingers, but it's no use; with a set this heavy, one must lay it flat on a plan table print side down and carefully roll it, starting with the bound side. I can barely feel my own hands. I ease along the last few steps to the ramp, swallow, and tread up the muddy diamond-plate steel slope. When I am safely indoors, I let the plan set fall with a heavy thud on the reception counter and wait for someone to come and retrieve them.

Sarah rounds the bend and issues me a polite smile and a nod.

"Hey Sarah."

"Hi Larry. Are you heading home soon?"

"Eventually," I answer. "The foreman left a lot of fittings and thread rod on the plan table for a mock-up. But he abandoned it, so I have to find the boxes for the parts and check against the inventory log in case anything is missing. You?"

That is the most words I have uttered to her in a single conversation, and they escape my vocal cords with such speed that I can hardly breathe. I can still barely feel my fingers, but now I'm hot and erupting with sweat.

"You know, always busy. But the weekend's coming."

"Such a relief—unless the subs have to work again. You don't have anything to do with the project schedule, do you?"

"Hard to miss it," she says. "But I don't make it. Maybe I can check it for you."

The engineers consult with the project manager and the owners to formulate the schedule, which is laid out in a series of colored bars on overlapping 11 x 17 sheets and tacked to the wall where everyone can see it.

"Don't bother; I've got to get back."

And just like that, I disappear out the front door, feeling somewhat less of a failure, but ultimately, it's another opportunity blown. I'm getting good at this.

Back in the skinny job trailer I shut the door behind me and rummage through piles of short thread rods, pipe clamps, insulation shields, fittings, channel struts and nut attachments. If I pile it all into the same box and guess that it is all accounted for, I may get an earful from Jamal. I don't really care that much since I am only an intern, yet my motivation to do the right thing always dominates.

I scroll through the log and find the estimated footage of strut, the number of nuts and bolts, and all the other assorted attachments. Jamal has used a couple of inches of small-diameter copper tube to sketch several circles, arranged in rows in a neat box with a cut-out corner, and then affixed a sticky note to amend his design once more before scribbling it all out and calling it quits for the day. He will eventually come up with an ingenious plan that will make everyone's life easier.

I issue a sigh, collect all the sundry items to deposit into their respective bins, and then return the hand-written notes to his office. His desk phone is blinking with a voicemail message, perhaps from the drafting office, with whom he had been exchanging phone calls all day. Instead of listening to it for him, I leave it alone, rearrange the notes in a row next to his keyboard, and give the plants a sip of water.

When I'm done, I shut off the lights, make sure both doors are securely locked, and make my way back across the lot to the parking area behind the general's complex. In the last hour the snowfall has intensified. I bite my lip and shiver against the wind as I trudge through the maze of piping and equipment. Bones Holdings does not require hard hats and protective eyewear on the staging lot after hours, so I tuck my gear under my arm and put my head down for the long walk to the parking lot.

As I reach the general trailers, I swallow when I spy Sarah's car. The engine is running, and the snow has all been cleared off the windshield, but there is no sign of her. As I walk towards it, the driver's side door opens and clumps of snow tumble into fluffy piles near the tires. I observe fresh footprints in the snow.

I try to focus on my own car, which is parked near the back of the lot. I angle my trajectory as needed to shorten the trip while I lengthen my stride. My teeth are chattering. Near the back end of Sarah's car, a plume of steam rises into the falling snow and then dissipates. The outline of a woman briefly forms against the night as the lights flicker overhead.

This is an illusion I'm unaccustomed to, and I don't know how to process it. Instead of saying anything, I try to quicken my pace as I walk past, but then out of the corner of my eye I see movement and stop instinctively.

Some unknown presence lingers there, like a transparent silhouette against a backdrop of snow and pavement.

I don't want to stare, but if this is Sarah's car and she's not here, then someone must be tampering with it. I turn slowly, thinking I will head back into the trailer and alert her that someone is trying to steal her car. Just then I hear a hollow grunt that sounds like a woman's voice.

I freeze to the spot as ice flashes through my veins.

If I'm wrong, I'm still an idiot, so what do I lose? Instead of breaking into a frightened run, I let my heart drop in my chest and speak as warmly and softly as I can.

"Sarah—is that—are you—invisible?"

No reply comes for what seems like eons. I bet against myself and hang my head low for the remainder of the trip to my car. I start the motor and gaze up into the brightly lit downtown towers, which have been blurred with fuzzy lines in the driving snow. The commute home is going to be miserable, slow, and dangerous, but at this point I may be ready for anything.

I wait, head still lowered, and turn on my blinker to turn right onto Washington Avenue. Behind me, headlights appear.

Sarah is alone in her car, fully visible, and is following me onto the busy street. When she is at last out of sight, I lightly slap myself across the face. If my friends were to hear about this, they'd have a good laugh, and *delusional* would be the nicest term they could pummel me with.

The guys are good friends of mine, with whom I have hung out for several years. We're as close as friends can possibly be. I share my life with them, everything from the highest highs to the lowest of lows. They mean well, attempting to raise my spirits by making fun of me, which almost always works to some extent.

I will have to travel to Joaquin's place for nachos and football on Sunday to explain what I think I've seen. That ought to be a riot.

But tonight, I have another plan: I relax on my sofa, crack open a cold beer, and turn on the television to find another cable movie to take away the sharp edges that the day has left on me. The demons blast me incessantly as I lie back and let sleep take me. Oddly enough, another night alone is exactly what I need. On Monday I'll go into the trailer and seek her out again to apologize for making a fool of myself, if I can stomach it.

It will be a new day and I will go in with a fresh perspective, and that will serve me well. For tonight, Bruce Lee and Dos Equis are my best friends. They suit me perfectly.

3

Aura of Betelgeuse

The snowstorm has cleared itself away, leaving behind partly cloudy conditions and a winter chill made only marginally better by the warmth of the sun. Some melting occurred on Saturday, followed by a deep freeze overnight that transformed even the well-traveled streets into virtual skating rinks.

I blink in a patch of driving sunlight and adjust my speed for an unbroken sheet of upcoming ice. Living in this climate, you adapt to frozen roads and treacherous conditions or you end up in an accident. There is no third option. Luckily Sunday traffic is almost non-existent and thus the journey to Joaquin's place is a relative breeze.

Saturday seemed like drudgery. Waking up with a headache is never a good sign, and when you mix it with paralyzing dreams and an otherworldly experience the previous night, you end up in a haze. Without the company of television or a good book, I knew the day would be a hellacious slugfest. The best way to assuage the demons is to bludgeon them, shoot them to shreds, and blow them up. If the videogames last all day, nothing is lost other than a few brain cells—but who cares about brain cells, anyway? With a life like mine, if you don't indulge occasionally, you become a shell of a human being in no time. If my normal personality can't attract women, becoming a veritable drone sure as hell won't.

The city is largely built from a grid of oblong, tree-lined blocks, sectioned into manageable neighborhoods and radially shooting away from the downtown skyscrapers. Joaquin lives in a historic district house converted to an apartment complex with on-street parking. Finding an open spot is always a gamble on Sundays, but with this type of weather I'll be lucky to parallel park less than a block away.

The little Saturday melting produced still puddles in potholes, now frozen solid in the night. The neighborhood's inhabitants have brushed the snow off their cars, leaving behind various piles of the crunchy white stuff. A young woman next door to Joaquin is laboriously chipping away at the snow and ice that has accumulated on her windshield. She is wearing a stylish black coat with black fur fringes and lining, which has an oddly slimming appeal. I could offer to help her but I'm still living in a delusion, and such an interaction might be dangerous for me.

I park about eight houses down, zip up my coat, flip the keys into my pocket and attempt to plaster a fake smile onto my face. The breeze greets me with a harsh reminder that I still hate the winter. To try to make myself feel normal, I offer a curse word that I subconsciously hope the young woman can hear. Combing a hand through my hair is cliché and always stupid, but it's like a nervous tic with me. I do a lot of things that under close examination would sound rightfully ridiculous. And if asked why I do it, I can only offer the patented, "I don't know." It's lame, but that's me.

Joaquin's landlord has scattered the sidewalk with rock salt and scraped away some of the loose ice, which has made the five steps to the front door somewhat safer. I cling to the railing without looking over my shoulder. Should I slip, perhaps I would brighten the young woman's day by tumbling backward in spectacular fashion. And when I would rise, covered head-to-toe with powdery snow, she would turn around and pelt me with predictable sympathy. *Are you okay?*

No, but it's cool.

Quin's door occupies the right-hand side of a short hallway on the left flank of the ground floor. The heat has been turned up, making the trek across the creaky floors somewhat invigorating. He has a hand-written sign taped to his door saying, "No beer, no service." I try to smile as I peck lightly against the hollow laminate with loose knuckles.

After a few seconds, he swings open the door, brandishing an array of remote controls and a beer bottle. He usually offers me a cold one when

I arrive, but he has already started on the bottle that's in his grip. I try to smile sheepishly, but the only expression I can muster is nothing more than a semblance of helpless indignation.

"Landlord take your puppy?" he asks upon observing my countenance.

I don't normally relate to sappy lines in country music, but I relent anyway. "And she stole my truck."

He shrugs. "Ah, well. Nothing beer, nachos, and football can't cure."

"What are the odds on the Kansas City game?"

My friends and I often engage in cheap bets and petty smack talk on game days. I open my wallet and fish out a fresh five-dollar bill before I sit down on the cushioned sofa.

"Chiefs by three. Over-under at thirty-seven."

"I'll take the points," I say, though I'm not entirely sure what that means. Oddly, it doesn't seem to affect my bottom line; without even knowing the odds, I'm about fifty-fifty on calling the outcome. And having a little wager on the line, along with a cold beer, turns the experience from tolerable to mildly entertaining.

He takes the money and swats it down, with his own five on top of mine on the end table.

"Go get yourself a beer," Quin instructs.

I shake my head and relax.

"How's the jobsite?"

I knew the question was coming but am still not prepared to answer. "Still a mess and pretty weird."

"What's the general contractor doing now?"

I force a chuckle. "I don't think even they know, which is typical."

He uncaps his drink and takes a sip before raising an eyebrow and effortlessly switching the channel to another game he is following. "Then what's weird about it?"

I gulp and start, in a shallow voice, "There's this girl—"

"Oh, shit! In love again?"

"Not exactly. She still calls me Larry."

"Sure beats 'Kerry'."

"Shut up, man." When he ribs me, I can take it as a sign of mutual respect. When friends don't joke about themselves, the relationship gets too serious and becomes boring in a hurry. When the insults vanish, the friendship is already on its last legs.

"So, *Larry*.... You going to ask her out, or what?"

"See, I'm this close," I explain, sounding pathetic. "But this shit just keeps me wishing I had what it takes."

"All you gotta do is ask. If she says no, there's always other fish in the sea."

I cough and glare at the television screen between glances at his wall posters. He's always rooted for Green Bay for one reason or another, despite never having lived anywhere near Wisconsin. When our teams meet once a season, we put the friendship on hold and ratchet up the attacks on one another.

"On second thought, maybe I should try fish. I hear they're less com-plicated."

"Tell that to my old man," he quips. "You'll get a hook in your ass."

Joaquin had once told me the story of his father and the trophy fish he'd had mounted, which was known to break out in song. It was one of those relationships that might stand the test of time: an old man and his singing fish. The thing was childish and flat-out cheesy, he'd admitted, but it occasionally dealt in barrier-smashing wisdom and ground-breaking frivolity. For him, football would have been sacrilege; the man lived for fresh air and quiet moments on a clear lake.

"What's her name?"

"Sarah."

"Sorry, did you say Sushi?"

"Bite me."

"Maybe later, if the Chiefs win," he says.

"You know," I explain, "I already thought she was different, but I guess I didn't know how different until the other night. I ran into her when I was leaving, or at least I think I did. It's sort of a blur now, but I swear to God she was invisible."

He chuckles. "So, an invisible girlfriend. You're still in high school, I take it."

Joaquin and I had known one another in high school but we hadn't really become friends until after he graduated college, from Temple University. I had gone a different route, electing to deliver pizza instead. We hadn't gotten along great in high school, but I'd never had an invisible girlfriend either. The only girl I'd gone out with in that era had treated me like a project, and when she'd failed her only assignment, she'd gone after the popular, valedictorian archetype instead.

For several minutes I can't speak. I struggle to stand up, walk into his kitchen to grab a beer from the refrigerator, and collapse on the sofa again before I open it. I listen intently to the color guy on the television analyzing Kansas City's defense while trying to think of a different topic that would make me seem like less of a dweeb.

"How did the whole thing go down?" he asks, the joking demeanor fading.

Sensing real sincerity in his voice, I attempt to sort out my version of events and put them into words.

"It was snowing when I returned the plans to the general's trailer, and she was the only one there. We chatted for a minute, and then I went back to clean up Jamal's mess and lock up. When I was walking to my car I passed hers, and I'm pretty sure someone was getting into it to scrape the windows. Then I heard her cough or something, but I couldn't see her. You know that feeling when you're sure someone is present, yet there's no solid evidence for it?"

"Yeah," Quin says, "Here in Philly, we call that a delusion."

"Well, on the West Coast it's something else."

I'd moved from Seattle a little over three years ago, thinking Philadelphia would be the perfect change of pace, in addition to being more affordable. The resultant lifestyle change had left me breathless but I'd never abandoned the core aspects of my personality. Within a year I'd made new friends, one of whom had introduced me to Joaquin. Only this time we became friends.

"And then I made a fool out of myself and asked her if she was invisible," I continue.

"Did she answer? Or did you?"

"No one did," I explain, shaking my head subtly.

"I stared at where I thought she would be standing, thinking she was looking right back at me. After I got into my car and drove away, she followed me out of the parking lot, so she was definitely there. What should I do?"

He tilts his head sideways as if to entertain the question. "Nothing. Wait a few days, see if she says anything. If she's super awkward, you'll *know* you made a fool of yourself instead of suspecting it."

"Gee, thanks."

Moments after the game kicks off and the Kansas City offense is about to take the field, the announcers start discussing some of the key facets of the team and the keys to victory. I don't revel in the specifics of what they say; to me it is nothing more than useless minutiae. I often defer to my more football-savvy friends to decode what the commentators are really trying to explain and focus on watching the plays instead.

When the stat sheet vanishes, my mind flashes back to Sarah: that peculiar smile must have prowled across her lips at some point during our interaction the other night, but now I cannot access the memory. Instead, I remember what she said, and—more importantly—how she said it. And then, like the infographic on the television screen, it all fades away in an instant as if being wiped out by a fierce blizzard. Only her car remains under the lights, as snow and ice remove themselves from the windshield.

"Bullshit," Quin mutters as the stats fade away. "KC blows. They won't be able to move the ball against this defense, superstar quarterback or not."

"Do you think I'm being overly dramatic?" I ask in a hushed tone.

He holds his beer aloft in one hand as if to make a toast, but his grin begins to erode when he sees my facial expression, as predictably grim as ever. "Definitely. You should mind your own business."

"Shit, I hadn't thought of that, Sherlock." My own sarcasm blows me away. Regret instantly rushes in because Joaquin, being the more educated between us, always wins these bouts.

"Elementary."

It takes only one word to reduce me to ashes, and my expression darkens as I squint at the screen. Kansas City's offense is now lined up on the field, and the quarterback is barking out signals over the din of the crowd in the seconds between the approving remarks from the color commentary.

"You don't get it yet, do you?" he says, searching my face.

Hardheaded as I often find myself being, I begin to fit the pieces of his opinion together. Then again, Holmes thrived on not minding his own business, especially when it really mattered.

"I'm just saying, what I saw the other night—"

"What you *think* you saw. The best offenses in football are built on misdirection. When teams these days are this dynamic, they need additional advantages. The best can take one simple play call, repeat it three times, and then on the fourth they give the same look but add a wrinkle and break it for big yardage."

"You should apply for the open color position at ESPN," I say dryly.

"You said you saw her invisible. She gave you a wrinkle."

I stare at him blankly. Quin may be well-versed in logic, or what often passes for logic these days, but I can see through it. When he is attempting to assert dominance in a conversation, which he always does, he references great works of literature and introduces jargon to make himself seem more impressive. Before the other person has a chance to build a rebuttal, they are wowed by his horse manure just enough to abandon their next point, or at least muddy it so the words start to mean something else. When we were in high-school I considered him pompous, but Temple University had ratcheted that up even more in the years that followed. I never win our arguments, but if I frame any discussion as a quest for facts, he's keener to educate me on what he feels is the truth.

"You think she did it on purpose?"

"Seems plausible," he says. "If it avoids another clumsy encounter with the likes of you."

"Shut up, man."

"You're so good at tripping over yourself that, if you get on the football field, twenty-one other players end up on the ground. But back to my earlier point: if you want to figure out what is really going on, go back to school."

"Do they offer Paranormal Activity 101 at Temple?" I ask, certain of his answer.

"There's this thing called the World Wide Web..." Joaquin says.

"Great place to learn how to be an even bigger idiot," I counter. "You can find information about practically anything, but most of it is garbage and simply not true."

"Depends on what questions you ask, and how you ask them. Maybe you need to think of a question and search to see how many others have experienced something similar."

I tilt my head sideways to consider the suggestion, as the Kansas City quarterback lofts a touch pass to a tight end for a modest gain. I know my luck by now; I have been called 'weird' so many times that I've started to believe it. Whatever the connotation, I have a unique ability to get myself into situations no human has ever endured before. The uncertainty is there to teach me a lesson, whether or not an afterlife or a higher power really exists. On that, my opinions are already surprisingly diverse, but not so enlightened that they cannot be shaped or guided by further knowledge. Remaining pliable, as far as I am concerned, is the best way to excel at all facets of life.

Then again, I do it with such regularity that absolute lies color my perception of the greater goal, thereby turning my journey darker and fraught with peril.

"In this instance you're lucky, my friend," Quin says.

Luck is a four-letter word if you ask me; it almost never applies, and on the occasion that it does, the situation is never so cut and dried that good fortune has a positive effect on the outcome. When I'm in over my head, luck only makes the consequences of my mistakes less severe.

"I know a guy; they call him Harley. Buy him a burger, get to know him—the man's got a thousand fantastical stories. He's not even on the internet, thinks it is some big government conspiracy or something, and he may be right."

"You're sending me to a crackpot street-corner preacher whose signs say, 'The end is near?'"

"He's right about that," Joaquin says. "Depending on your interpretations of 'the end' and 'near,' you can make that argument apply to anything. Don't like a bad situation? The end is near. But you can trust Harley."

I'll decide for myself whom to trust, and for what reason. Quin's suggestion seems like another prescription for failure, but then what do I have to gain?

Whenever someone asks hypothetical questions like 'What do you have to lose?' I flip it around to make the question seem more positive. The answer to the hypothetical is always some form of 'a lot,' but when the question is reversed, fewer and sharper scenarios begin to unfold.

Either Harley leads me down the rabbit hole of conspiracy, based on delusion and fashioned after fantastic 'what-ifs,' making me one more mindless drone, or he teaches me something true about the woman of my dreams. Trusting him can go south in a lot of ways, but if the positive is worth all the possible negatives, then perhaps asking him is not such a bad idea in the first place.

Damn Quin and his logic.

"Just like that," Quin says, unimpressed, as the Chiefs fumble the ball and the defense recovers.

According to him the handoff is considered one of the safest plays in football, but it's a low-risk, high-reward type of commitment. Teams that run the ball more effectively, he insists, enjoy a litany of advantages over those that don't. Still, in this league, that alone cannot decide games. Joaquin is right again.

"Is Harley homeless?"

Joaquin shakes his head. "Don't think so, but he's definitely on the dole."

"A conspiracy freak on government handouts? Say it ain't so."

"Not exactly what I meant," Quin says. "Talk to him. He'll tell you what's up, what's down, what's sideways, and some things that are in-between. Just be prepared for when they don't fit your expectations."

I shake my head and watch the replay of the fumble on the screen, ignoring the commentary on why the back fumbled the football and what it would mean for the offense during the rest of the game. If it happens again, Joaquin will be so overloaded with glee that being with him could become unbearable.

"Why not? I clearly don't have all the answers and Harley could give you a fresh perspective, which is what you really need."

"Wouldn't you call *Harley* 'delusional'?"

He shakes his head in turn. "There's a whole other word for what Harley has. If you don't want to be heckled, probably take it someplace quiet and off the street, because old Harley's been the victim of abuse for as long as I can remember."

"When is he out?" I ponder.

"All the time, but he gets the most attention on Sunday afternoons."

The conversation seems to wear thinner the longer I sit here. At last, I can relax. I sip my beer, place it carefully on the end table next to me, and attempt to immerse myself in the world of football. Using sport to escape something that could be considered a fantasy feels like an insane dichotomy, but I'm prepared to let it roll. The longer I watch, the more concrete Sarah's disappearance becomes. And for now, it seems only one man can help me determine a path forward.

4

Asteroid Crossing

In a little over three hours, the drone of the announcers picking at every detail of the game has become nearly intolerable. Joaquin's frown deepens as the fourth quarter draws to a close, and he shifts his feet uncomfortably as he perhaps yearns for another beer. The light in his living room seems to be dimming just as the Kansas City quarterback launches a deep pass toward the end zone. Quin draws closer to the edge of his seat as the commentators shriek with excitement. "Incomplete!" one says.

"He wants a flag ... I don't think there's enough contact there for pass interference."

"That's a good no-call. But what it has done is stop the clock. Now he's got a little more time to work with."

"The coach is going to line up a tight end in the slot and try to draw them offsides. If that doesn't work, expect a quick slant pattern, and then they'll call a time-out to set up the field goal."

Joaquin groans, but I silently wish the color guy would shut up and stop pretending he knows more about football than everyone watching at home.

"Back to pass, looking for the slot, pressure coming, and he *just* gets it off. Complete, but it looks to be a bit short of the marker."

"That's good coaching right there."

"Then why don't you coach?" Joaquin grumbles.

I could make a comment about how football announcers earn millions of dollars and perhaps more actual measurable fame than coaches, but I've lost interest in the game. The sooner the field goal kicker predictably puts it through the uprights in the last few seconds, the sooner my mind can shift away from football and toward something more productive.

When the light seems to flutter again, I shift my vision to something that seems to move across my peripheral vision. The urge to swat it away passes idly through my mind, but when I attempt to refocus, there is nothing to perceive. If my eyes are playing tricks on me here, they could just as easily have done so the other night. It is possible that the available light is altering my perception of movement. A little over a year ago I watched a television program that explained the way our eyes have evolved to perceive motion, and how our brains process light and color differently—or not at all—when motion has our attention. They tested the theory by showing a graphic on screen and asking viewers to keep track of what colors and shapes appear in the background, knowing that almost everyone would fail. There is something deeply upsetting about the fact that my own brain can't get around its own biases and preconceptions, as if I had previously convinced myself to believe I am better than evolution. But alas I'm just another human, easily deceived by my own brain. Do other animals suffer the same illusions?

The kick is good, and Joaquin leans back and offers a helpless *humph*.

"Good game," I say lightly, as my eyes begin to gloss over.

Quin barely notices I've said anything. His breathing has become strangely erratic, indicating an internal tension that I don't wish to investigate. He rests his head on the backrest and says nothing for several seconds.

"I think KC will go to the playoffs this year."

"They're good enough to win when the refs bail them out," Joaquin exclaims. "That should have been pass interference on the receiver. They're obviously paid off."

Never one to let facts get in the way of a juicy conspiracy theory, Joaquin drifts off into uncharted territory. I could alter the mood by bringing up something else, but perhaps the better tactic is to let Quin stew in his own rage until time settles him down.

After about fifteen minutes I scoot to the edge of my seat, and plan to announce that I have some other things I have to do.

Joaquin gives me the once-over, clearly expecting me to say something about my invisible girlfriend, but I currently have no interest in discussing her.

"I'll text you tomorrow after work," I say, stretching. "Maybe next week we can battle actual monsters."

"Yeah," Quin says, forcing a smile. "You kind of suck, but at least you're here for comic relief when you can't get out of a corner."

"Anything for a laugh."

"You going to find Harley? You might be surprised."

I shrug and trudge softly toward the front door, knowing he's watching my body language as I walk away.

Harley sounds like quite the character, but I'm not ready to commit to something that could prove to be a huge waste of time. Before I go that route, I need to do some more research. During my drive home I devise a series of questions to plug into the search engine in hopes of finding out whether anyone else has asked the same things.

After I park and climb the stairs to my apartment, I slip off my shoes, hang my coat on the hook and plop down on the couch with my laptop. A game I'd been playing remains on the screen. I hurriedly make sure my progress is saved before logging out and delving into the cavernous depths of the internet.

"What to do when someone disappears," yields millions of links to reporting missing persons, and even the suggested steps to take if one suspects that one's loved ones may be victims of sex trafficking. Clearly, this is the wrong rabbit hole, so I hit 'back' and hover over the search bar for several seconds trying to think of something clever.

When I type in, "Is there a way to become invisible?" I am only marginally closer to what I'm hoping to find. Most links appear to be based on superpowers, like x-ray vision and morphing abilities, although one science blog suggests that researchers have discovered a rare material that absorbs all light, rendering the wearer practically invisible.

My mind wanders back to when I last saw Sarah; trying to picture what she was wearing is easy. Even if she were wearing some dynamic polymer, she remained dressed in the same attire throughout the evening and it hadn't made her invisible earlier.

Then the topic of light creeps back into my mind.

Excitedly I hammer out a bit of garbled English, wondering whether it is possible for human perception of movement to change due to the presence of different types of light. I cross my arms as the links load in the browser. Believing that I am now on the right track, I read a detailed analysis of different brightness factors and colors of visible light. Much of the page rehashes the physics of light waves and how the light spectrum dictates the colors we see.

But our brains, it turns out, are good at filtering the information that we deem unimportant to our perception. Depending on our view of the lighting, perceived colors can vary from person to person, even when viewing the same photograph. I recall a viral meme that circulated the internet a few years ago, and how it had set off a weeks-long debate where one side insisted that the other was wrong—when in reality neither group was totally right or totally wrong.

Continuing reveals something important as to the way our brains perceive light and shadow: color, it seems, is mostly determined by the spectrum of light either being reflected or absorbed by the medium the viewer sees. By applying various filters to the camera, radical color changes can occur.

What happens, then, when motion is added to the picture? Pounding out this question leads me to a discussion page on a popular question and answer website, where users can post any question they can think of, and any other user can attempt to answer that question based upon his or her own knowledge.

One query seems relatively salient, but by the fourth answer, the internet conspiracy addicts have hijacked the discussion into some weird rant about how the government is trying to hide an alien species that is living among us—and how we can't see them because the government has programmed our brains to ignore their presence through use of clever brainwashing techniques in advertising, use of pesticides on crops, and possibly even the contrails jets leave behind in the sky.

I shake my head at the sheer idiocy of this, but I read on, completely distracted by the back-and-forth that is packed with logical fallacies and humorous retorts.

One poster claims that he saw a UFO once but that the government censored him for asking questions.

Four others then chide him for acting like an ignoramus, while another praises him for looking under the right rocks. "If you really want to know the whole, unvarnished truth," he says, "then it is your duty to dig deeper. Do some more research, ask the right questions, because the truth is out there."

I almost gag at the insinuation; internet trolls who have no relationship with reality often urge others to "do their own research," which I consider to be code for "look up the same conspiracies I believe in so you can fall victim to another scam." I may not be the sharpest tool in the shed but I'm smart enough to know when someone is trying to make me believe in something totally unfounded, just so that I'll start to fall for some of the deeper delusions.

Then again, the exhortation to dig deeper piques my interest more than the mindless conspiracies these people believe in. How then do I dig deeper, and with what tool? The more I think about it, the more convinced I become that I am woefully under-informed on the numerous possibilities that exist should I open new avenues of thinking.

Another poster claims something completely crazy, and five more people condemn him for being an idiot. I am almost ready to dismiss his views when he says, "Do some research," but his next post catches me totally off guard: "Talk to people on the street, get a second or a third opinion, and stop mindlessly believing what they want you to believe."

His insinuating use of *they* notwithstanding, I force myself to read a bit more of his diatribe. "When you allow yourself to converse with diverse individuals," he says, "you open yourself to viewpoints that cannot exist within your own head. You don't know what you don't know. Most people are not informed enough to know they are uninformed—this isn't some mindless conspiracy drivel. Knowing the real truth requires you to seek out multiple points of view, because each one is based on different skill sets, knowledge, and life experiences."

I sit back and brush my hand through my hair. If I'm seeking out an answer to this important question, I decide, then maybe this internet poster and Joaquin are both right. And what's the worst thing that could happen with Harley? That he might turn out to be one of those Bible-thumping old people warning others to repent because the end times are upon us? I don't know this Harley; he may turn out to be a kook, but what if he knows more and perceives light and color differently than I do, to such an extent that he is able to perceive subtle differences in the way people appear?

I swallow and consider the nearly endless possibilities, even as something in the back of my mind offers warnings that this endeavor could lead me to a land of 'fruits and nuts,' which was the way one of my high school teachers described California.

Sarah probably has no idea I'm doing this and it's probably better that way. Maybe tomorrow, when I see her, I will apologize for acting like a fool and questioning her existence. Some of the internet trolls may want to have me believe she is an alien species with reptilian DNA who is out to steal my thoughts, so I should stay away. I chuckle at the absurdity of this idea, but without knowing what Harley might know, I'm not prepared to face her again, much less engage in a discussion about her appearance ... or lack thereof.

A wordless debate begins to rage in my mind as the hours tick by. Before I realize what I am doing, I am opening another link to find more of the information that I'm missing, completely unaware that the hour hand has gone way past what I deem to be an appropriate bedtime.

As time passes, the cautionary voices in my head become louder and fiercer. Doing all this reading could lead me right to Crazy Town, where there's a skeleton hiding behind every rock. Damnit if Quin wasn't on to something; my own bias has taught me to listen to his musings on the nature of life and the occult. He claims to read a lot, everything from Jane Austen to HP Lovecraft. The characters and monsters he creates from nothing speak for themselves or scare me to death when I get just a small taste of the frightening intellect of my closest friend.

When I was in high school, Quin was a member of a dorky role-playing club, the type of kids that the jocks and debs would relentlessly make fun of. Quin didn't seem to be the type they all said he was, but he was smart enough then to act like a jerk, which irritated me. And his friend Kel was somehow crazier than he was, what with claiming he'd fought a mechanical wolf and a shadow monster in real life in order to save a kingdom from certain destruction. He was weird and I considered myself to be grounded in reason.

After Joaquin and I reunited, he reintroduced me to Kel. And Kel turned out to be a good guy, proving that I had perceived both of them wrong throughout high school. If I had been wrong about my two best friends, then it would be reasonable to suspect that I might be wrong about Sarah. Or, more terrifying, that I could be right about her: what if she is the answer that unlocks a whole new realm of truth? Am I supposed to pass that off as another paranoid conspiracy that might be embroiling me to no end?

I cannot simply sacrifice the thought that life can be limitless. After all, the universe itself has its own boundaries, as does its creator—if such a creator really exists. In this regard, perhaps I will never be able to understand the whole truth, if it lies outside the limits of human understanding. Maybe someday when I die, the afterlife will reveal to me everything that I am currently missing.

I know I believe in Sarah, and she is not a reptilian alien. She couldn't be. But what I don't know about her intrigues me so deeply that I must continually search for a deeper understanding, even if it leads me to Crazy Town.

Closing the laptop, I feel as though I am standing on a precipice, over a bottomless pit where darkened storms rage and the winds stir opaque clouds into a terrifying vortex of doom. What lies somewhere in the abyss may be the light I crave; or is it the darkness that will finally envelop me? Do I have the guts to leap, or do I hold fast to what I know and attempt to ignore the peril below?

I have never been a big risk taker, but sometimes I'm not smart enough to know the difference between danger and safety, or to separate knowledge from wisdom. It's a long way down, but perhaps instead of leaping I could dip my toe into the surface of the clouds and test the cliff for footholds.

5

The Sword of Ares

You don't often realize the sheer failure of fragile human memory until you're searching for someone you've never met based on a shoddy physical description. When your search takes you to a busy street downtown, that recollection can be futile.

After several minutes of scurrying along a crowded sidewalk from the garage I parked in, I catch my breath at the crosswalk and scan the throngs ahead for a stubbly-faced black man with a bald head. From my vantage point I can see four of them, so I home in on each for a moment so I can decide which to approach. The shadows of the skyscrapers seem to stretch on for blocks, bathing the street in a somber, post-dreamscape tinge of gray. The sun has melted away some of the snow from the previous night, but with the long shadows the temperature is beginning to drop. It will not be long before the puddles turn to ice and the fog of my breath further distorts my vision.

The first man of interest to me is wearing a sport coat and khakis and is hurrying along the various storefronts clutching a Styrofoam coffee cup while trying to dodge strangers and create a more direct path to his destination. I watch him until the crosswalk icon changes, then redirect my attention to the street to make sure the coast is clear. A dozen impatient strangers wait with me, engaging in clipped conversations or listening to music on their earbuds to drown out the noise of tires on wet pavement and distant horns echoing through the urban canyon.

A car speeds through the crosswalk, seemingly unaware that more than a dozen people are waiting to cross the street. Where are the police when you really need them? I grunt something barely audible, amounting to nothing more than a syllable from my favorite curse word, and attempt to retrain my gaze on the first man of interest.

In the fray of pedestrians, he has disappeared, either into the corner book shop or onto Fifth Street towards the tourist-ridden Independence Hall. In all my years living in this city I have never once visited that attraction; in fact, I have taken to the habit of consciously avoiding the area whenever I venture downtown, but Harley is said to like this area of the city.

When I finally reach the curb, I mindlessly kick a clump of ice off my shoe before pausing to scan Market Street from my new vantage point. The dozens of strangers have disappeared, only to be replaced by several more. I look on in frustration, past a crowd of spectators listening to the jazzy sounds of a saxophone on the street corner. I manage to peek through the throng to get a glimpse of the performer, who is a graying white man wearing a beanie. His carrying case is splayed out in front of him so that his adoring onlookers can deposit money into his account and keep him working.

I edge past a pair of women carrying designer handbags and wearing sunglasses, trying not to gaze at them for too long. A block ahead of me, another crowd has assembled to watch a caricaturist draw silly cartoons at the expense of his subjects. Who in their right mind would subject themselves to becoming a base stereotype so that a stranger can wordlessly make fun of them? I almost gag at the sight. Four women have formed a tighter huddle near the outskirts of the group, partially blocking an intense patch of sun that has scattered through the cluttered skyline.

I inch forward, careful to avoid stepping on the obnoxiously high heels of the woman in front of me, who has trained her attention not on the sidewalk but on the storefronts. A candy shop pokes a bright hole in the display windows, set back into the structure about five feet below the overhang of the residential tower above. It seems a good place to huddle from the biting breeze, so I enter and scan both sides of the street until I see a man vaguely resembling the description Joaquin gave me.

I had imagined a frazzled look, and a cardboard sign warning of the end times, perhaps with a shopping cart full of his personal property. He appears not to notice me even as I stare. A pair of cars passes by, slowing for the pedestrians. I step off the curb and hurry toward him, barely aware of the police officer who has been watching me. If he wants to nab me for jaywalking, he's going to have to do it after he finishes dressing down the other jaywalkers who have just obstructed traffic.

Few people are interacting with the man I'm looking at. When I reach the other side of the street, I glance up at the shimmering glass high above my head and marvel at how it interacts with the scattering sunlight that is filtering through the high clouds. I let out a puff of air and study him as I approach.

He seems cozy in the dim recess, adjacent to a closed-up shop whose owner has called it quits for the day. It feels weird to approach a stranger on the sidewalk and he doesn't seem happy about his situation. If I had any cash I would offer it to him, but all I have is my credit card. I swallow and wait for a father and three kids to casually make for the corner.

By now, the stranger has acknowledged my presence. For the moment, all I can do is nod at him, as though that act alone will make him feel somehow valued in a hurried world that reveres material possessions over friendly interaction. Life wasn't like this when I was in high school, but the world changes and sometimes not for the better.

He coughs when I get within speaking distance. He has taken his eyes off the crowd of people watching the caricaturist, and I can barely hear him over the tearing sound of tires on pavement or the saxophone music lighting up the late afternoon.

If we're going to have a fruitful conversation, it will have to be away from the din of downtown life, and the only way that will be possible is if I can lure him into the bakery a few stores down from his station.

"You there," he finally says, his voice sounding fuzzy and phlegmy from the cold. "You know they give tickets for jaywalking in this town."

"Yeah," I mumble. "Took a chance."

"Whatchoo want with me, man? Don't want your appearance to be assaulted by that know-it-all across the street?"

There's one thing we have in common.

"You Harley?" I take a chance, hoping against hope that I have found the right man, even though he somehow looks very little like what Joaquin described.

His eyes cross and he looks taken aback. "Some call me that, I guess. You can take your pick between 'vagrant,' 'hobo,'—or my personal favorite—'moocher'."

I try not to look startled, but his lexicon and speech patterns have already drawn me in.

He gazes at me, waiting for me to explain what has made me seek him out.

Words fail me; all I can do is stutter my friend's name and try to avoid eye contact should he feel insulted. Then again, he seems more interested in what I have to say than I expected. I shift my feet across a jagged crack in the concrete and attempt to haphazardly jumble some words together into what might constitute an actual sentence to someone listening closely enough. The cold breeze rushes against me, and to find refuge, I step closer to him in the recess.

"A friend ... he said he knows you, somehow. Said you might help me make sense of ... what is it ... a phenomenon? Something I have been experiencing."

"What kind of phenomenon? Astral, psychological, sociological, theological? You damn well look like you could use a word or two."

What's that supposed to mean? I try to hide my annoyance at the suggestion, but the applause for the street performers momentarily diverts his attention and shields me from a reaction.

"Maybe we can get a table in the bakery," I mumble. "My treat."

He furrows his eyebrows. "Nah. I'm not about charity."

"Get out of the cold, find some quiet for a change? If you have money, you can pay your own way."

"What makes you think I don't have money?"

This question hits me square in the chest, like a jab from a professional boxer. I can only deflect it by rehashing his own words: "Didn't you say they call you a hobo?"

"Never said they were right," he grunts, leaning back against the glass and glancing up at me.

I reach out my hand to help him up, which he refuses by simply shaking his head. He uses little effort in getting to his feet, which comes as another mild surprise. His jeans and overcoat on second glance don't seem to suggest abject poverty, merely casual comfort. I wonder what he's doing on the street if he isn't homeless, but he seems to feel the question coming.

"Watching people pitter patter on about their daily lives is kind of a hobby of mine; call it a social experiment. Long as I'm alone, no one even makes eye contact. I have a woman on my arm, I get a glance or two. But one time I gave a kid a piece of candy and suddenly I'm the talk of the block. People take social cues all the time, and you're no different."

I don't have a reasonable comment on his observations, so I can only walk in silence and pretend to peer through the shop windows of a clothing store hawking the latest trends in footwear.

"Brisk night," I say, shivering against the cold.

"You didn't come all the way down here for small talk," he says. "I take it you live in the westside district, in one of those midrise apartment communities."

His assumption is right on the mark, making me feel as silly as the people posing for caricature drawings across the street. I gulp and try to change the subject, but Harley has already launched another question: "What do they call you?"

His phrasing is uncanny. "It's Kerry, but I know a woman who thinks I'm Larry."

"This woman," he starts, "you in love with her or something?"

"Why would you say that?"

"She doesn't know your name, you brought her up to a complete stranger, and you didn't even have the nerve to correct her. Damn shame, if I say so myself, but you go get her."

"Actually," I stammer, "that's kind of what I was hoping to pick your brain about."

"Shit, I'm no love guru," Harley quips. "You'll have to wonder about the cosmos. I'm like Neil DeGrasse Tyson, but with a street mouth and a shitty attitude. Can you handle that?"

I nod. "Think so. So, she disappeared on me. I was walking to my car, and her car was running, and snow was getting scraped off, but she wasn't there. No one was, except I think she *was* there. Do you get it?"

We reach the bakery, and he visibly tries to wrap his head around what I'm saying. Somehow, having explained it, I feel even dumber, but a light seems to go off in his eyes for a split second. I realize by now that I'm not dealing with a street-corner preacher but an educated human being who has a knack for making some startling predictions.

"Ah ... that's a complicated one." He strokes his chin and considers a detailed response, while I pull open the door for us to file into the well-lit store. The aroma of fresh-baked cookies and muffins fills my senses and sets off a pang of hunger. I spy a delicacy behind the curved glass that seems to be making eyes at me. I decide to order the pastry while Harley surveys his options.

The cashier takes our money separately and hands out our snacks. "Two cups of hot cocoa," I add as she opens a glass door and grabs my pastry with a small square of wax paper.

"Stay or to go?" she asks.

"We'll enjoy it here," I mutter.

"Thank you. Come again."

Harley orders a small loaf of artisanal banana bread and together we find a table next to the broad glass so that we can observe the street. He takes a quick bite of his treat and swallows, before greedily reaching for his hot cocoa.

"So your phenomenon is a girl you have a crush on who seems to disappear?"

"Yeah. I asked her if she was invisible but didn't get a response. But I know she was there—I could feel it."

"You figure that she feels awkward about getting it out and tries to pretend you haven't noticed so maybe things will feel less tense."

I sense a pattern. Am I telegraphing my thoughts this readily?

"I guess you could say that."

"What happened when she disappeared? Did she dissolve, or just blur, or did her image turn off like a lightbulb?"

"Well ... I didn't actually see her. I'd talked to her earlier before I headed home. When I passed her car in the parking lot it was running, and I saw ice falling off the car like it was being picked at. And then in the rear-view mirror I see her lights turn on, and she's following me out of the lot. It would have taken her longer than that to get from the trailer to her car."

"You refer to the 'Ghost in the Room' phenomenon," he explains. "Psychologists refer to it as some sort of spatial awareness concept, where our brains tend to invent the presence of another individual. It's not as rare as you think."

"I don't think my mind was inventing her," I shoot back. "I know she was there. I was wondering if there was some visual trick with the light causing my brain to not register seeing her."

"Yes," he says, chewing, "Shadow and light and movement all have dramatic effects on what we think we see. But you say you didn't actually see her at all."

"It was like her silhouette or aura were still there."

"The aura thing is a joke made up by street mystics," he says, glancing sideways. "There's no rationality to it whatsoever."

I roll my eyes and savor a bit of sugary pastry while I listen to him. "Irrational—I guess that's as good a word as any. But there was like a swirl of wind or something from the storm."

"Now that puts a whole new spin on it."

I silently note his clever word usage and nod.

"Have you heard of the Legend of the Six, from Greek mythology?"

I zone out before he is finished with his question. Though I've always found mythology an interesting subject, it was useless in determining what was up with Sarah the other night.

He reads my expression before I even know I'm making it. "Didn't think so. When the Centurion guard were ransacking cities during a period of aggressive expansion of the Roman empire, legend has it that six warriors appeared to defend a town from certain doom, but five of them met their deaths. One woman, the Lady of the Six, as she was called, vanished after being punctured by multiple arrows."

I swivel my head to try to study him more closely. I remember shapes and colors from my recent nightmare, but more clearly, I recall the lingering dour feeling after awakening. That he has managed to bring it all back in lucid detail sends shivers down my spine. I cast my gaze sideways at my translucent reflection in the window while clutching my hot cocoa so tightly that my actions might accuse Harley of trying to steal it from me.

"No one knows where she went or if she even survived. Some say she's immortal, or she was translated to some other realm or some such bullshit, but she's long dead. You don't outwit the reaper by going invisible."

Outside, a pair of headlights illuminates a shadowy recess where a small group has assembled to either take shelter from the cold or to engage in conversation. When the light recedes, the shadow seems to elongate, revealing only vague silhouettes against the dark backdrop of the building skin. I nibble on my pasty as I struggle to formulate a response, which Harley is clearly expecting.

"Well, then, what do you think happened to her?"

"Most humans can't be translated," Harley offers, "at least not in the way suggested in the Bible, where a person lives such a great life that he is taken directly to the mythical place called heaven without experiencing death. Least it gives us a starting point."

"You're saying she's some kind of saint?"

He shakes his head and sips from his cocoa, before shifting in his seat and leaning forward. The gradual darkening outside has not gone unnoticed, and in about thirty minutes the bakery staff will have us leave so they can close up shop.

"I was giving you the expected parameters of passing on to a different dimension."

"A different dimension? Sounds like some kind of whacked out sci-fi idea."

"It's established physics," Harley argues. "While studying the behavior of subatomic particles, researchers observed something unexpected: you would expect electrons to be orbiting the nucleus of an atom in a relatively uniform fashion, with each on a different orbit so they don't collide. But sometimes an electron will simply disappear and then re-emerge a nanosecond later on a completely different orbit. They can't explain how this happens but theorize that the energy associated with their mass can cause some unexpected results."

"You're a physics major?"

"Not at all," Harley says, subtly raising a finger. "Just well-read. You'd be surprised what opening a diverse array of books can do for you."

I can only shake my head and glance out the window to the darkening scene on the street. From this vantage point I cannot see where the caricaturist is stationed, but the crowd around the saxophonist seems to have grown.

"I'm not smart enough for physics," I say, trying not to appear sheepish.

"I don't speak jargon. So I'm giving it to you in layman's terms. The point is, if electrons can alter their orbits, it seems to imply some kind of alternate dimension."

"What would that be?"

"Basic science knows of four: vertical, horizontal, depth, and time. But then time has a way of distorting the other three. It's why telescopes are basically stationary time-travel devices. Anything you see, you see it as it was thousands or millions of years ago."

"Sounds interesting," I mutter, not trying to dismiss him.

He continues without missing a beat. "Electrons jumping orbits in what seems to be an arbitrary manner might lead to many discoveries, and some theories, associated with particles of particles of particles, contend that there are at least five other dimensions. We exist in three and have evolved to perceive the fourth.

"Dimensional shifts occur more frequently than you might imagine. If particles can do it, why can't humans? Once you deconstruct what you think you know, you can experience a larger universe."

"Wouldn't the electron thing require more energy than the entire world can produce? Because it sounds like electrons can do it because they have low mass and high energy."

"It doesn't always take energy," Harley contends. "There are portals. Maybe at some point, your Missus wandered through the wrong portal and got trapped in some sort of dimension between dimensions."

"That's impossible."

"But then so is becoming invisible."

I roll my eyes and then glance at the cashier, who has begun packaging the day's goods for second-hand supermarket sales. In another dimension perhaps Harley wouldn't be making my head hurt, and then everything would make sense. And if that's the case, maybe the 'mythical' heaven Harley has described isn't such a bad destination after all.

"Are you an expert in philosophy?"

Harley rolls his eyes. "Those guys are nutjobs."

"You said something about a mythical heaven."

Harley settles in his seat and clasps his hands at the edge of the table, almost in a meditative stance. I half-expect him to wax poetic on the meaning of life, but what he offers instead is a stark reminder that life is more complex than organized religions often teach.

"It's mythical because what the Bible describes as heaven is an ideal; a depiction of perfection. You have to ask yourself what perfection even is. When you have a coherent answer, ask ten more people what they think heaven is, and you're likely to get ten different answers. So the ideal is not really so ideal. It's highly subjective to your interpretation of what perfect is."

"If you don't believe heaven exists, then I guess hell doesn't either." I pass it off, trying not to sound judgmental.

"Heaven and hell are extremes, offered as examples," Harley explains. "But life isn't a series of extremes, you ought to know that. It's always somewhere in between or generally associated. The Bible breaks it down into simple terms because it is intended as a moral guide between right and wrong: make enough right choices, you go to the right place after you die. Make enough wrong choices, you could be singing *Nobody Knows the Trouble I've Seen* with the devil."

"I guess that sort of makes sense." As long as he doesn't try to contradict what I know deep within my heart, I can listen to solid logic. His advice to deconstruct what I think I know seems more of a threat than a promise of greater knowledge. After all, that kind of thinking is what got Adam and Eve banished from the Garden of Eden.

Again, I allow myself a moment to process all the information he has just given me and fill the time gap with an unfocused stare outside. In the absence of focus, light and dark become blurred, and the world begins to lose color. Too much information seems a fantastic way to lose focus, which is an idea some churches warn against. If I don't even know what focus is, then how am I supposed to become more educated?

Then again, having focus is what guides the best research. By weeding out extraneous detail and only processing relevant information, a study gives a clearer picture. But then, what happens when one of those little details turns out to have a major impact on the data? I'm not smart enough to answer that question, and asking Harley is, ironically, a breach of focus.

"But back to what you were saying about portals," I drone on. "Where are they?"

"You never really know. Most people or things that go through them can come back, but it isn't something people do intentionally."

"I've always wondered what happens to my socks in the dryer," I quip.

It is enough to elicit a smile, but I can sense that Harley knows more than he's letting on.

"So you're saying you can only go through a portal to another dimension accidentally?"

He shakes his head. "Just easier to do it that way, because almost nobody knows what they are looking for, and most people can't even do it. When you see the world in black and white, you are limiting yourself only to those extremes that you can see. You have to open your eyes."

"But where do I look?"

"Everywhere—under the stairs, in the attic, across the street, between the mattresses. There are numerous possibilities. Again, you have to be looking, and be able to understand what you are seeing. When you are out in the street, don't just look at the glassy storefronts, or the people, or the towers. Perhaps it's a black splotch from an oil stain on the street, or a wobbly lamppost. Look for the voids, those places where shape and texture can only be interpreted from within."

"Fine," I say, not certain that what he just said constitutes an answer.

"But fair warning: should you succeed, I don't have any idea what you will see. I don't know whether you will get stuck, or for how long. There may not even be an immediate way out. And if time is different wherever you end up, you could be there for years, or even a lifetime. On second thought, don't do it—you'll just have to accept your woman's fate and move on. Otherwise, it's an abyss you don't want to fall into."

His warning resonates with me. Sarah is just a little crush, and my life would resume with or without her. If I choose to pursue her across the dimensions, if that is even possible, I'm an idiot.

Then again, Harley has probably just led me down another useless rabbit hole, if I wish to reduce this interaction to a dumb cliché. But he has proven one thing—that he's good at provoking honest thought. If thought is a construct of human origin, one can reason that it can have far-reaching consequences, both good and bad. It might take years or decades for them to materialize, which proves another platitude: hindsight is always twenty-twenty.

Aside from the fact that human memory disproves the cliché, it seems obvious to me that Harley has given me some valuable insight. Next time I see Joaquin, I'm going to hit him in the head with a metal water bottle, and he'll deserve it.

The cashier looks up from her perch behind the register after she has finished bagging and boxing leftovers. She doesn't even have to part her lips before Harley and I rise from our seats in unison and gather the last of our purchases to leave.

With little conversation, I offer a courteous smile to the cashier and we venture outside. I'm tempted to walk Harley back to his nook before going to the garage, but he stops me and looks deep into my eyes, as if searching for whatever kind of trajectory he might have put me on.

"Come back, my friend. I don't have a lot of people to interact with, and it's killing me."

I can only gape at him in shock. How could such a wise, knowledgeable man be left with no one? The heartache slithers into my senses before I can contain it.

I shake his hand and look up into the deep blue sky. A flock of birds crosses a low-hanging cloud and soundlessly disappears behind a glass tower; down at street level, the crowds have steadily begun to disperse, leaving Market Street a humbler and more mainstream urban place, and the saxophone performance slowly winds down. Fewer people has strangely revealed more to look at. Across the street, an odd nook seems to have been needlessly carved from the corner of a building by some architect who thought he was creating something unconventional. The crease traverses up to a third-floor setback that separates the residential portion of the building from the commercial. A lone pedestrian passes by without acknowledging its existence.

Further up the street, the empty crosswalk counts down the seconds until it is unsafe to cross. I gather my coat across my chest as the wind pummels me with an icy blast.

A few stragglers litter the streets, walking home or to their cars. The sound of the saxophone has faded away, leaving the normal din of street life to continue unabated, and the water from melting snow and ice on the pavement has refrozen, making for a slippery drive. Blocks away, a car slides right through a red light and miraculously gets through the intersection unscathed. It rights itself quickly and continues as if nothing has happened.

The garage looms ahead, tucked between and beneath a pair of adjoining office towers. The lighting inside the parking levels reveals opaque gray horizontal stripes, interspersed with soft yellow light. A high-pitched squeal indicates that a car is rounding a bend slightly faster than one should drive in a garage.

As I make my way there, I witness a black square punched into the side of the building. The falling darkness has made it impossible to see in without entering it. I carefully stroll to the edge of the dark, place one toe in the shadow, and swallow. This could be the proverbial first step of the rest of my life, if I am ready to take the plunge. If I disappear, will anyone really remember me?

With one foot in, nothing untoward occurs. I survey my foot to confirm that is still attached and then take one more step forward. The wind howls outside and again nothing happens. The texture of the brick and the dim light reveals that I have entered a narrow alley between high-rises. I follow the wall to a terminus, which appears to be an unlit overhead door for loading.

To my right, the wall adjoins another, constructed of mismatching brick. From a chipped concrete base, a black stain rises three or four feet. I slowly approach to examine it, feeling the texture of the brick with my fingertips.

I turn around and head back to the street in silence. I blink and something seems to have happened to the overhead lights; they seem dimmer and softer, as though a thin gray bedsheet has covered the bulbs. The sounds of tires on pavement have gone silent, and I can only hear my own footsteps and muted breathing.

Terror swirls within, and I close my eyes before stepping out of the alley, but the street is normal, and life has gone on without me. The revelation makes me shudder. Nothing about the alley seems ethereal, but the rest of the world does. I can only determine now that Harley has offered me an understanding that I will never part with. If that is going to create an impact on the remainder of my life, then I can only hope for a positive outcome. Still, I know nothing, and fear has stunned me.

6

Lupus Fangs

A billion points of light shine from the heavens, to reflect on the still waters of a forested lake I have never seen before. Ripples on the surface occasionally blur and distort the shattered rays as miniscule waves lap at the rocky shores. I hold a broken piece of eroded river rock in my right hand, turn it over several times, and reflect on why I am here alone in this unexpected wilderness.

More importantly, *how* did I get here?

On Sunday night after football, I visited Harley downtown, or at least some distant part of me remembers that interaction. The music has faded, the throngs dispersed, and Harley's face has transitioned into mere echoes of humanity. It seems like it has been ages. And on Monday I worked late again, cleaning and organizing supplies for the next day's shift.

Earning a thumbs up from Jamal, if I could distinctly remember it, would have been an accomplishment. I know I was there, but again the memory has faded like the starlight on the waves.

Amidst it all, I don't even remember if Sarah was there in any sense. I swallow when another memory prods at me. If it is a concrete memory, it is surely something I have never experienced; but like a lucid dream it crowds my vision, as though a specter of reality has sliced it away from another life. Allowing myself to ponder on it feels like a betrayal of everything I am, and yet I cannot stop its reflection from bearing down on the gently lapping waves of my soul.

Abruptly I try to push it away.

This lake must be somewhere in Pennsylvania, perhaps in the far northwestern corner of the state, where Lake Erie affects the weather six months out of the year.

The moonlight washes the waters to a glimmering shade of white, and in the distance, mist rises from the surface to obscure the thick greenery on the far shore. Nearer to where I'm standing, rows of vacation houses make the area like a rustic resort. Few seem to be occupied, as no lights are visible inside the windows.

About a quarter mile away, near the end of the row of shake-sided houses, a canoe is moored to a poorly constructed floating dock buoyed by heavy foam blocks. Its oars are visible inside it.

Not a single other human being graces these shores. Solitude tends to do funny things to the human brain; it is only by unwinding and obtaining a fresh perspective that we can open our minds to our vast potential.

Further away, a deer forages on some exposed grass before disappearing into the shadows of the deciduous trees. Before doing so it seems to pause, looking directly at me and deciding that safety is the best policy. How can a deer be so startled by one unarmed human standing thousands of feet away?

In deep humility, I look down at my feet and survey the exposed lakebed gravel. The stone I am clutching in my right hand sports a spotted flat side, rounded at its rough corners as though it had broken away from bedrock centuries ago and undergone erosion since. Wrapping my forefinger around the curved edges, I allow myself a moment of remorse for something I have never felt.

It is an agony that has been carved through my heart for more than a decade, an invisible yet indelible hurt that has transformed me into something I hardly recognize.

Frustrated with myself, I clutch the rock tighter, step back like a pitcher winding up his throw, stretch my arm back, and fling it as far forward as my muscles will allow. The rock seems to tumble in the air as it flies. The angle of its momentum is not high enough for the stone to make a heavy clunk in the water; instead, it skips, one, two, three, four times before soundlessly disappearing beneath the surface.

The sounds of the surrounding forest seem dull and strangely unappealing. A flutter of wings disrupts the silence, followed by the caw of a raven from deeper in the trees. The road that leads here feels abandoned. It winds through a maze of forested hills, densely populated with deciduous trees, and makes its way back to the nearest populated area.

Scanning the shore to my right reveals an ages-old wooden pier spanning from a grassy moor out into deeper waters, and beyond that, a glassy arm of the lake disappears behind a rounded knoll at the shore. Upon closer inspection I see the knoll is a forested island, disconnected from the shore by a narrow channel that cuts it off from vehicular access. The island strikingly conforms to the landscape, offering little charm. On warm days canoers might row out to the island to explore.

Stuck somewhere in the thicket of trees on the island, a stony rectangle juts up out of the canopy. This must be the little cabin—

A cabin? How do I know there is a cabin?

The memory collides with my consciousness and temporarily washes away the billions of stars reflected there. It seems so eerie and ethereal, yet something within me remembers this place. The pier, stretching from the tall, reedy grass in shallow water out into the deep; the cabin; and the row of summer homes on the shore. The spectacle of nature pierces my heart with foreboding memory.

I gather my strength and lunge forward, immersing my shoes and ankles in the cold water. If this isn't real, how can I be experiencing it? All at once, I feel terror enveloping me. Harley might have mentioned unexpected results from traveling into another realm; not only have I traveled here unwittingly, but I also somehow remember it. The possibilities play out in my mind as the frigid water numbs my ankles.

I wade deeper into the lake until the water covers my knees. Bending down and reaching into the black surface, I grasp at mud and stones, then gather a double handful of cold water and splash it onto my face. As if by instinct my mouth opens wide as the shock further bewilders me. I could be stuck here forever in this faraway place, and what if no one back in the real world even remembers me?

If this truly is another realm, it should be sparking with energy, yet it all seems so dead. The raven's cawing should be echoing through the trees and off the water. The deer should not have even been there, and its reaction to me should have been more measured. It acted as though it had not seen a human being before in its life, a strange occurrence for a habitat so closely enmeshed with the shrines of humanity.

My heart beats faster as the cold water constricts my muscles. To shield myself from hypothermia, I wade back to the shore and step onto the rocks, before falling into a cross-legged sitting position with the toes of my shoes touching the water's edge.

I can only do one thing, now. Pondering on a life filled with surprises should have been invigorating, yet I can only meet it in frightened silence. This realm—Harley had called it a different dimension—is more than un-nerving. I shudder against the cooling air and fold my arms across my chest. If I just close my eyes, perhaps I will awaken from this nightmare in a sweat and be able to text Joaquin about it.

My eyes wedge themselves open after only a few seconds. If the freezing water hadn't snapped me awake, attempting any sort of second-dimension sleep would have been sure to fail. It was all real: dazzlingly, crushingly real.

A fish jumping out of the water a hundred yards away seizes my attention. The resultant ripples radiate across the surface until they gradually fade away. I watch for it again, but at whatever time of night this is there are few fish that are active.

I had read something fascinating about some species of deer years back: they are crepuscular, limiting their activity to dusk and dawn, partially due to human interference in their habitat but also to take refuge from the heat of the day. They live on this schedule for their entire lives, despite the changing of the seasons.

This knowledge alerts me to the fact that if any of these homes are occupied, people should be awake. I survey the nearby shore once more. There are no lights in any of the windows, no hints of motion, and no cars on the road. The silence seems to pulsate with an unseen energy. Thinking hard about it reveals more than I originally let on. I must be trapped in a parallel memory of an event that hasn't happened yet.

The suggestion is enough to dizzy me. I can do some rudimentary calculations in my brain; if this memory is from some future dimension, I must be in my forties. Still, my body feels the same. I feel no unexpected pains, no new sensations, and my thoughts seem unmarred by future events. If I can still be so pure and untarnished in this realm, then I must have been recently plucked from another plane and randomly assigned to this one, where the only apparent life belongs to me, the deer, the fish, and the raven.

No. It must be a hallucination. Harley isn't that smart ... is he? My body is idle, yet my mind is traveling at a million miles per second. Memory from only days ago is beginning to fade away into pitch black, replaced by strange recollections that seem to float on the ether directly into my soul.

Acting on anything at this point seems to me a terrible mistake. I can only try to stay calm, but again—what if I am trapped in this limbo forever? The more I ponder, the more my past seems to vanish. What happens when there is nothing left of me? Would I become a stranger in a host body I don't even recognize?

I reach out into the darkness and refocus my attention on the millions of shimmering stars. My inadequate understanding of the cosmos notwithstanding, the constellations appear to be unaltered. Reaching out further, my vision seems to stretch away from me. A mysterious orb appears, at first with a light side and a shaded side, but in time all of it begins to burn as if set afire by the gods. A planet transformed into a star in the blink of an eye. When I close my eyelids, I imagine myself orbiting it to study it in all its detailed glory. Except that this doesn't come at me like idle imagination; it interacts with my spirit like dizzying memory.

One can spend hours marveling at the complexity of space and time. Ironically, space and time are all I have. Then again, somewhere in the vastness of this reality, even if at an atomic level, there are possibly several more dimensions lurking unobserved.

Feverishly I pry my eyes from the glowing orb and watch the waters as I rise to my feet. I once heard advice on taking a step into the unknown. As if dozens of years have gone by, it still reverberates in my memory: "Take one step into the fog, and then another. You can never see as far as you want to, but only enough to take the next step, and then the next, until you reach your destination."

Who had said that? Was it from philosophy, or religion, or a book? I scour my memory bank and settle on a middle-aged white man with a neatly trimmed gray beard and wire-rimmed spectacles. He stands somewhat taller than me, thin and lanky. His stature would seem unimposing to the unaided eye, and yet he intimidates me. Reaching through my mind to find a name filed away somewhere is more difficult than I expected. Was he a David or a Mark? No, it seems like an R name. Reginald, Richard? No, Ronald. Yes, it was Ronald. If I can somehow escape this memory, I can track Ronald down and meet him. Apart from the fact that Ronald may be a false memory, and finding him therefore impossible, I begin to formulate a plan.

I search the shoreline in vain, looking for a pocket of black that I can disappear into.

Look to the island, a voice in my mind says. I peel my eyes away from the nearby shore and study the isle in search of the cabin. If it were that simple, I would be shocked. Swimming to it would likely result in drowning or hypothermia, or both, but there is a canoe still lying about a quarter mile away, forgotten and unused.

Stepping over a chunk of rotting driftwood washed against the rocky shore, I keep my eyes open for wildlife and signs of a human presence, making my trek in the dark more difficult. Within only a few minutes I stumble, tripping on an exposed boulder and crunching loudly on a broken-off stick from one of the thousand trees. I pause in my tracks and look around. Why hasn't the noise spooked the wildlife? Then again, what if the wildlife was nothing more than a population to fill in a landscape that shouldn't exist in the first place?

My thoughts trail off as I resume my journey, resolving to step more carefully. A tiny splash in the depths peels away my attention but disappears by the time I can look in its direction.

The darkness behind the windows seems more and more unsettling as time goes by, as if ghostly vestiges of human existence lie trapped inside, longing for the freedom of the open water. This landscape should exude peace, but instead it chills me to the bone.

In ten more minutes, I step onto a strand of more refined gravel, which leads to a small sandy area that serves as a manmade beach, where children could play and swim if there were any here. Imagining the sounds of screams and laughter is almost enough to make me crumble. My heart clenches as a low groan emanates from somewhere in the woods beyond the houses, and then dissipates. A delayed flutter of wings follows, and then a snapping twig.

I freeze to my spot a mere twenty feet from the dock. "Hello? Who's there?"

If I were expecting an answer I would be deluded, yet still I'm stunned when none comes. Even in a dimension populated by humans, stalkers rarely announce themselves, especially when the mark seems to have discovered them.

I carefully step onto the dock, and it rocks and vibrates with my weight, sending ripples radiating outward to crash against incoming ripples from a fish jumping. The starlight reflects on the chaos with splendor and beauty. In some respects, staring into the reflective waters is like peering into my soul. Within it there is nothing but black, but the surface reflects all visible light, including from—*is that a pair of headlights?*

I swivel my neck and nearly flip into the water like a fish on a line. Terror drenches me as I look at the light. It momentarily bakes the landscape in luminescence and casts mysterious shadows over everything.

No land animal can make that kind of brightness. I strain to examine the source of the light, which has vanished as quickly as it appeared. A lone human silhouette stands at least five hundred feet away, draped in black from head to toe. It silently draws nearer, and the wildlife pretends not to notice.

Panic swells within me. The intruder could be here to help me out, but I don't count him as friendly. Wordlessly, I flee to the end of the dock, where the canoe gently rises and falls with the shifting waves. My nerves feel like an icy pincushion as chills race through every part of my body.

Assuming the intruder can't fly, he will be close enough for me to recognize or for a ranged attack before I can row into the safety of the water.

The boat shifts under my weight and the water sloshes violently as I grab at the oars. Struggling to untie a narrow bit of twine, I look up to the stranger every two seconds as he drifts nearer. If he had a gun he could shoot me at this range, but if movies are any indication, then cloaked villains skulking along a lakeshore prefer melee weapons to the inhumanity of ranged instruments of death.

Again, I grab at the oars; one slides over the edge of the boat and splashes into the water. I dip my hand in the cold liquid to grab it while attempting to push away from the dock as the menace approaches me.

He isn't real, I try to reassure myself. But when I blink, he is still there, seeming to gather darkness to him. My heart is on the verge of exploding as I steady the canoe, stick the blades in the water, and begin to paddle backwards toward the island.

But this doesn't appear to deter the stranger. Seconds drift by as the canoe floats steadily away from the shore. Within moments, the dock has disappeared from my view, yet the stranger still nears. He stops. Surveying the depths and then his prey, he steps away from the shore directly towards me—walking on the water? "Shit."

The first word I have uttered throughout this whole ordeal, and it happens to be a swear word that seems to die like a whimper in the dull wind instead of echoing on the open waters.

"You there!" the stranger shouts. It is the voice of a woman, and her pitch and cadence suggest a modern accent. The reverberation fills my heart with sorrow. How does her voice carry this far without dying like mine?

"Don't go!"

"I'm going," I whisper. "Anything to get away from you."

Still, there is something disarming about her voice; a certain sense of familiarity vibrates within it, emanating outward almost with warmth.

I drift farther away from her, slowly approaching the island behind me. Still, she approaches, as though the water has simply delayed each step. I steel my muscles to row faster, sending stronger waves toward her. Behind me an owl hoots and the darkness swells; the millions of speckles on the surface of the water shatter and fade as the oars kick up spray. I am faster than her, and that bodes well.

When I reach the shore, I don't bother to look back as I splash into shallow water and wade toward the rocky shore of the island. She appears to have given up, but even so seems to be reaching out for me. Terror rocks me when she calls my name.

"I know you. Please don't."

No. She is going to drag me into another realm. I scurry upslope as the cold constricts around my ankles. The island is a dense woodland, steep-sided and inhospitable to humans, yet someone has constructed a cottage-like cabin structure deep within the trees as a sort of refuge. A writer could feel comfortable here, in an idyllic realm where thoughts run as wild as the deer and the wolves.

Refuge. I stumble up the slope, grabbing at tree roots, branches, and rocks as I ascend. The silhouette of the visitor has disappeared into thin air, offering me a sense of relief. When I reach the dilapidated building, a stark feeling of madness seems to prowl at the edges of my mind. The boards creak as I move toward the front door, bypassing a dusty cobwebbed window. A musty scent fills my nostrils as I push open the door and look into utter blackness. I feel the near wall next to the door for a light switch and nervously flick it up. Nothing happens. As if my body is emanating some kind of artificial light, I inch forward through what seems like a kitchen area toward a square of black that could either be an open closet or a descending stairway. Even from less than a foot away I can see absolutely nothing. I reach out to feel for a wall and when I feel nothing but thin air, I proceed cautiously, expecting to step downward. Instead, my foot stumbles on hard floor, sending me tumbling.

Anticipating pain, I let out a preparatory yelp, which seems to die in dead air as I continue to fall through open space for much longer than I should.

A subtle whisper of a breeze vibrates at my eardrums. I close my eyes to prepare for an impact, but land on a soft cushion, which resists the force of my falling body and springs me back. Light explodes when I flit my eyes open. I am in a dimly lit bedroom, clinging to the lamp as if to throw it at any stranger that enters. The light grows, and someone next to me shifts violently. I howl when a hand wraps around my waist to pull me closer.

"It's just a bad dream," she says. Why does her voice sound so familiar?

I can only stammer as the cold batters at me. I flip out of the bed, crashing onto the floor and scurrying on my hands and knees toward the door. I dare not look back as the woman sits up in bed, flicks on the light, and watches.

I must flee the cabin as though my life itself hangs in the balance. Except that now it's clear I am not even in a cabin; I am in a well-furnished, fully occupied, three-bedroom home overlooking a serene lake with a secluded island. I peer out the window as panic settles within me. The island cuts a jagged silhouette against the reflective waters, complete with a square shape nestled within the trees.

7

Lyra's Instrument

Bedspreads and sheets rustle in the other room as the soft glow of warm light emanates from behind me. It shrouds the spectacle of the lake in blurry reflections. The brush of bare feet on soft carpet signals the woman's approach, but I pretend not to notice. My heart races. Somewhere out there, the stranger wades on open waters, alone with the wildlife, yet I cannot see her. I should be safe in this hallway, in this home, but I fidget and clumsily attempt to slide past a bookshelf.

The woman alters her trajectory slightly and cautiously as ice shoots through my veins. A warm hand settles on my waist, but I nearly shriek in terror.

"Honey, come back to bed."

An uncomfortable knot works its way through my back as I spin to face her. Her voice sounds the opposite of threatening, lingering in the air with a low, graceful pitch and an even timbre.

"No, I'm ... I'm fine," I stammer, turning to face her and pressing my back against the corner of the windowsill, where grapevine-patterned drapes hang silently to frame the opening.

Though she's in shadow, I can pick out some facial features. Her face is slender and oval in shape with high, unremarkable cheek bones and a somewhat pointed jaw. Her eyes seem to shine in the darkness like glowing sapphires. Dark hair curtains the sides of her face, curling behind the ears and falling in straight streams to her bony shoulders. Shapely hips and a firm belly indicate that she is beautifully fit. I don't bother to guess her age.

She whispers something that sounds cold and distant, yet perilous. "It's just a bad dream, like the ones you always have."

How could she know about my nightmares? I avoid eye contact, and yet to give me comfort she places her hands on my hips and leans into me. My eyes flit in both directions.

"Who are you? And where am I?"

She tilts her head sideways, allowing her sleek black hair to slip from her collar and hang loosely near her shoulder. "We're at the lake house and it was your idea. Do we need to make an appointment with a psychiatrist?"

Her accusation hits me like a fist. "Whoa. Who are you to make that kind of diagnosis?"

"Um, your wife?"

"I don't have a wife. I've never been here before. Wait—are you the one who was following me when I was canoeing to the island?"

Her eyes widen and her eyebrows arch higher as she lets her hands slacken and peels herself off my chest. She reaches for my hand, but I refuse. "Let's talk about it in bed."

"I have to get out of here," I mutter, shifting sideways and breaking my gaze away from her face. The bookcase is an ornate, brown-stained masterpiece housing a fine collection of genres, everything from Agatha Christie to JK Rowling, and a sparse grouping of knickknacks. Most of these seem to represent Southern California, which I have never visited. "How do I get back to Philly?"

She tries to smile, but the emotion behind her expression is strained, making her look less authentic. The gray carpet pokes out between her manicured toes, contrasting against her pink nail polish.

"You escaped that hellhole when you married me."

"No, I gotta find—what's his name? I was talking to someone downtown the other day. I think so, anyway ... or maybe not. I can't remember anymore."

She backs away slowly and seems to peer carefully at the edges of my soul. "You haven't been to downtown Philadelphia in years. Did you hit your head on something in the middle of the night? I can kiss it better."

She reaches for my hand, and I instinctively recoil.

"Gee, thanks."

"It's not you," I stutter, useless words churning inside my skull. "Okay, it *is* you, whoever you are, and I swear to God, if you kidnapped me and brought me here to brainwash me, you're going to regret it—"

Something freezes me to the spot. A lanky young child with matted black hair sleepily saunters down the hall with wide eyes and wet splotches on his cheeks. He seems to be about four years old. My "wife" carefully kneels in front of him and wraps both arms around him for comfort. If I were in a state of mind to acknowledge this situation, it would melt my heart.

"No it's okay, Mommy and Daddy aren't fighting."

"Daddy? What the...." My voice escapes like a dry croak that somehow fuses itself to the insides of my cranium.

"Let's go back to bed," she whispers, taking him by the hand, bending at the waist and leading the boy back down the hall.

This is my chance. I step sideways, my elbow brushing against a soft plant that feels like plastic. Feeling my way toward the front door, I struggle to make sense of the floor plan. The kitchen faces the road and offers a limited view of the woods beyond via a small, metal-mullioned window that likely fogs up in the winter. The dining room sits below a small ceiling fan, with a single large picture window facing the lake. A small bathroom juts off the hall, next to the kitchen and across from a comfortable living room with an aerial rug and soft matching furniture. A black television graces the wall above a gas fireplace, which ties the décor together into one common theme. The designers clearly ditched the cliché rustic appeal for something post-modern, but with subtler lines and the softer hues of tans and deep browns. One could spend hours deep in conversation with loved ones in this room and barely notice the passage of time.

I reach the front door and hear the woman hurrying down the hall, checking the master bedroom as she approaches. Instead of fleeing, I wait for her, the pitter-patter of my heart gently subsiding.

The blue glimmer in her eyes dances majestically, vibrations that gently subside as she speaks. "Where are you going? You don't even have the keys to the car. Are you going to abandon your family?"

I let myself look into her shaded eyes and feel a pang of regret. "Look, lady, I don't know who you are. I'm sure your husband is one lucky guy, but you have me mistaken."

"Come on, Kerry."

"How the hell do you know my name?"

"Because you told me when you introduced yourself at that party eight years ago?"

I struggle to fight against her; everything she says reeks of sincerity and truth but contradicts everything I know about my own past. I frantically look past her, at a tall potted plant next to the living room bay window that stands out, inviting a curious yet comfortable gaze. Behind the plant, I see tiny glint of light on polished steel. It can't be—

Casually stepping around her, I zigzag into the living room, by-passing the dining table, the long tan couch, and the square, dark-brown end table, which holds a lamp and a pile of mailed coupons.

The artifact lies on a cubby shelf in front of a row of movies, whose titles I do not remotely care about. I grasp it, holding it between my index finger and my thumb, slowly turning it over to admire it from all sides. I thought I had lost it more than a year ago. Tears well up in my eyes as I clutch it in my palm, spin to face the woman, and soak her in rage battered with sadness.

"I don't know how you got this, you sick—you stole it from me and I'm taking it back."

She hangs her head low, as if to admire the carpet, and clutches her bare elbow with her left hand as both fall slack at her hips. Her body expression communicates something morose, yet arrestingly familiar. Sympathy dances on her face as a weary tear touches the corner of her eye.

"Look at it, Ker."

I peel my eyes away from her long enough to open my palm and admire something I'd made with my own hands, that means something specific to me and only me. It is an emotion I have never shared with another soul, not even my best friends.

"Circles," she says, describing it. "Symbols of eternity. No end and no beginning, welded together by electricity, which you would have thought to be impossible. You pressed the button, and the spark was strong enough to create a bond that can never be broken, no matter how hard you try."

Tears well out of my eyes and drip down my cheeks as she describes it to me.

"You remember when you made it," she says. "You know that the circles represent us."

What she is saying is entirely true. I shudder and attempt to avert my eyes to hide my tears. Only a few lights are reflecting off the shimmering waters of the lake, coming from some of the houses that line the shores. To my right I spy the pier reaching out from its reedy shallows to create a barrier between the gravelly beach and the grassy moor that stands beyond. They say that wildlife frequently hides in these grasses, where few humans ever trespass.

The welded circles are a pair of small washers. The interactive museum display sported a box of them. The exhibit was a well-constructed box of dovetailed plywood planks, with a tongue-and-groove bottom lap-jointed to the sides. Several basic mechanisms lay carefully placed within the box, whose clear plexiglass lid offered a detailed view of everything that happened to make the charge. A copper wire was wrapped around a coil, attached to an anode and a cathode—similar to a pair of battery terminals, but this display was neither connected to an electrical outlet nor a battery of any kind.

I remember turning the crank, a black plastic handle on a simple, bent round bar that punched through the plywood side of the box. The wheel spun what appeared to be a miniature turbine, and the charge was ready after between ten and fifteen turns. Pressing a button closed the circuit briefly, and the energy zapped brightly, accompanied by a puff of gray and black smoke. Pressing another button released the clamps that held my creation, and a hinged plastic doorway gave me access to retrieve it. The creation was warm to the touch but not hot: the electricity alone had fused the two metals together, and little residual heat was left over in the material.

I remember placing the creation in my pocket to be admired later. Perhaps someday, I'd thought, I would give it to someone important as a sentimental gift. Had I given it to this woman? And when?

My head spins with the memory, or the lack thereof. I have never seen this woman in my life, but she clearly knows me so intimately that she understands my most closely guarded secrets. Understanding cascades into my heart as I wrap the pair of washers in my palm and attempt to make eye contact with her.

"Do I look younger to you?" I ask casually.

"You look like you've had a rough night," she says, breathing softly and placing her hands on her hips.

"I mean, do I look younger?"

She peers at me with questioning eyes. "Maybe, but it's late. I can't tell."

I step subtly toward her, keeping the washers constricted in my palm. "What is your name?"

"You know my name, Ker."

I almost choke. "Some people call me Larry."

A coy smile erupts on her face. "You told me."

Another question bolts to the front of my mind, but I hold it idly inside with the assumption that revealing Sarah's name will cause her heartache—in case I've ever told her about Sarah.

"Your name?"

"Kerry.... It's Susanne Rebecca Gearhardt, nee Freeman. You always said it was a pretty name. Do you really not know me?"

"I—God, this is a nightmare. Come on, slap me." The memories of future years blast into my consciousness like a cacophony of confused screeches. I know the lake, and I know the island. Somehow, there is an infant face hidden within the madness. Becky was gasping and crying, and the baby was, too. Wrapped in tiny white blankets, he kicked his little feet and offered a comfortless exhalation through gently parted lips.

Tears well up in my eyes. A lacy, flowery white dress fades like a bright echo, and the scent of a hundred different kinds of flowers wafts into my nostrils. It all passes by me in a flash.

It is enough to make me fall to my knees, but I stand rigid and nervous instead. I brush away a tear and start toward the front door, which is made of one solid CNC panel and studded with a semicircular array of pie-shaped windows at head height. I silently pull at the handle before I turn to face Becky.

I don't know what my face is showing right now, but I need to find answers. The name rings in my head, louder and louder until I blurt it out, which feels cathartic in a way. "Ronald. Do you know him?"

"I don't think so."

"He gave me some advice, and now I need more from him. Think about it: can you remember him?"

She shrugs softly. "Maybe if you tell me what the advice was?"

I cannot recite it word for word. In fact, now that it exists only in memory, the sentences fade together into a viscous mist that elicits base emotions. What was it? "I think it was something like, you're walking in the fog and you can only see a few steps, just far enough to take one more step, and then another."

She offers a knowing nod. "I remember, Kerry; I was there too. You hadn't met me yet, but good listening."

"Who said it?"

She wracks her brains for a moment, furrowing her eyebrows and concentrating. "There was no Ronald. The speaker was quoting the words of Jeff L. Martin, the church pastor."

"There was more to it than that," I say. "I need to get the rest. How do I find Mr. Martin?"

"You remember, don't you? He died shortly after we met. That was in one of his last sermons."

"It was like he was speaking directly to me. Who was the speaker who was quoting Mr. Martin? I need to know."

"I don't remember, Ker. Worry about it in the morning and come back to bed."

I shift my feet and begin to turn the doorknob. "I can't. I'm going to go find him and he's going to tell me everything."

A somber look drifts across her face. She draws her bare heels together on the carpet and her toe bones seem to buckle. Staring into my eyes, she emits a sense of vulnerability that temporarily fixes me to the spot. She offers nothing in rebuttal, but if I were to simply storm out, the vulnerability will transform into a cascade of tears.

I cannot say anything to reassure her. Still clutching the welded washers, I glance down into my fist and then gaze back at her. "Becky, I'm not who you think I am. This is some kind of parallel universe for me, but somehow I can remember certain things that have never happened to me. I'm trapped and I have to get back to my own time somehow. And this is all in pursuit of—someone." I dare not utter Sarah's name. "I swear to you, I'm not crazy. I'm just lost."

"Kerry."

"I have to go."

"I love you."

I wish I could say it back, but with no meaning it is only three little words that are smashed together into a sentence that only marginally makes sense. My eyes might offer a million words, but I cannot even utter three of them because they are not in my heart.

Without speaking I nod to her, open the door, and step out into the darkness alone, to aimlessly wander until I find a promising road. Memories flood my soul as I saunter toward the pavement, past a single streetlamp, and plunge into the shadows of a million trees.

8

The Rod of Asclepius

Wisdom is an unattainable abstract, which sates my conscious mind with visions of what it might be like to know more. Foraying into an alternate universe where I'm trapped in some nightmarish future has been devastating. Exactly how did I get here?

I remember crossing the lake in the canoe and the woman pursuing me, and then the dark cabin afterwards, but now it all seems to blur into what this realm was like before I crossed the lake, where humanity seems to no longer exist. I shudder as I consider the implications.

Limping along the winding road allows my mind to wander; Becky said I had met her at a party, but I have no memory of that. If memory is truly as pliable as the philosophers say, then surely it is a tool one can use to shape the future. But what can I do when both memory and future are intertwined in a paralyzing dance that makes me question everything I've ever known?

But that's where wisdom comes in: religious leaders talk about wisdom as though no one has it, and dangle it like the proverbial carrot in front of our faces. One can never grab it or taste it because it only exists in the future.

I rub my forehead as the chirping of dozens of crickets fills the rapidly thickening air. The temperature is beginning to drop further, to a level suitable for mist to form over the lake. No breeze whispers through the trees; other than the chirping, an eerie silence fills this realm.

A network of cracks in the pavement radiates in jagged spiderweb arms from what appears to be the impact site of something heavy. The divot in the center of the damage confirms it. I nearly trip over the uneven roadway but regain my balance and slow my gait to avoid future interruptions.

If I am making for Philadelphia, I have a long way to go. Hitchhiking is something I have never done. They teach its perils in school, but the unwitting victim in all those 'what if' scenarios is always the driver, never the weary pedestrian. This truth only strikes me now because *I'm* the one stranded and desperate. What if a crazed driver with an axe to grind comes to pick me up, stops in a corn field to dismember me, and then stuffs me in his trunk so he can later throw my remains into the ocean? And when fishermen find the pieces of me, the police can only chalk it up to another rogue shark attack? I'd consider myself lucky.

The hum of an unseen motor rumbles in the distance, behind a dozen bends in the road. The beam from its headlights does not illuminate anything. After a few moments, it fades and drowns away in the chorus of chirping, the noise I am making by walking, and the creaking trees.

Without light to accompany these sounds, the chill tatters my nerves and erupts in icy goosebumps. The vehicle has either turned away on some winding side road or been parked and switched off.

Breathing more heavily, I pause to survey my surroundings and attempt to concoct a reasonable escape strategy to get back to Philadelphia. There I can talk to Joaquin and put together a plan to find this pastor Becky was talking about. Wherever he is, he holds the key.

The darkness seems to swell as I stand there, glued to the shoulder of the road along the white line and trying to make sense of this realm. Deep in the tree line, the land gently slopes upward, sweeping gradually steeper as the vegetation thickens toward the hilltop. The dark reveals only a hundred yards or so, if the undergrowth and deciduous trees aren't creating a wall closer than that. The tree trunks create a mesmerizing effect of shade in blackness, which seems to linger like the aftereffects of a perilous nightmare. It somehow calls to me. If only I could dare to take a single step into the dark....

The hell with everything. If my 'real' self were watching all this unfold, he would be screaming at me to not step off the road, because the dark is where people meet their worst fates. What would happen if I died here? Would I die there, too? I can't fathom being dead. What would I think about, and what would my soul yearn for? There must be something after this, or it is all for nothing and we are but rats scurrying through a closed maze with no ending.

When I reach the bottom of the steep-sided ditch that protects the pavement from runoff, I nearly trip over a large protruding rock that accompanies a sawn-off tree branch with the leaves still attached. This would make an acceptable poking device for the inevitable spider web I will step into. The feel of the silk on my skin makes my flesh crawl. Numerous nightmares have had me traveling in strange, spider-populated wastelands for some unknown reason throughout my life. When the nightmares become too real, my blood curdles, and fear makes me do things my rational self would never consider.

Carefully stepping upward, out of the ditch, I use the stick for balance and pull it up after me by the gnarled end. Stripping it of loose twigs and leaves takes me about a minute, after which I am ready to explore the wilderness.

Again, I stop: my muscles seize up as the motor hum returns, but somehow it seems less mechanical and more bestial. God, it could be a bear, and if that's the case I should drop the stick, get back onto solid pavement, and run. Yet the dark lures me onward.

The groaning fades away, leaving my nerves a wreck of smashed ice. The beast is still out there, but if I change my heading to take a less direct path to the summit, perhaps I can still evade it. When I look to my left, the path appears easier. I walk carefully in that direction, clutching the stick tighter with each step. I reach the tree line and stretch out the stick in front of me to destroy any cobwebs that might obstruct my path. The underbrush grows thinner here than further up the slope, where it would take a machete to hack away a walkable trail. At this location the brush consists of relatively sparse bushes, surrounded by grass and low carpeting plants. Acorns, various tree nuts, and twigs crackle beneath my soles as I tread deeper into the trees.

I reach a point where I estimate that I've traveled fifty feet, peer down the slope, and then upward into the dark. Beyond the trees, the blackness seems to cocoon a peculiar block of granite. I inch forward, careful not to startle all the wildlife, and the slab of granite gradually becomes clearer.

Again, I halt, trying to make out what appears to be a shape carved between two huge boulders. It looks like an imperfect square, something that nature could never form, but its outline is fuzzy and indistinguishable from the surrounding dark. Again altering my trajectory, I make for the square.

Someone once told me to pay attention to the recesses, those dark corners that hide so much of the world. Who had that been? I can only shrug as my mind comes up blank. Still clinging to that piece of advice, I step over a loose pile of rocks, under a heavy branch, and closer to the stone. Tendrils of swaying silk tickle my arms. I frantically try to rub them away, but now the square is coming into clearer focus.

Ten feet away, then five, and then I'm close enough to reach the narrow end of the stick into the dark, and it becomes clearer. The black shape is an alcove carved into the rock. Curiously I feel the surrounding stone for carvings of some kind, but find nothing. Clearing away any cobwebs in the recess, I gulp as the harrowing growl returns, only closer. Have I stumbled on its lair? If it finds me, it will maul me to within an inch of my life, but I have nowhere else to run. There is only hope, and I cling to it desperately.

The groan lasts longer than my brain can discern without mentally counting the seconds. The sound echoes in the trees and reverberates off the nearby rock. A scent of drying blood rises in my nostrils as I glue myself to the granite. Fear consumes me. Within another moment the animal will bear down on me; its shadow casts a pall of thick blackness on everything below, consuming it all in inescapable dark. It covers my hand like an oily stain, drenches the trees in soupy bitumen, and towers overhead where it devours the moonlight.

I let out a scream as I scurry backward into its lair.

I stumble and then I am falling, head over heels as the air changes density and temperature. The darkness swirls like muddy water circling a drain. As it leaks away, I collide with something heavy and sharp.

The same breeze sounds in my ears and a dozen passersby stare as I open my eyes. The cityscape stretches above me like billions of glittering stars. The monster will strike at me any second now. It reaches out a knobby black hand to shred my soul and panic folds up within me. I scramble away from it as ice floods through my veins.

"Jesus, I'm only trying to help, you damn freak."

"Are you okay, sir?"

"Where did you come from?"

I cannot answer. When I've scrambled to my feet, the monster is no longer there. The black hand that was reaching out to me is attached to a human, who is now walking away shaking his head and mumbling under his breath. A woman hovers nearby, watching intently as I glance upward into the thousands of illuminated windows of the downtown towers.

Now I recognize it as the financial district, where the banks and brokerages chip away at the soul of the neighborhood by constructing oblique, utilitarian towers that draw attention to themselves by towering over the old brick residential midrise buildings.

The sound of music emanates from a street corner a block or two away, yet it sounds muted and foreign. Have I really transported myself instantly back to present-day Philadelphia? In any other circumstances a sense of victory would have rushed through my veins, but the implications are stark. What was it my so-called wife told me about? I check my pocket, where I deposited the welded washers what seems like an eon ago. The cold steel is secure in my grip, unchanging as ever it should be.

As I gaze up at the illuminated high-rises, a woman bumps into me. I can feel her hair brush against my arm. When I spin to apologize, she is gone as completely as if she has simply vanished into thin air.

I can only make for the music as I gain my bearings, repeating the name of the pastor over and over in my head until it sounds like a foreign language.

A couple straggles toward me, stumbles into the shade of an awning for a quick kiss, and then disappears. An old man with a cane swaggers toward me, looking comfortably unaware of everything that surrounds him. Within seconds, his image has faded into mist.

Terror fills me as I search for a familiar face among these hundreds. Thousands, even. Each of them scurries about their own business and pays no heed to me. This is downtown Philly, but it feels so wrong. The music on the street transforms from smooth jazz to somber piano, and then fades to a droning ambience like the soundtrack to the apocalypse. I cover my eyes as a tall black man jogs toward an alley. He briefly sets his eyes on me as he stumbles toward a dark recess and dissipates.

I clench my jaw and make way for a thinning throng of strangers enjoying the nightlife. A couple dances away their troubles near a crosswalk. The lights overhead dazzle and flood the street with their artificial brightness. High atop a lamppost, a black crow stands watch, innocent yet wise.

When a drunk-seeming man slams into my shoulder, I feel myself blur. My hands vibrate themselves into thin air and become solid again. This can only be the border between realms. Blocks ahead, the lights begin to turn off.

Blackness invades the city. A stifled, tortured groan stalks me in the distance. Onlookers, somehow blissfully unaware that their city is about to be ravaged by an extra-dimensional being, hurry about their lives while the groan intensifies.

I hurry away as the music fades to a complete, soulless silence, now enveloped by the expanding dark. There is no escape; I scream as it licks at my feet, erodes my shoes, and tries to consume all that I am.

Ducking from its grasp I cower, stepping backwards into a darkened storefront. A light flashes behind me, but when I swivel my head to see it, the blackness vaporizes what is left of me. I watch, detached from my own body.

My heart racing, I clutch at a nonexistent doorknob and whimper in terror. The light behind me turns on again, flashing blue, then green, and then it drones in multicolored fear as I step backward.

Everything hurts; my body aches. Spinning around to face the source of the light, I find myself in my own living room. I stare at the television, which has sat idle so long that its screen is glowing green and blue, asking if I would like to keep watching.

I pick up the remote, turn it off, and collapse on the couch to writhe in pain. The ache dulls my muscles as I move, invades my heart, and makes breathing uncomfortable. An invisible pain seems to tear away at my side.

Lying back, I lift my shirt and touch my tender skin. I look down in panic as sweat begins to run down my forehead. Somehow I can remember speaking with a man called Harley. It seems that it has been ages, but I remember ordering from the bakery and chatting with him. He would be interested in what I've just experienced, but it has been years. If he remembers me, I will be surprised.

The tender skin throbs as I dab at it. In the scant light from the living room window, an oblong scar boils red like a days-old burn. What the hell?

I kick off my shoes, thinking I should go to sleep on the sofa before it all makes too much sense. The same scars, yet older, have appeared on one foot. And my forearm.

My temples ache. Instinctively I press at them with my index and middle fingers squished together. I pull them away when I feel the sweat sticking. My eyes gloss over as sleep overtakes me, and the last thing I see is blood on my fingertips.

9

One Head off the Hydra

My vision blurs in and out as I lie staring at the ridges and bumps on the ceiling beyond the fan. An ache throbs behind my temples and I try to make sense of the nightmare.

Shaking my head, I grab for my phone to check the time and make the mistake of glancing at my feet, seeing the burn scars livid against my skin. Shock pours through me as the pieces begin coming together: it hadn't been a nightmare. The scars are the evidence. But where had the scars come from? Before I fell into the other realm—were there multiple?—I'd had no scars.

The city traffic rushes by on the street three stories below my window. As I do every morning, I shake as I rise to my feet, make my way to the window, and survey the neighborhood and the weather. A light dusting of snow has covered most of the cars and the sidewalks, but it clings only scantly to the pavement in the street as the heat from the cars compresses and melts it away. But the clouds remain, casting a foreboding gray over the city. It all looks so strikingly normal. No black stain devours it, and I observe no signs of a dystopian future.

A neighbor across the street brushes a film of snow off his windshield and half-glances up at me, as if he can feel my gaze.

I remove my fingers from the blind slats and walk away, headed to the shower. As the hot water pours over my skin, I study an old bump near my waist. It feels swollen and tender, burns an angry red, and appears to have become infected overnight.

I need answers. Harley might possibly be on Market Street today, but I don't know whether I will have time to visit him. Instead, I think of Joaquin. Around five he will be off work, and possibly contemplating a beer and a video game. I decide to drop in and accuse him of something, even in the knowledge that I'm not about to confront him. Frustratingly, none of the plans in my brain come to fruition.

The drive to his apartment takes less than ten minutes, even including that annoying stop light that the city engineers apparently can't time to prevent traffic backing up. I skid to a halt two houses down and huddle against the biting wind as I make my way over. Joaquin occupies a first-floor apartment in a large house that was converted to a four-plex at least twenty years ago. I imagine dwelling here in the pre-renovation period and it tickles my spine. It is reminiscent of a Victorian-era home, where the qualities that typified the style have been stripped away, leaving only brown wood siding and sterile red brick, punctured by rickety doors and drafty windows. If the rent weren't far cheaper than the going rate in this section of Philadelphia, Quin would likely move. He makes enough money to live in the suburbs but likes the city better.

A neighbor hurries out the front door of Joaquin's building, avoiding eye contact with me, and mutters something under his breath. I swallow as I enter and slowly saunter to his door. He pulls it open before I can knock, wavers in place for a moment, and studies my expression.

"You look like shit, dude."

Instead of a witty retort, all I can offer is a hurried, "Yeah."

"Find Harley?"

I pace past him, kick off my shoes, and rest myself on the sofa next to a loose-leaf tablet he uses to track character traits and make quick sketches of weapons. I glance at the paper and a young, female elf stares flirtatiously back up at me, the moonlight glinting off her polished bow as she aims an arrow at the empty white of the page. Below, Joaquin has scribbled a brief description of her personality. Anything to distract from her disproportionate eyes and breasts, I imagine.

"Interesting you should mention that," I say, trying to remember what Harley looked like, and drawing a blank. In the other realm, I could barely remember him. Now the memory has returned, but only a shadow of it.

"Did he help you find your girlfriend?"

I'm going to kill him. Playfully, I swipe his notebook off the couch and watch as it lands on the floor, crumpling the page with the elf-warrior. I swear her expression changes from coy compassion to indignant sadness as she falls. "Found something else," I say, searching my pocket for the fused washers. I could toss my creation to him, but I have never told him anything about it, so to him it would simply be junk.

"What's that?"

"Shit you could draw for your RPG this weekend," I say, glancing at the folded notebook. In the other realm, my "wife" hadn't been a disproportionally chested elf, but perhaps the woman who walked on the water was. I dared not say a word to describe any of it, because as imaginative as the mind of Quin may be, he is surprisingly rigid about real-life facts.

He looks taken aback. "You went to Comic Con without me? You bastard."

We are both scheduled to attend the event in a few weeks, unless I have fallen into a different timeline where the festival has already passed me by. The look on his face says it all. He knows he's joking, but he's reacting to my stolid expression.

"Okay—so did he, like, show you some figurines?"

"Didn't show me anything," I snipe. "Just told me to pay attention to the shadows or some shit. Before I know it, I'm at a secluded lake, then there's a bear or something—no, wait."

"Don't know Harley that well," Quin says, "but I didn't know he was into drugs."

"Not drugs," I say, clumsily defending him. "But you would think so."

"Then what did he say? Throw some glitter at her and maybe you'll be able to see her?"

I shake my head at his suggestion, not quite buying into the humor, but saying nothing. I can only contemplate Sarah and my last interaction, if I could actually call it that, what feels like a millennium ago.

"Fine, don't tell me. But you want to, otherwise you wouldn't even be here."

I lower my eyebrows and try to recall our conversation, which is already subject to the whim and folly of my own memory. I decide to wing it: "He didn't say much about her, but he started talking about Greek mythology and a 'Lady of the Six.' And then he goes on about how little we know about the world we inhabit, simply because we don't want to know. So he told me to start looking in the shadows. I went into an alley, but then everything got convoluted.

"It was like I was transported somewhere else, to a lake upstate, where the only other human was some woman who was going to kill me, so I entered a cabin, but the next moment I'm in bed with someone I don't know, and then I'm cowering before—I don't even know how to describe it."

"In bed with a woman?" Quin grins. "Talk about your Grade A delusion."

I'm in a mood to offer him a stock two-word response best accompanied by a waving middle finger, but I let his snark invade my brain instead.

"Brave men don't cower. They fight."

"Yeah, and wise warriors don't battle invasive demons completely unarmed," I counter.

"You know, I specialize in demons, so spill it."

I shake my head. "Thought it was a bear before I saw it. It was a shadow. Just dark, expanding like an oil slick, eating away at everything, but I backed into its den and then I ended up downtown where people were vanishing, but the street somehow kept its population up. And then the black again, devouring it all into nothingness."

Quin looks intrigued. "I'd say you've been reading too much Lovecraft, but I think Kel might have met up with such a creature one time or another."

"Don't bring Kel into it."

When we were in high school, Kel had had a vision or two related to a role-playing game competition when Joaquin was on his team. I don't know more than that, but Quin insists that Kel is perfectly normal. Kel and I didn't get along until we became reacquainted in Philadelphia.

"Whatever," Joaquin says dismissively.

"You?" I scoff. "Head character creator and Game Master, and you don't have a clue?"

Joaquin shakes his head and stares at the blank television screen for several seconds, clearly attempting to make rusty wheels turn in his brain.

The sound of a car horn outside distracts us briefly and causes my eyes to flit around the room. Instead of saying anything, I wait for Quin to build me an idea, which is his forte.

"Are you familiar with Greek mythology?" he asks, recapturing my attention.

I shake my head slowly, trying to remember some of what I'd learned in high school, but failing to scratch the surface beyond some of the most famous legends.

"What you've described ... it sounds like a Shade, but a bit more concerning." Upon surveying my unchanged expression, he shrugs and expounds on his idea. "Shades are the spirits of the dead in the empire of darkness. I've never heard of one consuming everything, though, even if it's the Elder Shade."

"So ghosts, then?" I ask, trying not to sound incredulous. "What weapon do you use to defeat them?"

He stretches his hand and studies my expression for a moment while glancing down to his notebook on the floor. "Maybe it will help if I sketch something out for you."

In high school I'd watched his ideas flowing from his brain into the paper through his magical pencil more than once. The way he wielded it always exuded grace.

Groaning, I reach down to fetch the pencil and notebook from the floor at my feet and strain to hand them to him. He sits back and works his fingers before grasping the pencil. Seconds pass away as he lightly drags it across the paper, creating baselines, and then gradually shades them.

"Shades are more than ghosts; they're dead, held in captivity, but if they are allowed to run free, they can terrorize the living—because those they've loved can still recognize their presence, even if they can't see them. It's like when you're alone in the dark and someone you love enters the room. The ambience changes and you can feel them. But you saw one."

"It was more like a monster," I explain, watching him stroke black lines into an abdomen.

"The Elder Shade," he continues, "is like a normal Shade, but more advanced. That guy is a lot worse, and he'll be bigger because the darkness feeds him. Legend has it that it can take many forms, but the living still know exactly who he is."

"If one were rampaging through the streets of Philly, it might get pretty big," I reason. "But then again, I don't know whether it was expanding or just trying to overrun everything in its path."

"The Shades are slaves," Quin reiterates. "They are controlled by Erebus, the god of darkness."

I nod slowly. The name rings a bell, but I cannot be sure whether I remember it from high school or later. Dismissing this detail as unimportant, I wait for Joaquin to finish building his character sketch.

"Shades don't need the weapons of mortals," he explains, pausing briefly, before coloring in the background with darker shadows. "Some may wield chains, possibly even black swords.... Remember Marley from Dickens's *A Christmas Carol*? Dickens never said it, but Marley is a good example of a Shade that has been able to take physical form so that only Scrooge can see him. But we know who sent him—you see, they don't really need weapons, because their presence is normally enough to defeat enemies."

"One cannot beat death," I say coldly. "Only delay it. Do you become a Shade when you die?"

He shakes his head. "Not really. It takes a commitment to the dark. Once you make the pact, whether or not it's a verbal one, you sign your existence over to Erebus. Erebus is not known to be a patient dude."

I watch his reflection on the television for a while before I manage to utter anything resembling good sense. Beyond the screen, the drapes hang low, shrouding the room in an eerie, pale gray light that softens the sharp edges and colors the room with just enough uncertainty to make me feel as though I'm right back there in the clutches of the Shade. I squeeze my eyes shut and try to imagine it eating me. What would I feel? Pain? Sadness? Grief? Despair? Or would I feel the darkest emotion of all—nothing?

"The Elder Shade," I repeat, turning my attention back to him as he blackens the background, accidentally snapping the tip off the pencil. He sighs and sets it aside, blowing on his creation to remove the graphite dust. "It can ... eat people?"

"Not in the way you think. If it's possible, it would be more like it could be absorbing your soul. In essence, you'd become beholden to Erebus against your will."

"Then what does it do? Why is it so dangerous?"

Quin sighs again. "You were there. Ultimately, your experience means more than theory, but legend has it that they feed on dark emotions, growing more and more powerful. And when they're dark enough they can literally tear you apart, atom by atom. It would be an excruciating way to die. Unchecked, they could destroy the human race, because humans are so predisposed to darkness.

"Now the thing about battling dark beings is, you can't expect the same weapons to inflict that much damage, if any. Aggression and fear only strengthen it because they are negative emotions—darkness. You can't hope to defeat darkness with more darkness. Only light can do that."

"Isn't that a Martin Luther King quote?"

"Some variation of it. King was a wise man."

"Shit," I gasp sarcastically. "Guess my staff doesn't light up anymore. Is there a quest for a new crystal to make it work again?"

"Maybe just be kind to it?"

"Somehow, I don't think asking it to coffee and then chatting about the weather and weekend plans is going to stop it from swallowing everything whole," I quip.

"Maybe if you try to keep your feelings neutral, it will avoid you. Or better yet, focus on hope or justice or love. The Shades don't know what to do with that, because they aren't in the realm of Erebus."

"But then I also heard once that neutrality doesn't really exist. Some seminary teacher or other, not that it relates to mythology. He said that you can't stop evil by standing by and letting it rampage through everything. If you're not taking sides, you're taking the side of the dark."

"You going to listen to someone literally trying to indoctrinate you with religion, or are you going to take the word of someone who knows what he's talking about?"

"Then again, what you know is theoretical," I say. "Because you don't know anything about parallel universes or time travel, or whatever the hell I'm going through. I'm betting I know someone who does."

"I sent you to Harley because he has a solid physical understanding of the world around him. But I doubt he knows much about this *parallel universe* business."

I shake my head dismissively. Harley hasn't steered me wrong, but then again, he hasn't given me enough information as to what I'd be facing should I embark on the journey by choice. If I made that trek by accident, he'd know even less. Still, he was a kind man and an engaging conversationalist.

Thinking about monsters and death has devoured my senses, almost making me forget the proverbial fog that some religious leader had once talked about. Does he even have a name? Cold invades me. The memory is dying, as if being extinguished by new dimensions of thought. Focusing on it once again is futile. The fog is dissipating, and now I can see where I'm going, I may not need the help of a religious leader after all.

That this is all about a girl who happens to have turned invisible in front of me has me squirming on the couch. How could I let myself be so overtaken as to set my entire life on the backburner? Maybe I should just forget about Sarah. If she wants to show herself to me again, I'll let her, and that will be good enough for me. Chasing the slaves of darkness is not something I can do if I plan to remain employed and advance in the construction industry.

"I need to try to get back to real life," I say slowly. "Sarah and this monster are going to put me in the unemployment line."

I have scarcely finished my sentence when I glance down at my fore-arm. A burning pain has erupted and spread across my scar, reminding me once again how frighteningly real it all is. I shudder as Joaquin folds his notebook closed and pretends not to notice the fear running through my body.

If Erebus requires a commitment, I'm already in danger. The scars prove it; I've already made the commitment and I cannot undo that.

10

Corvus's Wings

Police officers are blockading the intersection with Market Street as I approach, so that no cars can get through. Watching nervously, I try to gauge whether the cops will allow me to access the street via the sidewalk. The cold breeze disturbs my hair and presses against my back as I reflexively shudder.

The sun is not distributing an abundance of rays overhead, and without help from the reflective skyscrapers, the gray aura further bathes the scene in an unshakeable chill. A throng of onlookers has assembled to witness what appears at first to be a car accident, but their horrified faces suggest something worse. Keen to inspect the tragedy, the masses on the pavement shove their way to the front as the police sort out the scene.

To avoid the crowd, I hug the storefront and shimmy behind a tall woman who is standing on her tiptoes to observe the accident. An onlooker moves aside, allowing me a split second to view the carnage. A pedestrian is lying on his back in the crosswalk with his legs in a disturbing position, bent backwards at the knees and his shins angled the wrong way. Blood has poured from his scalp onto the street, and the officers snap dozens of photographs before the ambulance arrives. The lack of a siren suggests that the pedestrian is already very dead. I swallow a lump in my throat as I keep an eye on the overhang Harley favors.

The inset in the storefront offers shelter to window shoppers while providing a tantalizing view of the newest products the retailer sells. Shiny pottery vases of nearly every size and shape stand neatly arranged in a double semicircle, with the tallest in the back. Before them stands a handcrafted table built of polished and sanded oak strips. Approximately a foot and a half tall, it supports a decorative steel knickknack and a fake plant with shiny leaves and knotty branches. A lone magazine adorns the table next to the plant, and on the other end of the display, a high-backed riveted leather chair awaits, with a stylish woven throw carefully draped over its arm. A pair of shoppers is visible through the display, which has a black backing panel that does not cover the whole window.

By now, Harley must be keenly aware of what the market peddles, but he pays no attention and instead casts his gaze on the throngs lining the sidewalks.

"Saw it happen in real time, like it was slowed down," Harley says in his normal timbre. I have barely had a chance to look his way, which suggests he was anticipating my arrival.

"Somabitch didn't wait for the crosswalk, just tried to run for it, so now he's paint on the street."

"Damn," I say heartlessly, training my gaze on his beard. Somehow, he looks older than he did mere days ago, yet my memory is fuzzy to the point where I can barely remember what we discussed. Switching between the realms has had a disturbing effect on my memories and emotions. I twitch suddenly as he stares into me and leans his head back against the cold window in front of the urns.

"But you didn't come here to talk about that," Harley says, perfectly reading my expression.

"You said something about minding the recesses," I say quickly, standing over him and bowing my head as if in reverence.

"Did it do you much good? From the looks of it, I'd say no."

"What do you know about Shades?" My bluntness briefly takes him aback, but he nods and shuffles his feet. "Why didn't you warn me about them?"

"They are always there," he says softly. "Pay them no mind and they will ignore you."

"You know about them," I prod him again, lowering my eyes.

Again, he shuffles his feet but lifts his head away from the glass so that he can get a clearer image of me. I'm shaking with repressed fury as I remember the blackness consuming the entire city.

"The border dimension is not for the faint of heart, so don't go there."

"The border dimension?"

"Lots of people end up there without knowing it."

"I don't even know if a recess is a portal or whether it will transport me. Is there ever a sign as to where you're going?"

He shakes his head slowly.

"Rumor has it that souls in the border exist in at least three dimensions."

"Length, width, and height," I guess.

His stare increases in sincerity as he draws away from the glass, and with an effort he tilts his head back to look up at me. He runs a hand through his beard for long enough to consider an explanation. Somehow, he looks more haggard today, as if worry has crept in to replace rationality.

"Every alternate dimension is scattered in time," he says, clasping his hands and breathing slowly. "You're going forward or backward, to your own future or past. Your location is arbitrary, I think. You're here, now, in the present, are you not?"

I raise my palms subtly, attempting to make sense of every realm I've already visited. "I guess, if you say so."

"It means your future and past selves don't exist. But if you're in the past or the future, I think it is possible that you disappear from the present."

Memories of Sarah and her auburn hair push their way into my mind and let a faint aura of warmth invade my heart. Still, it wrenches me, knowing she was there and yet so far away. I frown at Harley but try to hide it as he presses his palms against the cold concrete and slowly, painfully, rises to his feet.

For a moment he simply gazes skyward, where a lone blackbird gracefully dances overhead before disappearing to perch on a high parapet.

"Never been to the border before," he says. "But I imagine that you're interacting with your surroundings while possibly remaining obscured by the veil."

"People were disappearing," I say. "Like they didn't even know it, but the people leaving were being replaced. And none of them could see the Elder Shade."

As I speak, Harley trains his gaze on shoppers across the street, who are visibly trying to avoid looking at the tragedy by the corner. My last two words snap his attention to my face. He has not been expecting that phrase, and it shows.

"Elder?"

"Like a Shade that consumes its surroundings, whether you're an innocent bystander or not."

"No such thing as an innocent bystander. If you stumbled into their dimension, you're an intruder and they're likely to treat you as such. It doesn't make a lot of sense, I know."

"They're slaves to Erebus," I repeat, but Harley doesn't appear to be surprised.

The shop door opens, allowing some of the warmth inside to sneak out into the recess where we are huddled. A lone woman pushes past the open door. She is tall and lanky, clutching a small vinyl bag against her waist, and she lowers her designer sunglasses and steps past without even peeking at us. All at once I understand Harley's experience, and I allow my gaze to stretch and my anger to fade away.

"How do you know about Erebus?"

I'm slow to acknowledge that my gamer friend knows a thing or two about mythology, which helps him to create multidimensional characters with interesting arcs.

"Read up on some Greek mythology," I lie.

"*Obscure* mythology," he says. "A man with a master's in anthropology can go his whole life without hearing about Shades."

"Same man," I start roughly, "who probably went his whole life without being attacked by shadow monsters. Is Sarah in the border?"

"Hard to know without witnessing her directly. Even if you were to describe her perfectly, which is impossible."

"Because your memory is confused by the time jumps," I finish for him.

"See that dead guy over there?" he asks, nodding. The ambulance has arrived and the EMTs are busying themselves loading the deceased into a black body bag while carefully regarding the evidence. Some of the onlookers have dispersed, and the scene all at once drains away the chatter of the shocked spectators. A pair of wings flutter overhead as I observe. Then a crack in the pavement below my feet steals my attention. A tiny, matted weed has forced its way up through the crack, as a tiny vein of nature in a city so heartbreakingly devoid of it.

"It happened right in front of me. Ask me what kind of clothes he was wearing, color, size. Facial hair, shape? Ask me."

I hesitate.

"It was a red jacket, long toward his knees with shiny buttons and slimming pockets. Black beanie, salt-and-pepper goatee, mismatching socks, holey denim jeans. Sound accurate to you?"

"Sure," I say, silently acknowledging that I hadn't had the chance to get a good view of the victim. A splash of yellow seems to have tinged my memory but it has been erased by Harley's description.

"That was all utter bullshit," he says, biting his lip. "You saw what you thought you saw, but when you listened to me it all went away, didn't it?"

"What are you—"

"Because human memory is notoriously fallible. Eyewitness testimony isn't even all that useful in court. Every one of those idiots will swear they saw something different, so whose version should you, the jury, believe?"

"Maybe all of them are accurate on average, but most people don't do details so easily."

He nods and stretches his back. "The human mind is wired to ignore minutiae. It's evolutionary: information that our brains deem non-vital gets deleted faster when others can fill you in on their version of the details. And then you spread that lie to someone else, without knowing it's a lie, and pretty soon the whole of society is nothing but billions of liars too uneducated to know how ignorant they all truly are."

"It's sad."

"It's human nature," he snaps. "I just proved to you that you I and are no different, even though we think we are. Sometimes learning tears apart who we want to be, so by our nature we cling to what we know, endlessly defending ourselves against the onslaught of new information."

"How do you fight the Shades?" I break in, broaching the subject so suddenly that Harley seems visibly shaken.

"You don't. You're in their world; the longer you stay, the keener they are to make you a permanent occupant."

"If I do, I cease to exist," I say shortly. "You know how paradoxical that sounds?"

Harley furrows his eyebrows. "But it isn't, though, is it? That you made it back here proves that."

"I'm not sure I remember all the steps," I say. "I remember being by a lake, in a cabin, then arguing with a woman over something, I don't even—shit, what *was* it?"

"What's wrong?" Harley says coyly. "Having a little trouble with your memory?"

I flash him a scowl and instantly look away as I mouth a curse word, which he either ignores or has not even noticed.

"But there must have been something else, because now I have these burn scars, and I didn't have them the other day." I pause and hold out my forearm to him.

He studies the mark and softly groans. "You've been somewhere that has destroyed your memory, and it must be from the past."

"How do I undo it?"

"You don't read as much as you claim to, do you? You don't undo anything. Even across multiple dimensions, the laws of physics are absolute. There is no way to create an ordered state out of disorder."

"Maybe physicists don't know everything."

"Now you're catching on."

I flit my eyes in all directions as the ambulance slowly pulls away, leaving the spectators staring at the wrecked car and its aftermath. Police officers have taken the driver to the sidewalk to take his testimony, as the investigators work to discover the truth of what has happened. If what Harley says is true, there is no way to prevent the tragedy from happening, even by traveling to the past and altering the course of the events leading up to it. Then again, what if my environment is truly untouched by my own presence? And what happens to my future self when the present me is there? If we meet one another, the consequences could be disastrous.

"I don't need to know any of these lessons," I argue.

"You do, or you wouldn't be learning them in the first place."

"I have to find her," I shout. "I'm going with or without your help. She needs it."

"Who needs it more? Her or you?"

"I don't have time for this. I have to find the Reverend Jeff L. Martin. I'm going, God damn it. Shadow monsters and ancient Greek gods are not going to stop me, and neither are you."

"*Larry?*"

I roll my eyes.

"Be careful. If there are as many dimensions as some claim, you can get lost and never manage to come back. If that Elder Shade gets you, he erases you. Everything about you, just gone. You're not even history, you never existed to be written or thought of. If that fits in with your agenda, you're welcome to it."

I steel my nerves and clench my jaw. "It does."

"Then God be with you," he says, as if he really means it and knows there is a God so fully that even casually omitting him will destroy his humanity.

The crowd steadily thins. The towers begin to glisten, as sparse rays of sunlight punch through the low clouds. The raven had returned to the rooftop, to keep watch on everything transpiring below. I peer up towards it at it spreads its wings to take flight.

11

Crown of Ariadne

My route back to the garage takes me past the alley that I suspect first led me to the lake, as it offers the most direct access to the elevator with the least amount traffic getting in my way. With my mind racing, I make for the same doorway from Market Street beside which the police and EMT's had loaded the body into the ambulance so they could finish their investigation and clear the scene.

I step lightly and try not to look at the pattern of blood on the concrete, and the cops carefully measuring and collecting evidence as though something stomach-churning had not taken place there.

The alley juts off the street between a pair of glass condo high rises encased in orange brick. Beyond the overhead door, the warehouse sits silently beneath the condo towers, which had been built partially on top of the facility. The sturdier structural elements have been repurposed as the engineers have determined them to be of adequate size to support the weight of the high rises. Normally the crews would raze existing buildings for the sake of gentrification, but in this downtown district special care had been taken to "preserve the neighborhood characteristics and historical architecture," resulting in a block of mish-mashed styles.

When I reach the entrance, I sigh audibly. If I want to find the pastor, it makes sense to go into the future, but where and at what time I would emerge seems like total guesswork. Then again, the alley seems fantastically appealing to me. If I give in to that desire, would my life be derailed again? Would I even run into Becky—*Becky? I don't know anyone by that name*—again?

Standing still and breathing deeply, I place my toe on the pavement just beyond the seam where the blacktop meets the concrete of the sidewalk.

Stupid decision. Inevitably, going back to the lake will lead me back to the cabin, which will lead me back to the vacation house with the woman claiming to be my wife, which will lead me to the lair of the Shade, which will then lead me to the border realm where reality itself is consumed by the blackness.

In frustration, I turn to walk away. I've only taken one step before I hear hushed voices coming from the end of the alley. I stop and peer into the shaded recess, which lies nondescript and derelict beneath the pair of luxurious condo towers. The walls, constructed of weathered orange brick, are somewhat chipped and repaired due to years of neglect or abuse. The brick fronts rise some fifty feet before meeting the steel parapet caps, which reflect sparse, chilly rays of the sun and amplify them in tinges of gold. Beyond the walls lie two businesses, one of which specializes in medieval-themed knickknacks and pewter gaming figurines. The owners have aptly named it Corona's. Though the alley-way dead-ends with an overhead door for shipping and receiving, the light doesn't spread evenly to all corners of the recess.

I listen intently to try to get the gist of what the strangers are discussing, but their voices have died out. Slowly I step into the alley, listening for helpless breathing or soft whispers. Peering into every cor-ner, I realize that I am alone. There is no one. Unless the voices had come from the setbacks beneath the condo towers, I try to convince myself that they were a product of my imagination.

Still, if real humans had made those noises, they surely must have been transported. I squeeze my eyes shut, altering my decision at the last second. If they are in danger from the Shade, I must warn them. Swal-lowing, I step forward slowly, reaching out in vain toward a darkened corner where the brick veneers have been stained black as if by soot and smoke. I imagine it coiling upward, above the spires to the sky, where a million blackbirds join in clouding the city below in murky gray.

I have nothing to lose. Ten more steps will lead me to an alternate dimension. Fear crosses over me and my hands tremble. The strangers will be there, cowering in terror over their mistake.

A car tears past on the street behind me, exhaust echoing through the urban canyons like a fighter jet, and the sound lingers for longer than it should. I reach the corner and press my hands against the damaged walls.

Nothing happens, other than the wispy sound of a slight breeze filtering through the alley. I pry my eyes open and press with my palms for any sign of magical interference, but there is nothing. A pair of cigarette butts smolder at my feet, lending a dry musky scent to the air. I attempt to not breathe it in, but my heart kicks into overdrive. Has this alternate dimension merely transformed the city around me into some version of its former self, where the strangers I heard don't even exist?

Evidence of their departure seems to hint otherwise, but I can't be certain. I glance around at the lifeless alley. A pair of ravens lands on the parapet cap high above my head. The sunlight reflects around them like the streaks of the sun's corona during an eclipse. The noise from the cars on the street has not ceased.

I somberly tread backward before shaking my head and returning to the street. Nothing could have prepared me for this. I gulp and take one last step from the blacktop of the alley to the concrete sidewalk. The sun's angle has changed; it is now preparing to set on the city's western horizon and casts shadows longer than the buildings.

The sunlight glints off the glass of a hundred towers, as if I have ended up in New York. The skyscrapers stand idly as the sun bathes their residents with a warm, intimate light. I ache for comfort as I embrace the cold that seems to lift with every step. From Market Street, I can still hear the throngs: thousands of people are enjoying live music. Cars are honking amid the fray, setting off the celebratory mood. What all the fuss is about, I cannot be certain.

Overhead, heavy wings swoop over me. I cast my eyes upward to the blue sky between the towers. Whatever had made that noise has already vanished beyond the glass and steel. I shudder when a car speeds by on the street; it is a model I have never seen before, and it tears past almost silently, accompanied only by the roaring of its tires on the smooth pavement. A half block away dozens of cars are parked, and I can recognize only a few of them. A brand-new Mercedes, an aging GMC SUV, and a modified hatchback with a goofy-looking wing spoiler, intended to make the driver feel like a racing legend.

Is this some kind of car show? I swallow and realize too slowly what has become of the Philadelphia I have always known. The city has been gentrified beyond my wildest dreams. The gritty neighborhoods have been replaced with an extensive financial district and a hundred high rise residential buildings clawing at the sky with their shiny spires, cutting a jagged skyline against the fluffy clouds. Any sign of crime has been pushed to the fringes of the city's core, where I live.

A police car silently idles past, and a barren feeling creeps over me. This realm is heavily populated. If what Harley described were remotely accurate, there shouldn't be many people here, at least people with whom I can interact.

I make for the source of the music by crossing the street, forming a theory in my brain as to why there are so many people here. When I turn the corner, nothing can prepare me for the onslaught. The people are not just partying. They are smoking, drinking, dancing, kissing, and shouting. Plunging myself into the chaos seems to be a poor choice, but I must do it in order to test my theory.

I purposely bump into a woman, just to gauge her reaction. She spins to face me, her smile drooping. To shield myself from the resultant shame, I scream nonsense at no one in particular. Dozens of revelers pretend not to even notice me. Again, I dive in, slamming against a younger black man, who seems hellbent on pursuing a voluptuous blonde with hair fluttering as she bobs up and down to the bopping music.

He spins and effortlessly wrestles me to the ground. I can barely manage to fight back before he lands a fist to my forehead. I shove him as forcefully as I can, but he counters by grasping my wrist and rolling me onto my stomach. "Son of a *bitch,* don't even think about it," he screams, forcing my chin into the rough pavement. I ache as I writhe against his strength, at once agreeing with myself to disengage.

Lying prone on the ground face down can only prolong this altercation. I twist my abdomen, vying to shield my face from his fists, but he presses his full weight into my hip, which shoots a jolt of pain through my spine. I groan and twist harder while he pummels me with fist after fist to my back. I tremble with agony as he vents his rage, and then inexplicably he climbs off me—no, he falls off.

I flip over violently, expecting another barrage, but he has rolled onto his back and his focus has been taken completely off me. To defend himself from his unexpected attacker, he folds his knees and places his feet squarely on the ground as he crosses his fists across his abdomen. The attacker, a woman dressed in a modest T-shirt and metal-plated skirt that shimmers golden in the sun, silently stares him down, turns her back, and then walks away.

Struggling to my feet, I aim to thank her; but as the bumpy concrete punishes my knees, I search in vain for my defender. She has vanished. I suppress the urge to scream, yet there is something vaguely familiar about her memory that stops me in my tracks.

Around me the party intensifies. The shouting and dancing has transformed into a rhythmic chant, thousands of people awaiting a deity. The warmth seems to spread, yet I am shivering. Any moment now, the Shade will arrive to devour them all. There is nothing I can do to save them—if they would even agree to accept my help.

Instead of showing fearfulness, they seem overly gleeful. The chants again transform into a tempest of uproarious cheers. They stand together as an army to receive marching orders.

I croak dryly as the heavy wings return. Straining my neck to look upward beyond the towers, I spy flecks of gold that seem to dance in the sky. Surely this can't be real. The crowd cheers when the bird comes into full view.

Its beak shines as golden as its wings, which unfurl against the sunset in an alarming blur of golds, oranges, reds, and blacks. It squawks to the adoration of the masses as it rises, gathering the sunshine and focusing it into a blinding ball of energy.

The pain in my back clenches as the bird continues to gain altitude, stealing the sunshine as it ascends. The crowd shouts and cheers louder as the darkness spreads. Terror cloaks me as further chaos unfolds. The cheers gradually dissipate into warring chants, and then further devolve into jarring rage, each combatant keen to outdo the others vocally. Fists begin to fly, bodies violently writhing as in the mosh pit at a heavy metal concert. The people around me join in, pulverizing each other bloody, screaming obscenities, and polluting the darkness with strains of blackened rage.

To defend myself, I press backward against a shining storefront. Before me, someone screams. I shield my face as he approaches in the dark, and the windows behind me shatter. Fire erupts from his hands as he charges, illuminating the air around him in a terrifying orange glow.

The fire shoots outward, directly towards my head. I duck just in time, allowing the ball of flame to lob directly over me, where it explodes in a cascade of fire and smoke against the building's skin. All around me is an inferno, charring the world black as I bleed. Terror sinks in as the fires build. The city is destroying itself, but the destruction ceases abruptly while I am planning my escape.

Calm has fallen over the masses, as eerie silence replaces utter chaos. Somehow the silence only builds the terror further. The wings cascade above, transforming into thunder, while the sunlight gradually reappears. The thousands of people watch patiently, allowing the warmth to spread across beaten, charred flesh and mangled hair. If this is a ritual, I decide, it is so disturbing that I can only mutter *calamity* under my breath.

Suddenly I am falling backward into an abyss, a familiar face lingering over me, her pale cheeks and auburn hair reflecting the glowing sun. She reaches out, mouthing my name as she disappears, and the world around me twirls into starlight.

The breeze whips past me into a whistling whirlwind. A painful crashing impact leaves me stranded on gravelly sand. I scurry to my feet to fight against an unknown enemy.

She stands above me in the dark, hovering over the glassy surface of a tranquil body of water. I freeze as she regards me, carefully observing my pain and the scars. "Kerry William Gearhardt," she says peaceably. "You must leave this place."

"It was Sarah," I croak. "She was—"

"An illusion. Free yourself. Go back and never return, or you will be trapped here forever, seeking a love that does not exist."

"She's real," I argue pitifully. My voice trembles as I speak. Her words are plain, but her tone is gently menacing. "I'm going to save her, and I don't need your approval."

"I know whom you seek, Kerry. Find him. Heed his words."

"What do you know?" I ask, suddenly aware that my flesh is erupting into millions of icy goosebumps. "What is his name?"

"Jeff L. Martin? The pastor. A wise man."

"I remember him, but I don't—" I try to explain, but to no avail.

She shimmers as she hovers over me, lighting the lake with a pale aura of white, which seems to attract the fish.

"I don't need to know," she says, her serene voice drifting out of focus.

Desperate, I dig my nails into my palms and silently plead with her to stay. "Who are you?"

Her voice trails away as her sentence seems to vibrate the surface of the water into a circle of sullen ripples. "I am the daughter of Minos, keeper of the...." The last word is garbled and muffled so greatly that I can barely hear it as a watery, baritone grumble. The fish scatter as her aura radiates outward and vanishes.

Terror twists in my brain as I stare out at the waters and the dense forest beyond. The island awaits, with a single, eerie canoe parked at its shore. I prickle at the sounds of wildlife urging me on. Here there are no humans, only ghosts. The only way I am getting to the island is the long way, through the reedy marshes where the deer normally hide.

Gulping down a knot of uncertainty, I flex my muscles, square my jaw, and begin the silent, agonizing journey.

12

The Fall of Phaethon

The reeds brush lightly against my arms as I tread through knotted grasses and sink into the soft, muddy soil. I trample a mat of twisted blades, which glisten eerily in the moonlight. Because this corner of the lake is relatively unexplored by humans, game animals forage and hide out in these grasses to avoid human interaction until after sunset, when they dare to wade in the low-lying portion adjacent to the open waters.

I groan as the humidity increases, holding my breath to avoid disturbing whatever wildlife inhabits this marsh. Beneath my sole, something moves. Instinctively I lift my foot, and in so doing I lean backwards so far that I have to flail my arms to avoid tumbling into the mush. Regaining my balance, I steady my gaze and peer dead ahead through the tall grasses and the pussy willows. About a hundred feet away, a lone stag pokes its head up but remains motionless for too long. It had to have heard my near accident and should have noisily sprinted away, even if its habitat has always been devoid of humans. The moonlight seems to gather on its antlers, creating twisted, disorienting shadows and pale bluish streaks.

Uncertain of which direction to tread, I cautiously step forward. The stag doesn't move, but its antlers seem to grow larger. If I get too close, it could trample or gore me, or worse.

I swallow a breath of dense air. The mud squishes under my feet. Trying to dull my breathing through my shivering and ruthless pain, I watch as my hands tremble. I pull back a thick clump of grass, listening to it rustle as

I move. Still the deer doesn't react. As I draw nearer, the shapes and shadows morph again. There is no stag. I peer helplessly at the cold, bare branches of a dead tree, suffocated by too much water and the grasses that hog all the nutrients in the soil.

Light has again tricked my eyes into seeing something that isn't there. If light can impair visual function to such an extent, then what Harley has told me about memory makes more sense. If my own memory can so thoroughly fail me, then what can I truly rely on? Is Harley even a trustworthy source?

Moments ago, I'd spoken to him, watched his body language, and communicated with him eye to eye. It was concrete and real, yet now his image seems to undulate in the perception of my memory, as if he were fading away from the firm reality inside my head. Clinging to him and hanging on his words proves to be of little use. As the seconds tick away his image flutters, the sound of his voice wavers, his body language disappears, and his eyes transform into glassy orbs of solid rock.

The dead tree stands motionless within the sea of reeds and tall grasses. Overhead the moonlight touches the scene with a moody blue light, the hue of mysterious crime dramas and cinematic vampire legends. Wings flutter somewhere in the distance, deadened by the tall grasses.

For a moment I can hear only my own breathing.

I shiver when I look up, to peer at a dark structure above the tips of the grasses. The trees grow thicker on the island, which seems to me untouched, even amid the growth of vacation homes. The cabin predates them all.

Filling my head with wondering over who had erected the house and lived in it seems a poor use of my time, but the noise is a welcome reprieve from the muted sounds of wildlife and the clinging silence. Based on what is currently in my memory, I can only surmise that the cabin dates to the late nineteenth century, possibly imagined as a makeshift hunting outpost for the wealthy citizen of a nearby town. It is perfectly situated to observe both the water and the populated areas where game animals graze. A studious hunter with a good rifle and a keen eye could take down a fine, prize animal by simply stepping out his front door and keeping to the shelter of the trees.

The mud seems more viscous as I step carelessly forward. When I look down, the squelching noise confirms my suspicion. I wrestle my foot free as I peer over the rippling waters. I am standing in it ankle-deep. It is not thick enough to prevent me from pulling my foot out, but I must alter my trajectory toward firmer footing, which will lead me further away from the island. From the beach, I recall having seen a gravelly bar adjacent to the reeds. From that point it would be a short row in a canoe to the forested slopes of the hill.

I begin to sweat beneath my jacket, even as the cold chills me to the bone. This could be the beginning stages of hypothermia, but I cannot focus on that.

Once again feeling the soft, mushy mud around my ankles, I turn my head to examine the island and to plan my trek. Straight ahead, a cold, hunched figure awaits me. It must surely be a peculiarly placed rock, but its presence indicates firmer ground and a clearer vision of the path I should take. Steeling my nerves, I head in that direction. Again, its shape gradually morphs in the moonlight as I approach: seams of black and folds of gray absorb my attention as I study it.

After about ten steps, realization dawns on me. This is not a rock, but a piece of manmade cloth, carefully draped over a clump of shorter grasses. I reach out my hand slowly as I tread closer over firmer ground.

Moments later, my fingers touch the rough fabric, a plastic-infused gray canvas with heavy sleeves and a fur-rimmed hood. A jacket. Its position in the grass indicates human presence. Excitement swells within me, even as dread curls somewhere in my heart.

Who could it be? I look around for clues, glancing down at the muddy soil where the sparse grass grows. A set of interrupted footprints trail off through the rocks toward the water's edge. She could be there, I tell myself, thinking her name sounds foreign and wispy in my brain, and built out of one or two extra syllables so that it begins to resemble an unfamiliar language.

I dare not speak. I follow the trail of footprints silently until I can no longer differentiate them from the muddy soil.

A hundred yards away, the rocky bar extends about a dozen feet into the water, but no canoe awaits. I step on something that seems too sharp, and when I look down in surprise, I realize that I am already falling. Instinctively I sprawl my hands out to shield my body. They plunge painfully into broken gravel. I yelp as my knees collide with the rocks. A soothing yellow light erupts from somewhere ahead; I glance up and see it disappear into the canopy of the island. My head begins to spin and pain shoots through my limbs. Struggling to my feet with the same resolve, I steady my nerves and tread on toward the rocky bar.

Trembling in pain, I wade into the icy, grimy waters that quickly cover my shoes and cleanse the mud from my feet. The cold is instant and numbing. If I make it to the island with any feeling in my toes, I will consider it an accomplishment. It stands in the dark about a hundred yards away.

Before long, the water is lapping at my waist, and then at my chest. Another few steps and I lose my footing. Launching off the invisible rocks below, I angle myself forward, swinging my arms. The cold blasts every part of my body as I try desperately to keep my head above the water. Even so, it wets my hair and makes my breathing more difficult.

As I swim out across the depths, something unknown brushes against my leg. I splash furiously as the island draws nearer, desperate to escape whatever creature prowls the depths. Every second seems to draw out toward infinity as the freezing liquid batters me from all sides. My feet collide with rocky earth again after what seems like an hour; regaining my balance is not as easy as my mind wants to believe. I stumble and fall face-first into the cold water, submerging myself. After a second or two of flailing, I gasp in a breath of heavy air. The waters across the lake from me emit an eerie gray mist that dances over the glassy surface and obscures everything beyond it.

Wading in toward the island, I spy the shore a hundred feet to my right, where the lone, forgotten canoe rests on the gravel. Continuing my trek toward the boat promises to be a waste of energy. Instead, I focus on the island: the cabin will be a hearty climb over mossy boulders and through dense undergrowth. From my vantage point I can only see the silent canopy stretching upward like a greenish black mountain surrounded by the black water.

My breath murmurs as I begin the climb. Pain pulverizes my side as if a spear has been driven into my flesh. Mindlessly I pat at my sodden clothes to feel for blood and let out a subtle sigh of relief when I feel nothing but icy moisture. I hold my elbows against my body and shiver. The cabin may be abandoned, but its shelter promises a tantalizing warmth that I will not want to leave all that soon.

The climb is arduous. I slip on a muddy section of flat rock and my knees crash against the stone. I can only whimper as the last of my memory of the street party vanishes, to be replaced by a sickening feeling of familiarity.

Struggling to make sense of it all, I see new images flashing before my eyes as the pain digs deeper into my knees and hands. She is mouthing something to me; her black hair falls on my shoulder as I stand cautiously next to her. Green stretches in all directions, and then, as the tan grasses spread across the horizon, a stark gray building emerges. Together we gape at it, and then vanish into a soup of tan and green.

I climb twenty feet, and then fifty, before the slope evens out and I can stand once again. Slipping through a knot of narrower tree trunks, I inch upward to reach a set of wooden steps. The planks rise another ten feet, but this climb proves easier.

I don't bother trying to peer into the blackened windows of the cabin. The house should have a portal to another dimension; I remember it keenly. The closet in which I fell occupies the main floor, beyond a small kitchen. As I turn the brass handle in my palm, the metal doesn't seem as cold as it should be. It might be due to the hypothermia that is building inside of me. The knob turns easily and slowly. Pushing into the darkness, I cast my eyes in all directions. One chair is pulled out from the tiny dining room table, beside which sits an old, forgotten book, and a clear glass that contains about an inch of water.

"Hello?" I call out to no one. Of course I am alone; that is the story of my life. Alone to observe the changing world around me, as if I'm immune to its perils but utterly subject to its agony.

The air seems thinner in this room. I casually wipe a thin film of dust from the table and lift the book until I can see its title. "*The Soul of the Baron*," I read under my breath. I have never read it, but as I hold it in my grasp, memories pour through me. I have held this book in my hands before. We were at a bookstore, and she had handled it seconds before placing it back on the shelf. I'd picked it up and flipped through the first several pages. The count had kidnapped the king's daughter and locked her away. It is the start of nearly every fable ever written, as far as I can tell. Before I can casually recognize why it seems so familiar, the reason appears before me. A young, slender boy with matted black hair and a curious expression is tagging along behind us. He has read so many of these kinds of books that they have become cliché.

I clear my throat as quietly as possible, wedging my body against the end cabinet and bending my elbows at my waist. "Are you here?"

What was her name? I furrow my brows, trying to remember, and come up empty. If she has a name, I decide, I have not used it in ages. Closing my eyes, I allow viscous memory to wash over me. There is her veil again. And then, years later, the baby bump. She is wearing a blue T-shirt with a pink heart.

"Becky? Is that you?" The sudden memory barely registers in my brain.

The cabin is so still and silent, feeling as though no other soul has stepped inside in eons, except for me. I study the patterns of dust on the floor to look for footprints. Her footprints must be here, but in the dim light I can only see my own wet, rugged pattern pressed everywhere. Sliding down the cabinet slowly, I drop to my knees to peer closer. At the right angle, the prints will be more readily visible.

I lower myself as quietly as I can, arching my back, and nearly press my cheek against the creaky floorboards. Fixing my gaze on the baseboard behind the table, I let the low angle bend the light rays relative to my position and study the shoeprints on the floor. I should be able to see my own prints from a day or two ago, but I can only see one set. I emit a deep breath and lift myself back up to rest against the cabinet.

My breath has disturbed some of the dust on the floor. When it clears away and settles, I can see a subtle, dirty ridge where the dust seems to have stuck to the floorboards. Excited, I press my fingers against it. It is a caked line of dried mud. I examine the room as thoroughly as possible. The ridges appear in other places, but there are only a few. I cannot tell whether they were made by a woman's shoe, but the shape seems to indicate smaller, petite feet.

Terror pulses in my veins, and the darkness seems to fold inside itself, shading the footprints and the book until they are nothing more than opaque shapes. I can only croak helplessly as I realize that my memory of this cabin has faded, beginning to shake as the moonlight briefly reappears. The room is in an odd disarray: barren furniture, caked with years of dust, lies strewn about the floor, covered in dirty cobwebs. The fold-out bed in the other room looks to be decades old. Rips in the fabric reflect the moonlight, and dust has dyed the cotton stuffing to a nasty brown. The spiders have found a home inside its arm and back. Millions of streamers of silk drape from the cloth upholstery to the dusty floor. A clock that once must have adorned the wall has fallen and broken. More dust coats its hands.

"Becky," I repeat quietly, as if to reassure myself that I am alone. Realization hits me as I stare at this disarray. I have never set foot in this cabin—not in the current timeline, anyway.

I begin to worry as I scan a nearby hallway that serves as nothing more than a narrow aisle that passes between two short walls. Two doors open out of this passageway, one on the left and one on the right. At the end of the corridor, a single door leads to a bathroom. Behind the kitchen cabinets, another door hangs open.

Pain rips through my knees as I rise to my feet again, swallow, and step gingerly into the corridor. Both bedroom doors are firmly closed, looking as though they have not been opened in years. The dust on the floor lies undisturbed in this section of the cabin. Still, I cannot help myself; the doorknob squeaks dryly as I turn it, and the dust sticks to my hand. I brush it off on my soaked jeans and press the door wide, revealing a twin-size mattress and no blankets. Dozens of black spots are scattered across the puffy surface. The other bedroom is in a similar state, though a thin sheet has been draped over the bed and a fluffy bedspread lies somewhat folded into a rough ball near the corner of the floor. There are no footprints in this room.

I shake my head and press open the bathroom door. It creaks loudly as it swings, and icy chills race down my spine. The darkness strengthens as I survey the bathroom. There is no mat on the floor, the mirror is caked with dust and cobwebs, and a single towel hangs from the rack near the tub.

The cabin must have been in use when it was abandoned. Did the hunter never return, or had he planned to when death got in the way? The possibilities seem endless.

Quietly, I back away from the trio of doors and peer into the black abyss of the closet. Readying myself for the fall, I clutch at my shoulders with both hands and wedge my eyes closed.

Gravity takes over, yet it doesn't feel like falling at all; instead, I feel weightless, as if the effects of gravity have been dulled to oblivion. When I open my eyes, there are millions of pinpricks of starlight surrounding me. I attempt to spin myself around in midair. Behind me, a red planet with icy white rings drifts slowly away from me. The arc of my travel suggests that its gravity is tugging at me subtly.

Floating in infinite space, I let my feelings soothe me, until it all disappears. When I open my eyes again it is dawn, and I am lying in bed atop a warm blanket. The pain in my knees hasn't dissipated. I roll onto my back, sit up quickly, and allow my eyes to adjust to the cascading sunlight. I am in a hotel room and there is noise coming from behind the wall adjacent to the door. I hear a bang that sounds like a bar of soap dropping to the bottom of the tub. Carefully, I rise from the bed.

My sodden clothes press against my body beneath my jacket, and when I turn to survey the bed, I see water has seeped out of my clothing, creating a huge, body-shaped wet patch on the sheets. I run a hand through my hair and approach the bathroom, ready to attack anyone who jumps out at me. There will be a towel I can use to dry myself, after I take off the soaked jacket.

After tossing the jacket into the open closet, I gather my senses and press the door open. A robed woman with black hair faces the mirror, dabbing foundation at her cheeks, and pretends not to notice me. It is as if she knows she has a partner. I stare at her longer than I should. Her wet hair hangs limply at her slim shoulders as she hunches over the vanity. Droplets of water drip to the floor at her feet. The voluminous robe reveals a pregnant belly. She opens her eyes to apply eyeliner and glances at me through the mirror.

Terror flashes through her eyes and she grips the eyeliner pen as if to stab me with it.

"Why are you wet? God, you look awful."

As though I have never set eyes on her, I back away. "I—I don't know how I got in this room. I'm sorry ma'am."

"Kerry? What's going on?"

"How do you know my name?"

She smiles sheepishly, drops the eyeliner, and turns to face me. "You're teasing me, aren't you? So sweet last night, so mischievous this morning. That's why I love you so much."

Love? Me? Other than my mother, no other woman has uttered those words to me. I shudder and back away step by step as fear races through me.

"Ker, what the hell are you doing?"

I stutter. "I'm—I—I'm lost. Help me."

She smiles, but then the humor in her face drains away, leaving a sad, concerned frown in its wake. Ready to leave, I wedge my hand around the doorknob and freeze in place.

She follows me out of the bathroom and flings her arms around me. She speaks slowly into my chest. "I take it you're ready to leave." Her tone drifts lower. "Let me get dressed and then we can go down and grab a muffin."

After a comfortless moment, she pulls away from me, tightens the robe around her, and plants a wet kiss on my lips. I stand paralyzed, unable to move. Realizing that I have not uttered a single complete sentence this whole time, I return to the bed. "How did you sleep last night?" I say, trying to sound conversational.

"You snored in my ear," she says, her pitch rising. "And you whispered something."

Her suitcase sits atop a knee-high metal rack inside the closet, whose bifold doors are hanging wide open. I make my way there and rummage through it to find a pair of men's jeans and a tee shirt.

Returning to the bedside, I quietly strip off my soaked clothes, tiptoe back to the suitcase to find a pair of dry underwear, and dress as quickly as possible.

When she opens the bathroom door, she looks radiant. Suddenly I can remember her name.

I try to fake a smile and say it out loud. "Becky."

She rushes toward me, flings her arms around my neck, and kisses me.

13

Altar to the Titans

The aroma of freshly prepared omelets fills the narrow corridor as we saunter past food service carts, each bearing entrees in reflective stainless-steel lidded trays. One hotel guest has opted for a fine wine in a new bottle doused in ice, accompanied by a pair of fragile, stemware glasses. Becky visibly smiles and lowers her eyes to the orange and red semi-circle-and-star pattern in the decorative carpet. She treads quickly, showing both purpose and panache.

A room service cart carrying fresh linens and cleaning agents is parked two doors down from the elevator. We alter our trajectory to stay out of its way and then dodge a woman hurrying out of the elevator, carrying a muffin and a steaming cup of coffee. She barely makes eye contact with Becky, who issues a brief smile and a courteous nod.

"That's some dedication," she says in a voice so quiet only I can hear her.

The elevator door remains open, and we step inside before either of us utters another word. I know what I need to ask, but she beats me to it.

"Do you want to do both the power plant and the prison today?" She has clearly made plans already, possibly with input from my actual future self, who has disappeared to make way for this version of me. In case it was my suggestion in the first place, I nod in silent approval and feel her growing nearer.

Within moments our hands touch. Her warmth is astounding and comfortable, as if it were something missing from my life all along. She clasps my hand tighter by interlocking our fingers and pressing her hip against me.

During our previous interaction, when I left the house with the welded washers in my pocket, I asked her about the pastor. At this stage of the future, before our child arrives, she likely knows the story should I choose to retell it. Instead, I can only offer faint bits and pieces of it, which would leave her confused and wondering why I would choose this moment to bring it up. I let the thought vaporize in my throat before mentioning it anyway.

"Do you remember Jeff L. Martin?"

She nods. "Of course I do. What about him?"

Trying to think of a way to hide my anxiety while speaking quickly and passionately, I lower my voice and gaze at our interlocked hands, clasped together like the two welded rings. "I need to find him."

A subtle laugh escapes her lips, but she suppresses it at the first sign that I'm being serious. "You don't just *walk up* to Jeff L. Martin. He's got aides who have other aides who have even more aides. You want to talk to him, you have to start at the bottom."

"He's that famous?" It doesn't seem to fit the situation, since neither Harley nor Joaquin indicated, whether verbally or otherwise, that they knew who he was.

She shrugs. "You know as well as anyone."

My eyes narrow. "What's that supposed to mean? You have to talk to me like I was born yesterday because I literally was, at least in this reality—"

"Jesus, what do you mean?"

Instead of staring at her, I watch the numbers on the door header light up as we pass the second floor and lurch to a stop at the ground level. Now that she senses something is not quite right with me, it would probably be an opportune time to bomb her with the truth. Then again, the truth might get me in even more trouble.

If I alienate Becky at this point in the future, would my life trajectory really turn out all that differently?

"Nothing," I say, my voice devoid of meaning and nuance. Instead of letting the thought linger, I scan her visually, particularly her jeans pockets. If she carries a smartphone with her, reason would have it that I could look up how to contact Reverend Martin. Then again, using the normal channels could take weeks or months and I might not be around long enough to see his response.

"Nothing, my foot. What's gotten into you? You get out of bed soaking wet, don't even bother taking a shower, and now you're standing here talking about—I don't even know what. Was your nightmare that bad?"

I can remember no nightmare, unless you count trudging through the muddy reeds, climbing the island, or—hell, *any* of what has happened recently.

The elevator door glides open, and we step out hand-in-hand. The lobby is abuzz with two families checking out a sundry of travel pamphlets, each excitedly pointing out attractions they want to see and trying to encourage the dads to fund it all. A little girl, not getting her way, grabs a pamphlet showing a scenic beach out of her brother's hands, swings it high above her head, and then throws it down on the floor in a dramatic quest for parental attention. When her mother doesn't immediately respond, she breaks out in tears, which I don't remember being entirely effective when I was a child.

The father nods and relents. Parenting must be so easy in the future, so I thank God I'm not around to dilute the waters.

"You know, you get nightmares too," I guess accusingly, perhaps out of a defensive urge.

She sees through this, too, and presses. "Nice try. This is about you and why you're acting this distant, this ... *aloof.*"

"Cut me some slack," I plead sarcastically. "I've been traveling." The intended double meaning predictably passes over her head.

Instead of prying further, she eyes a tall man holding two cups of coffee and leads me around a corner. We enter an expansive seating area, complete with dozens of tables, each adorned with the customary wire-mesh basket containing salt, pepper, and sweetener packets. The tables are topped with a faux marble veneer, and rimmed with ribbed stainless-steel bands, just like the counters seen in those kitschy, nostalgic themed diners that serve bland food and milkshakes. Along the far wall, behind the reception counter, an array of hot bars stands adjacent to a bakery basket and a trio of coffee machines. About a dozen guests wait in line at the hot bar to gobble up questionable processed meat, starchy pancakes, and scrambled eggs.

"If I'd wanted food, I'd have ordered room service," I remark, turning my nose up at the toast a young man is consuming alone as we make for the bakery basket.

"This, coming from the guy who used to eat frozen burritos four times a week before I introduced him to the new-fangled technology called cooking?"

That's a low blow. I happen to like frozen burritos, and they're better with a nice picante sauce. They have a palette of great flavors, unlike those disgusting fast-food packets.

"The muffins look decent," I say, picking out a lemon and poppy-seed monstrosity with a napkin. She grabs at a chocolate muffin and finds the juice tower. She silently fills a cup and stands back so that I can stare uninspired at the predictable choices of apple and orange, and eventually choose neither.

We stalk to the back of the room to an isolated table, far from the television that is yammering on with its political commentary and advertising. The only bit of it I recognize is the abject stupidity and lack of clear concepts. This future is a true dystopia, except for the woman I'm with.

I marvel at her sleek black hair, which she spent about ten minutes drying and styling. She lets it drape down to her shoulders, but occasionally brushes a strand or two behind her ear. Her makeup looks rushed, yet it shimmers in simplistic beauty. Nibbling at her muffin, she makes eye contact with me and offers a coy smile.

If this is what being in love feels like, it seems most appealing, except that I feel nothing—and how could I, seeing as how my current self has only known her for a grand total of an hour, give or take?

"The beach is so overrated," she argues, almost as if she's hoping an innocent bystander hears her.

I shrug. "If you can curl up with a good book and warm sun without five hundred people screaming and yelling in your ear, it might be enjoyable."

From the clues around me—what the hotel guests are wearing, the pamphlets in the lobby, and the general sunny quality built into the architecture of the hotel—a beach resort doesn't sound like a bad guess. A younger man with tan lines, wearing a pair of plaid shorts, a New Jersey T-shirt, a baseball cap, and sandals, seems to prance past the hot bar, glancing our way for a split-second.

"So, what do you do?" I say, changing the subject again. "Call Mr. Martin and leave a message so his aides' aides' aide can ignore it?"

"On Sunday, you could find where he's giving a service and make a scene, but don't act like you're a threat. Maybe you could meet him."

I smile; a good idea with a high likelihood of backfiring spectacularly is my idea of a good time.

"I think he's doing a tour of the East Coast next summer." She bites into her muffin, peels back some of the paper, and furrows her eyebrows as if deep in thought.

I'm not about to wait around in this future for a whole year. If I don't figure out what happened to Sarah, I'm doomed to a future of misery, and I'll possibly lose her forever, if I ever even had a chance.

When we step out into the summer air, a scent of bracken wafts into my nostrils. The high rises stretch out along a major boulevard, more tightly clustered several blocks away. Examining the metropolis, I quickly conclude that we are in Atlantic City. If this was indeed my idea, it makes sense. After all, this whole time-swapping business figures to be one huge gamble, with the promised payoff of finding Sarah and bringing her back to the *real world*.

As I approach the parking area, Becky clasps my hand more tightly and guides me to our car, a smaller SUV crossover. She opens the passenger's side door for me, and letting go of her hand I climb in. A gentle chuckle escapes her lips as she closes the door. Wordlessly, she climbs in behind the wheel and starts the car.

"Didn't feel like driving?"

I shrug. "Don't know where we're going."

"The power plant, right? State of the art, brand new, enough green energy to supply Eastern Pennsylvania and most of Jersey..."

She trails off and I don't bother to look dumb. "Yeah, but where is it?"

Another chuckle. "You MapZilla'd it yourself. You're the navigator, because I'm going to get lost."

I have no way of accessing the internet so that I can pretend to understand what she's talking about. "Right, can I borrow your phone?"

"What about yours?" She glances over her shoulder as she cautiously backs out of the parking spot. A sheaf of hair falls from behind her ear and flops on her shoulder.

"I seem to have—lost mine," I say sheepishly.

"Didn't you have it when we got to the hotel? I could have sworn I saw you looking at it during that show we were watching."

With that information in mind, it seems likely that my future self's phone is still somewhere in the hotel room; yet if we go back and look for it and I have no idea where it is I'd look incredibly stupid, which would cause Becky even more alarm.

Instead of entertaining the idea, I nod and wait. She'd deposited her purse on the center console. I don't bother asking before unzipping it and digging in while keeping my eyes fixed on the boulevard.

Feeling its glossy screen, I pull it out and tap a few icons. I can guess that I may be up to five years into the future. The feel and design of her phone doesn't differ much from the one I'm accustomed to, albeit from a different manufacturer and with a strange operating system installed on it.

I bring up MapZilla and start typing in 'power plant,' which the application remembers. I click on it and a detailed map pops onto the screen, zooms out, and then highlights the best route with a thick blue line. Off to the side, a set of directions appears. Within the app, a voice button offers to speak the directions in real time. So that I don't get her lost by inadequately relaying the information on the screen, I let the voice assistant do all the work. I sit quietly in my seat, gazing out at the towering hotels that stretch along the beachfront instead of speaking.

If we live in Philadelphia and vacation in Atlantic City, the power plant is almost the same distance from both, but perhaps a bit farther from the beach. To confirm my suspicion, I clear my throat and speak softly, noting the name of a familiar business behind the ritzy hotels. "Do you think that's as good as the one in Philly?"

She looks at me, seemingly perplexed. "We went there a month ago, at home. But we haven't gone to Philadelphia in years. You know that."

I don't dare ask her where we live, for fear that the answer will disappoint me—or worse, reveal that I'm fully committed for life. Judging from what little information I have, she seems kind, and someone I could see myself settling down with, except that my eyes are on another woman. The image of Sarah's auburn hair lingers in my memory. Perhaps it is familiarity, but even with all the years that must have passed between then and now, I remember every detail, right down to the tone of her voice. A flash of snow falling off an idling car passes before me and my heart flutters. In contrast, a vague face from perhaps the same era haunts my memory. His salt and pepper beard dominates his image, but his eyes have disappeared. Still, I remember Harley's name for some reason.

"Of course. I used to go to the one in Philly, you know, before we moved away."

"*You* moved away," she said, "to be with me, remember?"

Did we have a long-distance relationship? I swallow and say nothing more. The suburbs stretch miles from the oceanfront. I watch the street signs pass by as Becky listens to the instructions from the virtual assistant and turns onto a freeway entrance ramp. The sun lingers high overhead, and the air is warm and humid. The trees are a dark shade of green, indicating late summer, perhaps August or September. Quietly, I let the scenery pass by, feeling Becky glance at me once every few minutes.

After about the third glance, she speaks again. "What are you thinking about?"

Classic conversation starter, but a complete failure. My mind can only draw a blank, as usual. If I tell her what I'm really thinking, she's liable to drive off the side of the road in horror.

This future isn't as strange as some of the others I have stumbled into, but for some reason I can only remember flashes of them now. If this realm becomes too comfortable, I can only be in greater danger the longer I stay. The Shades will be back to ravage the city tonight, possibly in search of me. I try to gulp away my sense of foreboding and simply watch the country foliage pass by, as Becky speeds along the highway.

At my best estimation, an hour and a half has passed by since I drifted off to sleep. Although not totally unexpected, the effects of tiredness hadn't consciously registered. I stir in my seat and scan the densely forested hills that stretch out in all directions.

Seeing me move, Becky glances to her right and flashes a smile. "How was your nap?"

I don't answer. She turns off the two-lane highway onto a local street, bypasses a gas station, and then switches onto another country road at the voice assistant's command.

"What's wrong? Did the nightmare keep you up last night?"

I offer a silent nod. In fact, sleep has been a rarity for days—how long? I try to specify non-verbally by rubbing my eyes, which Becky is watching out of the corner of her eye between long glances at the highway.

"Well don't go back to sleep now, we're almost there. Look, you can see the stacks."

I peer directly ahead. Behind a shallow hill, steam is rising from a pair of tall, tapered cylinders. Construction of that behemoth of a power plant would have to have gotten off the ground at least five years ago, but I can't remember seeing it mentioned in the news, although I'm not exactly diligent in reading it every day. The cooling towers suggest a nuclear plant, which is supposed to be dangerous from what the politicians say. They hype green energy so much, yet they fail to understand that nuclear power is one of the greenest forms of energy ever devised. Some seem more than content to prop up coal, which is a dying and inefficient industry. Based on what I know, natural gas is the most effective means of powering cities, especially in this northern latitude. Solar would be spotty, and wind wouldn't be sufficient. With few hydropower projects, the northeast doesn't have a single reliable power source and depends heavily on coal and gas. Nuclear would provide a huge boost, but the masses don't trust nuclear projects because of the negative publicity that surrounds every meltdown. Chernobyl, Three Mile Island, Fukushima and the rest were all huge press events, but, of the thousands of reactors all over the world, the disasters represent only a tiny fraction. They may actually be safer than coal and gas, but their reputation still suffers.

For the next few minutes Becky thinks out loud, offering short, clipped sentences until she has parked the car in a giant parking lot that is about halfway filled with cars. If the power plant is pushing heavily advertised tours of the facility, perhaps the fear of melting down is stunting attendance.

The cooling towers come fully into view. After we get out, Becky slings her purse over her shoulder, clasps my hand, and walks straight toward what is obviously the main tour entrance. A few other couples are migrating that way, some with children. Two hundred yards away, separated from the parking lot by a shady street and buffered by rows of low-growing shrubs and native trees, a line has formed. At least fifty tourists are waiting to get in and learn how their power is generated.

I don't know why I suggested this tour, if it really was my idea. Green energy is not something I'm generally concerned about, though the idea seems more appealing the more thought I give it.

The line moves quickly as we file in behind an older couple with no children, who seem entirely too cheerful in their interactions with other people's kids. The old woman bends at the waist, shows a wide grin, and dotes on a little girl, who is showing off her new doll. "She's so beautiful! You must take such good care of her."

At this stage of life, I barely acknowledge that kids exist, and I have no idea how to interact with them, having forgotten almost everything about my own childhood. I vaguely remember crying in the final inning of a baseball game that my team is losing. *There's no crying in baseball,* I can hear my coach yelling, but in my head, he sounds like Tom Hanks. For our team, there wasn't much winning. Out of a dozen games I can only pick out a single instance of enjoying the thrill of victory.

The line moves, until only the old couple is left in front of us. The family with the little girl has disappeared through the glass doors, and I let my grip on Becky's hand slacken. She nudges me with her hip, flings her left hand up to my neck, and plants a quick kiss on my cheek. Before I know what I'm doing, I'm leaning in. She feels so good, so fresh. I let go of her hand, wrap both arms around her shoulders, and lean into her, kissing her lips three times with my eyes closed.

When we're done, I can feel several pairs of eyes drilling into the back of my head.

"Wow," she says. "You haven't kissed me like that in a long time. It's like you haven't seen me in weeks."

"You have no idea," I mumble, so softly that she cannot hear.

After about a five-minute wait, the glass doors open again and a tour guide welcomes the old couple, the two of us, and another large family behind us into the facility.

"Welcome to Green Mountain Power Systems," the guide exclaims gleefully. "The newest, most state-of-the-art facility on the East Coast. We'll walk you through our methods and systems to inform you of our proud commitment to powering our communities responsibly while contributing nothing to climate change.

"The first room we will show you is our operations data center."

He leads us through a set of double doors and down a broad, industrial hallway where a network of pipes crisscrosses above our heads.

"This is where we monitor current usage trends and predict peak demand based on weather forecasts, up to a week in advance. Using climate data from the National Oceanic and Atmospheric Administration, as well as historical population growth in the region, we can accurately predict demand and tailor our energy mix to best meet that need.

"As you can see, a lot of science and calculations are applied so that we can efficiently power your homes and businesses. Does anyone have any questions?"

Someone from behind us pipes up: "How do you account for when the forecast is wrong? Weathermen are basically paid to stand in front of a green screen and tell us they really don't know what is going to happen."

"Good question," the tour guide responds. "Meteorology may be an inexact science, but a large part of our equation is based on the NOAA's heating and cooling data, which is a factor of average temperature, humidity, dew points, wind conditions, and population density based on over a century's worth of past observations. Have you heard meteorologists use the term 'Cooling Degree Days'? The NOAA calculates this data historically, monthly, and daily, to track the usage needed to cool homes during these hot summer months. The same happens in the winter with a similar calculation, called the Heating Degree Days.

"Any other questions?"

I keep my head down and try to internalize the information the tour guide has so happily given us. He leads the group down the hallway past a dozen or so doors, some of which are labeled with the four-diamond symbol generally used to indicate hazardous materials.

"The second piece of the puzzle is optimization," the guide says. "By accurately predicting demand based on weather conditions, we have the ability to mix services on the wire. When the sun is shining on our solar arrays, we can collect that energy and add it to the mix. If the wind is blowing, one of our four wind turbines helps boost supply.

"We have five general services we can pull from at Green Mountain," he explains. "I mentioned solar and wind, but we also use a pumped storage hydro system, which is operated by one of the other four services. A lower reservoir, which you will see out the window on your right, collects water runoff from an upper reservoir."

The reservoir consists of a broad pool about ten feet deep, contained on three sides by gravel dikes. A fifty-foot-high concrete wall is built into the hillside beyond, and a pair of huge pipes penetrates it to lift the water to the upper reservoir, which remains out of sight atop the hill.

"During off-peak hours, we pump water up from the lower reservoir to the upper, and in peak hours we let it run off through the turbines to generate energy."

"Some engineers must have had fun with this one." I snort derisively. I poke at the engineers because their understanding of construction consists only of the basics. Though involved in scheduling and product selection, they mostly stay off site and judge our work based on a few paltry visits.

The tour guide laughs. "That is a fact."

"Our fourth service takes advantage of our earth's natural magnetic field. Again, using power from the other four services, we generate electromagnetism, which we harness to create constant energy."

He leads us to a set of double doors and points to a stainless-steel rack that holds dark blue smocks in clear shrink wrap, boxes of cloth shoe covers, and hearing protection. "Before we go any further, you will need to smock up. Place the booties over your shoes and make sure the smock is zipped up all the way. Hearing protection is also required beyond this point. If you are unsure whether you're doing it properly, please ask for help and I will gladly assist you."

He watches the dozen or so people on the tour crowd around the rack to grab at the required equipment. When I'm dressed, I see that the children in the back are finishing up and the group is ready to move on.

"This room is our Electromagnetic Generation room." He pushes open the door. "This is a semi-circular room because of the properties of electromagnetism. Each of these cabinets harnesses magnetic motors that react with the Earth's geomagnetic core. The motors run off of servos connected to the turbines located in the next room. We have ten cabinets in this room, with capacity to add two more for future demand."

His voice trails off as I wander amidst the cabinets in awe. Suddenly I hear a voice calling to me, lost somewhere in the loud drone of the electromagnetic motors. I can sense that the group is moving on without me, Becky included.

I can barely move. I stare in all directions: smaller cabinets around the perimeter of the room supply, monitor, and transform energy from the motors, while a thick web of conduits, pipes, and ducts crisscrosses like spaghetti overhead, so deep that I cannot see the ceiling. The diamond-patterned steel floor tiles are arranged intermittently in the aisle. A pair of orange caution cones and a ladder gather dust in a nearby corner.

Each of the cabinets is fitted with a small window, through which power engineers can view the equipment and monitor whether service will be required. In one, a red LED light pulses like a constant heartbeat. I stare at it, transfixed, while it transports me to a strange realm. The gray and silver equipment surrounding me evaporates into a fine mist as I stare, and the flashing red light becomes a constant glow in a sea of black. I gaze out in every direction, my feet disconnected from the floor, if there even is one. The red aura gathers into a glowing orb in an ocean of stars. As I gaze, the red giant grows and the voice returns.

"I am Cygnus," it seems to say, like a wispy, whispered response to a lover. *"Transformed into a swan by Apollo after the fall of my friend—follow me."*

I stand in the ether, transfixed by this orb that bathes me with its red heat. I reach out for it, certain that it will lead me to Sarah, and close my eyes. I can feel her hair tickling my arm, and the sound of her voice, echoing as if trapped in a steel box.

When I open my eyes, the red light is flashing again. The voices of the others have trailed away, as the guide has led the rest of the group through a set of double doors. I nearly trip on something as I work my way around the aisle, not bothering to look inside any of the other cabinets. The pipes and conduits swarm overhead, seeming to coil like a thousand snakes in a bucket. I twitch in sweaty agony as I push open the door and find myself in a spacious room populated by a huge set of whirring turbines. The group is examining one of them. I see Becky standing alone, staring toward the top of a cylindrical tower at least twenty-five feet tall. An array of pipes and conduits connect to this tower through dozens of ports and nozzles, each fitted with a pressure-indicating device, heavy motorized valves, and an array of peripheral equipment.

I silently walk up next to her as she stares at a huge valve overhead, supported by a cage of square columns and channel beams. The flanged inlet and outlet, covered by a thick white coat of insulation, grow to larger diameters at either end of the valve. Next to it, dozens of metal conduits cling to the frame of the cage and snake their way to the various ports on the turbine head.

Marveling at it, I can barely speak—and even if I did, Becky could not possibly hear me over the roar of the turbines.

I hear a booming voice that grabs our attention. The guide is barking out instructions to follow him through another set of doors. We follow into the next room, a quieter one filled with a broad arrangement of tanks, pumps, and equipment. Networks of piping, from tiny stainless-steel tubes to impossibly enormous diameters, fill this room.

"The cooling equipment for the fusion reactors is sensitive to the slightest temperature fluctuations, and the flow needs to be electronically controlled so that the reactors don't overheat," the guide shouts.

"If the cooling supply gets above forty degrees Fahrenheit, an alarm is triggered to let the engineers know that an adjustment to the chilled water flow needs to be made manually at one or more of the chillers. The pumps are monitored through frequency drives, which electronically dictate water flow from the pumps. When the pumps cycle, the flow and pressure increase, which cools the reactors.

"The reactors are located in the central core, surrounded by three-foot-thick, lead-lined concrete walls so that no radiation can escape. This process is normal and completely safe, despite what you may have heard. Keep in mind that we live approximately ninety-three million miles from the largest nuclear fusion reactor within a light year.

"All five services combine to create a power supply that dwarfs nearly every power plant on the East Coast. We supply twenty million homes and businesses, in Pennsylvania, New York, New Jersey, and Delaware, with a mix of unrivaled clean energy. We expect other suppliers to mimic our process when they see how much energy we produce at such low consumer cost. Are there any other questions?"

No one speaks.

"That is entirely expected," he says. "That is a lot of information to take in in thirty minutes, and a lot of it probably sounds like unintelligible jargon. At least now you know the basics of where your power comes from."

He leads the group into a room with row upon row of merchandise and memorabilia. Another great way of capitalizing on eco-tourism is through the sale of bric-a-brac. I consider grabbing a T-shirt until I nearly choke at the price tag. Becky controls the purse-strings because I have nothing. She eyes a miniature replica figurine of the power plant and shows it to me. "How cute."

"Cute? I guess if you think a heavy industrial money-making machine is cute—"

"What's your problem?"

I shrug. "I don't know, I guess it's the humidity and the prices."

This is not a lie; only hours ago I was swimming in icy water, and the real timeline I traveled from is in the middle of winter. The heat and humidity is normal to me in the summer, but now that I'm pouring with sweat and nearly dizzy from the constant screech of heavy machinery, my mood has soured. She elects to purchase the figurine for us, but I decline her invitation to buy something for myself.

With our purchase ensconced in a clear plastic bag, we exit the gift shop and dive into the sun outside. The heat blasts me as I walk, and her fingers coil around mine until we find our way to the car. Our day is only half over, and I know it's going to get worse. If the Shade arrives while we are touring the penitentiary I'm never coming back, no matter how urgently the Swan calls out to me.

14

The Arrow of Apollo

The radial corridor spins beneath my feet, and the blank gray walls blur into streaks like they are the only things moving. Except *everything* is moving, and I am running on a giant circular treadmill. The section from the public restrooms to the metal detectors seemed like a different world, but now I am here alone, in a circular prison block rotating faster than a pulsar. A harrowing whine lifts into the silence as the walls, doors, and openings whiz past my face, so quickly that I can barely recognize the presence of a building. Gravity pulls me sideways, toward the outside wall, as if the Earth's pull has been flipped laterally, yet I remain on my feet.

My leisurely saunter has become a stumbling gait, and my heart rate intensifies. Becky and I were separated when I wandered into a bathroom entirely clad in stainless steel and filled with electronic devices to control the fixtures to prevent tampering and conserve water. She was gone when I exited into this different corridor. Wherever she is, she must be having a different experience. Pain is roaring through my head as the rotation winds down, like a last coda on a carousel. Attempting to regain my balance, I stagger toward a drinking fountain, but it whirs right past me. Avoiding it requires that I push off against the stationary wall, the momentum of which spins me so that I'm facing away from the direction of rotation. Still running, I find my progress has halted.

The motion slows further as my pace overcomes it and I run past the drinking fountain again. The world staggers back and forth as I chart my course toward the end of the wall's curvature, back to the double doors. The faster I can make it out of this spinning top, the better.

With one jarring click, the motion ceases, causing me to clumsily lunge forward and trip on my own legs. Avoiding a face plant in the hallway is a feat I can reflect on later. At the end of the curve, the doorway stands where it always has. I breathlessly make for it as my heartrate begins to slow again. Gulping down shock and attempting to wipe perspiration away from my brow, I clutch at the steel-latched door handle and yank it toward me. Nothing prepares me for what I see next.

Instead of a line of tourists I am faced with a maze of black walls, decorated with illuminated, jagged red pinstriping and flashing orange lights, expanding beyond the limits of my eyesight. The main corridor has been inexplicably cut off from this hallway.

Wandering through the darkened halls, I hear laughter echoing from somewhere. A high-pitched cackle precedes a barrage of grunts, followed by silence, and then another round of quieter chuckles. Changing my course to find the source of the sound, I plunge further into the darkness. This corridor must not be entirely straight, because the light that should be cascading through the wire-meshed glass windows in the door has disappeared, leaving me in a wasteland.

I saunter cautiously toward the laughing sounds, and then the perimeter wall at my right-hand side breaks into a wide opening. The room is devoid of light, save for that annoying pinstriping, which seems to glow like a blurring reflection.

"Don't bother taking from me, cuz I'm gonna win it back next hand anyway," a high-pitched voice barks, clearer and nearer to me.

"So drunk you can't tell your wrist from your hand, Tiny?" a man with a deep voice growls.

"Gonna take all your money anyway, Pops," Tiny replies, his voice coming to me clear yet somewhat slurred.

A poker game amongst prisoners might not be entirely unexpected, I reason, leaning my head in closer to listen to the exchange of coins clinking and bills shuffling as if on a baize tabletop.

"Call," crows Cackles. "You in, Stitch?"

"For fifty. Lay 'em down."

Cackles shrieks as though she's been had.

"Maybe that'll teach you to be more conservative with your hand!"

The growler takes this as a joke and roars with laughter. "Tell that to Tiny."

In my imagination Tiny is an obese, tattooed man with a bald head and terrible manners, yet he speaks like he's in his early thirties at best and likes to party.

Leaning in closer, I can almost smell them from around the corner. Thinking better of witnessing a prisoner card game, I turn around and follow the red pinstriping back to the main corridor, which the red lights present as a comparatively brighter environment.

Trudging deeper into the wasteland, I quietly pass a dark alcove and press on at least a hundred feet. Another gap in the wall to the right reveals a starker red light. Hoping this will lead me back to Becky and the rest of the tourists, I turn, without considering the ramifications.

Sitting atop a rocky ledge that slopes toward the black ceiling, two men seem to be in the midst of some kind of philosophical discussion. "Don't know what it means to be a deist," one says. "If it means you think God's real, then you're still part of the machine."

"It's all a scam," the lower of the two voices says. "They convince you to part with your hard-earned money and tell you everyone's after you, and you believe them while they buy a bigger yacht and give the rest to the most arrogant of politicians."

"My man, that's the machine talking again. They want you to hate religion because it serves the same purpose. Long as you ask no questions..."

I step away from the approximately eight-foot-tall rocky cliff, which is constructed of real, hexagonal pillars of basalt, stair-stepping towards the rafters. Their discussion breaks off when one of them sees me.

For the briefest moment I gaze into his fiery eyes, and they reflect the red lights, making him appear demonic. The resultant appearance is unnerving. I step backward and haphazardly apologize for being intrusive.

"Another damn tourist," the older of the gentlemen surmises dismissively. "But like I was saying...."

"What do you think, young'un?" the younger man says, his black skin seeming to morph into the rock. "Is there a creator that controls everything?"

"Magic Skydaddy," the older man scoffs through his grizzled beard.

They wait for my reply, but I have nothing. I back away instinctively. The men are not shackled; they are as free to wander the corridors as I am. No bars separate this room from the broader corridor. I shuffle backwards until I collide with a rolling table. Flimsy steel crashes to the cold concrete floor behind me. The lights barely seem to reach this corner of the room.

"What's the matter? Skydaddy going to smite you?"

"N—No, look I'm sorry, I didn't mean to intrude."

The younger, black, man seems to bore into my psyche with his stare. It silently carves its way through my heart, leaving me utterly speechless. "Look around, there ain't no tourists or guards, or other ... prisoners here. Might as well humor us."

"S—Sure," I stammer. "Maybe there is. You know ... probably doesn't control everything."

"Now there's a novel idea," the bearded man says, his voice oozing sarcasm.

"And that's the problem," the black man, whom I take to be the more reasonable one, says. "Nobody understands nuance. Everything has to fit into one of two little boxes. Either it's all fake, or it's all true. Maybe some of it is fundamentally true but it's wildly misunderstood. Seems like a more acceptable conclusion, don't you say?"

"I—I wouldn't know." Nervously, I allow my voice to waver.

"We ain't gonna kill ya, son," Beardy says. "Or maybe we will. Been a long time since we had good barbecue around these parts."

His laughter is corrosive and haunting. I can't even stammer a reply before the reasonable man piles on.

"Couple cells away, we got an actual cannibal. No one knows his name, so we call him Lecter."

"His name's Luther, shitforbrains."

"Maybe. But maybe that's what the guards want you to call him. The only thing real in this shithole is you," the black man says patiently, his eyes once again piercing mine.

I step sideways to avoid the worst of it, but Beardy has already caught on. "Sure, go back to your McMansion."

I hurry away from them as the basalt cliff face blends into the dark and both of them vanish. Backing into the corridor again, I let out a small exhalation. Another twenty feet along the pinstriped corridor reveals twin openings. Yearning for Becky, I take the second and step into black. The stars twirl overhead and the wind rushes as I fall through empty space and land firmly on—

Grass?

My eyes flash open and the world floods me with hallucinogenic light. A meadow stretches onward about two hundred yards toward a shaded canopy filled with dense deciduous trees. I stop short and survey the environment for signs of life.

Fear fills me as I stare toward the tree line. The beginnings of a wooden structure lie in ruins in the shade, with logs and cut lumber strewn in every direction, as though a hurricane has ripped through it. I detect no obvious human presence, but there must be people here somewhere.

I hear murmuring to my left: a woman steps out into the clearing, brushing a sheaf of dirty, matted hair behind her shoulder. She dares not approach me in case I am an enemy, but I barely pose any threat. Instead of saying anything to her, I eye her carefully.

She is wearing a ragged dress that seems draped over her shoulders and which had once been white. A man steps out next to her within a few minutes and gestures to me. His hair is caked with dust and sweat.

Silently he points to the tree line, where the shack has been destroyed. Rather than trying to talk to these strangers, I make my way in that direction.

Ahead, the trees begin to sway as if being sucked inward by a vicious wind. The shambles of the structure were once a house, left in ruins by what seems to have been either a fierce wind or a blunt object. As I approach, I witness charring on some of the timbers, amongst the white, splintered wood, fragments of which have been spread in every direction.

Peering into the ruins, I am beckoned by the glittering remains of a lost home, shining like treasure in the sun. I reach out as I step into the debris;

the wind in the trees howls and then settles. Before long, the trees disappear, as if they are falling slowly into a void of black, to be replaced by a terrible shadow.

The Shade.

I cower away as it strikes at the broken ruins, consuming them whole. Every fragment vanishes into the cloud of darkness, expanding outward. Seconds tick away as I consider running, yet something someone once told me seems to stick in my brain: *you can't beat fear with more fear.* Instead of fleeing, I hold firm and fight the worry engulfing my soul.

Evil is already licking at my feet before a guttural roar erupts in the trees. The Shade seems to waver, just long enough for me to slither away from the splintered and charred ruins. Silently it changes its course, as though its appetite has changed.

The roar booms again in the trees and the Shade follows, eating away trees, roots, rocks, and vines, leaving only emptiness in its wake.

From the canopy, a column of black smoke spirals into the warm sky, as if invading the blue. Terror begins to envelop me. In this landscape, I am alone with the two strangers. There is no escape; the Shade will return and devour me in the name of Erebus.

Cold is swallowing my heart, even though the humid heat still blasts my exposed skin. I must get back to Becky somehow. I imagine her trapped in that hellish prison and my body begins to ache.

My only recourse is to help the terrorized strangers to safety, because the Shade will not spare them. If there is a portal or void anywhere, it must be hidden in the restless trees. I break into a run towards the man and the woman as terror washes over me. If I am a victim of the Shade in another dimension, what happens to the real me in present-day Philadelphia? The question has no clear answer, and that is perhaps the most disheartening truth of all.

15

Draconian Heart

The wild bleeds vitality at every pore. Millions of trees grow together as if they are one sentient creature, content to live out its span in observance of the utter chaos beneath the canopy. It is teeming with life. The humidity cranks up when we reach the shade of the branches, and so too does the heat. The strange couple manages to navigate the forest with remarkable dexterity. A low-hanging vine is something I can negotiate with, but avoiding the obstacle distracts my attention from the knobby root protrusions at ground level, which are cloaked with a dense undergrowth. I nearly step into a patch of carpeting plants when the woman holds me back with a firm hand.

Silently, she redirects me away from a shallow pond and toward a steady incline. A roar emanates from somewhere to my right near the pond but dies away. Birds chirp overhead as the brush leaves rustle directly in our path. Heading right towards the disturbance, the man hunches down and creeps along defensively. Waving a palm at her partner, the woman urges me to follow his example. Bypassing the expansive brush, we take a steeper route up the slope.

I hold my breath and walk as quickly as I can manage without my feet becoming tangled in roots and sharp rocks. Spider webs crisscross our path, and I walk face-first into a grimy web.

Howling, I double over in horror, imagining dozens of venomous monsters crawling through my hair and tickling my back. Lost in the confusion, I roll my ankle against something hard. Pain rockets through my left foot and I let out a string of obscenities that the strangers don't seem to understand. I attempt to straighten my posture, but limp backwards right into the sharp, jutting branch of a tree. As a new round of pains stab at me, I shift to my right and fall face-first. My knee collides painfully with a rock and then a root. Under the canopy of carpeting plants, the light seems dimmer. Mushrooms sprout up in front of my nose, and tiny flowers bloom only a few feet away.

The shadow is awash with motion. Thousands of tiny creatures scurry in every direction, some carrying tiny chunks of green on their backs. They seem not to notice my intrusion, but they scuttle away when a darker threat enters their domain: a giant, hairy spider with a hundred eyes creeps along at the roots of the plant stalks, sizing up its prey before striking. The pain swells within me, but a firm hand grips my underarm and pulls me up.

My heart beats a million miles per hour as he studies me, perhaps questioning my urban upbringing and how utterly unprepared I am for this wild jungle. Yet still he says nothing. His dark brown skin carries droplets of sweat, kept in place by a gauze of dust. His eyes are still and serene.

He escorts me to a small clearing where there rests a solitary rock that I can rest on. Breathlessly, I sit down and pat him on the elbow to thank him.

He says nothing, but his partner speaks in a language I have never heard. Her body language urges haste. She waves her hands to her right, where I perceive the Shade to have invaded the forest in search of fresh meat. Her shoulders twitch as the mane of matted hair sticks to her brow and falls in her face.

I conclude that this couple speaks no English, but it is the only language I have ever known.

"The Shade," I say, motioning in the same general direction the woman just had. "How long has it been here?" I tap my wrist as if they can understand that it means time. When they fail to grasp it, I change course. "Tick, tick, tick.... Long time?"

The man shakes his head and stammers, using his hands and arms to describe something monstrous as he yammers away in his own language.

"No? I don't comprehend. Must get to a dark place." Surveying the undergrowth, I search for a dark shape, and finally find one in a narrow, rectangular slot in an ancient tree. Excitedly, I point to it. "There. I will take you to safety."

They hesitate to follow as I stand up from the rock, stretching and charting the easiest course. The roars and chirps of jungle life seem to blossom in the shadows. I stumble on rocks, regain my balance, and reach the tree.

The dark inside it beckons as the Shade crests a distant hill, gobbling up the forest and speeding our way. I grasp the woman's arm to her partner's chagrin and draw her in as I wedge myself into the slot. Instantly, black surrounds us. Terror flashes through her eyes, which are momentarily the only visible part of her. Two shining, fearful orbs with pits of black flit in every direction as I grasp her hand. The stars around us swirl, and the distant sun burns into our flesh as we drift to an uncertain destination.

We arrive in a familiar alleyway. This is downtown Philadelphia, and it feels like the present—the real present, where I live my life unceremoniously and drone along day after day.

The woman shudders at the cold as she gazes up in wild fancy at the skyscrapers, the cars, and the hundreds of people that pass by on the sidewalk.

Terror strikes me once more when I realize that we are alone. Her partner has not escaped the other dimension. I groan as I imagine him being eroded, consumed by the Shade.

The woman's palm erupts with sweat. Instinctively I let it go, chart our course, and decide that Harley will be our closest ally. Just in case the woman's partner will emerge from the square of black behind me, I wait as a dozen cars roll past on the street beyond the mouth of the alley.

The woman is awed at the tops of the towers, the idling cars, and the apparel of the Philadelphia citizens. Enraptured by shoes, jewelry, and the glass and stone skin of high-rise buildings, she dances around in a tight circle before burrowing her eyes into mine and asking me a question I can barely hope to understand.

"Chawangaitzeliannacompas.... Timego puclo?

"*No comprende*," I say, trying out one of the few Spanish words I can remember.

She appears nonplussed, but when she gestures to the sky and then lowers her palm to the city street, she is clearly asking me where we are and how we got here.

Certain that she cannot understand me, I mutter my response. "This is called Philadelphia. The City of Brotherly Love. We have been ... transported here ... I guess you could say that. And it might be a thousand years in the future for you. Tick, tick, tick." I point to a futuristic building in the distance to indicate a long time.

After more than five minutes, the man hasn't emerged. I gulp slowly, knowing deep down that he has succumbed to the Shade. The woman will not be safe in this environment, just as I was not safe in hers. I grasp her waist and hurry her along the cracked, oil-stained concrete toward the sidewalk. As far as I can tell, it is evening, and the sun is inching down towards the pinnacles of the tallest buildings. Cars bustle by on the street and a dozen passersby continue their daily lives, having not even noticed us.

I make for the busiest portion of Market Street, squeezing her hand as I dodge strangers, orange cones, and an open manhole cover, beside which a bright yellow truck is parked. Turning onto Market Street hand-in-hand, we avoid the throngs of tourists and hurry toward the alcove where Harley hangs out. By now, he seems to be a distant memory. That I can remember anything about him at all surprises me.

When we reach him, he seems surprised—not by me but by my companion.

"Gotta just keep coming back, do you?" Harley says, grinning and stroking his stubble. He stands carefully and offers the woman his hand.

To her, this is obviously unexpected, but from the way I had grabbed her hand and led her through the city, she assumes that hand-holding will lead her somewhere, so she grasps his hand like a lover and holds onto it before stepping toward the street corner.

"Shit." Harley understands. "What have you done? You're not supposed to bring anyone back, unless this is your world-famous crush."

He sizes her up and surveys her knotted hair and dirty dress as I speak. "Had to. They were there, and so was the Shade. The Shade was coming for us."

"You ran into another Shade? And lived to tell the tale?"

"Goddammit," I stammer as she slowly releases Harley's hand. "Becky. She's gotta still be there, in the prison."

"Holy hell, how many people have you been interacting with?"

I glare at him and ready myself to verbally accost him. "You know that feeling when you fall into bed with a random woman out of nowhere, and she tells you she's your wife, but you have no idea who the hell you're talking to? You'd think a savant like you would have warned—what do you call people like me? Time travelers?"

"I have never been transferred to an alternate dimension, Larry. Rumor has it only a few people can actually do it, portal or none."

"Good Christ." I hesitate. "Wait, did you say 'rumor'? Who told you? What do you know?"

He shrugs and steps backward into his alcove so that a trio of tourists can pass, looking for a shop to spend their money in.

"Talked to a woman a day or two ago," he explains. "I mentioned you and your ... girlfriend. She knew what I was talking about, and next thing I know we're dating and she's coming in for a really great kiss—"

"Focus!"

"Yeah, anyway—turns out she's something of an expert, having hopped timeframes a few times herself. But she's never run into a Shade—if they even exist."

I inch closer to him and frown before pointing a finger right under his nose. Remembering the structure of our last conversation is surprisingly easy. He hadn't even acted surprised at my mention of the Shade, and in fact spoke as through he was quite familiar with them himself. "They exist. And they eat everything in sight."

Realizing my error at last, I back away slowly, curling my way into the inner part of the sidewalk so that I can lean against a dusty storefront. The dwelling at the edge of the forest belonged to this woman and her man. They indicated as much, but now that I'm in a more familiar setting, the pieces are falling into place. The simple fact that the structure was destroyed, and not eaten entirely, suggests that they didn't even know about the Shade, because the Shade did not destroy their home.

What other beast in their world could have done that kind of damage, to splinter heavy timbers and char wood? A dragon? The real expert on dragons is Joaquin, but I have no interest in talking to him right now. To get to the bottom of the latest string of events, I need another source of knowledge.

"Where is she?" I say, my mind broken and my body aching.

"Right here," Harley says, motioning to the woman I've brought. "What did you say her name was?"

"She doesn't speak English," I mutter. "I'm talking about your friend. How do I find her?"

"Piers, Callahan, and Roberts. Six blocks away, on Tenth. Hazel windows and white marble, you can't miss it."

The name of the business rings a bell: it is a century-old investment firm headquartered in Philadelphia. If I'm to talk to anyone there, I'm going to need a change of clothes, because poor construction laborers like me may not elicit welcoming stares.

"Her name is Vanessa Clark," he says. "Or was that her sister? No, it's Vanessa. You can ask the receptionist. She's tall, with gorgeous black braids all the way down her back and sparkling eyes."

"I get it," I say, walking away.

Rather than driving all the way home just to change clothes, I consider my options. Tourist-oriented clothing shops would be my best option. It's likely that disguising myself as a tourist might just get me in the door.

Finding a clothes shop is not that difficult. I see a sign for one across the street and kitty corner. Turning back to Harley and my new friend, I mutter something cold: "And keep track of her, will you? She's never been in a big city like this before, and she'll probably get lost. Maybe you could give her a name that makes sense."

"Of course," Harley says. "She can stay with me. See you again in a couple of days?"

I shake my head, unwilling to commit to a timeline. My next task is to find Vanessa Clark and ask her the ins and outs of time jumping. If she can offer me precious insight for my journey, perhaps I can avoid the Shade.

The man I've left in the jungle must have left no remains, but now that I've departed that timeline, does it even exist? What if the alternate realms I have traveled to only exist while I'm there, and are unconnected to geography or history?

The woman who claimed to be my wife would have a different insight, but what if I never catch up with her again in that same timeframe? The implications seem to hollow out my chest as I walk away, uncertain of my next steps, but I know the larger destination still offers a glowing aura of promise.

Clinging to that light can help me find my way, but if that light turns into darkness, I could be lost in time forever. And if I don't bring Sarah back from wherever she's disappeared to, I will never know what real love even is.

The yearning rises in my heart as I enter the clothing store and search for one of the most obnoxious tourist T-shirts and shorts I can find.

Finally I settle on an overpriced, white "I Heart Philly" tee with bold, red serif lettering and a beating heart that suggests brotherly love. The only shorts I can fit into are a pair of grey cargo ones that would not draw much attention in California or Florida.

I pay for them at the register, considering it lucky that, after all I've already been through, my wallet is still with me. I can change in a nearby alley, I hastily decide. I find an unoccupied one a couple of blocks away and deposit my filthy clothes in a dark corner while I slip into the more comfortable outfit. It's still winter, even if it's a much milder day, so these clothes quickly prove to be a ridiculous choice. If anyone asks, I'll say I'm from the South where clothing is mostly optional for men.

The chill in the air bites at my legs as I walk, progressively numbing my shins as I trek the six blocks to the building Harley described. Passersby mostly ignore me, except for an overweight woman who smiles as I approach. "Ain't you cold?" she asks.

I nod and dodge a couple in the midst of a daytime spat, tiptoe over the grated iron tree planter covers, and avoid a busy area of sidewalk dining. The building looms amidst a trio of skyscrapers occupying a single block. The structure that houses Piers, Callahan, and Roberts rises above the other two, coalescing into a shining spire at the top of a glossy parapet.

Alternating between glass and glimmering marble, the sheer building skin rises at least fifty stories. I step through the rotating glass doors into an ornate lobby with expansive marble floors, a luxurious seating area, and generous artificial greenery. A small reception desk fronts a back-office area staffed by an unarmed uniformed guard. I make my way to a pair of wide television screens that display the names of the tenants and their corresponding suites.

The brokerage firm is easy to find, listed as occupying three successive floors from thirty-one to thirty-three. The elevators stand behind a wall, decorated with local art and the name of the building backlit in white light. My ride to the thirty-first floor stops at floors nine and sixteen, where two people enter and exit.

Piers, Callahan, and Roberts is fronted by a clean glass curtain wall, which separates the thirty-first-floor lobby from a wide open-office cubicle area. A half-height divider separates each workspace. The receptionist, a younger blonde woman in a sharp striped blouse greets me as I enter. Without delay I ask her how to find Vanessa Clark.

"Let me check," she says, punching Vanessa's name into her keyboard. "Thirty-second floor. Go in, take a left, and she will be in the third office on the right. If her door is closed, have a seat and she will be with you shortly."

I nod graciously and hurry back to the elevator. It lurches to a halt as I prepare myself. Again, a broad glass curtain wall greets guests as they disembark, and following the receptionist's directions is easy.

Vanessa's door is open. She is poring over some documents in a manila folder through her wire-framed glasses, which are down at the point of her nose. She pushes them up as I greet her. Long black braids on her head are pulled into a tight, stylish ponytail, and reflected light glints off flecks of glitter beneath her eyes. She looks little like I had imagined. She is slender and fit. Though her desk is mostly free of pictures or knickknacks, a few ornaments decorate a shelf behind the cushy, steel-framed chairs. I dare not sit down unless she invites me to; instead of saying anything, I gaze over her dark complexion and drag the toe of my shoe over the flat carpet.

"Good afternoon," she says. "Can I help you?"

"I'm—not really into investing," I stammer.

She leans forward to listen.

"A friend of mine knows you. Harley."

She smiles and nods. "The man on Market Street. I'll have to thank him for the referral, though you look a bit underdressed as far as our usual clientele is concerned. Looking to update your portfolio?"

I shake my head slowly. "I don't have a portfolio. I don't know how to say this—"

"Say whatever you like," she says, smiling.

"I have been—I don't know what to call it. Time travelling? Harley says you know a little bit about how it works."

"Time travel," she repeats, sighing. "Wondered when someone might bring that up."

I wait for her to continue as she waves for me to close the door and take a seat. I do as directed and exhale slowly, resting my palms on the clear plastic protector over the polished oak surface of her desk.

"It was a late night," she begins. "A bar fight. A friend of mine's drunk ex stumbles in, smacks someone he accuses her of 'seeing' in the face and starts threatening her. I come to her defense, but he doesn't like that too much. He punches me in the face and when I get up, I'm suddenly feeling a bit woozy. So I go into the bathroom, or what I thought was the bathroom ... and everything goes dark. Next thing I know, I'm riding on a horse with a group of soldiers headed for Appomattox."

"The Civil War?"

"Apparently an ancestor of mine was a somewhat important figure in the Union Army, and they'd just gotten word that the Confederates planned to surrender."

I narrow my eyes as she tells the story, pausing long enough to add flourishes to the tale with details. When she's clearly finished, she expels a breath and waits for me to speak.

"How many times have you done it?"

She shrugs. "Maybe a couple of times after that, never the same place or the same time. From what I understand, most people aren't capable of ...'time travel,' not that they would really want to. A woman I met in the future explained to me that you have to have a really good reason to do it, like it's a part of your destiny, and you're gifted. Or something to that effect. But people have been doing it far longer than anyone even knows."

"Hundreds of years?"

"Try thousands. According to Greek legend, anyway."

I struggle to utter the words. "Well, I ran into someone ... I guess in the future I'm married to her, but I didn't know where the hell I was."

I hurry through the story so quickly that I don't have time to emphasize any details. She nods at certain intervals to indicate that she's still listening. I speak more quickly when I get to the part about saving the strangers from the Shade, which seems to surprise her.

"What is a Shade? You say it like it's important."

"Don't know how to describe it," I stutter. "It's like a black stain that just sucks in everything, leaving only blackness. It is controlled by Erebus."

She flashes a smile. "You know your Greek mythology."

"It's real. I need to find someone my future wife talked about. But I don't know how to get back to that time. Can you help me?"

"Like I said, I've never been to the same place twice." She relaxes against the high-backed mesh chair and picks up a pen. "So I'm afraid I won't be of much use to you. Still, depending on how you got there, you might try going to the same place."

"It's not consistent," I say, dismissing it. "And—oh my God."

She sits up alertly, as if my remembering it has just jolted her awake.

"I think I've been transported from dimension to dimension, within a dimension."

"Doesn't seem implausible," she says, nodding intently and frowning. "But I'd caution you against going back too often, because just from the logic of it, you could get lost."

I frown as the realization pulses through me like a shockwave. As if in disbelief, I lower my voice almost to a whisper. "I think I already am."

Vanessa sits up and waits in vain for me to expound on that point, but I let it simmer for so long that her only option is to force the conversation to continue.

"Think about how you got to her," she says.

I allow my mind to wander. Was it the alley that had sent me there the first time? Wracking my brains, I settle on it and decide to stick to the portals I know. Even if it takes me ten years to find Becky again, I must do it. The pastor can help shed some light on the *why*, or at least I presume he can. But without knowing how to get to him, I'm like a ship on a storm-tossed sea, untethered to anything resembling objective reality.

16

Pisces Eyes

I lean back in the comfortable chair as if to stretch my back, while trying to appear interested in continuing the conversation. Seeing this, Vanessa makes eye contact and subtly shrugs, as if she already knows what I'm about to say.

The sun beats in through her floor-to-ceiling window, casting oblique shadows from the books on a shelf behind her. I eye her carefully and consider my options as she waits for me to speak.

"You don't think you could ... I don't know, show me where you went?"

She doesn't look the least bit surprised. Instead, she nods and considers it. "The bar led me to history. I'm guessing you want the future."

I nod. "I guess about five years from now would be ideal."

"You could try the harbor yards by the river. I met a man there once who claimed to be a long lost relative. The portal led me only a few years into the future, where I was standing behind someone inspecting a pipe trap for leakage. He knew who I am and why I was there.

"You have to show an ID at the gate."

"And you have one?"

She nods suspiciously. "From a couple of years ago. Didn't really see it as useful at the time."

I mull it over. The sun glints on her braids, casting a strange reflection throughout the room. The shimmer lasts only a moment, barely long

enough for it to register in my brain, but now that I can see it, it is burnished in my memory forever. What could have caused such a reaction?
"I guess if you think it could be a success."

"I get off whenever I want to," she explains. "Give me about ten
minutes to cancel my afternoon and change, and I'll meet you in the
ground floor lobby."

I incline my head, back out of her office, and wander between
rows of cubicles filled with overworked professionals stuck in tiny cages,
staring carelessly into the blinking monitor lights. That could be me
someday, if my dreams ever align with reality. I could be the one re-
searching products, producing schedules, and planning personnel usage.
I would be good at it, too—that is, if this time travel business doesn't
leave pieces of me in every dimension I've seen.

Riding the elevator down proves uneventful. A pair of businessmen gets on a few floors below where I'd met with Vanessa, and a few
floors below that, a professional young woman with a plait of shiny
brown hair and a tight skirt gets on, mindlessly browsing through her
smart phone as the businessmen ogle her between bits of shop talk.

I don't wait for the elevator to stop before pushing away from the
wood-paneled back wall, bending my hip against the golden handrail.
The door slides open as I patiently halt in front of it.

Entering the luxurious lobby, I spy an open leather chair next
to a huge rectangular planter which seems to be growing real trees. Its
position in the lobby, sufficiently far from the other occupants, provides
a modicum of privacy. But it does not shield me from hearing them talk.

"I assure you, Mrs. Walker, that your investments are in good
hands. We'll touch base next week to go over your options."

Mrs. Walker, an older woman with graying hair, lets her shoulders
droop and offers him a warm smile without extending her hand for a
shake. "It is good to meet you," she says, glancing distractedly in my
direction.

A lawyer with a briefcase fumbles with a ringing phone as he
hurries toward the elevator, nearly colliding with Mrs. Walker. He barely
makes eye contact with her before spinning like a running back and
juking through the lobby.

A young man with a computer tablet smiles while craning his neck to stare at the video on his screen. Sitting idle while the present flashes in front of me seems a poor usage of my time, but I can only wait. The minutes tick away until Vanessa emerges from the elevator, packing a tote by the straps in the crook of her elbow. She shoves her phone into her back jeans pocket, still looking as stylish as ever.

As I am parked at least a half-hour away on foot, I follow Vanessa to the crosswalk a few hundred feet from the front doors. She darts through the crowded sidewalk and watches the red hand on the other side of the street. A beep signals the okay to proceed, and she hurries across, bypasses a comfortable coffee shop, and makes for a glass-doored vestibule next to one of those blue derelict newspaper boxes. She brushes her braids behind her shoulder, punches a code into the reader, and briskly pulls the door open. We enter a concrete-floored elevator lobby with a single public service announcement poster about scams, and I study a tiny crack that zigzags across the floor toward a painted metal rim member bolted to the concrete.

The elevator soon arrives and whisks us up three floors, where her car awaits. I imagined an expensive luxury car but am taken aback when she presses a button on her key fob and the rear lights of a newer looking Honda flash in the gray darkness.

The garage is mostly silent; this early in the day, the investors and executives will not yet have left for the suburbs. Vanessa waves me to the passenger side door while depositing the tote that holds her change of clothing, purse, and shoes in the backseat. We carefully pull out of the parking stall as she looks in all directions. The tires seem to shriek on the smooth floor as we round a series of bends before emerging onto a busy street. She taps her knuckles on the steering wheel, waits for an opening, then punches into traffic. The acceleration presses me back against the seat and she flashes a smile.

The minutes wear away quickly as she drives, interrupting the silence with an offhand comment about a billboard getting a facelift near where the interstate juts toward the river.

She handles the turns with ease and guides us safely to the harbor yards, which stand behind an eight-foot-tall chain link fence topped with barbed wire that spans the perimeter. The narrow driving lane slices between stacks of blue plastic pipe and rebar before snaking through towers of blue-and-orange shipping containers waiting to be loaded aboard a ship.

She rolls the window down as she approaches the entrance, consisting of a lockable, wheeled sliding gate with a derelict shack at the driver's side window. The white siding is peeling, and the aluminum window needs to be replaced. A man behind the window scans her identification across a magnetic reader and an orange and white lift gate swings upward to let us in.

Vanessa finds the right place with ease. A rust-red shipping container with cut-out doors has been repurposed into a public restroom facility. Next to that, an unused, heavily damaged yellow container rests with its rod-locked door ajar. She smiles, parks the car, and bypasses the restroom.

"The man I met who claimed to be my long-lost cousin was standing here, looking like he didn't know what to make of this place. His eyes were focused on this yellow container. I was there on a business errand to introduce a tailored IRA plan to the freight employees when nature called. So I stepped in to investigate what he was looking at, and suddenly I'm on a busy pier along the beach and a tall man is reading a paper about events that I know have never happened. Almost immediately we're in a club dancing, he leans in to kiss me, so I slap him. And then of course I'm the aggressor. The cops apprehend me, accuse me of assault, and cuff me while little girls look on. It's humiliating, but the woman in the jail who takes my possessions seems curious, asking me a lot of personal questions. We become friends within hours. But I don't remember anything after that, just shapes, colors, images. It's like your past is slowly erased and repainted with memories that don't even exist. And then when you leave, you forget most of it."

Her story is not altogether unlike mine. I allow myself to satisfy my curiosity as she opens the car door and tiptoes over chipped, gravelly concrete toward the yellow container. I gulp as she grasps my hand and leads me into the darkness. Stars swirl and bend as we twist through the nothingness together, and a glowing red orb seems to siphon off gases from a nearby moon as we drift.

Landing feet first is a welcome change, but there is no pier and no beach. It is an industrial hellscape, with tall stacks belching black smoke into the night sky that obscures the moon and stars. I try to breathe lightly. Police lights flash up ahead and instinctively Vanessa darts to a rectangular opening behind which metal clinks against metal along with the brutish whine of machinery.

In an instant the blackness dissipates, and the factories collapse into piles of soot that disappear at our feet.

We are standing in the middle of a grassy area, at an intersection between brick-paved paths that weave between towering green trees. A bus awaits us at the end of the path, and she leads me in that direction.

Horns honk and riders disembark to allow for new passengers to board. When we take our place in line, the humidity seems to peak. She grasps my hand tighter as the bus driver greets her with a pleasant smile. "Good morning again, Vanessa."

"You've been here before?" I whisper.

We take our seats quietly and she nods. "The future me must come here somewhat often. And I probably don't look that much different now."

Our destination unknown, we ride toward the center of the city, a weary-looking Philadelphia; the skyline looks as I have always remembered it. We pass a billboard depicting a happy husband and wife, and my mind wanders. The white dress reemerges and then fades into a flowing hospital gown. Becky's brow sweats as she gasps, pushing at the doctor's behest. As I look on, the image blurs with tears. The little boy is being born.

The infusion of new memory confirms that we are in the correct time frame. I am tempted to instruct Vanessa to find her, but I have no idea where we live, or if we even live in the city.

The skyscrapers seem to sway in the breeze as the bus makes its way along the crowded boulevards. When we disembark, I frown. A young man handing out flyers printed on yellow paper accosts us. I try to back away, but he persists, shoving one of his flyers in my face. One simple word catches my eye and I snatch the paper from between his fingers. A minister will be giving a Sunday address today in Philadelphia.

Over eons of history, it can only be simple luck that we've landed on the right day in the right place to hear the reverend speak. I read over the few words on the invitation before I pass it to Vanessa, who rolls her eyes.

"It's not like religion is totally innocent," she passes it off, perhaps referring to the bold lettering imploring us to "Join the Crusade."

"I need to hear this message," I say. "If it's really fate that brought us here."

"Fate?" She grins slyly. "I don't know what you're talking about."

Moments pass and I refocus my attention on the flyer. The acne-faced kid has taken no offense at me snatching the flyer out of his hands and busies himself passing them out to anyone who dares step near him.

"You're not religious, are you?" I mumble, uncertain whether Vanessa can hear me over the bus's diesel engine and the chatter of the disembarked riders who are quickly fleeing to their cars.

Waiting for her reply, I study the skyline and look back to the flyer to gain a clear understanding of where the mass is being held.

"Mama was a Southern Baptist," she explains, her voice dropping. "God rest her soul. But no, I haven't had anything to do with it for years. Not thinking of going, are you?"

I try to offer a smile, but only a forced curvature of my lip results, making me look like I'm sneering. Seeing her reaction, a half-step backward and a blank frown, I speak quickly. "Oh, I'm joining the crusade."

"You traveled all the way here to find Jesus?" she jokes, but her eyes demonstrate a serious sense of dismay.

"Not Jesus," I snap. "Jeff L. Martin—the pastor."

Vanessa looks nonplussed but allows herself to show her curiosity anyway. "What do you want with a mega pastor?"

Not in the mood to explain my interest in a disappearing girl to yet another stranger, I look down to study the flyer. From the position of the sun, I surmise that it must be late in the morning. The service starts at noon. Figuring that Martin will be the last speaker, I estimate that we have perhaps an hour to get there.

"How fast do you think we can get to St. Peter's?"

She rolls her eyes. "We can get a cab to the airport, and maybe get on standby for a one-stop flight to Rome, but—"

"Not the one in Vatican City. The one on Pine Street."

"Pine and Third," she says tilting her head back. "From here on foot, it's a good hour." She pulls her phone out of her pocket and analyzes the time. "Allowing for daylight savings time, you're not going to make it."

"Unless we get a cab."

"I ain't going in that place," she argues, shaking her head and causing her braids to sway back and forth at her shoulders.

"I'm going to need your help," I say, formulating a plan. "We're going to cause some mayhem. Enough to get Pastor Martin's attention, and probably the cops, too."

"You want to go to jail in whatever year this is? You're crazier than I thought."

"What?"

"You come into a power brokerage in an outfit like that, in the dead of winter, you've got a screw loose. Now you want the law to have their day, probably shoot me? No, you don't even have a screw."

I furrow my brow and wait just long enough to ensure that her rant is over. When she folds her arms, I can tell she is back to listening, albeit defensively.

"We're going to need a seat in the middle, closer to the front."

She nods. "You got a change of clothes? They're going to take one look at you and condemn you right to hell."

I shake my head. If I'd taken my old, dirty, tattered clothes I'd been wearing instead of leaving them in an alley downtown, perhaps we'd get a front row seat and serve as proof that the church wanted to give aid to the homeless.

"You?"

"Still in my bag," she says. "At least go buy some jeans."

I frown. "Shit. I guess I don't have any money to invest."

"You're sick," she says. "Just go. I'll lend you the money, two hundred percent interest calculated daily."

She scans the bus stop and searches for a taxi. When one rounds a corner, she hurries toward the crosswalk with me almost jogging to keep up with her. The heat is starting to build, and I erupt in a sweat.

We dive into the backseat and Vanessa directs the driver to a clothing store on the way. Gazing at the clock on the dashboard between the seats, my heart begins to beat faster. I will barely have time to browse for something my size, especially if we want the driver to wait for us.

When we arrive at our destination, she nearly pushes me out the door. I dash across the busy sidewalk, fling open the glass door, and weave through rows of racks sporting men's clothes. The area with blue jeans is directly ahead. Most of them are designer labels for which I'd have to shell out plenty of Vanessa's money, but within moments I've laid my hands on a nice pair of dark blue comfort-fit jeans and am rushing to the register. The cashier is busy bagging a purchase for a younger-looking woman with straight black hair, trailing to a point midway down her back. I tap my toes impatiently as she bids the cashier goodbye, and stubbornly approach her.

"You in a big hurry?" the middle-aged black woman says. She pushes up her glasses and waits for me as the fluorescent light seems to glow on her curly, silver-tipped hair.

"Going to church," I say breathlessly.

She examines the jeans and glances at my "I heart Philly" T-shirt and exudes sarcasm. "Solid choice."

"Need to change in the dressing room," I say, handing her the cash and waiting for her to shell out change.

In case I need the cargo shorts in the future—or the past—I tuck them under my arm and hope that Vanessa will store them in her bag for me. Hurriedly I rush to the changing booths, pull off the shorts, and shimmy into the jeans without bothering to remove the tags. Somehow I look even more ridiculous, and my hair looks like it's been through a sandstorm in the Sahara. I swallow my pride, thank the cashier on my way out, and fall into the backseat of the cab while Vanessa eyes me.

"Yeah," I say, reading her expression. "Got room in that bag for these?"

"I don't even know where they've been," she says.

"They're new. I bought them about two hours ago, back in the present."

She shrugs. "Give them here." Stuffing them into her bag, she exhorts the driver to make his way to St. Peter's Episcopal Church.

I can barely contain my nerves as we stop for light after light, inching closer and closer. The gathering crowds give it away. A sign on the corner indicates that the service will be broadcast on an obscure local television station.

The driver stops at the curb, and we are greeted by throngs in their Sunday best. The church is an historic three-story edifice constructed of red brick; horizontal and vertical grooves stretch along a portion of the skin to break up the sheer wall and give it a subtle hint of curb appeal. Plain arched windows with gray keystones stack up the front and sides of the bell tower, overlooking a narrow grassy area where the crowds await. The doors are open and a pair of young boys in black suits and colorful ties usher the families in. I nearly stumble on a crack in the sidewalk as we approach the ushers. They don't show much interest in my apparel, or even Vanessa's. I try not to look like my nerves are frayed, but it doesn't matter.

The boy on my left greets me with a generous smile, offers an enthusiastic "Welcome," and lets me pass. The foyer is a narrow corridor with a cloakroom positioned off the corner. Dressed in an ornate white wood finish and sporting neatly arranged flower vases on decorative buffet tables between wooden benches, it adds an aura of nineteenth century mystique that I can't explain.

From what I understand, most mega pastors choose to hold events in giant arenas where they can really pack in the crowds. When they pass around the baskets, they can rake in a lot more money for their mission to save the human race—or maybe to buy another sports car. I don't know anything about the Reverend Martin, but I don't envision him being that different from the mainstream.

We make our way through the foyer, following a young family. The father, wearing a gray sweater over a clean white shirt, clasps the hand of his bride, an attractive, petite woman standing slightly shorter than Vanessa. She has donned a pink and white floral dress that flutters in the breeze down by her knees. Her heels click on the solid brown hardwood floor as she walks into the open chapel.

The pews are laid out in sections, separated by a broad central aisle. At the partitions between the pews, shaded by an extensive mezzanine, there are decorative white wooden columns intermittently supporting the balcony, where a group of about a dozen ten-year-old boys are observing the proceedings. The mezzanine wraps around the back wall and is bathed in bright light from the high windows.

I settle into a white bench pew near the aisle and wait while Vanessa departs the chapel in search of a bathroom where she can change.

When she returns, she somehow looks even more handsome than she had hours before in her office. I watch as hundreds of people filter in from outside, casually taking seats in the pews. A choir of boys and girls assembles at the front of the room, with the suit-clad boys occupying a wide area to the right of the pulpit, and the girls arranged to the left. The pulpit seems to glitter in a patch of sunlight and is decorated with a simple cross beneath the microphone.

The choir gently starts singing as a grey-haired, bearded man leads them along with a shiny black wand. I can barely watch as my nerves start to bristle.

After about ten minutes, a man in his forties appears behind the pulpit. He taps the microphone and waits for the crowd to settle down and the noise to die away.

"Good afternoon, saints!" he exclaims.

In a loud drone, the congregation responds enthusiastically, "Good afternoon!"

He smiles and strokes his speckled beard. "It certainly is a beautiful Sabbath afternoon. After the invocation, our wonderful choir will grace us with a number, and you are encouraged to sing along. Then I will offer a few words before Reverend Jeff L. Martin offers his insight. Jamie Hancock will lead us in prayer."

A hush falls over the mass as Jamie appears behind the pulpit and humbly thanks God for the wonderful weather and the opportunity to hear from the famous Reverend Martin. Her voice cracks as she stumbles on, and then she looks up. High on the wall behind her, ornate stained-glass windows shower her with colored light.

Moments after she finishes, the choir erupts into song. I tap my toes throughout the hymn and wait for the middle-aged man to return.

He speaks about the grace of God and how scripture can guide us through our trying times, relating stories from what sound like decades ago, and quoting the prophets of old. I swallow when he exhorts the worshippers to stand their ground in a world of chaos and evil, to represent God faithfully in the face of persecution.

I am unaware of the persecution he insists is happening in real time, but I dare not say anything. Intermittent shouts of "Amen!" rain down from the mezzanine as he speaks.

I wait patiently while Vanessa checks her phone and scans through social media without looking up. When the pastor disappears, I nudge her. She slides the phone into her bag next to my shorts and suddenly sits upright to act as though she is paying attention.

"Reverend Martin," someone exclaims.

"Brothers and sisters, I am pleased to have the honor of addressing you today. God has given us wonderful weather and I'm happy to see all your smiling faces."

I watch him without listening carefully and begin to formulate my plan.

"Glory be to God in the highest. Years ago, I had the pleasure of speaking with a group of young Christians gathered for a service project in the heart of this gorgeous city. Their spirit was remarkable, and their dedication sturdy. On that morning, a girl of fourteen approached me with a smile. 'You're a great representative of Jesus,' she said, the light of angels in her eyes. I was humbled by her approach and her candor, but when I thought about it, I was struck by that simple truth that in that situation, I was not the representative of Jesus. She was.

"We talked at length that day as she gleefully invited me to her family's barbecue, which I was not able to attend."

"Why didn't you go?" I grumble.

Reverend Martin stops mid-sentence to stare at me as if in shock, but his demeanor doesn't appear to be one of anger.

Now that I have the attention of the entire congregation, I ramble on. "Take one step at a time through the fog, and you will eventually find your destination," I recite, uncertain if the words are accurate.

"Indeed," he says with a smile. "But back on topic—"

"It was about finding the light! How do you stand here now and pretend that never happened? Or was it just words? God will be the judge, not you."

"Young man, I'm sorry if I have upset you, but these wonderful people have gathered to hear me speak."

"Because you're a celebrity!"

"Boo!" Someone behind me shouts.

"Sinner!" another scolds. Still, I'm not ready to end my scene.

"They pay you good money to fill their heads with all this garbage about the world going to shit, when your church is a big part of it," I continue.

"Christ's work can never be done—"

"And your work? When will that be done?"

He waits for me to finish, drawing a hand through his salt and pepper hair and exhaling deeply. "Young man, if you would like to speak with me privately about your grievances, I will be all ears. But may I finish first?"

"No," I say with a furious frown. "Let's talk now."

"I will do so, if you promise to leave peacefully and not interrupt my sermon again. Do we have a deal? Will the back room suffice?"

I nod and he backs away from the pulpit. I leave Vanessa looking dumbfounded as the congregation chatters. I follow Reverend Martin to the classroom to the left of the pulpit while the middle-aged man returns and starts to ramble.

I shake my head as I enter the dark classroom, where the Reverend has taken a seat behind a polished broad-topped desk. The chairs are all folded and stacked along the softly decorated beige walls. As the thoughts fill my brain, I plot a course forward, but regret fills my mind as I unfold a chair and face him silently. The darkness seems to grow as we regard one another. Within moments the woman on the lake is calling out to me over time and space: "Don't go, Kerry."

17

The Assault of Typhon

Sunlight leaks through the partially open horizontal blinds and spreads softly in all directions, making the desktop shine. Reverend Martin's eyes reflect off the polished surface and catch my gaze. For a moment, which begins to seem like an eternity, neither of us speaks.

I imagine that by now, Vanessa has risen from the pew and escaped the eyes of hundreds of parishioners into the warmth of the sun, where she will be waiting for my discussion with the reverend to conclude. Still, I am in no hurry. The pastor owes me a full explanation, but now that I am facing him, I can barely remember the words he spoke.

"You are a troubled young man," he says, stroking his beard before returning his palm to the desktop.

"I've travelled the past, present, and future to find you," I mutter, trying not to look mesmerized.

He sees through the mask and attempts to comfort me. "The past can be painful, even if properly addressed. The future can offer as much hope as it can gloom."

I slowly shake my head, glance down to the reflection, and then allow my eyes to study his. They are like marbles cut out of a monolith and polished to perfection. "I mean literally. I'm in the future now."

He furrows his eyebrows and breathes deeply. "The future is now."

"What year is this?" I wait only a half second for him to respond, but then rattle on anyway: "I live in 2020 Philly. It would take all day to explain how I got here, and you wouldn't believe me anyway."

Shrugging slowly, he lowers his voice and speaks. "You might find that I'm a trusting individual. Trust is something lost in the pages of the Holy Bible, but it's as much a virtue as love."

I swallow and eye a stack of chairs along the wall in the darkened corner behind the pastor's right shoulder. "It would have been a year or two ago by now," I say, changing course. "I met someone at one of your sermons. In a few years, she told me about that message, where you tell a story about walking through the fog—"

"I remember it well," he interrupts. "It's a message on revelation from God. We always think that only the prophets of old were capable of such, but regardless of our journey, God has a plan for us if we trust in him. Even if we cannot see where we are going, we only need to take a single step to see far enough to take the next, and then the next, and so on, until you finally find your destination."

I nod slowly.

"God knows what's in our hearts."

"What if God only wants to confuse me?"

He shakes his head. "That is not the work of God. The devil may have a hand in it, but oftentimes what we are sure we know is far enough from the truth that it conflicts and blurs our path."

I'm not interested in religious dogma. The existence of God is irrelevant to whatever I'm trying to find. The voice of the woman on the lake is fading into murky waters, muffled by time and my own memory. Was it Becky?

In this timeline, I know Becky. She is probably worried about me, since there's no way I told her where I was going, if it's true that the me in this timeline has disappeared.

"Who did you meet?"

"My wife."

A smile spreads across his lips and his eyes sparkle. "The Lord works in mysterious ways."

"A little too mysterious, because I'm here now trying to find out what happened to a woman I know back in 2020. One night after work I wanted to talk to her, but she was—invisible. Because I think she was in the future. Where if you stay too long, your past self gets erased."

Reverend Martin doesn't speak for several moments, as if he is trying to piece together everything I have just said and compare it to what he knows and doesn't know.

"Does your wife know?"

"I don't know her in 2020," I counter. I can feel the welded washers in my pocket. Transferring them between sets of clothes had been so automatic that I hadn't realized I was even doing it. The significance is not lost on me. I pull the contraption out of my pocket, turn it over in my fingers, and drop it in the center of the desk for him to examine.

"I made this in an interactive science exhibit circa 2017." Although I'm guessing the year, its only relevance is establishing that it was long before I met either Sarah or Becky. "My wife says that the two washers represent forever, like some kind of predetermined destiny. And you can't break them apart."

"An interesting point," he mutters.

"So clearly I gave it to her in the future, and now I have it back."

"You took it with you from the future?"

I narrow my eyes and tilt my head subtly sideways. "What if it was never meant for her? What if I was supposed to give it to my 'invisible girlfriend?' That's why I'm here. What does this revelation say about her?"

He clears his throat. "We are free to choose our own journey through this life; that is God's guarantee. In that regard, there is no such thing as destiny. I think there is such a thing as preordinance, where God has selected us to have certain gifts, but our choices still reign. I think it is up to you to determine who is better for you. Ask God for guidance, of course, but the choice is yours."

"So your speech about finding my way through the fog doesn't apply?"

"It applies in the sense that the next step is the only one. You will find your way."

Again I narrow my eyes: "But what happens if that next step that I can't see is in front of a train, or off a cliff, or into a woman carrying groceries? In the real world, that's a good way to get lost, or worse."

"You are thinking literally, my friend," the reverend admonishes. "The whole story is a parable. When we introduce factors of our own imagination, the outcome is inevitably altered."

An inexplicable darkness shrouds the room. Instinctively I shift my eyes to the window. A thick shadow passes before the sunlight returns. There is only one explanation for this: the Shade. It is going to eat everything—the church, the whole congregation, and Vanessa too if we don't escape.

This part of Philadelphia doesn't offer a lot of voids that could be used as portals. Finding one before the Shade consumes us seems unlikely.

The reverend seems wholly unperturbed by what has just happened. Does he not see the Shade?

I abruptly stand and clench my fists while Reverend Martin remains seated and crosses his arms on the desktop.

"It's going to devour us," I shout, grabbing the washers and stuffing them into my pocket.

Still the reverend doesn't move.

I sprint toward the door without processing what is happening. To my horror, the congregation is sitting in enraptured silence while the choir sings a perfect melody. They cannot tell they are in danger. I swallow and try to scream at them, but only a high, raspy screech escapes my lips.

My heart is beating a million miles an hour and sweat is beading on my brow. The light coming from the transom windows in the mezzanine dims and shines again intermittently. The monster is just outside, enveloping the city in blackness.

If Vanessa is still alive, we have only seconds to find a portal.

Lowering my eyes and feeling my heart pounding inside my ribcage, I crash through the double doors into the chapel, dart through the foyer, and leap into the sunlight through the open doors.

Vanessa has wedged herself between the church building and a quaking tree, which is losing its leaves to the tempest. I don't bother trying to explain before I grab the crook of her arm and dart into the street.

Terror engulfs us in waves as we dodge cars driven by people unaware of their impending demise. Panic often leads to questionable decisions, and this time is no different. I cast my eyes upward as we run arm in arm to the other side of the boulevard. A set of scarlet eyes puncture a swirling veneer of black; giant wings swoop overhead, pushing a forceful wind through the streets of the city.

It bears down on us, lowering itself to the street, and belches fire at the pavement in front of us. Scrambling to safety, we sprint toward a bus parked on the street, kitty corner to the church. The monster roars as its wings carry it aloft, bathing the streets in bleak shadows. The smoke burrows into my nostrils as I pant and gasp.

Vanessa screams as she trips on the curb. Her bag topples to the sidewalk, spilling its contents, including my change of clothes.

Grabbing her by the armpits, I drag her to her feet as the monster lunges at us. The darkness seems to flare. Multiple eyes highlight the growing abyss as another inferno erupts from its jaw.

Regarding its victims with loathing, it takes in the hate and the squeals. Car horns, rumbling motors, shattering china, children's screams, and the voice of the Reverend Martin himself join in the ear-splitting din.

This is no ordinary Shade. I breathe heavily as I position us behind the bus, but the monster swoops higher, overturns the vehicle, and burns it to cinders as we scurry away.

The smell of molten rubber and black smoke drills into my nostrils and the extreme heat sears my back. Vanessa clutches at my arms and screams as her braids flutter in the wind of the attacker's wings. The only available direction of escape is along the block, beyond a row of old houses that are uniformly set back from the sidewalk via a five-foot wide strip of grass divided by walkways to the front doors.

Pursuing us through the air, the monster howls again, and I swear I can hear Becky's voice amidst the deafening squeal towering over me: "Don't go, Kerry."

I weave along the sidewalk, surprised that Vanessa can keep up. She is panting as I pull her around a corner, before the house next door combusts. Flaming debris and melted shingles fly off the roof in every direction, raining down around us like fiery meteors. The resultant heat boils at our sides before we have a chance to dodge the incinerated shards of wood. We both hit the deck, diving into the grass as the monster roars overhead. The house rages, with flames towering at least thirty feet high, fully engulfed and emitting a crackling roar. Agony pushes its way through my joints as I spy what appears to be a square, black hole cut into the grass behind the nearest undamaged house.

A shattered array of flaming wood particles crashes in the grass between us and the hole, impeding our path to possible freedom. We hunch lower to avoid the rising heat and bypass the pile of burning wood.

Seeing us, the monster rears backward in order to incinerate the next house and trap us between two infernos, but vile blackness creeps up behind it. The beast's wings flutter in the black smoke rising from the bus, and seem to bleed into the darkness behind it. I swallow and guide us closer to the hole. The creature belches smoke and sparks as it swoops its heavy wings to carry it higher and higher, far above the burning houses.

Sirens wail in the distance as the Shade attempts to rise, but it seems to be held back by gravity. The winged monster's means of escape is upward, while ours is downward. As if it can feel us, the Shade inches forward to douse the flames and smoke like a creeping oil stain that devours everything it touches.

Vanessa offers a colorful curse as she gapes at the hole in the grass. I grip her tighter as the heat begins to dissipate. The Shade lunges and pauses in mid-air just long enough for us to reach our exit point.

The church should still be prominent from this angle, but it has disappeared into a shroud of pitch-black smoke, as if the Shade has erased the entire building. The fleeing monster screeches, and Vanessa instinctively covers her ears and screams into oblivion. Safety seems to hover just in front of us, and the Shade knows what we are doing. Still, Vanessa freezes to the spot in terror. I drag her the last couple of feet through the grass on my hands and knees by wedging one arm into the crook of her elbow, scooting her towards the pit.

I hold on tight as the monster swoops away, flying higher and higher as the Shade obliterates the city below. Vanessa whimpers when we reach the hole. It appears to be a square well dug into the grass, with sides of reinforced concrete. The Shade lurches toward us as it scoops up the huge pile of burning refuse that had once been a home and causes the burning bus to vanish inch by inch. I shove Vanessa into the abyss and watch her disappear into a vortex of dark before I dive in to follow.

Falling feels like misery. The stench of the smoke follows me down into space, where billions of stars twinkle. The red planet reappears briefly close to me as I twist through nothingness.

I blink to take in the light of eternity and feel a tug at my elbow. Vanessa is lying next to me, whimpering. Her braids emit smoke, and the dirt has smudged her makeup and mascara.

For the moment we are safe, surrounded by an industrial wasteland. The surrounding dark seems to invade as the distant screeches of machinery add torment to the night. Pain rocks my whole body and I struggle to sit upright. Vanessa still clings to my arm, yet determination has beaten the fear out of her eyes.

In the distance, the sounds of beating wings pummel the dark. I pull her to her feet, and sprint towards an ominous structure built of soot-stained cement masonry blocks. It has stacks of black and white piping scaling the walls in a cage of black-painted square steel tubes.

Certain that it is locked, I let Vanessa lead me to the door, hoping that the warehouse will provide safety from the lurking creature. I can feel her body heat at my side as we navigate the cold wasteland, and distant screams pierce the night. Failing to push the door open, Vanessa creeps along the foot of the building, clutching my arm tightly.

We round the corner and find a shattered streetlamp, leaning from the impact of a badly damaged, abandoned car. A half-dozen other vehicles are scattered through a small parking area beyond a loading dock, which is protected by a gray metal railing of welded pipe wrapped in thick black foam.

Heavy rubber snubbers protect the concrete foundation below the overhead doors. A lone door lies in a far corner, next to the overhead doors, with a set of concrete steps leading up to it.

Hoping that the door is unlocked, I let my grip on Vanessa slacken and follow her willingly. She curls her fingers below the bent plate handle and tugs. The door scrapes against the metal jamb as she wedges it open. The monster ignites a distant building as we enter the dark.

The inside is a maze of gloom. Racks of white and copper piping crisscross overhead, darting between huge sheet metal ducts covered in shiny batts of insulation. A spacious room juts off to our left and we limp in that direction, where a series of doors is arranged between points of connection and insulated white pipe and stainless-steel tubing puncture the metal wall.

Along the walls, shiny stainless-steel grate racks reach upward toward the rafters, bearing the weight of dozens of sealed cardboard boxes.

Vanessa turns the wheel handle on one of the doors and examines the darkness. She steps over the bulkhead into the black, grasping my hand tightly as I follow.

The darkness swirls, and we emerge breathlessly into a dense urban neighborhood, populated by rows of midrise apartment blocks. I recognize it instantly. It is my neighborhood at night, yet a tower crane I don't recognize looms like a shadow rising into the dark. The silence is alarming. My building lies two blocks away. Allowing my grip on Vanessa's hand to slacken, I lead her to my home, where we can recover from the scars and burns inflicted by the beast.

"What was that thing?" she asks.

I cannot answer, so I let the silence speak for me.

"And then it fled." She pants as I walk briskly along the cracked sidewalk beneath the trees growing out of round holes in the concrete.

"From the Shade."

"I don't like this," she says, trembling.

I silently agree. We quietly climb the stairs to my third-story apartment, and I decide to let her rest on my couch while I snooze the rest of the night away in my own bed. The pain digs into my knees as I turn the key in the lock and push open the door.

18

To Callisto with Love

The night is fraught with the painful memories that once plagued me.

The only time I had ever deemed high school worth the torment was when Quin would set up his video game console and we'd spend hours rotting away in front of it to save the princess. Such nobility was only bestowed sparingly, since Kel often passed the time dreaming up roleplaying game characters, a talent I was neither inclined toward nor blessed with.

The bullies were another problem: Iron Side High School had scarcely been known as a just institution until after Kel and that new girl had upset the power structure, and suddenly bullies like Jason were more frequently held accountable. Then again, Jason hadn't been the worst of my problems. A guy he sometimes hung out with had seemed hell bent on making my life as miserable as possible by daily pushing me against the lockers, or making wisecracks about my looks or my mom. Though it sounds trivial in retrospect, every tactic had worked. I went to a behavioral health counselor for a year trying to whisk away the demons that had me convinced the bullies were right about me.

My head aches as I sit upright in my bed, listening to the sound of running water from the bathroom. The clothes I was wearing when I arrived home now lie in a heap on the floor at the bedside. Pain racks my knees as I struggle to remove the blankets and sit upright.

Last night is a blur. A demon followed us into another dimension, and when we escaped that, we ended up here in present day Philadelphia. Before I retired to my bedroom, Vanessa and I made uncommitted plans to call a cab to drive her to the shipping yards where she'd left her car, and on the way, she would drop me at the garage where my car has been parked for what seems like years.

I quickly dress in a fresh set of clothes, slip on my shoes, and elect to wait for Vanessa on the couch, where the blanket I'd loaned her lies neatly folded on the armrest.

Within a few moments of the water turning off, she cracks open the door to notify me that she will be right out. I elect to pass the time by reading the news.

If I'm lucky enough to still be employed at this point, I'm going to owe Jamal a major explanation, which he will ultimately not believe, because monsters from the underworld are not well-known occupants of Philadelphia. At least not yet.

The news is uninspiring. I scan through a half-dozen articles before a sinking feeling of déjà vu clicks in. After opening another article and perusing the first paragraph, I touch my fingers to my forehead. I have read this story before, and sure enough, the date below the headline indicates that this story was first printed three years ago.

"Oh hell," I mutter, refreshing the page repeatedly, in the hope that current news will soon appear on my screen. My phone's data connection must be acting up again. Add that to the list of worries I'll have to address in the coming days.

Frustrated, I put the phone away just in time for Vanessa to emerge from the bathroom running fingers through her sleek, braided hair. She has dressed in the same clothes as she had on yesterday, though her attire now only seems vaguely familiar. I try to offer a pained smile, but she beats me to it.

"Is your boss going to have an issue with being late?" I ask.

"Mostly I'm my own boss," she replies, flinging her hair behind her and dabbing at the back of her neck with the towel I let her borrow. "You never told me what you do. Fancy telling me about it?"

I shrug. "The glamorous world of construction labor has its limits."

"Hammers, saws, and drills can be fun," she says, indicating a desire to spice up the conversation with something hopeful.

"Not like I'm allowed to operate them. I arrange and catalogue supplies, deliver plans to and from the general job trailer, and sweep the floor after everyone's gone for the day. Not really the investment type."

"Who manages your 401k? Can't be those bloodsucking pirates down at Howell Max." She grins as she says it, underlining a vein of sarcasm.

"Don't even know if I have one," I say, shaking my head and glancing at my phone on the end table to my left.

"You know, there's a way to change that," she whispers, sitting down next to me with her head hunched over her lap, supported by her elbows. "Any more battles with monsters on the radar today?"

Of course, last night was hardly a battle. The memory of it is already beginning to fade. If Vanessa weren't here sitting right next to me I might be inclined to believe it had only been a dream. There was something about a pastor, and a beast of some sort, and I remember using the names Becky and Sarah. I wrack my brains to put faces to the names, as I must have met those women before, but frustratingly I come up empty.

Asking Vanessa about it seems like a terrible decision, but I open my yap anyway. "How much do you remember about it?"

"About last night?" Seeing my slow nod, she continues: "It was daytime, and you were in a church. And then ... there was a factory or something? On second thought, this doesn't make a lot of sense."

"I doesn't make any sense," I grind out. "I shouldn't even remember you."

"Why's that?"

I don't like where my brain is headed, but I don't dare tell her about it for fear of inciting panic, a fight, and the summoning of the police. It is a dark conclusion, and I must figure out for myself whether my assumption is true. That means going to meet Joaquin. This time of day, he won't be home, but I know he works about eight blocks from Vanessa's office. I'll have Vanessa drop me off there.

"I'm not sure," I mutter, realizing that my eyes have glazed over. "Do you mind dropping me off to meet a friend of mine? He might have some insight."

She lowers her head somberly. "If you think so, I'm coming with you."

"Can't keep you away from work too long."

"It will be a leave of absence," she reasons, leaning back, and glancing into my eyes. The fire present behind her pupils tells me she's as passionate as ever.

I consider testing her by mentioning someone I vaguely remember, but his name is not something I can access in my memory right now. It's like I have been locked out of the present by my own thoughts. The only way this can be true, I guess, is that I have somehow gone back in time. Impossible.

She can see the wheels turning in my head and decides it the best policy to head me off by creating a different line of conversation.

"Who's your friend?"

Trying to make sure my memory is accurate, I ramble, "Insurance salesman, I think, avid RPG player. You'd like him."

She flashes a weary smile, reaches for the straps on her black canvas tote at the foot of the couch, and exhales. "Sure about that? We don't know a thing about each other. So maybe, on the way, we cover the basics."

I relent by standing, stretching my legs, and meandering to the bathroom. Vanessa has left the seat down and wiped the vanity mirror clear of fog. Lifting my shirt momentarily, I study my clear skin, and notice a bruise that wasn't there yesterday. How did I get it? My mind plows through the possibilities, eliminating them one by one, and decide that the haze of last night must have left its mark on me.

Stopping by the refrigerator on my way back to the couch, I spy her scheduling a ride pickup in about fifteen minutes. I offer her a drink while taking a bottle of water for myself. Downing it offers a sense of relief, but an inexplicable dread is working its way through my brain.

Accepting the water, she thanks me, unscrews the cap, and takes a long, uninterrupted sip. "I'm not liking this at all," she says after pulling the bottle away from her lips. "Why can't I remember?"

"I have a theory on that. But before I tell you about it, I need to talk to Quin."

We share small talk until the cab arrives and use the twenty-minute ride to formally introduce ourselves, as if we're on a first date. Expected topics like 'What do you do for fun,' generate little real discussion. Revealing past events proves more engaging.

She details growing up in a Southern Baptist household in rural Georgia, and dealing with the horrors of racism, both subtle and overt. Her father had left town for a job in Atlanta, and the next thing she knew he was the victim of a violent shooting and she was left to raise her young brother while her mom dealt with suicidal thoughts. But through determination, she says, she'd made it through in one piece as a stronger version of herself. She'd moved to Baltimore as a teenager and left her mother's home to settle in Philadelphia only a couple of years later.

By comparison, my upbringing seems entirely sheltered; I barely have the nerve to talk about my family, whom I have not contacted in years.

When we reach Joaquin's place of employment, Vanessa offers a cash tip to the driver and digs into her pocket.

The lobby sports two upholstered metal chairs beside a long table with a decorative floral centerpiece and a small stack of magazines. Beyond a curving half wall there sits an idle computer. A security guard paces from the storefront doors to the security office and back. The elevator awaits in a wide corridor beyond the security desk, next to a set of bathrooms and an unmarked janitor's closet with its door ajar. We ride the elevator to the third floor, check in with the receptionist, and meander through a maze of beige, half-height cubicle partitions. The workers type away, mostly without glancing at us. I don't remember ever setting foot in this building, and the framed motivational posters along the full wall about fifty feet in front of us seem to confirm it. Quin manages a well-decorated workspace, in which he has displayed an array of hand-drawn sketches of monsters and warriors, and photographs of a famous basketball star whom he's never brought up in conversation.

I read his nameplate silently and swallow without saying anything. Joaquin spins in his chair and offers a hand to shake. The work on his screen seems to flutter and I glance at it briefly. "How can I help you today?"

His greeting is not altogether unexpected; it is simultaneously too polite and not polite enough. It is like he is trying harder than necessary to greet a possible customer, and being forgiving enough to nearly confirm my suspicion. Looking somewhat younger and clean-shaven, he regards me with cool eyes, waiting for me to tell him why I've come.

"You know me—Kerry. Some people call me Larry."

"Kerry? Yeah, that's right. I remember you from high school, man. What brings you to Philly?"

"You've got to be kidding me," Vanessa says, shrugging. "This is your friend?"

I pretend not to feel like an idiot and fail, stammering something about visiting from another era, before we became friends. "We're friends."

"Look Kerry, I don't know what you're talking about, but it's been a lot of years. Maybe we can catch up over drinks sometime. You can tell me what you've been doing."

"Right, whatever." I wave my hand subtly towards Vanessa, who tries to look busy by tying her braids into a ponytail with a spare rubber band from her bag. "This is Vanessa. She's a broker."

Vanessa stares at something at eye level, which for her could be a hundred feet away in another employee's workstation.

"You came here to talk to me about my investments? Sorry, but now isn't the time." Joaquin seems skilled at turning us away without making it sound personal. I could commend him for that, but he has just proven my theory correct.

I nod and forget about shaking hands with him. I will run into him another time for sure, but I can't decide how. I lead Vanessa out of the cubicle area the same way we entered, matching stride for stride until we are safely out of earshot of these strangers, before I tell her the secret.

"I bet you already know it," I guess, "but we are not in our present-day Philadelphia. Screwed up as it sounds, we've been transported back to Philly three years ago."

She nods, as though this information does not strike her as shocking. I regard her suspiciously and gaze at dozens of buttons in the elevator before selecting the ground floor.

I grit my teeth. "I suspect that if we stay too long, monsters will catch up with us and erase us from existence."

"A bit of a drama queen. That's not really what happens. You don't know what's going on?"

I can't believe what I'm hearing, but I listen anyway. The elevator seems to pick up speed as the air begins to circulate faster.

"This isn't my first time. I've been further back than this and I stayed over a week. There was never a monster. Never seen one before."

I shake my head and gape at her. "You ... time travel? Last night ... why don't I remember it?"

She rests a palm on my forearm to comfort me as I tremble in cold terror.

"Because it hasn't happened yet, and that's not the way memory works."

I back against the wall and try not to look at her. "What are you talking about?" I mumble breathlessly.

Vanessa filling in the gaps of my knowledge is not something I'm prepared to accept, so I can only avoid eye contact as if she's a total stranger. Finally fitting the pieces together, the truth strikes me like a brick hurled from nowhere as the elevator stops. There is no way we know one another unless we have interacted before. I swallow and allow myself to tremble in realization of this important fact.

If destiny has anything to do with what is happening, Vanessa and I are already closer than either of us know, and that strikes a chord of terror all the way to the bottom of my spine.

Then again, her experience, if genuine, may yet allow me to experience something resembling a future—if it even exists. For now, I can only be a passenger on her journey. If I can't trust her, the price of peril will be too steep to fathom.

19

Following Artemis

Vanessa sits across from me at a round glass table, shaded by a lime green umbrella in the shadow of the towers downtown. She looks pale in spite of her complexion, but nonetheless expressive, folding her arms and leaning back. Her eyes seem to sparkle, suggesting that she's inviting me to ask her some more questions.

All I can get out is, "How?"

The shadows grow shorter as the minutes pass, and we wait for the waitress to bring us tea from inside the crowded café. In this cold weather few have elected to sit outdoors, though there is no wind, and the sun is shining brightly enough to make it feel several degrees warmer.

"You don't understand," she says.

I scoff. "Explain it like I'm five."

She nods and narrows her eyes. "You know a bit about Greek mythology. What if I told you I was there?"

When I don't respond, she relents and digs deeper. "You and I aren't just travelling in time. We're entering alternate dimensions, which is why what happens in the past, with us, doesn't affect the present in this dimension. And I've been through a few. You want to know how old I really am?"

I shake my head, knowing I'd never considered asking, and try to appear disinterested despite her offer.

She leans closer, and gently rests her palm on my arm. "Over two thousand years."

"But your mother—"

"The one in Baltimore," she says. "She always knew me as her daughter, but she had a surrogate. I grew up with her, but I discovered some things that I've never told anyone."

"You don't have to tell me anything," I mutter, glancing up into the relative darkness inside the café, where our waitress is chatting with a co-worker while carrying our tea. I shift my feet and try to let the silence resume.

"If it's about your destiny, I don't have a choice."

"I don't believe in destiny," I say, biting my lower lip and furrowing my eyebrows.

"Destiny is a word that takes many forms. Some call it just dumb luck—being in the right place at the wrong time. Some say it's really called predisposition. But you've seen enough to know some of it must be true.

"Take me, for instance. It was my destiny to grow up in this century, to interact with many wonderful people. But I'm from the stars."

"We all are," I argue.

"Literally. I was sent there by Zeus. People all over the world know me, some by the name of the Great Bear."

"You're ... Ursa Major?"

"It's my astral name, anyway. Here, my name is Vanessa. I'm mortal. Before I became the Bear, I knew Zeus. I was in love with Artemis."

"How do you know all this? Am I really supposed to believe that you're not just a good broker? No offense, but I don't buy it."

She shrugs and waits for our server, a tall woman with blond and gray hair, who gently sets two cups of tea in front of us and wishes us a good day. If a two-thousand-year-old lover of Artemis is really sitting in front of me, I could count myself as either eternally lucky or endlessly cursed. Wrapping my head around the possibilities makes me weary, but I dare not rub my eyes in front of her.

"Maybe someday I will prove it to you, but today—we have to get you back to our present-day dimension."

I gulp. "I don't want to go back, because I'm a hunter." So many thoughts fill my brain that expressing any one of them seems an exercise in futility.

"If you say so."

Stammering, I belt out a sentence that I already know isn't going to make any sense. "It's just that I don't know what I'm trying to find. And I still don't really understand how we ended up here."

"You don't know because your memory of the future has been erased," she explains. "Memory is a terribly subjective way of recounting past events. The older the event, the less reliable the memory. It works the same way when the memory is from a future dimension. We've been here for over twelve hours, more than long enough for your memory to be completely removed.

"And when you're in a future dimension, your brain naturally fills in the memories that you've missed."

"Travel a lot, do you?"

"Not a *lot*," she says, sipping her tea and squinting in a patch of sun that has appeared on her face, leaking through the gaps in the umbrella. "Not much reason to."

"So how much do you want from me? You're going to tie me up in a van, demand some kind of ransom, and when I do finally pay up, I'll be floating face down in the Philadelphia River none the wiser."

"You do have a wild imagination. I'll give you that."

"The hell I do."

"You're a construction laborer? How long you been doing that?"

"I guess about a year now. Give or take."

"You've looked at building floor plans? Know how they evolve?"

I let out a slow breath and try not to appear too tired. Her grilling seems to be going nowhere, but for now I can only let her speak, since she is the one loaded with useless information and I know practically nothing. "I'm somewhat familiar with it. There's a process: the foreman looks at the job specs, and when he sees a requirement that will be difficult or costly to achieve, he writes a Request For Information to the architect or engineer. When the RFI is returned, it sometimes comes with a supplementary release. But even by the time the subs get the work, the entire plan set could be on its third or fourth iteration. Then they change it again, because the general requires the subs to document as built conditions."

"Good explanation. Do the plans ever go backwards?"

"Never." I shake my head and frown. "Even if an RFI successfully alters the plans back to an original design, the documentation stays in the system; it never gets erased. The PMs make a lot of money carefully documenting everything."

"Then what happens when you join the project midway through? I expect there's training that briefs you on the history of the project?"

"Sometimes."

"So then you start to remember some things you weren't there for."

Again, I breathe out. "What are you getting at?"

She offers a subtle smile, which purses her lips and makes her look more thirty than two thousand. "You'll see in about three years."

"If you're really reincarnated from two thousand years ago, how do you remember it?"

She nods and exhales, a sign that she has been expecting this question. "Only the structure of it; who I was. Nothing on the day to day. I don't even remember Artemis. It's been lost to time *and* a different dimension."

The conversation gradually turns tedious as the minutes slip away. She sips her last bit of tea more than ten minutes after I've finished mine and leans forward out of the shadow so that the sun highlights her face. A certain spark of wisdom I haven't yet seen seems to blossom in her expression before fading away. She leaves a healthy tip in cash under her receipt and eyes me as I strain to get up.

As if lost in the city, I tread through the shadows of the skyscrapers and marvel at how concrete everything seems to be in a universe with endless possibilities. Vanessa walks quickly next to me, dodging strangers and glancing in some storefront windows. We chat little about time or memory. She paces with purpose, as if she has a destination in mind as we walk closer to Market Street.

The pedestrian noise kicks up the closer we get: cheers and shouts echo from a few blocks up, followed by the steady thumping of a bass drum to get the crowd riled up. She leads me in that direction, closer and closer until we can no longer engage in normal conversation without raising our voices. The nightlife in this district is notorious for being even more chaotic than the tourism. When the crowds grow ever denser, she takes my hand and squeezes through a throng of young women dancing the afternoon away.

We enter an alley, and she hesitates before prying open a back door and disappearing into the dark. Unable to predict the future, I follow tentatively.

The bar is lit with dim neon and glowing beer signs. She nods at the bartender, a muscle-bound white man in a tight black T-shirt, then passes the bar, a few wooden tables, a jukebox, and a single billiards table topped with green felt and an Eagles logo, as she moves towards the bathrooms.

I let go of her hand as she pushes open a door next to the women's room. The inside is a rectangle of black. She grasps my hand tighter, pulls me closer, and vanishes into a wispy dark vapor.

Red lights flash all around us as the stars swirl. Gravity has lost its hold as we float in the ether, until it all disappears entirely, and the night has resumed. I sit next to her panting. Confusion tatters at every corner of my brain.

The abandoned sidewalks stretch for blocks, and not a soul stirs. Cars sit idle, parked in rows along the curb, at least two with the driver's door open into the street where no traffic prowls. At any time of the year, and any time of night, this would be a rare sight. Now it's making the goosebumps ripple across my flesh.

Vanessa rises to her feet and stretches. She blesses me with a sheepish grin and then reaches out her hand to pull me up. I groan as I rise, my bones creaking and my muscles aching.

The city is dead, but this observation barely registers on her face. I look around squeamishly in the hope of setting her attention on the bizarre scene, but she has other ideas. Looking up and down the sidewalks to determine her bearings, she glances to the sky, where a thousand dim stars sparkle overhead. Then, once certain of her surroundings, she points at the shadowy overhang of a movie theater marquee that has gone dark.

"What the hell?"

"Say we catch a movie," she says, looking only mildly surprised. "Think they're open today?"

"Gonna go with no," I guess, the sarcasm implied in my tone. Still, she leads us in that direction. The wind chills my bones as we pace the empty sidewalks, past dozens of idle cars, and look up at what are normally illuminated towers stretching into the darkness above us. Only a few of the thousands of windows are lit up, and I wonder why. The idea that some buildings are built with always-on emergency lights flashes through my brain and causes another chilly ripple to spread through my skin.

Vanessa grasps my hand tighter as she quickens her pace. A familiar sound penetrates my eardrums amid the clicking of her heels: the distant swoop of wings playing in harmony with the breeze filtering through the abandoned streets. The sound seems to rise into the skyline, even as it comes near, sailing over the low-rising buildings as if to sneak up on us.

Hearing this, Vanessa pulls me closer to the storefronts, into the shadows, in case the monster flies overhead. I hold my breath, stepping lighter and faster in response to the gentle tug of her hand. The theater marquee covers a broad, angled setback in the glass storefronts to provide shade and subtle warmth for crowds to wait in line.

The wind picks up as wings flutter overhead, beating heavily against the breeze. *Don't look up,* I plead to myself, but I cannot avert my eyes for long. The beast sees us, patiently looking down as Vanessa approaches the canopy. She pays no attention to the monster, but I get the feeling that she knows it's there, eyeing us cautiously.

By now, if it had seen us as a threat, it would already have incinerated us. I glance up as its wings flare out and it glides straight toward us. Its huge talons stick out and a blunt beak creates a conical outline of shadow on its feathered face. The eyes, glowing pearls of fiery orange, study me. Gently, with the breeze, its wings float upward as its body slumps toward the pavement. A heavy *clack* echoes through the streets as it touches down and peers thoughtfully at us.

I remain frozen to the spot as Vanessa tugs at me impatiently. For a moment, neither of us speaks. I marvel at the beast: a ten-foot-tall bird with enormous, powerful wings of dark gray, blue, and burnt orange. It takes a single step forward, lowers its head, and waits for us to move.

Vanessa creeps backward into the overhang as I pant harshly. "Come on, we gotta get out of here," she says, her voice trembling with fear.

"It's okay," I say, squaring my shoulders and regarding the creature.

It squawks in approval and my heartrate settles. Vanessa tugs at me again and I relent, backing into the canopy with her.

Memory flashes into my brain out of nowhere—I see the wings beating against the dark night, the orange and gray feathers rising to obscure the setting sun as a violent mob rumbles in fury. Punches fly, and fire erupts. Thousands of people join the fray, shouting and chanting as the creature rises into the sky.

Again, my blood runs cold. The beast seems to lure me as Vanessa grips my hand more tightly. I offer what little resistance I can muster as she wills us toward the storefront doors, behind which blackness reigns.

Somehow, I feel that we have landed in this dimension for a reason. The winged messenger silently nods at me, wishes me well, and squabbles as it stretches its long, feathery wings skyward to launch itself from the street.

A low rumble echoes in the distance. I swallow as the bird soars higher and higher, and the beating of its wings fades into the distance.

Chills race through my spine as Vanessa flings the door open and drags me into the darkness.

The interior of the theater is a black den, with expansive marble floor tiles in a chunky mosaic pattern, between curved accents of stainless-steel and flat, red felt carpet along the colorful walls. The wall sconce lights, spaced about ten feet apart high overhead, remain dark.

The concessions counter is bathed in gloom. Hunger pangs constrict my stomach, though the scent of popcorn has long since dissipated. The morsels left over in the vat look cold and disgusting. Behind the counter, something slender and black slithers along the wall.

Vanessa wastes no time in plumbing the depths of the halls, gradually working deeper into the dark as we proceed away from the windows. A ramp and a railing appear along the left wall near us, providing access to an elevated walkway perpendicular to the lobby. She grasps the cold stainless-steel and scurries up the ramp toward an opaque opening cut from the blackness.

"What was that?" I ask, murmuring.

"You don't want to know," she says, yanking my hand as she struggles up the slope.

"I've seen it before," I admit, letting my guard down.

She stops and studies me, as if in horror. In this dim light I can only see the whites of her eyes, but she looks dead serious as if trembling with dread.

"You know," I murmur accusingly. "Why do you fear it? It meant us no harm."

"You don't understand what it does to society," she says, lowering her voice and pulling me closer. "It has caused cities to collapse into chaos until they destroy themselves."

"Is that why the Shade wants to eat it?" I can barely understand the words coming out of my mouth. Hoping that her response offers clues, I let my mind slowly and subtly fill in the cracks in my memory until it all becomes clear.

She steps further up the slope and nearly twists my hand when she crosses the wide, carpeted corridor. Her hand shakes in mine yet settles when I squeeze it reassuringly.

"Tell me what it is," I demand, squaring my jaw.

"There's a long backstory," she admits, leaving me breathless and pausing in front of the opaque black rectangle, which appears to be a single, unmarked doorway. "I'll have to tell you about it later."

"Then just tell me what the creature is called."

She sighs and waits for several seconds before relenting. Squeezing my hand limply, she raises her chin as if to stare into the dark ceilings overhead and to signal compliance.

"It's the Icarus," she whispers.

I silently nod while I take it all in. The tone in her voice is one of dread. She clings to me in the stillness, draws me nearer, and steps into the doorway. In seconds, we are floating in freefall, together spinning through a forest of shining stars until there are pebbles scattering underfoot.

20

Flight of the Icarus

I know where we have landed before I open my eyes. Vanessa remains silent, as if uncertain of how to react. She breathes deeply and I can feel her gaze falling on me while she nestles her body against mine to share my warmth. The world under my eyelids is a bright shade of blurry yellow.

The sun is beating down on the lake as I open my eyes. With Vanessa standing at my shoulder, we look out on the once tranquil waters, now covered with lapping waves as the distant hum of motors destroys the ambience.

On the island, the chimney of the cabin peeks above the canopy; one could visit these shores a hundred times without realizing the home is even there. By now I'm assuming that foot traffic has beaten dusty trails through the trees.

A motorboat towing a water skier rips across the bay towards the reeds, takes a hard right towards us, and sends its thrill seeker tumbling into the choppy waters.

I barely move as I take it all in. Behind me should be the home in which I first met Becky. I turn sideways and shield my eyes from the sun. The shore has been transformed into a vacation paradise: broad swaths of the pebbly banks have been converted into sandy beaches where sunbathers can soak up the rays, and beyond that, a three-story hotel has cut a rectangular white wall against the verdant backdrop.

I gape at the scene silently. Vanessa doesn't bother to speak.

"God, they've ruined it," I gasp.

"Where are we?" she asks. "*When* are we?"

I shake my head. "At least ten years from now. My last visit, the place was all but abandoned. A half-dozen vacation homes over there, no beach. And—"

She waits for me to expound.

"And one other soul."

"Who?"

"Becky," I say breathlessly. "That must have been her when I was rowing to the island."

Vanessa glances at the forested isle, which stands as tranquil as ever, its dense thicket of dark green deciduous trees shading the old timbers of the porch.

From beyond the island, a pair of personal watercraft speed into the open and disrupt the path of what appears to be a canoe carrying two relaxed fishermen. In the distance the lake stretches to the far shore, which is now dotted with several cabins overlooking the waters, each with its own private beach. Canoes and inflatable rafts are moored in front of two of the houses. A motorboat idles near the far shore, as if the occupants are studying the buildings, and then it speeds away.

At what I perceive to be the lake's outlet, nearly a mile away, a pair of sailboats lazily bobs up and down on the waves created by fellow adventurers.

At my side, Vanessa's eyes wander back and forth before falling on me once more.

"Icarus made his wings," she explains, "out of wax and feathers, but he ignored his father's warning. *Don't fly too close to the sun.*

"His wings melted, and he crashed into the sea and drowned. The beast we just encountered is what remains of his soul—rebelliousness—chaos. They say that he ignites civil wars simply by his presence."

"You believe that?"

She nods, again casting her eyes towards the shadow of the trees on the island.

"I met his father."

The memory of the future realm blasts into my consciousness, as if reawakened from a deep slumber. The riot was severe, the people chanting and screaming, engaging in brutal fist fights, and launching flaming projectiles at storefront windows. Thousands of people churned in un-fettered violence as the Icarus rose into the sun, turning the futuristic Philadelphia into a war zone.

"Why did he let us escape?" I ask.

"It was Philadelphia like I've never seen it before," she says. "Abandoned and isolated."

"And it looked like the desertion happened recently," I finish for her, centering my memory on the open car doors and the fact that everything still looked reasonably clean. "Does the Icarus just come and torment random cities?"

She shakes her head. "There can only be one reason."

"What's that?"

"Helios still dominates him," she explains, tilting her head back and letting her braids dangle behind her shoulders. "The sun—to remind him that he's still inferior. When he's present, there is light."

I nod and drag my feet through the pebbles. A young boy, perhaps ten years old, runs toward me, looking behind him to track a spinning plastic disc, which he intends to intercept. I catch sight of his eyes momentarily and regret fills my heart.

Those eyes look familiar.

In response, I glance up and down the shoreline in search of another version of myself. The person who has thrown the disc watches in amazement as the boy leaps to catch the toy. From afar, I study the man's movements. That can't be me, because if Harley is right, the me residing in this dimension has disappeared.

I scan the shoreline fronting the vacation homes and the hotel, guessing that the boy's mother will be close by. I spy her waiting in the shade of a thick oak tree in front of a house two down from the hotel. She wears a striped blue one-piece bathing suit. Her black hair is tied in a neat bun at the back of her head, and she applies lotion to her silky-smooth legs. I gulp, hoping she has not noticed me.

Turning away, I can almost feel her eyes on me. Her presence alone alerts my senses with a familiar tingle. Why didn't I feel that the first time I ventured here? The answer is plainly obvious by now. The woman walking on the water wasn't Becky. It was Sarah. She must know I am searching for her.

I search the faces of dozens of strangers, aching to catch a glimpse of her amber hair and pale skin. No one looks remotely like her.

This entire dimension seems bright—so bright that the Icarus could emerge from behind one of the low-hanging cumulus clouds at any moment.

Before I can finish imagining it, the sound of wings beating in the sky echoes from beyond the island. The black creature swoops upward, crests the isle, and sails toward the more populated shore.

I gasp at how quickly it has found us. What has given me away?

The only logic that penetrates my brain now is that it has somehow followed us. Like a tempest, it seems to gather itself in a shroud of dark that battles the sunshine. My blood runs cold. I instantly recognize the beast as the monster that raged through future Philadelphia just before the Shade attacked.

It squeals as it glides toward us, locking its numerous glowing red eyes on me alone. Despite all the innocent tourists, it has picked me, and the tourists barely acknowledge it, if at all. Vanessa seizes my hand and squeezes. Adrenaline courses through me as I take off in a sprint toward a single canoe tethered to a newly constructed pier beside the flooded reeds.

The sun seems to filter through its mighty wings as the beast circles above us, bares its hundreds of fangs, and begins to settle.

As if reading my intentions, Vanessa squeezes my hand and then sprints onto the pier. She doesn't bother to slow down when she reaches the canoe, but flings herself in the air, does a near total forward flip, and lands painfully on the seat boards. I busy myself untying the ropes as the monster swoops overhead. I can feel its many eyes burrowing into the back of my soul as if to puncture me with a million needles.

The screech cannot be far behind. I gulp as I feverishly work at the rope, while Vanessa reaches for a long wooden oar. She holds it aloft like warrior, as if daring the creature to attack us.

It obliges by gathering altitude, and dives straight toward us at it howls a mouthful of shattering glass, honking horns, jet planes, children laughing, and the sound of Sarah calling out to me, all at the same time. The din batters at my ears, resulting in a hollow-sounding ringing.

The creature rages, belches fire into the air, and continues to zero in on us. It is flying faster than its own flames can travel. It isn't seeking to incinerate us this time, but instead to devour us before the Shade arrives.

I push the canoe away from the pier as Vanessa aims the oar at the creature's head.

It screeches immediately as a thunderous boom rocks the lake, catching the attention of every soul within earshot. Swinging my head around violently, I see that Vanessa is wielding a shotgun instead of an oar. She loads another shell into the chamber as the enemy vaults higher into the sky.

She aims at its heart and blasts another scattering of shot into the sky. As if unamused by this assault, the monster belts out a piercing roar. I can only shield my head as it dives, again aiming straight for us.

Smoke billows from its thirsty maw as it angles its wings behind its massive body.

Vanessa can't hope to unload another shot in time to fire at the creature; instead, she grasps the weapon with both hands, positions it in front of her face, closes her eyes, and turns her head. The enemy thunders and plunges headfirst into the water not ten feet away from our vessel.

Its wings submerge in the turbulent water as it thrashes its limbs violently. It gurgles, and the water bubbles under like boiling mud.

The lake begins to build a massive wave, the monster swimming underneath us. With another huge splash, it lunges out of the surface. The weight of the water has dampened its wings, inhibiting the beast's ability to fly higher.

It flails and screeches as Vanessa loads another shell into the shotgun's chambers. Seeing this, the monster belches fire to preempt her attack. The surge of flame narrowly misses behind her, and dissipates into thick smoke. She cocks the gun, aims at the creature's head, and fires.

The scattershot audibly pelts the thick skin of the attacker. It screeches in angry pain as it slaps its heavy wings against the surface of the lake. The resultant banging blends with the torture it unloads from its mouth as it struggles out of the deep and slings itself into the air once again. I take the remaining oar and paddle as fast as I can. A knot of pain quickly works its way through my muscles.

Vanessa wastes no time in loading the shotgun in case the creature should take another dive at us.

Anticipating this, I row even harder. The portal in the closet can offer us shelter, but I already know the risk: if the monster burns the house to the ground, it will eliminate the portal, and we could get stuck in the in-between forever.

The water splashes as I work to propel us toward the island's shore. The monster swirls around high above, blocks the sun, and screeches like tires on pavement amidst a raging thunder of wildfire. In an instant, the light from the sun returns.

The beast circles as another set of wings joins in the fray.

The tourists have fled the shore at the sight of the violence, and the hum of motorboats gradually falls to silence amidst the isolated screams.

The monsters lock talons high overhead, pelting each other with heavy blows. The black beast's many eyes glow red as it launches a stream of fire at its assailant, which responds by flipping itself over and jabbing its beak straight into the top of the monster's skull. I row harder while the black monster prepares itself for another dive. Vanessa angles the shotgun toward it, unloads a shot, and misses wildly. She shrieks and lays the gun down as if in surrender. Out of shells, she readies herself for another assault. Instead of attacking us, the monster unfurls its wings and glides over the choppy waters.

The dark creature glides near the surface of the lake while its attacker circles overhead. I let my eyes wander upward as its wings unfold against the sun's disc above. The Icarus is not our enemy; instead, it seeks to shield us from harm.

The monster glides away from us, doubles back, and eyes us impatiently as the Icarus circles. If it can get in just one more attack, it can barbecue and devour us. I gulp as it swoops towards our canoe. The hull of the vessel scrapes against rock as we reach the island. Vanessa grabs my hand to hoist herself to a standing position, jumps into the knee-deep water, and waits eagerly for me to follow suit.

Our assailant launches more fire in our direction as we splash to the rocky shore, and the canoe bursts into flames. Our defender dives toward it. To prepare itself for battle, the black creature turns itself over, flaps its wings violently, and stretches out its talons.

The Icarus angles its wings backward, sinking a single talon into one of the beast's red eyes. It screams in terror, trying to defend itself, flips upright, and attacks. Fire erupts amidst bloodthirsty screams, howling sirens, and the heavy blasts of a ship's air horns. Dozens of voices begin to chant as it pummels the Icarus with well-timed hits. The bird will succumb to the water before it surrenders us, I decide.

It launches itself skyward as the black creature gives chase.

Vanessa and I flail as we climb out of the water and onto the pebbly shore. I angle my eyes upward and begin to climb the steep slope as she grips my hand uncomfortably. My breathing has gone cold and erratic.

Howls erupt overhead, high above the canopy. For now, the monster has lost sight of us. My muscles ache as we creep up the slope.

A lost hiker is resting against a tree trunk and gaping at us as if we've just committed mass murder. He lowers his eyes as we pass. The Icarus strains overhead as the monster roars, singeing its wings with a bright orange flame.

I stammer while Vanessa bypasses a boulder, bumps against my hips, and climbs the steeper gradient under the green canopy. Spiders have spun webs on many branches to gather feasts of insects. Vanessa seems to whimper as we near the house.

Screams echo above us, mingled with the whine of heavy machinery and artillery fire. We climb onto the wooden porch of the house together, and black smoke wafts through the trees. The attacker has expended its wrath in the woods to stop us, but not being able to see us, it is a shot in the dark that misses and ignites the greenery instead. We will be lucky if the entire island doesn't burn black from the assault before we reach the closet.

I swing open the front door and spy a red arrow painted onto the floor. A woman cowers and weeps in the corner as if loss has reduced her to nothing more than a wispy vapor of tears. I cringe, release Vanessa's grip, and approach her.

Seconds pass as the stranger locks her gaze on me. The sad eyes seem to hypnotize me. Together, we levitate softly above the wooden floor as a chilly mist encircles us. The pale skin gives her away while her tears drop to the ground. The vapor swallows her whole and seeps away into the dark.

Vanessa impatiently tugs at my hand as I float toward her. She drags me into the open closet before my feet can touch the floor; the quiet howl of a whipping wind penetrates my ears before the cabin goes black.

I flip head over heels in the dark and land in a soft bed. Vanessa grips my hand and rolls over—we struggle out of the covers, cross the hall to the window, and overlook a lake of fire.

21

The Kingdom of Hephaestus

The horizon is mottled in hues of orange and red, the scattered rays of a sun that is clouded with smoke over a canopy that has been transformed into a raging inferno. Vanessa grips my hand as we overlook the chaos. The flames rise from the waters themselves, at least twenty feet high, and rapidly advance toward the lake houses and the hotel. The tourists are nowhere to be seen.

"God, it's hell," I gasp.

"Or the work of a certain god," she whispers.

To make sure I've heard her correctly, I turn my head slightly and gaze at her. The heat from the fire is radiating through the window and it suddenly feels hot enough to melt plastic. If this is real, the house will be incinerated within moments.

"Gotta get out of here."

"I know a portal," I say sharply, remembering my solitary walk through the woods after leaving Becky, when I'd taken the washers. "But we'll be crispy by the time we get there."

"Be a good time for something that flies," she breathes.

I can feel the heat of her breath on my stubbly cheek. At any moment she may kiss me. I almost don't dare to look at her, but a tearful sadness seems to float in her voice, catching me off guard. The moment our eyes meet, her grip on my hand tightens and her lips tenderly lock against mine.

"In case we die in this abyss," she says softly, the pitch in her voice rising toward the end of her sentence.

Trying to remember the architecture of the house, I wrack my brains. The boy must have emerged from somewhere. The home is a small one-story vacation cottage with up to three bedrooms. If I'm lucky, one of the closets can serve as a portal.

The living room is awash with the same orange glow that dominates the outdoors. I start in that direction, before turning on the balls of my feet and making for the boy's bedroom. When we reach an open door, we take a hard right. The bed is unmade, and a small pile of clothing is gathered at the foot of the bed. The closet sports a vented sliding barn door. Without thinking, I slide it open and gape in dismay as the oranges and yellows from outside bathe the well-organized shelves that hold clear plastic bins containing sundry toys.

I slide the door shut forcefully, letting it go as I turn. Vanessa is staring at something atop a bedside dresser next to a lamp. Following her eyes, I find myself staring at my own face in a picture frame. I look somewhat older, and my hair is longer. Visible flecks of grey pepper my sideburns and a joyful smile parts my lips.

"Handsome," she says. "Are you sure you aren't destined for her?"

Her question almost makes me choke. The flames atop the choppy waters seem to have abated, revealing reflective waves. I grasp her hand and make for the hallway. When we turn right, we face a bathroom door, which stands ajar. I push it open, scan the bathtub, and stand there puzzled.

She has taken this moment to study the hallway's ceiling. Tugging at my arm, she whispers something that my own thoughts seem to blur.

I spin and let my gaze rest on what she has seen, a black outline in the textured ceiling with a small metal handle positioned at the front edge.

"Go get at chair from the dining room," I say breathlessly. With every second wasted, the heat seems to increase, and the scent of smoke grows stronger.

She lets go of my hand and throws her palms up helplessly.

"Please, go get a chair," I amend.

"A woman's place is in the kitchen," she snaps sarcastically. By now she must regret kissing me, but I can still feel it, as the warmth has lingered on my lips.

She darts away and I study the dark outline of the rectangle. In a house like this, the only thing this could mean is attic access. An attic, I guess, may contain something resembling a portal, but our chances might be slim.

Moments after she disappears, I hear wood scraping against tile, the click of legs bumping over a metal separating strip, and then the shuffling of wood against carpet. She drags the chair backwards and positions it beneath the trap door.

I gaze upward, balance myself on the soft upholstery, and tug at the handle. Nothing happens. I yank harder and decide to angle my force toward the back of the door, should it simply be stuck in the jamb.

As I work it loose, the fixed wood begins to squeak. I groan as I pull at it and smoke wafts into my nostrils. At the end of the hall where Vanessa had just emerged, the reflection of the flames glows brighter.

The door finally comes loose as I gulp. The darkness above us seems perfectly capable of transporting us out of here. If we can find a way to wedge ourselves into the hole, we may escape this hell.

Understanding this, Vanessa kneels on the front of the chair and applies all her body weight. "Stand up on the back."

The chair rocks as I plant my right foot on the wooden, arched back-rest, yet when I pull myself up using the door as leverage, the chair remains steady. The last six feet will be challenging. I reach my hands into the dark, grasp a wooden jamb, and strain as I attempt to pull myself up. When my weight has eased off the chair, Vanessa stands and hoists my feet higher.

"Shit, hurry," she yells.

The darkness is emitting a dry heat that feels like an oven. In minutes we will be aflame. Groaning, I let my knee rest on the wooden door framing, pull my other leg in, and then struggle to turn myself so that I gaze down at her.

When I'm in the right position, I reach out my hand. A roar from outside suggests that the roof has finally caught fire. We may not even have thirty seconds to live. She wastes no time in climbing onto the back of the chair, using my hand to steady herself. Once her weight is balanced, I pull myself backwards and lift her high enough that she can wriggle herself into the void.

She pants as she inches higher. Again, her face bumps against mine and I back away. If our lips lock again, there will be no letting go while the flames devour us. Hephaestus will not relinquish his victims so easily.

"Damn it," she breathes, as if pain has erupted in her knees. I turn around and crawl into the darkness as the smell of smoke intensifies. The floorboards creak as I make my way toward what appears to be a framed, sheet-rocked cube in the center of the house. She scurries behind me, and I take a left. A loose nail in the floorboard painfully punctures my knee. I cringe and yelp while continuing to propel myself forward. When I round the corner, bright orange flames lick at my face.

The backside of the cube hosts a square opening, behind which a veil of darkness seems to undulate. I decide it is wide enough for us to sit hip-to-hip and fall in backwards. I waste no time positioning my body so that I'm facing the growing flames. She gazes into the dark over her shoulder as she presses her weight against my side, grasps my hand as tightly as ever, and leans back.

We fall at least fifty feet through the dark. Weightlessness makes my senses tingle as a single second seems to stretch for a full minute. I close my eyes and let my grip on her hand slacken. The jolt of hitting a soft landing bounces us upward.

Again, we lie in the same bed, staring at the ceiling.

I fling myself into a sitting position and peer around the darkened room. The decorations are slightly different, yet the same painting adorns the wall.

Vanessa understands where we have landed before I say anything. The blankets have loosened from our landing, yet they seem loose enough already to suggest that we aren't alone in the house.

Terror tickles the base of my spine.

She emerges from behind the wall adjacent to the kitchen, her face shrouded in dark, and her hair dangling wildly in front of her. She looks pale and forlorn, like a terrifying shot from a psychological horror movie. She is wielding a cast iron frying pan. I launch myself to a standing position in defense, but not before she swings the pan right for my face. I gasp as the metal collides with my cranium. Staggering backward, I gape into the hollow, bewildered eyes of what appears to be a wraith. She screeches as she lunges for me. Vanessa gathers enough momentum to propel herself into Becky's path. They lock arms together and fall to the floor as the pan clangs to the carpeted floor.

Gathering my senses from the shards of my shock, I draw in a breath and shout Becky's name.

"*Noo!*" she screeches. "*Noooo!*"

In the chaos, Becky has twirled several of Vanessa's braids around her fist. She straddles my companion, rears the fistful of hair backward as far as she can reach, and punches her dead in the face.

Vanessa squeals with the pain and tries to wrestle herself free, but Becky does not relinquish her braids.

"Becky! Don't. It's me, Kerry."

"You bitch!" Becky ignores me and smashes her fist into Vanessa's face again. Vanessa lets out a squeak of pain as she looks at me through swollen eyes.

Still, she is not ready to give up: as Becky rears back for another strike, Vanessa grabs her wrist and instinctively twists it as a concentrated sneer overcomes her lips. Rage boils in her eyes as she twists Becky's forearm.

Vanessa grips the frying pan now lying at her waist by curling the fingers of her left hand around the handle. If she gets the correct angle, she can put Becky out for good.

"Who are you?" she yells.

"Vanessa, no!"

Too late. The metal clunks heavily against Becky's scalp and she collapses with a look of enraged horror pulsing through her eyes.

Vanessa is panting as I reach out my hands and pull Becky upright. She twitches wildly as I hold her body in my arms.

"She was going to kill me," Vanessa breathes heavily.

"Becky?"

"Kerry, we have to leave her."

I speak slowly and softly, without looking up at Vanessa. "I'm not going anywhere." I gather my wife's wet hair with my fingers, push it behind her ear, and bend my neck downward to kiss her forehead.

She lies sleepily in my arms for several minutes while I try to formulate a haphazard plan. Still, without knowing *when* we are I can barely get a single step of a strategy into my head. The future has sealed itself off from the present, and anticipation is impossible beyond a few seconds.

"Kerry?"

I don't bother to glance at the woman who has just pulverized my wife with a frying pan.

"I'm sorry, I didn't mean to—"

"Callisto," I say, lowering my voice.

"Please don't call me that."

My mind wanders as I graze my fingers softly against Becky's pale face. The moments seem to pass faster and faster into history, where demons were pressing against Sarah's perfect face. Before I understand the emotions that swirl within my own brain, a tear forms at the corner of my eye.

Vanessa kicks away the frying pan and grimaces as she scoots across the floor toward me.

I eye Becky's damaged, bruised scalp. Fear torpedoes inside me. She may die in my arms. This is my future wife, a beautiful woman who has reacted in terror at her home being invaded by two strangers from the past.

Trying to remember everything that has just transpired, I breathe slowly. The memory of flames and smoke seems to gather into a soup of dark gray and orange, glowing like viscous lava. It is already beginning to fade away.

I study the colorful painting on the wall, which depicts a bulbous vase with cutoff sunflowers, interspersed with lilies and roses. The combination is eye-catching yet serene. Again, I well up.

In the hall, sniffing and whimpering invades the silence.

Vanessa turns her head to encounter the stranger. In the dark I cannot see him, because he lingers beyond the door against the wall. I cannot call out to him because I do not know his name.

"It's okay, son," I say, trying to inject strength into my voice. "She's going to be okay. Come in here."

"You—you tried to kill her."

"You don't understand," I say, with sorrow dripping through my voice.

He emerges from around the corner. Terror has whittled his emotions so thinly that he looks primal. His hair is a mangled mess, and tears shine on his cheeks. He stands about four feet tall and is wearing baggy pajamas that drown his bare feet. I recognize them as a pair of pajamas I had worn as a child, yet I have not seen them in so many years. The futuristic *Star Wars* spacecraft swirl in a vortex of black, as green blaster bolts zip through the vacuum. It somehow evokes a smile, even amidst the chaos. I cannot place how he got the pajamas, but he looks great in them.

As I stare on, Becky wedges her eyes open, and realizing that I am holding her tight, she struggles in my grasp.

Vanessa sits upright as if to defend herself, yet I let Becky get away. She hurries to free herself from me, staggers to her feet, and rushes to the boy's aid.

For the briefest moment, her fear sparks against mine, evoking another pang of regret. I can only watch as she wraps her arms around our son and wipes away his tears. Agony crushes my soul when I look back up at the painting. Had it been there the last time I had fallen into this bed?

"Get the hell out of our house, Kerry," Becky grates. "You left us. Do it again."

"I—what?"

She trembles as if with rage. "Take your new girlfriend and get the hell out before I call the cops."

"Becky, I'm sorry."

She sniffs, curls her arms around the boy, and speaks sharply. "You never are."

22

Realm of the Naiads

Becky trembles before me. The moonlit glow from the window across the hall bathes the bedroom in a pale blue haze. Tears are streaming down her face as she attempts to comfort the child. His empathy is palpable, even though he is looking on with confusion. He blinks twice, wraps his arms around his mother, and continues to gaze at me.

"We gotta go," Vanessa says, tapping her wrist as if to remind me of the time.

Wherever we are, time seems unimportant, yet if the monsters have successfully followed us to other dimensions, they will surely track us to this lake. I don't know how many times the portal in the attic will work, or if it will land us back in the bed every time, but the most promising means of escape would be the recess in the rock. It seems as if it has been eons since I first found it, and stumbling on it a second time would require the kind of luck that has never been on my side.

I shrug subtly at Vanessa, who gently rolls her eyes and leans back against the foot of the bed.

"Becky," I whisper.

She ignores me, but the boy suddenly looks comforted and loosens his grip on Becky's shoulders.

I rise to my feet and approach him. He flinches when I take my first step but doesn't move. Taking in this signal, I stop, glance at Vanessa, and drop to one knee. I spread my arms as if to welcome him in an embrace, but when he still doesn't move, I let my arms slacken.

"Everything's going to be okay, son," I say, locking my eyes upon his with sincerity. Lying with such ease is not a product of my normal personality, and his reaction is jarring.

A sudden, single nod amidst Becky's sobs ensures me that I have earned his trust. Realizing that I have never even heard my son's name, I devise a simple solution that could have disastrous consequences.

Again, I carefully rise to my feet, pace toward them, and rest my hand on his shoulder.

He squeezes out a single tear and lets his shoulders rise warmly against my palm as he inhales.

I swallow and then lower my voice to create a somber tone with the expectation that the reaction will be muted. "What's your name?"

His head flinches and he darts his eyes to Becky and back before attempting to pull away from me.

Becky moans in a deep sob, picks up her son, and carries him down the hall. She is going to call the police. If they catch me here with Vanessa, we will be locked up in separate cells until the monsters return to devour this entire dimension and we will both cease to exist.

"Becky, wait!" I shout.

"Get out!" she screams.

"I want to know his name," I say, without realizing that I'm shaking with a cold fury.

Vanessa follows me into the hall and stops to gaze out the window.

Trailing behind Becky and my son, I sigh with sorrow pulsing through my veins. In this moment, nothing else seems to matter. My heart beats irregularly and the chills race through my veins.

"Daddy, you already know my name is Ian."

"Ian, come back and give me a hug. I miss you."

These words fall on deaf ears.

From the hall, Vanessa sounds more worried than she has the entire time. "We might want to … you know, take her advice."

When I glance back at her, she remains fixed in place, staring out the window as if in terror. The house is still alight with the blue glow, suggesting that the fire has not returned. I raise my palms and remember the welded washers I still carry in my pocket. The last time I reached for them, I had been showing them to the reverend before his church and all the parishioners were eaten whole by the Shade.

I reach into my jeans pocket, wrap my fingers around the cool steel, and slowly approach the kitchen table, where Becky is shakily dialing the phone. When I have her attention, I place the keepsake on the table to remind her of that old dimension where I'd met her for the first time and taken it.

"For old time's sake," I say, breathing lightly.

A tear drops to the table and splashes next to my homemade trinket. The indication that she remembers it at all suggests that all these dimensions in which we have interacted are somehow connected through time or destiny. I swallow and make the mistake of glancing up at Vanessa, who has covered her mouth with her palms and is still gazing out the window.

Becky finishes dialing the police as I return to Vanessa's side.

"What?" I say impatiently.

She says nothing. Fear boils up in her expression, causing me to peer out the window to my right. My reaction doesn't match hers, but terror still spikes within me. The lake is boiling with millions of reflective bubbles, splashing violently as the moonlight dims.

"Get to the attic," I say, but before I can finish the words, slender figures begin to emerge one by one, and then by the hundreds.

Bodies rise out of the waters like flesh-hungry zombies, sloshing naked toward the shore. An army of women splashes toward the beach, even as more and more burst out of the bubbling water. They march toward the house as a single unit, thousands strong, dripping wet. From this far away I cannot see their expressions, but their veins seem to burn blue against the dimming moonlight.

The Shade cannot be far behind them. It has awakened them from a deep slumber and sent them to bring us down and drown us in their home.

"Jesus," I breathe.

Instead of turning towards the end of the hall where we'd climbed into the attic, Vanessa sprints in the other direction, right towards Becky, who has begun speaking into the phone. If I leave her and Ian alone with those women, they will not be spared.

I grasp Becky by the shoulders, rushing to the front door as she shouts into the phone line. If we're lucky, we won't be here when the police arrive. Instead, they will arrive to a turbulent lake as the thousands of angry women return to their watery abode.

"He's kidnapping me!" Becky screeches.

"Trying to save your life!"

She drops the confusion, grasps Ian's hand as tightly as she can and struggles as I rush out the front door with Vanessa's aid.

Vanessa takes Ian's other hand as we assemble on the porch.

The women shriek in unison, streaming over the beach and closing in on us. Together, we sprint. Becky still struggles, until she lays eyes on the women.

Her jaw drops and the much-needed terror kicks in. Before long, the Shade will be here to devour it all. Will it eat the warriors it has sent to drown us?

I have no intention of seeing the answer play out before my eyes. My heart palpitates as we turn onto the road. If we simply follow the pavement, the demons of the deep will achieve the correct angle on us and drag us into the lake. Making this calculation is painful; if we are to have any hope of escaping, we must level the playing field by making them break ranks and battle through the forest with us. That tactic will surely mitigate their numbers advantage.

The shrieks intensify as we bound across the road. Vanessa has taken to virtually carrying Ian, but Becky matches my pace. I don't dare to release her hand. Subjecting her to time travel seems unwise, but somehow I love her, and her fate will be no different if Vanessa and I just leave her to deal with the women alone.

The thousands of voices echo in the night. Behind us, still more women splash out of the water. My blood chills and the moonlight is nearly extinguished. I can feel the heat of Becky's breath as I lead her into the woods, jump across the roadside ditch, and stumble over a broken tree branch, which is lying next to its parent tree still attached by splinters of white wood and bark.

"Come on, Ian," Vanessa shouts. "We can make it."

"Callisto, we can use your magic," I yell.

"I don't have any magic, Kerry. I'm mortal."

"You're ... how?"

"No time to explain," she says, swinging Ian over the branch and darting into the shadows with us.

The army has already advanced up to the road. They rage behind us, scurrying like thousands of mice, and darting in and out of one another's paths. Their arms reach out behind us as they run, impossibly fast. We have no hope of reaching the recess in the rock at the rate they are gaining. An ally must come to our aid, from somewhere, but the forest is eerily silent.

We struggle through the undergrowth, and the women begin to climb up over each other and bounce off the trees like the viscous waves of a rising tide. They trip on the roots and advance on us, screaming into the night like a tempest of a thousand screeching voices, rushing through the trees.

Naked limbs seem to gather into a flailing ball that rolls inevitably toward us. I shove Becky forward as sharp fingernails begin to claw at my back. Pain leaps through my skin and hundreds of hands hold me aloft. I float on dainty hands as I glance sideways at Vanessa, who is still clinging to Ian while attempting to battle the women of the deep.

They have begun to carry me back down the slope to the waters. Becky disappears behind a hundred wet bodies, and I scream helplessly. The dark seems to pulse with an eerie energy as they carry me away, approach the road, and separate me from the sight of Becky, Ian, and Vanessa.

The women shriek and pause at the roadside as if spooked.

Agony floods through my soul; it can only mean one thing.

The women assemble in masses, crawl over one another, and form a wave of human bodies that ebbs spectacularly towards the refuge of the waters. In the process of rolling away, one of them loses her grip.

I use this moment of sudden freedom to fight my way loose, despite sharp fingernails clawing at my legs and forearms, tearing my clothing, and drawing blood. A fiery surge of pain shoots adrenaline through my veins to battle it. In a rage, I kick at dozens of hands that attempt to grasp at my legs.

They heave me aloft, higher and higher until I am at least twenty feet above the surface of the road. They cover the distance with such alarming speed that if I do manage to free myself, I will be near the beach when I hit the ground.

Screaming into a shroud of blackness, I glance into the canopy, which along the hilltop has begun to be invaded by a sucking storm of dark.

"Becky!" I scream, punching a woman in the face.

Her eyes seem to roll back in her sockets as another wave of adrenaline surges through me.

She squeals in vicious agony. More hands grab at me, but the pressure has ebbed, and the bodies have begun to thin out as the women teem back into the waters to flee the Shade. When I hit the grass adjacent to the sand, at least eight women begin to claw at my ankles. I kick them away, inching up the slope until few enough fingernails claw at me that I can stagger to my feet.

The success is short-lived. The women scream and splash back into the water without me. On the horizon, the Shade is eating away at the trees, which vanish one by one into a cloud of expanding coal dust.

The only direction I can go is directly toward it. The squeals dissipate and the water splashes behind me with the thunder of crashing waves. Breathing deeply, I sprint up to the road, dart across it and disappear into the trees, discovering the three of them breathlessly clinging to a fallen tree branch. Becky's clothes are torn and her hair, which had been sleek and wet, has dried into an unkempt mop of tangled strands caked with sweat and dirt.

Ian whimpers as I scoop him up. Vanessa lets me lead the way up the slope. Trying to remember how far away it is, I sprint through the trees as vines attempt to tangle my feet. Running faster, I conclude that the trees' roots have come loose to flee the coming beast, which bears down on us from the ridgeline.

"I thought they had you," Vanessa shouts.

"They did, but they were just afraid enough to allow me to fight my way out of it."

"Afraid of what?"

The trees groan. In the distance, they begin to break, snapping off at the trunks to be towed into the black. My rage allows me to run faster than I thought possible while carrying a sixty-pound kid on my shoulders.

Becky appears almost dumbfounded, but she runs behind us as more trees snap in the distance. The cold has transformed into a sudden heat that seems to be propelling me forward. I dodge a thicket of low-hanging branches, hurl myself through spider webs, and feel the roots scurrying beneath the soil. Some of the fallen leaves and loose vegetation begin to vibrate before being lifted into dozens of tight cyclones that whip painfully against my bare calves.

Becky and Vanessa scream in unison as an uprooted tree whizzes right past their faces. In no time we will all be scooped up into the violent abyss.

It closes in. In the distance, I begin to make out the rocks; sprinting in that direction seems easier when the wind is literally sucking us that way. It lifts us off our feet before dropping us a few precious steps closer to the rocks.

The square of black seems to loom hazily in front of us as we are swept off our feet once again. We crash through heavy tree branches as a lull in the storm deposits us at the base of the rocks. I waste no time in shoving Becky through the portal. She vanishes into fog as I lift Ian off my shoulders.

He struggles mightily as I shove him into the portal.

"Daddy, *no!*"

"We're out of time," Vanessa wails as a wall of blackness seems to huddle over us, hundreds of feet high. But then it wobbles suddenly as a bright light erupts behind us. It has come to our aid at the last possible second, wielding a light so powerful that the Shade cannot devour it. Instead, it waits patiently as it wavers like an undulating cloud of soot. Vanessa scoots into the portal and vanishes as is I turn around to admire the source of the light.

It is blinding, creating an illusion that I am alone in a landscape of white, where I know someone waits for me, but I cannot see her.

She steps forward and the light seems to burst behind her as an eternity of white space. Coming toward me, her blonde hair flows behind her in the wind as her blue and white dress flaps against her ankles.

"It's ... it's you," I whimper.

She takes one more step and rests both her hands on my shoulders. "Take this gift. I trust you know how to use it."

Though she holds nothing in her hands, I somehow understand what she is talking about. My body begins to emit whiteness as I stand there, with the Shade fleeing behind me as the light pierces it.

"Let it go," she says, her voice wavering as though a ghost were stealing her voice and carrying it away to the lake.

"Glow?" I say, understanding that my ears have heard it wrong.

"It is a powerful weapon if used for the right purposes. I go now to my own downfall, having passed my father's most secret possession to you. Use it well."

In a spark of clarity, I remember her name: Ariadne. The Minotaur appears out of the blinding white behind her, pauses by her side, and gazes at me through its black eyes.

"Goodbye, Kerry," she says serenely. "Until we meet again."

Her voice flows away like water as she lets her own light obscure and cover her. Under the weight of my own breath and the pain stabbing at my extremities, I step backwards as the winds begin to pick up once more.

The light begins to drain away, and the Shade reacts by again swooping down the hillside to devour me. Confused and terrified, I hurry toward the rocks, step inside the square of black, and watch the lakeside forest vanish into swirls of green and black. The red star glows hotter and nearer this time as I freefall through the emptiness of space.

Gravity tugs at my feet and I descend. The star streaks away, and I expect my feet to collide with pavement amidst the sounds of car horns and rushing tires grinding against the grid of urban streets.

Instead, the landing is soft. I squeeze my eyes open to adjust them to the light. Three towering figures stand over me like watchful sentinels. In a flash, my blood runs cold.

23

Ruins of Aether

Shuffling backwards as fast as my feet can move me while I'm still sitting, I allow my instinct to protect Becky and Ian. They are somehow standing behind me, transfixed at the tall stone structures that prod the cloudless sky amidst a cool, oceanic breeze.

The figures gaze onward, upon the high bluff with the yellow grass grains flapping lazily at their feet. One has his arm outstretched, as if pointing to something important beyond the blue horizon. The third, standing slightly taller and of more muscular build, wields a pitchfork-like object and directs his eyes downward to the rocky shores some fifty feet below us. This island, if it is an island, must exist nowhere on earth, suggesting we have wandered into another dimension entirely.

By now I can no longer track how far we've gone into time. Different jumps and locations have already blurred together like the frayed edges of aging dreams.

"Is this Easter Island?" I stammer.

Vanessa has taken to studying the sentinels, cautiously stepping around their feet and grazing the hems of their stone robes with an outstretched hand. At least thirty feet above her, the guards pay no attention.

"Don't think so," she says. "They wouldn't replace *Maori* with Greek gods, no matter how strong the urge. We're somewhere else, possibly on the shores of Greece, and far enough back that they haven't toppled."

"Which means we've got to get moving," I groan, struggling to my feet.

Ian and Becky have gone eerily silent. The pain still slices at my ankles and calves, but it is nothing compared to the torture my heart feels for subjecting them to something they're not familiar with.

Being in the past I have found to be particularly perilous. Memories of past events become an unstable future. Stay long enough, and they all get wiped away and you forget how you got there in the first place, having no idea how to get back to what you call home.

"We're in trouble," I say, looking left and right before making the decision to step towards the cliff.

"No," Vanessa says. "We got here, and that means there's a way out."

"Greek gods?" Becky's voice has grown somewhat stable, yet she is droning as if her mind can no longer assign meaning to the sequence of past events. She lowers her face to the grass as I turn to face her. Seeing Ian's pained expression as he clings to his mother's dangling wrist is almost too much for me to bear. It prods painfully at my heart and contorts my face into something I cannot recognize.

"Dionysus, Poseidon, and Aether," Vanessa says, at once admiring the monoliths and lowering her face to avoid stepping on Aether's toes.

I ignore her and gaze helplessly at Becky. She has rearranged her face from rage and terror to something resembling rapt interest. She barely flinches her eyebrows as her bangs brush against her temples in the breeze, but for now, the emotion no longer mars the surface. All at once, she looks pleasant and as beautiful as I remember her.

"I don't know if I can explain it all," I say, careful not to let my eye contact linger for too long, should her anger return.

"Maybe best if you didn't," Vanessa quips.

Was she joking? If we don't get out of here fast, her memory will be toast and she will become a resident of whatever realm we wander into next. Perhaps if I fill her in, she will afford me greater trust.

Then again, in some future dimensional timeline, I left Becky and my son. I don't want to know where I went, but if she doesn't tell me, how will I be able to avoid making that choice when what I regard as my present tense catches up to that future?

"Tell me," Becky demands.

I sigh. Going against Vanessa's advice seems foolish, but I speak carefully without embellishing the how and the why, with which I still struggle.

"The black rectangle in the rock was a gateway."

"Seems patently obvious," she agrees, narrowing her eyes and kicking at a rock in front of Ian's feet, "but go on."

"It would seem that we're in the past. We have jumped to a different dimension, where none of us has ever been."

"At least it's light," Vanessa says, casting her eyes upward at Aether.

"Light," I repeat. "After you all went through the portal, I stayed long enough to interact with Ariadne and the Minotaur. She said she was giving me a gift, something to fight the Shade with. It repelled it."

"Outstanding," Vanessa breathes sarcastically. "How does it work against winged monsters?"

I shrug.

"M—Monsters?" Ian shudders.

"Not here, if we don't stay too long, but they will know how to find us."

"The black beast may not be on the same team as the Shade," Vanessa observes. "If we can get it to help fight the Shade—"

"It won't work," I argue. "There's only one thing that can beat something controlled by Erebus."

"Erebus?" Vanessa looks horrified. Her eyes widen as she slings her dirty braids behind her shoulder and steps away from the statues. "Forgive the expression, but oh God."

"I'm sorry," Becky says, "but I don't follow."

"You're going to have to roll with it, unless we have a week and a half to explain everything to you."

"Your girlfriend doesn't even understand."

"Not a girlfriend. Vanessa's a ... what? You seem to let slip that you're mortal, as though your two-thousand-year-long life is somehow threatened."

"I have not lived for two thousand years," she corrects me. "You didn't listen when I told you my backstory. Zeus sent me into the stars, where I was to live in eternity. You can still see my shape at night under the right conditions, but for all his deception, he isn't that smart.

"Some people can be ... reincarnated into flesh and blood if we conquer something in the stars. In my case, it was Arcas, sometimes called Bootes, or the minor bear."

"Shit, what?"

"He was my son. In the stars, I watched over him, gave him a home. Someone out there thought that was worth a reward. Today I'm as frail as anyone else, and when I die that will be the final chapter of Callisto."

"Forgot to mention it?"

"Wasn't relevant at the time," she excuses herself.

This exchange does not appear to have convinced Becky. She contorts her expression to one of deep confusion when I retrain my gaze on her, and her body has taken a defensive posture should either of us attack her.

"We're short on time," I say, trying not to callously dismiss her. "If we don't find that portal, we're going to be stuck here forever."

"We won't," Vanessa says. "I've been back farther."

"How far?"

She shrugs and allows her gaze to pierce me.

"To the beginning."

"The beginning, as in Adam and Eve?" Becky folds her left hand under her chin and appears to be considering something while she clutches Ian's hand.

"The beginning for me," Vanessa corrects. "Or, more accurately, when Arcas was born."

"You don't believe in Adam and Eve, do you? Maybe the story was always highly subject to interpretation, but that's still true, and you standing here claiming to be some kind of Greek Goddess isn't going to convince me otherwise. You know it too, Kerry, or at least you used to."

"I don't know what I believe," I say. "For now, I'd be good with figuring out which reality is the real one for me and going from there. We'll drop you off at yours on the way there."

"I don't believe any of this," Becky says, flinching. "I don't know you anymore, Kerry. It's over for us."

"It might be just the beginning," I suggest.

"Bring us back to the cabin and get the hell out of my life," she says, suppressing a greater rage. "We don't need you."

"We'll have to figure that out," I say, nodding between syllables.

Vanessa studies us and waits. "Let's get a move on before your memory disappears."

I shrug silently and approach what seems to be a cliff overlooking the rough waters. The ground itself seems to sway gently as I tread in that direction. A rocky outcrop juts out into the waters as a point of crumbled stone, about fifty feet down. A pair of seabirds are basking on the highest point of the rocks, dodging the spray from a crashing wave. Their wings flutter as they wait, unaware that they are sharing the island with at least four humans.

The shadowy portions at the bases of the rocks seem to cut vague geometric shapes out of the gray surroundings, but nothing that would obviously suggest a portal.

I step closer as Vanessa appears at my side, searching carefully in a different direction along the broken coastline.

Green mosses and lichens grow on the rocks closer to the water, but this high up, they exist in tiny, isolated colonies on vertical stacks of volcanic rock. This island is heavily eroded; any portal closer to the waves would likely have collapsed generations ago.

What appears to be a smooth beach occupies an alcove between two heaps of rock, at the end of which grows a lively crop of green and yellow grass that seems to be thriving in the shade. Getting down there would require a careful descent of the rock face, and if we then failed to discover the gateway, climbing back up would take longer than advisable, not to mention be fraught with danger.

Vanessa seems to be silently following my train of thought. She breaks her concentration on the rocks below and turns around to face the rounded hilltop behind the statues. I study her for a moment before I continue to scan the ocean below. From this point of view, another island pokes above the waves far in the distance, at least sixty miles away. Dionysus appears to be pointing at it, lending credence to the idea that the landscape is of some importance, however tangential. It would take us months to get there if we had to build a boat.

Becky and Ian follow Vanessa to what seems to be a ridge behind me. They have caught sight of something interesting, for Becky has shielded her eyes from the sun with her hand by placing it against her brow as if in salute. Vanessa gestures at something and nods as the wind whips past my ear. Instead of electing to climb down to the beach and join the birds, I choose to keep Vanessa company.

The summit sweeps away in a broad field of rolling hills, miles across. In the distance, toward another ridgeline, a small knot of dark green trees sways with the wind. Vanessa points her feet in that direction and waits for me to settle at her side.

"See the dead trees there? By the rocks?"

A mile away, the sweeping grassland gives way to a stray jumble of rocks, interspersed with tufts of yellow grass. The trees have rotted and fallen over the ages, forming a trapezoidal shadow that could be nothing or everything. Between the logs more grasses grow, yet the shadow is perplexingly dark. There must be a deeper recess there, one which would allow that kind of shadow to form at the foot of the fallen trees.

"What do you think?"

I study the horizon for far longer than I should, swallow, and relent. "Looks like it's your way or no way."

"Becky, Ian, you ready for a hike?"

"Daddy, are the monsters coming back?"

I rest my hand on his shoulder as we embark on the trek, first descending a shallow hill. The wind seems to pick up as we sink towards the valley. Another, shorter hill rises between us and the dead trees.

"So that will take us to the lake?" Becky asks, seemingly filled with hope. Still, her expression is all wrong. The confusion has given her trust issues, but her only option is to follow Vanessa and me on the journey.

"Maybe," I say, not wanting to lend false hope. "At least it's a start."

"I'm pressing charges when I get home," Becky threatens. "Think long and hard about that before interrupting our lives again."

"Becky—"

"I'm not talking to you anymore, Kerry. Just get us home."

I already know that if we do find a portal, it will not transport us back to the lake—instead, it will land us in another dimension, which will allow us to access another, and then another. Where will it possibly end? The only answer to that would be wherever destiny takes us, which could figuratively be through hell and back.

Vanessa trudges on more hopefully than I do. She draws her dirty braids along her scalp toward her shoulders as she steps over loose stones caught in knots of tall grass. The sun arcs higher into the sky as we walk, suggesting morning. It will take at least a half hour to arrive at our destination, if the monsters don't have other ideas, but for now they stay away.

I don't dare speak to Becky on the journey. Instead, I attempt to make small talk with my son. Does he play sports, have many friends, enjoy school? Is he into science and discovery? I know virtually nothing about him. Thinking about that causes a deep ache to throb somewhere in my heart.

When we crest the second hill, we pause to gauge our progress. Three-quarters of the way there, and the shadow below the dead trees has shifted from a rough trapezoid to an oblong circle that could be the mouth of a cave.

Every few steps, I glance up at the changing skyline. The trees at the far ridge appear to be the edge of a thriving forest made up of several arboreal species that inhabit the Mediterranean coast.

After another ten minutes, we arrive at the trees. The hole is broad and dark, and it seems to poke into a black void beneath the stones. If it is a portal and we are not instantly transported when stepping into the shadow, it will require a dangerous climb over a steep, shifting slope of shattered stone. No grass pokes up between the rocks. I offer to test the terrain ahead of Vanessa and Becky, who has no choice but to trust us.

The gravel slides a little under my weight but seems sturdy enough for the rest of them. Vanessa aids Becky in her descent as she tightly grips Ian's hand. After twenty feet or so, a cold blast of air flows out of the cavern as we descend.

I land on harder rock, reach into the darkness, and observe a faint rectangle in the gloomy distance. The trek looks like it could take another twenty minutes, but the distance disappears in darkness.

A guttural roar erupts within the den as I snake my way through piles of boulders, and shiver.

Looking back, I allow dread to wind its way through my heart, as the others have vanished. I am alone, reaching for a black square that I may never touch.

The roar intensifies just as a spinning sensation overtakes me. Terror envelops me as I tumble through a rotten abyss encrusted with blinking stars and collapse onto a stone floor. A dark ceiling arches high overhead.

"Vanessa? Becky?"

No answer. If I have abandoned them to the Shade or the winged black monster, I will never forgive myself.

Shaking in the cold, I step forward inch by inch until a false orange light filters through the den. The ceiling must be half a mile up, if one even exists.

"Shhh, it's okay, honey," I hear someone say behind me.

Becky's voice offers me a sense of relief, but it vanishes when my gaze falls on Vanessa's face. Her eyes are wide, and her braids have come loose, allowing frizzly little strands to poke out in every direction. It makes her appear older and more hardened, but there is no mistaking the ashen look of petrification as she breathes lightly. The dark envelops us as we stare headlong into the perfect hell—a catacomb a mile deep that is seemingly endless.

24

The Lair of Erebus

Becky and Ian stand wide-eyed and eerily silent, as if they've just seen an indescribable horror so deep it has rendered them speechless. Vanessa grabs my hand and tugs me onward, or the only direction that can be described as onward—deeper into the endless chasm. Her face somehow reflects the darkness, as if it has burrowed so deeply into her spirit that it has become part of her.

"Gotta get moving," she says quietly.

"Christ, what did you just see?"

She doesn't answer for what feels like ten agonizing minutes. In the interim, she leads me deeper into the void, eventually letting go of my hand. The floor supports no vegetation and little life, unless you count a million different types of microbes and possibly sparse patches of lichen. Instead, it is littered with loose, rough-edged stones as far as the eye can see. The 'horizon' may either be the limits of a dense, amber smog, or the very walls of the cavern themselves.

I'd imagined this dimension to be full of bats, but the ceiling is so high that I can make out no details. I dodge a thick cluster of rocks and gaze up into the hazy distance. This chamber should be utterly dark, I reason, but there is enough red-orange light to clearly illumine our path, as if countless hidden lanterns are casting a diffuse light in all directions.

My breathing intensifies when we ascend a gentle rise in the floor, which doesn't appear to have a terminus. The slope is steep enough to allow for flowing water, but there is none visible. The silence between the four of us is so deep and torturous that if water did exist nearby, I should be able to hear it. There is no gurgling of a stream, no dribbling against loose rocks, and no plipping of drops from the ceiling. We have covered plenty of distance, enough to require hydrating, and that might also serve to clear our minds. Then again, in a tunnel like this, no water could be reasonably safe for consumption. We will have to find another way out, and soon, because if my intuition is correct, this tomb may seal us in for God knows how long.

No one dares speak, but then Ian begins to complain about something under his breath, and it doesn't sound like "Mom, I'm hungry," or, "I have to go to the bathroom." When I glance back, Becky is drawing him tightly against her side and squeezing his shoulders against her waist.

Her face appears to match the damage of what she's just seen, but she doesn't carry it any better than Vanessa has. The minutes seem to tick on by to eternity until I hear a dull, echoing whine coming from somewhere ahead, far from any wall. It drones for a few seconds and lowers to a nasal whisper before dissipating completely. At our right-hand side, a jumble of heavy boulders marks what seems to be a trail—a winding clearance of rocks that hugs a tunnel wall.

For at least ten minutes, we follow this trail upslope, towards what looks like a distant ridgeline. Ian's complaints grow louder, but no less un-intelligible. Vanessa has not spoken for so long that my fear intensifies with every step.

"God, where the hell are we?" I ask, hoping to spark at least some somber conversation.

Vanessa seems to sniff. "Might not be relevant. I have an idea but hope I'm wrong." Her voice seems to undulate and crackle with terror. She swallows another thought and steps forward.

Behind me, a sound like wood or plaster scrapes across the floor and rolls to a halt. No rock could have made that sound. Becky has fallen to the ground, petrified, and I turn to confront her. She is staring in horror at what she's just kicked, a human wrist bone, disconnected from the rest of the skeleton.

I gasp when I study it. Shorter than mine, it might compare in length to Ian's wrist and is similarly slender. Not a good sign.

And then another omen: the scattered rocks in the distance have become a veritable graveyard of various body parts, all missing the rest of their skeletons. This catacomb may contain thousands of dead bodies.

I gulp, sidestep a rock, and quicken my pace while trying not to think about it. Vanessa matches my gait, and no one dares to speak for several more minutes. With every step, the scattered bones become denser. In the distance, about twenty feet off the path, a full ribcage, possibly with an associated pelvis, occupies the center of a pile of splintered bones. Vanessa keeps by my side and casts her eyes upward, where the ridge seems to carve a straight line across the cave itself.

The silence seems to deepen, and then there is movement, to my right. I have no time to swing my head in that direction before a bony hand grasps my ankle. Ice water pours through my veins, and I let out a helpless cry. Even with my earliest perception, this is no skeleton. Out of the darkness crawls the hunched figure of an emaciated man. His corduroy jeans and flannel shirt are tattered at the seams, allowing tangles of loose threads to dangle in the still, dry air.

Before trying to arise to a standing position, he lets out a raspy yawn and tilts his head downward as if to pray.

"Who are you?" I ask. "Where are we?"

"Th—the One," he moans, lifting his head off the floor and struggling upright.

The stranger stretches his back and seems to peer towards the ceiling. To get a feel of his character, I level my head and gaze into his eyes. Or at least I would if he had any. It is like they have been sucked out of his skull, leaving enormous, blackened holes encrusted with sagging skin and hundreds of rough-edged hairs.

Becky has clearly come to the same gruesome conclusion before I can even move my lips. She whimpers and looks away, backing herself toward the rocks with Ian clutched under her arm. He doesn't even dare to look at the man.

I take one step backward. If he could see me, he might be offended, but then again, how had he known we were here?

"The One?" I utter listlessly. "What are you talking about?"

"Not one for nuance, are you?" the man rasps. "Would call that 'typical,' but you know there's no such thing.... God, you're mortal!"

I shudder. "And you are?"

"They used to call me Chuck." His voice echoes dryly, as if bone dust is clogging his vocal cords. "But no one here calls anyone anything; we're all just servants. Some of us alive, some of us dead, others somewhere in between."

He frames his face with slender fingers as his last sentence clatters to a close. I look upon him with ruined disgust as chills race up and down my spine, so quickly that the changing of perceived temperatures might cause condensation to form on my neck.

"You're servants of 'The One'?"

"D—Did I st-utter?"

Vanessa probes him somberly by stepping forward, glancing at the scattered bones, and then boring into his eye sockets with a calculated stare. "Do the Shades come down here?"

"Sh—ades," he ponders. "Some of us call them the Vapor Spirits, collected dead that gather more servants of The One. On—Once you become his, it becomes your destiny. There is no other you, no other reality, just him.... All knowing."

Vanessa nods encouragingly.

I roll my eyes at his rough grasp of the English language. He's as well-spoken as anyone I've ever met, yet his raspy, stunted delivery makes him sound less than intelligent. "They collected you."

"Me? And every—everyone else 'down' here, as you put it."

"This is down," I wager.

At least it is for us, because we came from above, where the sweeping grasslands reflect a blinding sun as the Gods stand watch over the island. Others swallowed by the Shades would no doubt have a different perception.

"And 'The One,'" Vanessa guesses, "Is Erebus?"

"It ... has a name?"

"Holy shit."

"Got a feel you won't like what you—you're about to see, friend. Don't—take it personal. You all seem like fine people. 'Cept no mortal has ever ventured here. This place—it tears you apart piece by piece until you are nothing. Just—assemblies of loose body parts, stitched together enough that you can serve until time does that to you." He points at the ribcage and the pelvis. "Goodbye, Howard."

"There's gotta be a way out," I say.

"N—Not a chance."

"Tell us more," Vanessa demands.

But the stranger shakes his head and turns it in every direction, 'looking' all around at the dusty piles of bones, some caked with dusty cobwebs, others mashed into stones like fossils built into chunky pillars of volcanic rock.

In the distance, a chorus of howls erupts, followed by a fierce, echoing bellow filled with the sounds of everything, all at once. Screeching tires, clacking keyboards, droning engines, and the cruel chatter of a thousand souls.

We all freeze to the spot, wincing. And then there are wings: swooping higher and higher in the abyss, soaring overhead like an enforcer of death. Vanessa grips my hand.

"R—Run!" the stranger rasps.

But it's too late; the beast arcs higher into the cavern. Even from a half a mile away, it locks onto us, zeroing in with its hundred red, serpentine eyes.

Ian screams, his scratchy voice clawing into the darkness overhead.

The monster hears him. It lurches toward us, gliding. And behind it, in tow, the sludgy fog gathers into a towering figure of vapor five hundred feet tall. It leans toward us, following behind the monster and morphing its shapes as it goes. Now that it has locked onto us, we have no escape. We are sealed in.

I reach deep down for the only hope that still lurks within me. Ariadne's voice echoes in my skull like a wispy memory. Reaching for it gives me power. Focusing as hard as I can, I tense my muscles and feel my heart painfully screech to a halt. My fingers begin to glow as the beast hurtles toward us at breathtaking speed.

My glow sparks, flashes, and dies. But the result has given pause to the shapeshifting mass of smoke. It lingers in midair, leans away, and collapses into the figure of a giant human.

The creature roars with honking horns; repeating beeps like those from medical equipment, deathly whispers, and flowing gravel against rock.

Behind it, the Giant vanishes into nothingness, evaporating into the void.

The glowing eyes latch onto us as the beast glides closer. It belches a fire that illuminates a hundred lifeless skulls. The resultant smoke seems to flow backward, to join with the lingering fog. When Vanessa guessed that the Shades and the Monster were on different teams, she was wrong. They were competing for the adoration of The One, the black ruler of darkness, Erebus. And he is calling, channeling the air, the rocks, and the bones to rumble one sentence that will haunt every dream and memory for the rest of my existence—"BOW, SERVANTS OF EREBUS!"

But I have made up my mind; I will not bow. No God of darkness is going to control me. My destiny lies elsewhere. Focusing on the now-distant memory of Sarah and her lingering spirit surrounding her vanished body, I allow myself to glance at Becky and Ian. They stand transfixed, sparking with mortality at the precipice of doom.

Becky leans closer to Ian, shielding his eyes and ears the best she can, and allows vanquished tears to stream down her cheeks. Defeated, she moans into the hollowness.

Vanessa and I form a wall to shield them.

The beast lands on two massive, taloned feet, shaking the ground beneath us. The rumbling voice barks commands in an ancient language, and all at once the bones on the stone floor rattle. Some untold gravity collects them into heaps, and then the mounds erect themselves into human form, hundreds of giant skeletons composed of sundry shattered body parts. Now fully animated, they rattle to life to obey Erebus's commands. As if in a single motion, they join ranks and march on us.

Vanessa screams and starts in the other direction.

I reach down into the center of my soul to grasp a single fiber of hope. It ignites and catches my eyes, which seem to glow with a brilliant white.

As if uncertain what to do next, the skeletons pause. The nearest assemblage, with skull-kneecaps and vertebrae-feet, raises what seems to be a fifteen-foot-long sword clenched in a giant fist of carpals and fingers that resemble ribs. Screeching voices chant in the distance, far beyond the rise that I am now certain is a rocky altar carved out of the floor of this abyss.

It watches me as I glow and spark. The energy in me collects into a ball and leaches out into the void, bathing the million deceased beings in blinding white light, while my breath fails. The blast radiates enough heat to set the skeleton army on fire. Breathless, I fall to the floor, flanked by the only people that matter to me in any way.

Darkness floods my soul, and it's over. The monster screeches with the sounds of my own heartbeat and every horrible memory I've ever endured. Its talons grip me as I black out completely.

25

The Road to the Styx

The cavern flashes with sheet lightning, briefly illuminating an alien world far removed from the realm I've always called home. The darkness is utterly bleak—the kind that soaks so deeply into the soul that all sorrows and dread overcome everything you thought you were. Agony pelts me from all sides. I call out to my companions, starting with Vanessa, but no one answers, rendering me so alone that my body begins to convulse with waves of torture.

The lightning flashes again; about a quarter of a mile ahead, the silhouette of a dead tree paints a white crack across the horizon. As I reach out for it in the total darkness, the field seems to stretch away, and when the lightning returns, the tree is gone, replaced only by shadow.

My eyes wedge themselves open. In the darkness, she stands in front of me like a pallid ghost. Sadness eats through her demeanor.

"Sarah," I rasp.

But she does not answer.

I reach out to her, my fingers inches away from the sleeve of her dress or her amber locks, which disappear with a flash of lightning. The thunder that resumes will be the voice of Erebus—

"Jesus, Kerry!" Becky's voice lingers on a lonely breeze and vanishes before the walls or the ceiling can echo them back to me.

My eyes fall upon her ghostly appearance. All at once she looks frail, yet intact. A quality exists in her spirit that suggests she is being erased, pixel by pixel. She shimmers, and my body aches.

Casting my eyes in all directions in the dark, I search for Vanessa and Ian. "Where are they? What happened?"

Becky can barely speak. Her jaw seems to undulate and her lip quivers. She looks defeated, yet desperation still clings to her persona, intermingled with a fierce determination.

"They ... were taken." She gasps and her eyes erupt with tears. "Your girlf—Vanessa made me a promise."

Trembling, I slide myself up next to her to share warmth against the coldness of the cave. She doesn't pull away but hesitates to snuggle with me. Still, her comfort is welcome in this hell.

"Tell me you know the way home."

I can only shake my head slowly. "It's not looking too good."

"And Vanessa? I get the feeling she knows more than she's letting on, and that's saying a lot. You know her better than I do."

My voice breaks; the lack of water has rendered my throat scratchy and the roof of my mouth sticky. "We're lost."

She sniffs, grasps my hand, and tries to energize me, but ultimately fails.

"Has your memory changed? We've been here, what, a few hours? But everything still seems like it's in one piece. That suggests that—"

"There's no such thing as time travel, Ker."

I wrap my fingers around her fist and attempt to draw it toward my heart, yet she releases me and looks away. Her anger has not yet dissipated.

"I'm going to be honest with you, because you deserve it."

"First time for everything," she sniffs.

That simple sentence burrows so deeply into my heart that it seemingly rusts it all to a red iron powder, leaving a knot of emptiness in my chest. Searching the darkness, I find only emotion sketched out of rocks and musty lines, forming a horizon at least fifty miles long.

"I don't remember it all. But I think I'm from Philadelphia ... I have a job in construction where there's this girl, Sarah. One night she literally disappeared, but my friend says there might be a way to save her. And now

I'm locked in this maze of dimensions so complex that I don't even know what's real. And like, someday I'm going to wake up, go to work, and find out she's still there and everything will be proven to be a nightmare."

"You already told me about your job," she says quietly. "Don't you remember the dance? You asked me what I did, I answered, and then I asked you to explain what you did. I remember the passion in your voice."

Goddamnit, Kerry. You're an idiot.

I shudder in the cold. Something seems to swirl overhead like a gathering black storm, with clouds so dense and thick that they will drench us in hypothermia-inducing rain in no time. Instead of paying attention to it, Becky appears somber and introspective. She wipes tears away from her cheeks with her sleeve and blinks.

"I don't know where you went when you left, or why, but we have to find our son."

"I know," I whisper.

"Kerry?"

I don't dare answer, but I feel her words forming somewhere deep within her before she utters them: "It's all over, isn't it? You, me ... everything."

"If there's an end, I won't let this be it," I say through gritted teeth. "I'm going to find her."

"Ian."

I nod slowly. Hope seems so far away now that the future is totally black. Her warmth seems to be shielded from me, yet I sit beside her on the rocky floor without moving for several more minutes.

"Did you—see me do anything weird?"

She sniffs. "You fought them off, and it was like you exploded with light. How did you do it?"

I don't bother trying to explain.

"But that must have taken everything you had, because a second later you were limp, and the monster was carrying us away. The rest of them fell back, and all I remember is Vanessa yelling at me like I was hallucinating it all: 'I'll keep him safe.' Whoever she is, I guess she's a good person. You're lucky to have her."

"I don't *have* her."

"I see it in your eyes."

Her words could mean anything, but I lock them away somewhere in the rusting cage where my heart once resided, just in case I need to call back to them again.

"You don't recall what direction we came from?"

She shakes her head. "I was out, too, or sort of between consciousness and sleep? It's hazy."

A murmuring sound filters through the vast wilderness; I look up. An army of spirits is marching toward us. Panic leaps through my skin as I struggle to my feet. Becky follows and grips my hand. If I'm lucky to have anyone, it's her. She seems to radiate comfort, even in this realm where security seems impossible.

The spirits seem to dance on a lifeless breeze, inching ever closer. One of them grows a body out of the soupy fog, and then another. We turn to run away, but the spirits have surrounded us in an array of bodies sharing only one thing in common—their lack of eyes.

"God," she gasps.

RISE!—the void says, through vibrations in the ground beneath our feet.

The eyeless souls form a circle around us, while above them the swirling storm assumes the shape of a monstrous face with sagging skin, glowing red eyes, and a mane of knotted hair. It slowly descends to smother us in soot.

I don't dare to speak. Becky grips my hand tighter and whispers something in my ear.

The face begins to stretch out of the sky, growing fiercer and denser until it appears to grow cells one by one. These cells coalesce into a bubble-like soup as the smoke shrinks and morphs before us until it is only a face floating without a body between us and its army of dead servants.

"You!" it shouts like thunder. "You broke the barrier. And for that, you shall pay."

"I did that?" I say, defiantly. "Your world must be fragile indeed if an accident can turn it on its head."

"You shall not speak!"

My tongue is bound up within my mouth, twisting into a knot so tight that my face turns red and my fists ball at my sides. Becky whimpers next to me. Tears stream down her face and wet her shirt.

"Yes, it was you. And you will never find her; she is mine."

My thoughts bark at him: *I'm going to get her back, you evil piece of shit.*

His face tilts upward and a vicious grin parts his lips. Laughter erupts all around us, rumbling through the thousand reanimated spirits, the ground, and the air itself.

It can read my thoughts.

And control them.

Beside me, Becky turns her head and seals her eyes shut as the thousands of hands reach out to us, shaking, shimmering, and then vanishing into smoke.

Kill her!

I wrestle my hand free from Becky's grasp, wrap my arms around her waist, and draw her in for a kiss that will never happen. Her body trembles in my embrace, and her tears tumble onto my shoulders, leak through my shirt, and cleanse my skin of days' worth of dust, grime, and sweat.

For a moment I can taste the salt, and then the sweet. The tears soak into my skin, penetrating deeper until a faint light appears between us.

I hold her tightly and the illumination grows, brighter and brighter.

Feel the wrath of the Elder Shade.

The light is extinguished as the fog forms around us, towering so high that its limits cannot be seen.

Becky whispers again, through a heartbreaking sob. "The sticks—go. I'll be fine."

My tongue is still twisted in my mouth. I draw away and try to scan her face with a look of confusion. There are no sticks here.

"The river—the Styx. Go there. Find the boundary."

My heart trembles. I will not let her stay to be devoured and enslaved. Instead, I hold her tighter. The demon may be able to control my thoughts, but it will never defeat my actions.

Instead of walking away from her, I grasp her hands, pull them to my shoulders, and dance in the darkness. The underworld seems to twist away with every step, and then, somewhere in a field of glowing stars, a giant red orb appears. Our dance leads us directly towards it, as its gravity tugs on us. The energy begins to reform as we turn, as though we have been sucked into a cosmic turbine that transforms mere matter into pure energy. The orb glows brighter as we drift closer, settle into a steady orbit, and draw energy from the source. When I first saw the orb, I was touring a green energy plant with Becky. And now we are genuinely inside the energy plant, only it is supplying us instead of millions of households.

The field of stars grows starker, deeper, and wider. A smile appears on her lips, draining away her pain and sorrow. Instinctively I lean into her, with the bright red star burning in the background. The kiss only lasts a half second, but it supplies me with enough energy to fight through every monster, skeleton, and spirit, and prepares me to face the Elder Shade.

In the blink of an eye, we are standing firm on dry, rocky, rutted ground. I can feel a presence somewhere to my right, infinitely faint, yet attractive enough to guide me toward it.

The muttering voices return. Thousands of spirits flank us, but they dare not reach out. The energy I feel is replacing my heart and all thought, something this devil cannot control. Our steps seem to echo in the abyss as we tread down a gentle slope and watch a team of skeletons assemble themselves out of scattered bones. They join the throng, yet the energy inside me seems to repel them.

The pain leaks away; I cannot speak or even think sentences aimed at Becky, but somehow, she can feel everything that exists in my soul. I breathe in deeply, exhale, grip her hand, and descend to what appears to be a distant, fiery furnace. Tortured laughter and agonizing cries pierce the darkness as we walk.

The Elder Shade swirls above all, menacing as ever, yet it too can only follow along as though some strange electromagnetic force repels it. The energy in my chest reacts with it, gradually ebbing away as the cloud bears down on us.

It may have lasted an hour or even less, but we make a good pace. The energy still draws me closer to the presence. Its attraction grows stronger with every step, yet the power within me subsides faster as we go.

The heat builds as we near the fire. A pit of bubbling lava emits steam, and millions of souls form a path leading right to it. Within a few steps, the source of attraction separates into two distinct figures. Ropes are lashed around their hands and feet, and the spirits are about to toss them into the inferno, which will consume them until they are nothing but pure minerals.

Instead of walking, we are jogging; I can scarcely control my legs. Ian and Vanessa are drawing us in faster and faster. Three hundred feet away, our gait has become an uncontrollable sprint. The power in my chest sparks into life and my hands glow.

Vanessa looks horrified. Ian cannot even bear to look; his eyes are sealed shut. We arrive just as the energy begins to falter. I release Becky's hand to hoist my son to my shoulders, but Becky trips and tumbles face-first toward the inferno. I watch as the gases bubble up only a few feet from her skin, yet she doesn't fall in.

Vanessa is holding her, leaning above the fire, and slowly pulls her away, tumbling to the ground in a heap.

I reach out into air that seems hot enough to melt flesh and bone, help pull Becky to safety, and then wrap my arms around all three of them.

The energy is gone and the Elder Shade creeps in, lurking lower and lower in order to consume the horizon and everything upon it.

It bears down on us, sinking, and begins to tear off my flesh one cell at a time. Screams erupt in the distance, and galloping hooves and wings roar toward us. The hollow shrieking sound, combining every noise in the universe, deafens me.

The hooves arrive first, and the thousands of spirits close in on it. It kicks them away and blasts a fierce light throughout the cavern that sends shockwaves through the ground. The tall composite skeletons shatter with the shock, their thousands of bony body parts clattering over the rock and settling into dust.

The wings separate themselves from the throng. The monster launches itself higher to combat the hooved creature, which I now recognize as Ariadne's Minotaur. Its former master cannot be far behind. Light is beginning to leak out through the shadows, filling the cavern with a blinding glow more powerful than any I could ever imagine. It repels the eyeless spirits, confuses the Elder Shade, and envelops us. Invisible wings swoop overhead, and claws grab at me.

Ian, Vanessa, and Becky are hoisted away from the floor, as the winged beast soars above the briefly illuminated chaos below. The Minotaur has teamed up with the Icarus, and the battle begins to rage below us as we fly away from it all.

Millions of spirits clash in a frothy mortal combat that can have no end, because its participants are already dead.

You shall fall to your demise!

The wings carrying us aloft vanish in a cloud of smoke and feathers as the light flickers and dies. The four of us fall face down and collapse into a heap, and the soot gathers behind us. Without thinking, I team up with Vanessa to rally us away from the chaos. Millions of screams fight to be heard through the din as the soupy mass of smoke pulses toward us.

The river is within reach; I feel it before I can see it. Its babbling supplies me with a fresh flow of energy, which my body attempts to convert into light. It manages to keep the endless black at bay just long enough for us to jump into the black waters.

The cold rips through my skin, but I gather Ian in my embrace and fight against the current that tries to drag us away. The Elder Shade scours the shoreline, reaches out, and is buffeted by an invisible boundary. I can still see it, even as dim sunlight appears over the far banks of the river.

We have escaped, but the monsters are still out there. They will not let us win this easily.

26

Tartarus Rising

Ian splashes helplessly as the current attempts to carry him away. His arms flail, and when I grasp hold of him, he is breathless and cold, his heart beating a million miles an hour. I angle my trajectory upstream to the far shore, where Becky and Vanessa wade in the shallows.

"Ddd—ad," Ian stammers. His eyes flit in all directions, revealing a certain darkness that I can barely cope with. It is as though Erebus has reached into his soul and clawed out all that was clean and hopeful, allowing the void to be filled with unbridled terror.

The current sweeps us about a hundred yards downriver before I feel the sodden earth beneath my feet. Still fighting against the stream, I wade towards the shore as painful knots form in my thighs.

I reach up to grab the roots of some brush on the bank and pull myself upward, with Ian nestled against my shoulder. He is trembling and thrashing as though a violent hypothermia has set in. While it's true that the water is cold, it doesn't seem cold enough to quickly inflict hypothermia, even with total immersion.

But I already know, painfully, that it is not hypothermia. If the monsters, the fifty-foot skeletons, and the Shades have not been enough to induce post-traumatic stress in him, I might consider it lucky.

"Talk to me, son," I groan, trying to make myself seem calmer than I am.

But it is no use. His eyes seem to flicker as they lock on to me, and I can suddenly see more of him than I could ever have imagined: the embers of hope have been extinguished, their smoke choked off by an airstream of sadness.

My demeanor isn't helping. I am shaking from the cold, the nightmare in the cave, and the thousands of women washing ashore like a surge that tried to carry me to a watery grave.

You cannot save him.

The words of Erebus come as a rigid explosion in my own head, blasting me with a dark truth that I cannot escape. The pain skyrockets as I pull myself up from the water to cuddle with my son in the golden grass.

How can Erebus influence my thoughts across dimensions? Then again, we hadn't really stepped through a portal. Instead, the river seems to have created a boundary between his realm and whatever world we have emerged into. I glance back at the far shore, which is nothing more than a black shroud, creeping into the sky like an oil stain on canvas.

Ian convulses as I hold him, but I cannot extinguish my own tremors.

Sparse conversation lashes through the weeds from upriver, like barbs sawing through sensitive flesh.

"You didn't see it."

"I was there. Where ... and who the hell do you think you are?"

The arguing causes a lump in my throat. I tremble and attempt to massage the pain in my temple with one hand while ignoring the cramps in my thighs.

"Mm—mmm."

Ian is trying to call for his mom, but he cannot speak. Still, I try to comfort him by wrapping an arm around him. Realizing that I have no happy memories with him flashes a deep trauma through my soul. I have nothing with which to fight the pain and dread away. Hope is quickly vanishing, and the energy that had swelled within me before has sputtered to a pitiful flame on the edge of being extinguished entirely, moribund and cold.

"You don't have any idea who I am! You're a fraud. When we get back home, I never want to see you or him again."

"Becky."

One word Becky delivered to Vanessa strikes me: "When." I hold it in my head for nearly a full minute, allowing the broken timbre of her voice to penetrate as if to make it mean something else.

'When' is a word of hope, whereas 'if' suggests doubt. I admire it until the sound becomes something eerie that I cannot wash away.

They emerge from the tall grass next to a stubby, fluttering olive tree, which seems to cast opaque lines against a dark blue overcast sky beyond the sunset. I expect their faces to be sparkling with anger. Vanessa's appears first, and she bites her lip at the sight of us. The bindings holding her hair in braids have broken loose, and strands of her hair have turned to a wiry frizz. Her shoulders lurch when she hurries toward us, leaving me to gaze at the marred specter of my future wife.

Her hair is mangled, muddy, and knotted. The river water is streaming down her face, undistinguishable from the tears I know are already there. But they are not tears of sadness; the ferocity in her eyes tears me to shreds. Her lip quivers with rage, terror, and agony, all mixed into a poisonous sludge that drowns out her real self. My eyes narrow as I watch her step closer.

She kneels in the soft, muddy grass next to Ian, combs through his hair, and wordlessly instructs me to let go of him.

In an instant, the anguish vanishes. She whispers words of love, which I can barely understand.

When I pull away to sit up, Vanessa reaches out and draws me into a loose embrace as she crouches next to me. This should be the time to plot our next move, because the monsters will not just let us go. They are going to follow us back to the time and place I consider the present dimension to be, which is starting to stretch further and further away like a mere point on an endless horizon, a safe distance from where an observer cannot see any detail that sets it apart as real.

Ice water washes my soul, but Vanessa is understanding. For at least three minutes, she says nothing and simply rests her open palm on my forearm as we shiver in the cold, drenched from head to toe.

"Ian, you're scaring Mommy."

"This is hell," I croak.

Vanessa shakes her head, allowing a moment for hopelessness to morph into thoughtfulness. It the meantime, she presses her shoulder into mine.

"You wouldn't think the borders to the underworld would be roses and rainbows, but all is not lost; we've just got to find another portal."

She gazes in all directions and allows defeat to gradually creep over her face.

"Where are we?"

I shrug so abruptly that shockwaves course through my torso. "Other than lost..."

Instead of answering, she levels her gaze and studies the horizon toward where I imagine south to be, where the river meanders and stretches before dropping below the horizon. We are in a broad plain, but to our right there are dark hills, sparsely populated with deep blue poplars and cedars, rising to fold the landscape in beauty. I imagine a light breeze filtering through the grasses to warm me from the inside out, and the woman I want to be with lacing her arm through the crook of my elbow and softly resting her head on my shoulder. I picture her hair lightly and comfortably brushing against my shirt.

Vanessa doesn't feel so defeated, almost as though she's immune to everything that the monsters have unleashed.

"I know what the Elder Shade is," she says, twitching.

"Yeah, it's like this—wait, you *heard* that? It was in my own head."

She shakes her head again, and a somber calm passes over her expression. "*Heard* might be a stretch. It's like it was my own thought, manifested through vibrations. A strange power that I knew only one man to possess."

Somehow, I already know who she is talking about. I squeeze my eyes closed and feel the pain digging into my forehead and legs; perhaps standing would release the pain, but then again it could also spread it to other regions of my body.

"Which means she and Ian *heard* it, too."

She nods slowly.

And that perfectly explains why Ian is lying in a heap on the riverbank, nearly comatose. I suppose it's payback for what my future self did to them. Suddenly, I remember it. The visions play out painfully in my mind.

Ian is chasing a soccer ball on a green field while Becky cheers her approval from afar. And then it's all gone; the green, the smiles, and the joy blend into a field of grey where I sit alone, isolated from the world at large. Pain sparks through my spirit, and the night turns to rain. Cold, murky showers pulverize everything I thought I knew about myself. I give in to remorse, like watching Becky get on with her life from a distant reality, experiencing new joys, bigger smiles, and a warmer green.

The memory melts my heart. I can almost feel her heart racing twenty feet behind me, as she battles emotional torment to save our son from the demons of the underworld. Tears leak through my eyes, and I know Vanessa can feel it, too.

"We're not beaten yet," she says.

"If we die here, we die everywhere. We cease to exist."

"There must be a way out. Maybe up in those hills."

I shake my head.

"If there's a will, there's a way. Sounds cheesy as hell, but you know the truth about idioms? They're born out of the observation of truth. Sometimes there is only one way, and we can search our whole lives for it, but it's still out there and you hunt for it because you must. It becomes a part of who you are. The activity gives you a purpose, and there cannot be hope without purpose."

"Did the reverend burrow into your brain, too? You sound exactly like him."

Obviously knowing what I'm insinuating, she fixes her gaze on the hills and presses closer to me.

"I can never be yours," I say, lowering my voice.

"You don't think I see it? You're in love with her." She tilts her head subtly backwards and gazes sideways to indicate Becky.

I shake my head. "I broke her—in the future, I think. When she told me in the house, I could see the truth in her rage."

"How do you ... remember it?"

"Because we are far beyond that now. It's like we're at the limits of speculation, so far ahead that no human alive can anticipate what happens next. The horizon is the veil. You know it too, and so does Becky."

"You know something weird my momma always told me about the future? She said we can do anything we want with it. Throw a pebble into a river, and nothing happens. Throw in enough pebbles and you can alter its course. I think there still may be a chance to change it, even if you somehow remember it."

"I just need enough stones."

She tries to smile. "Weird analogy, but whatever."

I slowly exhale. "Then let's get going."

Energy sparks through my joints. Vanessa helps me to my feet while the horizon turns sour. The sudden darkness can mean only one thing: we need to run.

I dart back toward Becky and tug at her shoulder with both hands, but she swats me away. The river water has dried from her face, leaving behind only the flood of tears that is running down her cheeks toward her neck. She brushes through our son's wet hair and lurches in pain.

"We've got to go," I say slowly and darkly. "They're coming."

"I'm not going anywhere, you son of a bitch."

"Becky, please. I know what you're feeling right now. I know what you're remembering because I'm there, too."

"You're nowhere. Get the hell off me."

Vanessa gasps when she glances toward where I perceive north to be. "Maybe the spousal abuse can wait. We're all going. Forgive the expression but *run for the hills.*"

I almost don't want to know what she is seeing, but I cannot stop myself from looking.

You're going to die.

The horizon is clogged with smoke. It billows up from afar, towering so high into the sky that it is like a super volcano has exploded and we've yet to feel the shockwave. No, it eats at the sky, eroding it molecule by molecule, and replaces it with soot.

"Jesus Christ," I whisper.

Becky launches herself to her feet, wrapping Ian in a close embrace as she stares out with us. Still easily thirty miles away, the blackness extends like a wall, or a storm without end. Within its smoldering pillars of smoke, forked lighting bursts forth repeatedly, flashing across its blackness like rivers of superheated electricity. It is growing bigger, darker, and angrier, slowly pressing toward us in the shape of the most ominous thunderhead I've ever seen.

The wind will arrive well before the cloud does. My heart pulses with terror as I will myself westward. Vanessa laces her fingers through my palm as Becky drags Ian along. At this rate, the storm will envelop us before we reach the lowest of the hills.

Instinct takes over. I wrestle my hand free from Vanessa's grasp, hoist Ian to my shoulders, and voicelessly coax Becky to hold hands with Vanessa. A shrill siren erupts somewhere to the south of us. We are flanked. The winged monster has not appeared, but its call is unmistakable.

Our only means of escape is into the western hills. Pain rips through my knees and abdomen as I hurry in that direction. As I am carrying Ian, I cannot run because the pressure on my legs is too great to gain the necessary height and momentum. Instead, I sprint-walk as the raging storm erases the pale twilight.

The winds are coming; they kick up a blinding storm of dust that obscures the darkness behind it. The dust forms a curved tan wall that marches forward. In the distance, I imagine it uprooting trees and sending sticks and small stones hurtling through the air like shrapnel from a huge grenade.

I dare not look for too long, in case I trip on a root protrusion, a rock, or something else, and send Ian tumbling. The shock is still coursing through him, and a fall may put him out of it completely. "Hang on tight," I say, hoping he can hear me.

He wraps his legs around my neck and trembles.

The monsters are marching on the south horizon. Legions of them, arranged in rows, are grinding up the ground beneath their feet. Wolves howl in the distance ahead of us, as a cacophony of life splinters the false sense of solitude that has thus far permeated this dimension.

If life can find a way here, it can thrive anywhere.

I sense a tiny glow in my elbows as I clutch Ian's feet tighter and press his ankles to my chest. I can sense his erratic heartbeat even as mine steadily cranks faster. *Thump-thump. Thump. Thump, thump, thump.* There is no rhythm, but instead an impossible energy. If it can feed into me somehow, perhaps I can use it. First, we must make it to the hills, while our enemies close in around us like two advancing masses to smash us in the middle.

Pretty much a shit sandwich, only we're not the bread.

Life howls up ahead. A million birds take to the sky all at once, shrouding the orange filtering through the clouds on the horizon like a cloud of pepper dust. Their song erupts in chaos.

The monsters will devour it all. There must be a portal there somewhere, but hope is flickering. The energy in the surrounding chaos seeps into me in disorganized streams.

"You gotta be kidding me," Vanessa croaks.

In the hills ahead, huge chunks of rock have started rolling, gathering into masses, and erecting monolithic statues of sparkling granite easily a hundred feet tall. The golems assemble themselves rigidly to stand guard as sentinels of a sacred land.

They will not let us pass.

With hell behind us, troops of monsters to our left, and the raging storm to our right, we are trapped in a sea of utter lunacy. The land beneath our feet seems to roll with the shockwaves of an earthquake. Trembling agony swirls between us, and the millions of birds screech with one voice. A chipmunk flees a long snake at my feet; the snake launches itself forward into the grass to seal the chipmunk shut in its vice-like jaws, but it collides with a rock, which splits with a heavy *crack* that whips through the air like thunder.

Still moving, we begin to climb the slopes of a shallow hill as the golems stand awaiting us. They could crush us flat by simply falling apart in our vicinity. If we are going to make it out of this trap, Ariadne's gift will need to reveal a new trick.

Then again, the Elder Shade has learned a new trick of its own, besides the lightning. It rises black over the coming cloud of dust and coalesces into giant smoke wings that that swoop like rolling thunder over the plain below.

The wings rage and boil to form a face three hundred feet high, which then collapses into a tight vortex. This thing is going to devour this landscape and anything in it, including the golems and the monsters. I reach into my soul, breathe heavily, and close my eyes for the final assault.

27

Headwaters of the Acheron

The advancing dust cloud stains the sky ahead of the storm a murky tan, as the orange of the twilight fades into somber blue and charcoal gray. Ian's weight compresses my spine and causes a dull ache to begin to swell in my neck.

Even at the edge of consciousness, he manages to tug my hair and ears, sending arrows of pain through my head.

Unencumbered by the weight of a ten-year-old child, Vanessa and Becky easily outpace me, but fearing she will leave Ian behind to be devoured, Becky slows and dodges a few scattered rocks while trying to keep a low profile.

Vanessa shouts something as the wind kicks up. Within a few minutes we will be walking through a hurricane. A lump forms in my throat. To our right, the storm stains the entire sky pitch black. Lightning flashes through it like a pulse, yet it does nothing to illuminate the ground beneath it. In any other setting, it would appear that the storm carries on forever, yet this one has erased our view of the horizon completely.

To our left, the army of fifty-foot skeletons, winged serpent beasts, and scaly chimeras raise a colossus of noise. Every sound imaginable emanates from their direction. As I glance over there, thousands of red eyes prod at the falling darkness like lasers.

The pain arrives before they do. The ground buckles beneath our feet, sinking us into a field of sandy, rocky dirt up to our kneecaps. Then the shifting Earth swallows Becky to her waist, immobilizing her. Vanessa turns back to save her, but she will get sucked down as well. The only way I can help her is by setting Ian down on a nearby rock, finding a solid path, and pulling her out before she's buried alive.

I shriek as the wind whips into a fury. Sand in the air pulverizes my skin, filters through my hair, and irritates my eyes. Twigs and leaves, ripped from their parent plants, lash at my arms and face. A dirty patch of blood coats Vanessa's forehead. The soil wraps around her ankles as her hair flaps in the wind like a tattered flag. The sand in the air becomes coarser as I work towards them, just twenty feet away.

Having deposited Ian on a safe boulder, I reach out, trip over a rising stone, and fall face first into another one. Ian will be exposed to the dust storm for longer than feels safe, but if I don't rescue his mother, none of it will matter to either of us.

The pain makes me woozy; my head spins and my vision blurs. Vanessa's hair appears like a streak of black against a tan backdrop. She helps to raise Becky by slinging her hands under her armpits, but only manages to lift her a few inches while sinking in further herself.

Screaming in agony, I attempt to stand, trip again, and then flail haphazardly above the shifting soil. Becky grabs my outstretched hand, and I attempt to anchor myself to the rock by wedging my ankle in a tight crevice. Using all the strength I can muster, I pull her toward me. She grasps the stone with her free hand and climbs onto the relatively stable rock while Vanessa works herself free of the dirt.

Ian murmurs to himself while hunkering down against a jagged stone about twenty feet behind me. Looking back at his facial expression, I am haunted so deeply that the chills could evaporate my skin and leave me as nothing more than a skeleton fighting for survival. Becky issues a pained grunt and climbs to her feet. Pebbles kicked up by the ferocious wind pelt my face, along with more tiny sticks.

The wind must be moving more than a hundred miles per hour to do this much damage. Out of the corner of my eye I see a squat cedar fall. Half its branches snap off and become airborne, screaming towards me so quickly that I cannot dodge them. One of the heavier branches slams me right in the gut, which spins me sideways over the pit of tumultuous dirt and painfully twists my ankle within the rock crevice.

Laughter emanates on the howling wind, maniacal and vexing.

It feels like you're being scraped into nothingness. You pathetic fool.

"Go to hell!"

The laughter only intensifies. *Best idea you've ever had.*

Vanessa frees herself from the soil, hops onto the stable rocks, and reaches out for me while Becky nearly lands on Ian. She pulls him in a tight embrace as the storm and the approaching monsters split our ears with a din so loud that it drains the world of all other sound.

"Leave me," I croak, hoping that Vanessa can hear me.

Her eyes turn downward as she kneels at my ankles. For nearly thirty seconds, she rocks my ankle back and forth painfully. To prevent myself from screaming, I clench my teeth and grimace. She wrestles my leg free, helps me to stand, and hurries to rescue Becky before a snapped-off poplar limb can pummel them both.

She dodges the projectile by mere centimeters and before I even know what's happening, the wind has launched us airborne.

I sail at least sixty feet in the air, where the sand and debris seem thinner. Vanessa disappears while Becky and Ian arc skyward, surpassing me. Looking down at the chaos is like watching a war reduce a landscape to ashes. The blackness creeps closer and closer; spinning, I collide with a flying boulder, while another rock pinches my waist with enough force to crush me. I howl in agony, searching the chaotic skies for Vanessa while the golems pull me higher and higher. I pass one hundred feet of altitude in the blink of an eye before I can see the face of the golem frayed with dust. It grins menacingly.

The monsters squeal with every noise I've ever heard. Their wings carry them skyward to battle with the dust and debris.

I gasp as the horizon vanishes. The golem lumbers up a steep slope, traveling what feels like a hundred miles per hour. Even at this height, the sand and twigs punish me. I can feel the heat of the blood dribbling down my cheek as the wound cakes with burning sand. The other golem has seized Becky and Ian in one of its school-bus-sized boulder hands. Together, they march us into the hills, away from the armies.

Below me the ground begins to be stained black. The dust thins before I even know what's happening. But the storm is just getting started: sheet lighting erupts from all directions, highlighting shapes of billowing skulls, sneering lips, and menacing eyes. It erases the landscape as it comes, every ounce of rock, dust, trees, and sky converging into a frothing sea of dark.

Fire whizzes past my ear, singing the hairs on my neck. The resultant pain is barely noticeable within a split second. The blackness coils and oozes. Lightning flickers and thunder booms, and suddenly everything is light, and I am nothing but vapor.

She floats in the ether like a shining fairy ghost, shrouded in white and the flickering embers of yellow flame, smiling.

"You've made it thus far," she says, her voice echoing as though we are alone in a white cave.

I rasp and reach out for her. Her hands are grimy and cold, and her image undulates on an imperceptible breeze. Her eyes are like fireballs blazing with a paranormal energy that soaks into me. I can feel it growing, my skin glowing brighter and brighter second by second.

"I'm finished," I croak. "The Elder Shade.... It got me ... it got them. All of them. And I could do nothing."

"Look again." Her voice sprinkles me with clear warmth.

In an instant, I am floating in nothingness. No grass, no rocks, no dirt, no flying monsters. And no Elder Shade. It's all nothing. But they are alive. Becky and Ian float in an endless embrace as Vanessa looks on, shifting her gaze toward me, the glowing—whatever—that has saved them all.

"How...?"

I cannot find the words.

"Where...."

By now, Erebus must be grinning. He should be inside me, controlling my thoughts, but the resonance is gone. I am utterly empty.

Her energy radiates through me.

"You know how to find me. Go to the lake—"

"I'm lost, Sarah. We all are."

"You know how to find me."

"Sarah."

She floats on the breeze, flutters, and then vanishes. Her energy crackles within me, as if the lightning and her spirit have ignited me into a blinding flame.

Slowly I float downward. The rocks fall at the same pace, and the golems fall to pieces, every boulder tumbling down into the pitch black. They will crush the others flat, but the fact that I can see them makes me burn brighter.

Sarah's voice echoes in the ether. "You know how to find me."

The Elder Shade swirls away in defeat, but it will soon return with more ferocity than ever. We have only minutes before it reappears with a vengeance. The winged serpent monsters lock onto us as we navigate the newly strewn boulders higher into the hills.

A gurgling brook interrupts the comparative silence, before it blends with the sounds of train horns, thunder, and a million screaming babies. The cacophony digs into my brain. We run along the border of utter blackness, where the world has been devoured and grasses have been sheared at the roots by the hundred-mile-an-hour wind preceding the arrival of the Elder Shade.

Somewhere in the distance it is regathering its strength, but something within me has defeated my fear. I search the darkness for the sound of the babbling stream. A hundred yards away, I spot it oozing out of a twenty-foot-tall structure of moss and granite. The clear water catches the scant light and reflects it like the fringes of a hallucination that burrows into my soul.

Vanessa sees it, too. She sprints toward it, hoping for a drink of fresh water, but she doesn't make it.

The monsters attack. Fifty-foot-tall skeletons structured from a mishmash of ancient, splintered bones stamp on the ground, causing it to quake under our feet. Becky emits an ear-splitting scream as the sirens obliterate my eardrums, yet somehow I can still hear it all.

The monsters will not be defeated by whatever the lightning has done to me. It has retreated, and I am sparkling now like pure energy.

A knotted stick about six feet long lies in the windswept grass near my feet. It will not make a potent weapon, but if it can slow them down, even for a second, it can buy us enough time to make for the stream.

My back erupts in agony as I bend to pick up the stick. It seems to glow with an opalescent white as I grip it, as the energy that exists within me is being transferred into the wood. The nearest skeleton slams a foot consisting of ulnas and scapulae on the ground about ten feet away. I spin toward it, flinging the stick as sharply as I can at shins constructed of vertebrae and ribs.

Blinking, I scream and expect the stick to explode in my hands. Instead it effortlessly slices through the bones, which scatter as the rod of pure energy blows through their structure. The skeleton teeters and hops heavily on one foot, but otherwise manages to keep its balance until my weapon slashes right through its other shin. It stands there dumbstruck for several seconds before falling in a cascade of dusty bones, which settles into a pile six feet tall. Seeing this, the other skeletons hesitate. Some fall back, while others press their attack.

I beat the stick furiously back and forth like a drunken samurai, cleaving mismatching bones in half and sending fragments scattering in every direction. Before long, one skeleton flashes its five-foot sword straight at my head. It bursts into flame from the tip to the hilt as it meets my staff. Metal clinks as showers of glowing steel pitter-patter into the grass.

The monster seems to frown. In the moment of confusion, I press another attack, flinging my weapon through both of its bundled-fibula legs. It tumbles into a mound of shattered bones, even as more march on toward me. I have no time to revel in my victory.

The winged serpent beasts with their hundreds of red eyes circle overhead. One swoops down to grip me in its sharp talons. In anticipation of the assault, I arc my stick through its wing. It squeals, tumbles, and falls to the earth with a heavy thud, but even injured it poses a significant danger.

Gathering itself for another assault, the creature flaps its wings and belches a scorching river of flame directly at me. I barely manage to dodge it as the heat burns my back. The smell of bubbling flesh deters me. I fall face-first in agony, even while the beast is rearing back for another inferno shot right at my heart.

The stick is no defense against fire—

Except it is. Somehow, it absorbs the energy of the flame, making it glow like a white laser sword, while reflecting the excess heat at the attacker. It squeals in pain as its own fire burns through its other wing.

A second later I climb to my feet, launch myself at it, and swing the energy stick right at its hundreds of red, furious eyes. The energy slashes through its skull, rendering it silent before it explodes into a lustrous fireball that sets my clothes aflame.

Vanessa and Becky scream while trying to defend themselves from an army of chimeras, whose armored serpent heads on bulky, cat-like bodies lash at them. Fangs spit venom as one aims to bite Becky's arm in half. I spin in her direction, howling like a banshee as the monsters overwhelm us, still thousands strong. Gathering Ian, Becky, and Vanessa in a tight group, I fight toward the stream, past the flaming carcass of my winged enemy, even as dozens more swoop overhead.

You know how to find me.

I do, somehow. Fighting a rearguard action, I slice through several skeleton legs constructed of metacarpals, ulnas, and fibulas. Skulls rain down from above as they fall to the earth. Legions more march on us with swords raised high. Individually, they are no match for my energy staff, but I am severely outnumbered.

I yelp when I see the water; a splash indicates that it is somehow deep enough for us to have to swim across to the void of darkness on the other side, a circular black hole in the world of chaos that is more inviting than the water itself.

We will not have time to drink.

Getting the same idea, Vanessa hikes up the legs of her jeans and jumps into the water. The chimeras lunge at her but hesitate to bear down. I slice one of them in half while Becky takes Ian in her arms and wades in after Vanessa.

Smoke rages overhead; the Elder Shade has returned.

Lighting forks across a sky that does not exist, and millions of bones rain down from above as the thousands of composite skeletons burst in collision with the tendrils of smoky, billowing black.

Becky and Vanessa scream in unison. Instinctively I glance in their direction. A different kind of monster splashes out of the water and is wrapping wet, scaly tentacles around its victims. To battle the hydra, I splash in and feel waves of agony rip through every part of my body. The river is acid, and it slowly starts to devour the energy in my stick and my body. Fear swirls up out of nowhere as fire rains down on us. The winged monsters and the Elder Shade are ripping the world out from under us and eating the sky with their billowing blackness.

I wield little energy by the time I swing my staff at the tentacles that bind us. One of them rends in half as my laser sword cuts through it easily. The second writhes as my blade cuts through with more resistance. The third strike bounces off. I am now harmless, with the blackness lurching overhead as more fireballs thunder down from above.

I scream as I reach the shore, wracked with unimaginable torture. The others clearly feel the same thing. The hydra squeals as its dozens of alien, serpentine heads flail in the water. I wrestle myself free from one of the heads, kick it in what must be its face, and watch it stagger with confusion. Still, it lashes its tentacles at us as we flee onto the shore. The rocks around the circle of black are beginning to fade into coal dust by the time we reach them. I push Ian and Becky in first, make sure that Vanessa has scurried into the pit, and watch as the bodies of devoured monsters thunder to the ground while thick arcs of lightning flash all around. The billowing black washes away my shoes as I dive into the abyss.

We land on hard pavement and my entire body is still awash in agony.

28

Sword of Perseus

Chaos spreads through the night, like a rapidly expanding torrent of darkness. Distant screams and sirens shred the ambience, permeating the setting with a sense of foreboding. Black clouds lurk overhead, fed by multiple columns of heavy smoke. I pay little attention to it all, because a mere second after we land, Becky erupts in a wail of panic.

Ian seems stable, if not erratic, but Becky is peering at Vanessa and reaching for her head.

I gasp audibly when I look at her. Her scalp has cracked open, allowing a copious stream of blood to congeal in her hair and form a blackened, scabby mass of sweat, dirt, and gore on her forehead.

The blood flows toward her eyes, which dart back and forth as instinct draws her fingers to her temple. In the process of falling to my knees, I press at her injury and momentarily allow my hand to rest on Becky's. Seconds pass before I gather the words to calm Vanessa.

"It's—it's not that bad," I lie. "Probably got to get you to a hospital before too long."

Becky's heavy breathing barely registers, but out of the corner of my eye, I can see that she has cast her eyes skyward at the rising smoke.

"Get out of here," Vanessa pants, "I'm *dead* already. Leave me. Find another portal."

"Not leaving without you. You're fierce."

A coy smile passes over her lips before disappearing into pain. "Sometimes the bear dies. You know how it ends."

"Callisto ... you're stronger than a bear."

She laughs painfully. "Admitting frailty isn't weakness, it's strength."

"Ker—" Becky whispers breathlessly.

I try to wave her off so that I can give Vanessa the attention she needs, but the subject of Becky's gaze now fills my perception with a grim reality.

The factories in this blighted industrial district have been reduced to rubble. The warehouse Vanessa and I had transferred through remains standing, but only just. A sizeable portion of its roof has been sheared off, leaving crumbled concrete and mangled steel trusses strewn around the perimeter. The pipes that once scaled the tilt-up wall lie sideways on the ground, heavily dented, and emitting smoke.

The city is pocked with destruction. The embers of dying fires are belching black smoke from here to downtown. This time of the night, the skyscrapers should be shimmering with stacked squares of yellow light, but now they are glowing with orange flame. As far as I can see, buildings have fallen. The sturdier structures remain upright, yet skeletal, as the glass has shattered and the skins have been peeled off.

Philadelphia has been sacked, and I cannot even determine whether we have landed in the correct dimension. The panic sets in long before Sarah's ghostly words can echo through my soul. I squeeze out a tear and feel my chest heave. Vanessa's bleeding has slowed, yet the blood is growing darker. I press harder and she groans in agony.

"You risk too much," she rasps. "Get to a..."

Her lips purse as her eyes widen. The pain has contorted her face into an expression of extreme anguish. Her mouth quivers as she struggles to get out the words: "...the theater."

Where the Icarus had greeted us—the janitor's closet had taken us to the lake. I attempt to avert my eyes, but a knowing glance suggests she understands more than she's letting on.

"Go."

"You're coming with us."

"I'm just going to slow you down. I'll be fine."

"If you die in a different dimension, you disappear from all of them," I reason, as a searing pain shoots through my back.

I grimace, while Vanessa's hands rest gently on my shoulders. Her warmth presses against me as the soul in her eyes flickers. She will return to the stars as the Great Bear, I presume, but her life means more to me than the constellations. I visibly plead with her, yet she remains unmoved.

"You remember that night you first went to the lake? I was there. I saw you—followed you. I knew who you were, Larry. You have a destiny."

I shake my head and frown. "It's all hocus pocus. There's no destiny."

"You of all people should know better."

"Of all—what does that mean?"

She tilts her head backward and presses her hands tighter against my shoulders. "I guess you'll find out here in a few years. Sometimes people pass through your life—"

"And sometimes they stay," I say, knowing where she's going and deliberately altering her course. Power comes by various means, and it isn't always about glowing body parts and sticks transformed into veritable lightsabers. It can emanate from the soul, even in the darkest of times, if one remembers its source.

I visualize Sarah standing there in midair like a wispy vapor of ambient light. She somehow looks more beautiful than ever, but if the power that Ariadne has given me has any meaning, it must be used for the good of someone else or it can no longer radiate through me. I glance at Becky and back to Vanessa before making my own decision.

Gripping Vanessa by her underarms, I pull her to a standing position. She has at least two inches on me even without heels, so carrying her might not work.

She doesn't look surprised when she surveys what is left of the horizon. From here, we have more than a mile to traverse to reach the theater, which may or may not have remained standing. The skyline bleeds blackness amidst the glow of flame. I can feel it penetrating my heart, to replace all hope with dread.

Vanessa leans her weight against my shoulder and straightens her knees. I glance down at Ian, whose eyes are silently darting in all directions. A thin layer of sweat erupts from his forehead and reflects the light of destruction. He isn't making any noise but seems to be largely free of any physical injury.

Becky is another story. In her quest to shelter Ian from the carnage, she has caught the brunt of the damage. A red burn boils on her forehead, her hair and eyebrows singed only inches away from a narrow cut that must be stinging painfully.

I bite my lip as I study them. Failure to return them to their own time would be a catastrophe I can scarcely fathom. In the worst case, it could warp time itself, cause the dimensions to bleed into one another, and allow Erebus to enslave all of humanity.

Then again, their time could be at the point of any number of the interactions I've had with her. Determining the correct one is a task I cannot trust my brain to do objectively. The portal in the movie theater had led us to the lake, where I'd climbed the island, entered the cabin, and seen Sarah before she vanished into thin air. And when Vanessa and I had entered the closet, we'd fallen into Becky's bed.

I swallow my thoughts, steel myself against Vanessa's weight, and approach a debris-strewn sidewalk on the way downtown.

"God," Becky breathes. "Philadelphia was a hellhole before, but this—how the hell did we get here?"

"You remember when we toured the power plant?" I change the subject, hoping that a shared experience is real enough for both of us to remember.

She begins to shake her head before pausing, nonverbally admitting her mistake, and responding with a subtle nod. "Somehow."

A cool sense of relief spreads through me. "You remember when I fell behind, in awe of the many engineering marvels? I don't know if I ever told you this. In some of the equipment in that electromagnetism room, there was a red light, and the floor kind of fell away. I was in space, and the light was that red star. It was energy connecting the dimensions. That's how you know it was real."

She whispers solemnly, "And then when we toured the prison, you disappeared. They searched the whole complex for you as I drove myself crazy, and the whole time it was your idea of a sick joke, where you'd found your way home and acted totally innocent."

"Because I—*that* me—*was* innocent."

"And a couple of years later, you left us for good, Ker. There's no way to fix that, with all the time travel, alternate dimension, and BS excuses. It's over."

Agony sinks through me. It must be apparent on my face, because between glances at her, the anger seems to flush from her face to be replaced with sorrow. My heart feels as though it is buried in boulders a mile deep as my spirit suffocates within. Peering at Ian only makes the anguish travel deeper. In response, my muscles jitter and my pace increases, even with Vanessa weighing me down.

Perhaps one day I can prove myself right, if that's even possible. I consciously choose to put it off to another day or perhaps another year.

We reach the crest of a shallow hill, overlooking the destruction of downtown. The buildings that have not totally collapsed are only carcasses, with massive sections of concrete floors smashed, glass blown into billions of tiny bits, and composite exterior skins reduced to rubble. Somewhere in all that stands the tower where I am working as a construction laborer, but without context it may or may not exist yet. Searching the skyline for where that building should stand, I see bent pieces of red iron, buckling concrete, and a core of which entire sections have crumbled. Assuming it is the correct building adds context. This would be some point in the future for me, perhaps paralleling a stage after Becky and I will meet for the first time.

Narrowing my eyes, I propel us across an abandoned street lined with hundreds of burned out or idle cars. A blur beyond the buildings suggests that whatever has sacked downtown Philadelphia is moving north along the river. I already know what it is before I see it.

The black, winged beast—the mighty Typhon. It incinerates an entire neighborhood block in one breath and squeals in the distance with every sound I have ever heard, including Sarah's transcendent voice.

You know how to find me.

The trek is as arduous as any journey through the city ever could be. Instead of dodging throngs of pedestrians and tourists, however, we must navigate over mounds of debris from collapsed buildings and smoldering embers. At the outskirts of downtown, the destruction grows thicker.

Where once a modest twenty-story office high rise stood, a dusty pile of broken concrete now sits, fifty feet tall. It reeks of death. Heavy slabs have been cracked in a million directions, some separated into multiple huge chunks. Rusted and twisted rebar lies exposed to the elements as we pass, and beyond are more buildings lying in heaps of concrete and structural steel.

Without landmarks to guide me, I can do little more than guess where the theater may lie. Ahead I make out a jumble of painted bricks and concrete. When we near it, I can recognize it as the destroyed façade of an aging building whose side wall had been decorated in a fifty-foot-tall mural depicting clear skies, green trees, and soaring birds. The building is only a few blocks east of the theater.

Switching to a side street caked with destruction, I ease along shattered storefronts whose curtain walls have been utterly ripped open. Metal twists like the wires of a sheared chain link fence, and piles of glass are spread out from the curb to the darkened insides.

Above the storefronts, a fifteen-story building stands with concrete floors intact, but its face has been entirely removed. Two blocks away, a skyscraper seems to lean toward the river, as if about to tumble to its fate. Cars of various ages are burned out, smashed from fallen debris, or merely desolate, all lying along the street.

Breathing heavily, I make out the boulevard. The traffic lights have been toppled and lie as dark, tubular poles amidst the ruins. I swallow hard the moment I feel an eerie presence creep up behind us.

Darkness towers high overhead along broken streets, like a huge wall of billowing smoke. The wind whips up loose chunks of brick, concrete, and glass, flinging a storm of deleterious confetti at us, which could shred our bodies if we cannot find shelter.

It burns blacker in the night, a creeping stain devouring what is left of the city.

You shall not escape this time. You are mine!

"I can never be yours," I mumble, without realizing I am repeating something I had told Vanessa seemingly ages ago.

"We're going to die," Becky rasps out when she sees it.

I drag Vanessa onward as she trips over a heavy chunk of concrete with broken stems of embedded rebar. She manages to shake off the obstacle and keep pace with me as Becky trudges through the ruins parallel to my path. Walking in the center of the street offers a clearer, safer path to the theater, but the raging storm of glass and concrete dust could tear us apart before we make it. Then again, if we don't make it to the janitor's closet, the Elder Shade will make us all cease to exist entirely.

Electing to take the clearer, faster route, I step out into the street and attempt to shield Vanessa from any more harm, while Becky does the same for Ian.

A shard of glass digs painfully into my back before a large, heavy brick is heaved right at my head. It smashes against my skull with a weight I have never felt, yet I manage to stay upright until we reach the shaded entryway to the theater.

Our feet splash in running water at least an inch deep on the tiled floor as we venture into the ruins. We pass the concessions desk and meander through fallen pipes and ducts, twisted ceiling grids, and crumbled tiles, until we reach the carpeted ramp which runs parallel to a clean wall that once displayed posters advertising upcoming movies. When we are safe inside, the wind transforms into a steady howl interspersed with loud, heavy bangs from equipment colliding violently with the structure, or banks of piping falling to the floor in one of the auditoriums. I keep to the handrail along the ramp and climb quickly.

The Elder Shade is about to swallow the whole building in one smoky gulp. I shove Becky and Ian into the closet, the door of which has been removed from its hinges. They disappear into the blackness before I cross the threshold with Vanessa leaning on my shoulder. Her blood is staining my shirt, and she clings to me desperately as we vault through a vacuum of stars, where there is no destruction, no Elder Shade, and no us—only a big red star gently pulling our invisible bodies into its gravity. A second later, we crash down once again into gravel.

29

Asteria Rising

The surface of the water is like glass, reflecting millions of pinprick stars that seem to undulate in my perception. The sounds of nature are as calm as the water's surface, and no wind rustles through the trees. The ambience is unnerving.

Vanessa's blood still stains my hand red. Staring at it for far longer than I should lends a stark understanding of innocence lost and reminds me of mortality. Even goddesses are not immune. Her heart rate seems erratic as she leans against me, resting her bloody scalp on my shoulder and attempting to inhale.

Every empty moment devoid of conversation adds fuel to a growing paranoia that we are about to be attacked by a horde of monsters or water ghosts. Impatiently I scan the horizon for signs of the Elder Shade, but the nocturnal tranquility remains unbroken, except for the wordless complaints of four weary and injured travelers.

Pressing Ian's face against her dirty blouse, Becky issues a harsh sigh to comfort Ian as he aimlessly and vacantly stares out at the lake. I hope that any moment now Ariadne will appear and guide our way, but so far all is calm.

"Talk to me, baby," Becky whispers, standing up, glancing around at her surroundings, and taking Ian by the hand.

Before she has managed to take a step, I wager that she's about to make a beeline for the cabin and call for an ambulance, which may not be a bad idea considering the seriousness of our injuries. Still, being lost in time is not a prospect worth muddying with more dimension-bending.

I hold out one hand as sign for her to stop. "We are not there yet."

"Ker, this is—"

"Not the right dimension."

Her insistence on helping may be commendable, but if I don't get her home soon, the consequences could be too steep to imagine. To avoid thinking about it, I grasp Vanessa's shoulders and decide to explain my plan to any who will listen.

"We gotta get to the island."

"No one has ever been there," Becky says, perhaps believing in one of a dozen or so urban legends that no doubt explain the island's mystery.

"I know someone who has."

"It's her, isn't it?" Vanessa rasps.

I already know both of us are thinking about the same person. Chills race through my body as the memory catches up with me.

Suddenly, I can see her. She flashes me a warm smile while casting her eyes shyly at her feet, bending one knee as if to curtsy. Her flawless beauty is breathtaking. And then I hear her voice. *"Bye, Larry, it's been a pleasure working with you."*

And then, she drifts away like tiny snowflakes on a subtle ground breeze. She is departing, and sadness fills my heart.

I nod slowly as Vanessa glances up at me while clutching my shoulder for support.

"I should stay and call emergency," she says slowly, gazing out over the crystalline waters. "Then again how do I explain what's happened? They'd send me to the *other* kind of hospital."

"The only way is to come with me."

"You say so," she says, curiously leaving out the 'if.'

"Where's the boat?"

I scan the island's shoreline. Depending on where we have ended up in time, the canoe could be on this bank or on the island.

"Of course it's over there," I mutter. "We're never going to get there without drowning or freezing to death."

"Would be really helpful to have wings right about now," Vanessa says, probably only half-joking.

If only if it could be that easy. We could call on the Icarus to glide us right over, pay it our admiration, and end the ordeal. But the Icarus can only appear when there's sun and, judging from the positions of the moon and stars, I would guess it is somewhere near midnight here—long after Vanessa and I rowed to the island the last time as the hundred-eyed winged monster sought to eat us.

The only way is through the reeds. In the shape we are in, it will take us an hour. I start in that direction, still supporting Vanessa's weight. Begrudgingly, Becky trails along, holding Ian to her chest like a cold football.

"We're going to make it," I say, more to reassure myself than the three of them. Perhaps being a leader in this situation comes naturally, but offering vague, insincere assurances seems to betray everything I thought I believed about myself.

"Of course we are," Vanessa says. "You've always been the navigator."

I gulp. "We've known each other, what, three days?"

Her voice wavers as she speaks, but gradually grows steadier. "Give or take a hundred years."

I manage to laugh without smiling, which causes a heavy ache to press into my stomach. "I don't think it works that way."

"It does if it's in someone else's dimension."

My heart leaps at the suggestion. If she's alluding to what I'm guessing at, there is far more to our story than I know. I lower my head while shuffling painstakingly through the gravel toward the dock and the reeds beyond.

"I don't think I want to know."

"Destiny," she breathes. "It's always been you. I can't tell you how I know it, but it's true. It may be my truth, but that doesn't stop it from applying to you—if you can find it in your heart."

"I need to find Sarah," I stammer.

The boat dock seems to glow with the moonlight on its wet surface. No boats are moored to its columns, and removing a section to float across the waters would be impossible. We'll get to the rocky outcrop beyond the reeds before deciding on how to get across to the island. Taking on seemingly insurmountable challenges one task at a time serves to spread out the worry, making subsequent steps easier by comparison.

Deciding that Becky will be fine guiding Ian through the marsh, I grasp Vanessa's hand tightly. The activity seems to make her feel colder with every step we take, as though the life is slowly draining out of her.

"Not losing so much blood now," I say to myself, taking relief in the fact that her bleeding has ebbed. That could either be a good sign or a bad one, but the fact that she's talking makes it seem better.

Allowing new memories to invade my soul, I trudge through the muddy reeds, keen to grasp at steadier stalks. I am watching for the staghorn tree. We wade through the ankle-deep mud in silence for what feels like an age.

Becky's breathing gradually grows deeper and more erratic.

"Are you okay, babe?"

"Don't you,"—*gasp*—"call me that."

"You're still angry..."

"Not angry, just over you. Over us." Agony strikes at my soul. The bitterness in her voice seems to shred my conscience and press acid through my brain. If only she could realize that I don't *remember* her memory, we could be on the same page.

Before I can utter another thoughtless word, I remember what Vanessa had said to me moments ago. If this is my dimension, then the Becky in this dimension may or may not be the 'real' Becky. It sounds more and more confusing as I work it through my mind. If I had the heart to do it, I would ask Vanessa what it meant. Still, perhaps I'm better off not knowing.

The dead tree with its antler branches stands slightly to our left, indicating that we have trudged what I deem to be a safe distance from the water's edge. The gentle slope of the land has allowed most of the moisture to ebb away, leaving the mud firmer, thus allowing us to move faster.

I gaze up at the tree as we pass by. It seems to loom taller than it did the last time I walked through here. The memory of it is burnished in my brain by now. We can't be far away.

A slow, steady upslope begins soon after passing it, and as a result the reeds thin out and give way to taller grasses, which then yield to hard, rocky earth. We emerge from the thicket at the foot of the large rock with the hearty brush growing out of its base.

Hope flashes through me as we inch closer. The white, fluffy hood is mostly hidden, and the gray back makes it look like a protrusion of granite in the scant light. My heart leaps as I lay eyes on it.

"This belongs to you," I say to Becky.

She stares at it. "I've never seen it in my life."

"What? That means—"

"Larry?" Vanessa clutches my arm and turns me to face the rocky outcrop leading to the channel between the mainland and the island. I swivel my head in that direction and see a small miracle. The canoe is still floating at the base of the rock, tied to a stout shrub with a narrow thread of twine.

"Funny," I say. "I swear we left it on the island."

She nods. "We did. It's not there anymore."

"How?"

Becky starts toward it as our feet shuffle in the grass. "It's a tourist destination. Probably someone went out there on a jet ski and took it for a ride."

The solution to the problem seems a little too convenient for me to believe, but then again what with all we've been through, we should take a little relief without questioning how it came to be.

Carefully, we load Ian and Vanessa into the canoe. The oar Vanessa used to defend us from the monster still rests within. The shotgun is gone.

Becky nestles next to Ian, gazes out at the still water, and allows me to row. Vanessa seems content, but through her breathing and relative silence, I can sense that she's in pain. If she can just hold out a little longer, I can get her to safety. It doesn't occur to me until are halfway to the rocky island beach that I have not yet been back to my present day from this island. I don't know the way.

I had not thought about that fact when I made my plan to take Becky and Ian through the closet, climb into the attic of the lake house, and then land softly in Becky's bed safely in her present day before bidding them goodbye and continuing on to find Sarah.

My heartbeat seems to grow wild the closer we get to the island. When I splash into the water and help Vanessa out of the boat, a comfortable warmth fills me. A hope I cannot explain burns through my chest and begins to pulse.

My limbs have not yet started to glow, but the energy is surreal. It gives me the strength to help Vanessa up the steep slope, around large boulders, through dense brush, and under low-hanging tree branches.

When we've reached a gap between two huge trees, I feel eyes staring at me from the opposite shore. Hundreds of red eyes, homing in on us. The beast takes flight as an ear-splitting screech tears the ambience to shreds. Thunder rages from afar. Unaware of how fast my feet are moving, I help Vanessa climb until we reach the porch, and then double back at least a hundred feet downslope to help Becky and Ian.

The monster bears down on us.

Typhon will slay.

I lunge, pressing Ian up onto the porch, and then heave Becky upward so that she is sitting on the elevated planks looking back at me in confusion. The energy seems to radiate through my hands to hers. Within a split second, the anger and sadness flushes from her face. How am I doing this? I reach deep down into my heart to drag out what I really want to say, but I cannot form the words. The only thing I can do is gently grasp her waist and kiss her. Just one tiny peck on the lips—it floods me.

The monster flaps high above, locking onto us intently as Vanessa escorts Ian into the relatively safe cabin before reappearing at Becky's side. Breathing deeply, she grunts as she hoists Becky to her feet. I motion them to get inside the cabin before the monster incinerates us all.

Tucking its wings sleekly to its back, the beast speeds forward, belching an orange blossom of flame. Twenty feet above me, it pauses in midair and beats its wings to remain stationary. I hold one hand aloft to shield me from the flame that never comes. The energy pours out of my hand like a cool, faint white light. The red in the hundreds of eyes turns to pink.

"KILL."

The thundering voice makes the water at the shores vibrate and sends eerie ripples in all directions.

It again attempts to launch its attack, but the energy keeps it at bay.

Darkness roils in the forest. Helplessly, the monster inhales, pushes out a stream of flame hot enough to set my clothes on fire, and then slams itself to the ground, hoping to claw its way up the slope.

I leap down from the porch to confront it. Its many eyes grow hungrier as it struggles toward me, and I allow it.

The howl encompasses every sound I've ever heard: a chainsaw, an Air Force jet plane, screaming children, and Sarah's assurance. It emits another torrent of fire, belches smoke, and rears back.

Before I know what is happening, Vanessa has reappeared at my side. I bend down to pick up a rock at my feet that is slightly smaller than my fist. Holding it aloft, I somehow know what it will do before I hurl it.

I rear back, shouting in victory as Vanessa emits a blood-curdling scream. The energy pours into the rock as I release it, accelerating it to the velocity of a sniper rifle bullet. The rock smashes through the monster's head, obliterating its skull. Its wings and body ignite in a cascade of red flames as it falls to its doom below us.

Vanessa whimpers as I stare at the twitching, defeated creature. Spinning to help her back to the porch, I meet the horror in her eyes.

Something has happened that I cannot explain. She coughs up blood, bends over, and vomits a reddish pool of bile in the dust at her feet. Rushing to steady her, I whisper helplessly.

"Go," she whispers. "It was fun while it lasted, wasn't it?"

"No, Vanessa. Hold on."

Looking up, her eyes seem to bleed with untold sympathy. She lets her expression warm, staggers on her feet, and presses a look of serenity straight through my heart.

"You're a Titan."

"Vanessa! No!"

She loses her balance, releases her grip on my elbow and falls to the dirt at my feet.

"Vanessa! God, Vanessa!"

No response. My heart sinks into my chest as the energy drains away from me. I can only stare at her still body as her solemn eyes glass over. She stares beyond me into the vastness of space. The galaxies spin in her eyes as I search them for signs of life.

"Noooooo!"

My voice rasps in my throat. Every pain I have ever felt swells within me as tears roll down my face.

Becky stares on from the porch as I pour my heart into the heavens. Fear compresses her expression to a mere moan. Out across the lake, the darkness ripples.

The Elder Shade is here to finish the job. I am defeated; Ariadne's gift can no longer help me.

Becky silently helps me onto the porch, quivering in terror. I dare not open my eyes, as more tears stream from them. How can I be responsible for the fall of the Great Bear, Callisto herself? I'm too foolish to admit I'm a fool. Rage at my own weakness boils within me as the winds flatten acres of trees behind the row of beach houses.

I glance back as it erodes our lake house plank by plank, absorbing it into a billowing stack of heavy smoke.

We enter the darkness and encounter Ian sitting silently in a chair at the table. He stares down at a book held limply in his hands, blankly turning the pages, and glances back up to his mother. The terror he must be feeling is unthinkable, but for the moment it doesn't matter.

Pulling it gently out of his hands, I study the spine and turn it over in my fingers. *The Soul of the Baron.* Ian knows this book, and with a sudden flourish of memory I do, too. I relate to the Baron because he echoes something deep within me: silent resolve.

Flipping through the pages, I stand up and feel my fingertips tingle. The freshness of my tears feels cold against my face.

The Elder Shade will not have stopped, but for the moment it doesn't matter. Once again, I fling my arms around Becky, and whisper "I'm sorry" three times. Each time, it feels like a dart plunging deeper into my abdomen.

"Fear not."

These are not the words of Erebus. A higher power somewhere translates them through my brain wordlessly. I feel myself letting go of Becky, turning to the place I'd seen Sarah before as a spirit—sad and alone.

The warmth resonates through me.

When I open my eyes, she is there and we're alone on a cold night. She looks deeply into my eyes, wraps her arms around my shoulders tightly and lets it all flow through her.

"I must be hallucinating still," I stammer.

"It's real," she says into my shoulder. "You found me."

"I ... the Elder Shade ... I'm either dreaming or dead."

For a moment, she says nothing. Then, gradually pulling away from me, she takes my hand in hers. The energy returns to my fingertips.

"It was cold that night, wasn't it? They got the snow part of the forecast right, at least. I couldn't believe you could tell I was there."

"How?"

"I don't remember everything," she explains, staring deeply into my eyes. "One day, I was cleaning behind a plant at the office ... you know the one. The tall one with big leaves behind reception, at the general's trailer? And something tugged on me. Painful at first, but it led me somewhere different. And before I knew it, it was like the office was fading away. It felt like years had gone by, and I was somewhere in between times. Always right at the edge, between one place and the other. I think I saw myself flash a few times, but I could feel myself moving around. When I went home that night, it all felt normal. But then the next morning I went to investigate, and it pulled me right in. And I've been stuck in this limbo ever since. It's taken years, but you've finally found me. And I didn't even know you were looking."

"Of course I was looking. Sarah—there's something I have to tell you."

"I know," she says. "You don't have to say it."

Our lips touch gently and momentarily. She reaches up with one hand, dries the tears from my cheeks, and then places both hands in mine.

"Do you trust me?"

"I guess?" I stammer.

Silently we begin to fade, our arms, faces, and legs transforming into mist, molecule by molecule as the cabin around us stretches, waning as it goes. The stars whiz beyond us as we swirl around a giant red star that I know all too well. We are invisible, as though all the matter in our cells has been converted into energy. We hurtle around the star at impossible speeds, yet it feels like we are hardly moving at all.

My heart pulses as we near what seems to be a space probe. This isn't our sun, I think; how could it be? The gravity pulls us into a tight orbit, and all the while I stare into her eyes and feel her heart, even though we are both invisible. Again the scene speeds up, flinging us at light speed to the nearest planet.

Home—or more accurately, the office.

The steel columns rise four hundred feet skyward as a chilly sun leaks over our faces. A steady breeze filters through her hair as we look on at the clear plastic flapping in the breeze hundreds of feet up the skeleton of steel. When the building is finished, we will both be able to look upon the skyline of Philadelphia with pride, knowing what we have contributed to the rich tapestry of the city we love. We could live here forever if the rest of the memory weren't so hauntingly real.

Her next words prove it.

"I'm moving to Portland in a few weeks, to take care of my grandmother. She's resting well in the hospital right now, and the doctors say she has about a year left. Of course, you can come visit me, or I could come here. It might be fun."

"You don't sound too sad about that," I say, trying not to seem callous.

"I hardly know her, but she's family. And she only has me and my dad."

"I think visiting sounds wonderful."

Her mission has come to a fitting conclusion. If we end up in a long-distance relationship, I could find my way through it. Having brought her back successfully, perhaps I owe her.

But my quest isn't over. Becky and Ian will not know how to get to their lake house in the correct dimension. Frowning, I try to form a plan.

"Can you take me back to the lake? I mean, is that possible? I have something else I need to do."

"I think we can find a way. Come with me."

She grasps my hand and leads me up the diamond-plate steel ramp without placing her free hand on the railing. The plant is pulled away from the wall when we enter, and for the moment no other office workers are lurking. She pulls me behind the reception desk, crouches behind the plant, and an unexplainable force grips me around my midsection, yanking me into a black ether filled with a billion stars.

Within moments we are standing on a firm wooden floor as the room around us materializes. Becky and Ian are huddled at the table and flipping through the book, completely safe from the Elder Shade. Ian glances up at me, offers me a warm smile, and pulls me into a comfortable embrace.

30

Tethys Spring

The interior air smells dank and musty like an unfinished basement, yet the heat rises toward once-polished timber rafters covered by uniform roof slats. When Ian releases me from his grip, I kneel next to him so that we can speak eye to eye.

"Are you doing okay?"

He doesn't answer, but a glimmer of hope has touched his eyes.

"Everything that happened will take some years to process, but maybe that'll be better for you. I want you to promise me one thing."

Again he doesn't speak. Instead, he lowers his eyes and lets his shoulders slouch. Becky looks on with tears streaming down her cheeks. I catch my heart murmuring as I glance at her. It will be harder for her to let go than for Ian, and probably even me, but I know she has it in her.

"You keep everything up here." I gently rest two fingers on his forehead, looking perhaps more somber than I intended.

"It's still out there," Becky guesses. "I don't know where you disappeared to, but you were only gone for a few seconds."

A few seconds? It had to be at least twenty minutes to my perception. That's either a great sign or a bad one. I'm not interested in figuring out the math right now.

"Why hasn't it devoured us yet?" I wonder.

She tries to answer but fails to form anything resembling a sentence.

"Because it knows what I possess."

Ian nods slowly. "I won't tell anyone. It's a secret."

"I think you can discuss it with your mom in private. Maybe it will help you both to come to terms with it. And if I ever come back, you can confide in me."

Becky casts her eyes at the rocking chairs in front of the fireplace, before attempting to gauge how I feel. Then she drills a hole in my heart with a look resembling longing. "Are you going to come back?"

"Let's get you home. I know the way."

"We have to go out there?" her eyes widen, and her hands twitch at her waist.

I can comprehend the fear she feels; the Elder Shade is built out of fear. It feasts on it and grows ever more powerful from it. But fear has its equally powerful opposite that fuels the gift from Ariadne. Fear can never win an even match against hope if the latter is nourished and cultivated.

"I know another way: the closet."

"No," Becky says. "I'm not going through any more of this."

"You can't stay here. This is not home for you—or for me. You stay here and that *thing* gets you. I don't want that to happen."

My logic wins her over, but she visibly rehashes it in her brain before taking my hand. She and Ian breathe deeply before I tiptoe around the corner, push open the door into the darkness, and guide them in. After they vanish, I step in after.

Falling is always a remarkable feeling. The weightless sensation causes the nerves to spike, sending tingling throughout the body, and the fear of landing causes brain tremors. I land on top of something hard and Becky yelps in pain.

Rolling off her, I clutch Ian tightly in my arms. If my understanding is correct, we have one more portal to travel through. Becky slowly climbs out of the bed and looks at me as if through untamed anger. She slowly folds her arms across her stomach and waits for me to comfort Ian.

When he settles down, I ease off the bed and hold Ian's hand. He squeezes mine tighter than I squeeze his. I can't bear to look out the window over the lake, so I instead allow my heart to settle.

Guiding them out of the bedroom, I soothe my nerves the best I can. The chair is still in the hallway under the access door, which looks like a black square. The house should have burned down seconds after Vanessa and I fell through the portal, yet we stand in the hall and there is no orange glow coming from outside.

Have we emerged in a different dimension of the same time? That destroys the physical laws of time travel I have built up in my own mind. Harley is going to get an earful when I see him again—

I shouldn't be remembering his name, either. I have spent too long in other dimensions. The unease creeps up in my spine as I signal Becky toward the chair.

"You up first, then you can help Ian."

"Ker, why are we going into the ceiling?"

"That's the way home," I say, trying to explain it in the simplest terms possible. I know, but what I don't know is what it's going to be like once we're there. Dread builds within me, but I purposely suppress it.

Fear not.

"Are those—are the women going to attack again?" Becky's tone picks up toward the end of her sentence, indicating panic.

How can I assuage that with my internal hope? It is never going to work because Becky exists in a sphere outside my own. 'One flesh' had always been meant as a unit, but when a single unit has two distinct properties, how can those properties reliably interact? A unit of velocity is measured in meters per second, two distinct dimensional measurements, but when time is subject to distortion, how can distance remain so rigid?

"I can't stay long," I say, lowering my voice, without trying to feel how she will react.

"Why are you always running? Whatever you were dealing with, I would have helped you cope. All you had to do was ask."

She climbs onto the chair slowly, to test its sturdiness. Still shaky about the prospect, she climbs onto the armrest and pushes herself to stand while using the back of the chair and my right hand as a guide.

"I have to go, because I am supposed to be in Philadelphia in 2020. I don't remember the events like you do. It is just a series of images that have arisen in my brain. I don't know how to properly say I'm sorry for that—for any of it, but you have to believe me."

"We hadn't met yet," she says, steadying herself on the armrest before raising her foot to place it on the chair back.

I rest my knees near the front of the cushion and then use her hand to climb to a standing position so that I can act as a counterweight to keep the chair from falling backward. She can barely reach the wood framing at the opening so I will have to hoist her upward with my arms at least six inches before she can use the trusses to pull herself the rest of the way.

Wrapping my arms around her waist, I push my back foot down against the cushion and lift her up until she can grasp the framing members. Fearing to let her dangle, I hold onto her legs to steady them while she shimmies upward into the dark.

Getting Ian into the attic should prove much easier, yet he has clearly developed a resistance. He subtly backs away from the chair as I tower over him, extend my arm, and try to cover my face with a fatherly love, which probably doesn't look anything like it because I'm unfamiliar with the idea of being a father.

"Son, you can do this. There's one more portal, and you will be home safe and sound."

He relents after a moment's hesitation, yet not fully trusting me. I can feel his jitters vibrate through his hand and body as I lift him to my shoulders and wait for Becky to reach out of the darkness.

She grips onto him by the underarms and pulls him up. Together, they crawl away from the opening before Becky returns to help me. Pulling myself up using her hand and the opening frame seems easier than it was the last time. When my knees contact the hard planks above the ceiling, I wrap both arms around her and let the tension melt away.

"Becky, I can't say I'm sorry enough for putting you through all this. You deserve a better man than me."

She says nothing, but I can feel her heart beating faster and warmer. The energy once again builds within me. The luminance glimmers around my wrists. Instead of releasing her, I pull her tighter into an embrace I hope will never end. Still, it must. Staying here would damage time and cause even more destruction, because Erebus is still seeking me.

"We're going to go into the chute," I say. "Tomorrow, I want you to call a contractor and seal it. Stuff it with insulation and fill the hole with brick. The better you seal it off—"

"The more permanently you stay away."

"I never meant to hurt you."

She sighs and wipes a tear from her cheek. "You ... you still did. That's something that doesn't just heal in a night, regardless of how sincere your apology is. You can't ever put it right because it's done. And now you're saying ... I'm never going to see you again. I c-can't do this, Kerry. I love you too much to let you go."

Tears roll down her cheeks so profusely that my body trembles with untapped sorrow. How could I have been so foolish? Perhaps if I'd never ventured off on the wild quest to save Sarah, she would have remained intact, yet the experience of being with Becky for any amount of time is something I wouldn't give up for anything. It is clearer than ever, and I must admit it.

I heave with a heavy sob as I hold her tight. Ian looks on from a safe distance.

"I love you too. If I had to come back and do it all again, I wouldn't. And your memory of this moment will wash away eventually."

We must get moving. I lead the way toward the chute. The loose nail digs into my knee painfully. Within a minute, we reach the portal.

"You first," I say to Ian. "When you land, get off the bed immediately or your mother will land on you."

He nods and I position him backward in the opening. His eyes dart from side to side and his hands tremble. "It's not that far, and it's a soft landing. Trust me."

I can't believe I can say that with a straight face. In my experience, when someone demands you trust them, it is a bigger mistake to listen, because the truly trustworthy never beg for it—they expect it. Then again, I'm not trustworthy either. It will take a lifetime of learning to reach that milestone.

Becky kisses her fingers and presses them against his forehead seconds before he falls away into the dark.

"You next. I have to run out to that rock formation as soon as I land. Be ready because I don't know what's going to happen when I emerge."

She quivers as she pulls herself backward into the opening. I watch her fall away with agony writhing within me. If I never return to her, I don't know whether I'll ever be able to forgive myself. It hurts too much for me to survive as though nothing has happened, because it all did happen. I will grapple with that reality forever, and no amount of interdimensional time travel will ever be able to erase it.

Traveling through time is something I can never let myself do again, yet I have a couple of matters of unfinished business to attend to.

I wait a few seconds to position myself with my back to the chute, to allow Becky enough time to get out of my way. Then, frowning, I let myself go. Energy pumps through me as the sky sparkles with stars.

I bounce on the bed, gather my senses, and stare up at Becky and Ian, who share a warm embrace and wait for me.

"A promise is a promise," I say. "Everything is going to work out."

For once, I can feel the truth of my own statement brimming within me. I don't know how or when, but the cost of destiny is worth the reward. I gather them both into a tight embrace before backing away and fleeing into the hallway.

Living all this down will torment me for the rest of my life, but I guess I have accomplished what I'd set out to do.

Sarah will be waiting to see me at the reception desk. Would I ever want to have a relationship with her after everything that has transpired? I can't make that decision now. It might take years for it to finally make sense to me.

Running toward the front door, a thought pops into my mind. I stop and turn around just as Becky and Ian emerge from the bedroom. I can't believe it's still in my pocket.

I pull it out, roll it over in my fingers, and approach Becky quietly. She places one hand on my waist, plants a kiss on my lips, and holds her pose for what feels like a full minute. "Take care of yourself."

"I have something for you." I pull away a few inches, hold out her palm, and place the welded washers in her fingers. She clearly knows what they are without looking. Folding her hand loosely around it, she stares at me carefully for several seconds. "Always keep them near, and you'll remember me, because you'll remember what it means."

"What about Vanessa?"

"She's gone," I whisper. "I can't save her. If you pass on in a different dimension, you can't exist in any of them. I guess she's back home in the stars now."

"Is she really what she claimed to be?"

"A goddess. Callisto, the Great Bear. I'll never see the Big Dipper the same way again."

She smiles and lets her gaze linger on me for far longer than she should. Still holding the washers in her fingers, she drifts away, brushes a wave of tears from off her cheek, and lets me walk out the front door for the last time.

The trek across the road offers solitude and a chance to mourn Vanessa in a healthy way. She called me a Titan. I don't know what that means, but maybe it could mean a multitude of things. I can't be a Titan literally, because I'm not some reincarnated Greek deity, or at least I don't think I am.

Instead of dwelling on it, I think about Becky and Sarah as I make my way as silently as I can through the undergrowth. This portal will take me back to the beaten in-between dimension, but suddenly I remember the alleyway and the storefronts that the rioters had smashed.

I pull myself up to the standing rocks, rest quietly in the void, and allow the millions of trees to wash away like pure water from a brand-new spring. The spring is life renewed, perhaps the real meaning of the Fountain of Youth. Ponce DeLeon would love to hear my explanation, but I am sure I'm never going to meet him, because I'm done with it all. I have one more task to embark on, and I already know the way.

31

On Atlas's Shoulders

At dusk, the streets of Philadelphia seem normal. Throngs of tourists, long since departed, have left patches of litter in various locations. At this hour, only weary pedestrians scurry home from dismal jobs or head out for drinks and dinner. Birds soar overhead in formation, casting polka-dot shadows on sidewalks already pock-marked with oil stains and blackened chewing gum.

A particularly amorous couple retreats into the shadow of an unlit storefront inlet, in front of a single glass door leading to an elevator vestibule and a flight of stairs. I pass them without looking and weave between smaller groups of walkers, who mostly keep quiet. There is no chaos here, as if the Icarus has kept away and there is no Elder Shade eating up the horizon.

Before I flee this dimension, I need to make sure it isn't an alternative version of my own home time. This may seem a tall task, but one tiny detail from my previous trek into the border realm cuts into my mind like a glimmering shard of glass. Three storefronts down, after turning the corner from the alley, an abused and graffitied news stand box stood in blue and stainless steel against a brick wall. In case newspapers exist in this dimension, I make my way in that direction, working through the crowd until I am left staring at it. It is completely empty and damaged almost beyond comprehension. The plexiglass window has somehow been cracked open, allowing thieves to steal what may or may not have ever been in it, and the door's hinges are caked with rust and lie half-detached from the metal frame.

I frown, turn my attention to the storefront across the street, and watch a red ticker line streak across a vertical surface. It mostly advertises low-interest loan deals and free accounts, but then shows sports scores. When the line flashes with the Eagles' football score, I peer directly at the date, twelve-ten. Of what year?

To help me gather that information, I look up towards the glass towers, which reflect a quickly darkening sky with ominous clouds lingering over what is possibly New Jersey. Nothing looks out of the ordinary. No new high rises populate the skyline. One could trick me into believing that this is the same version of Philadelphia as the one I live in, but it is December, and my previous foray into the border realm was in the summer.

I tiptoe around a rusted red planter grate surrounding a piti-ful-looking single tree lashed to a sturdier hardwood stake. The stake has been punched into the hard earth and the grate has been cut to fit it.

Red leaves skitter across the sidewalk.

Memory from my previous visit fills my mind with images of a billboard being absorbed by the Elder Shade. Today it advertises an upcoming concert by a local rock band, which the local radio stations are heavily promoting. The same concert on the same date as the one I'd seen last time. Either the sign has been left unkempt in the meantime or the concert is being replayed. It is a small detail that I don't care about.

I barely remember how I escaped this realm the last time, when the rioters were smashing windows with Molotov cocktails, kickboxing in the streets, and worshiping Helios. It was on this side of the street. A flaming bottle pulverized a store window as a giant thug came at me, before being tackled by a tattooed guy with a bad attitude. There would have been a recess, but the chaos was so immersive that I didn't care how I got out. I did, right before the Elder Shade came to destroy it all.

No, those were two different events. My memory is fuzzy, proving Harley correct all those years ago when he described what the victim on the street had been wearing. He had made it all up but was so convincing with the details that he'd had me believing it.

How exactly is my memory supposed to function in this realm? If they had been two separate events, why can I remember both?

I have an idea why, but I need Harley to explain it to me. Chances are he still has that woman I rescued from another past. I can't leave her in modern-day Philadelphia and risk destroying time itself, and possibly the entire city.

Taking my chances that the two events happened near the same timeline, I go with my instinct to trust the clearest memory, when the rioters were on the rampage.

An open storefront, now abandoned, stands just before me. The overhang seems dark enough to support a dimensional portal. The door is set back some ten feet under the overhang, providing ample shadow for me to disappear into. A couple materializes out of thin air, and a small group of people vanish into the storefront. This is the only one that makes sense.

I swallow, gather my nerves, and step into the blackness.

I emerge into full daylight, with the dueling skyscrapers built atop older brick buildings cloaking the alley in shadow. The low roof parapet of the nearest tower rises about ten feet away from the tower's main trunk. A bird flutters through the air and lands on it; I am home.

The walk back to Harley's station takes longer than I'd anticipated. I'm not in a big hurry. Instead of rushing through traffic and fighting the crowds, I take my time so that I can appreciate every detail of being home. The memory and the importance of it drives energy through my heart.

On the street, the sun glints off the glass windows and stainless accents of a dozen tall buildings in the financial district, and beyond that, the historic streets are awash with tourists, all gravitating toward the famous Market Street.

The parking garage, where my car should still be, stands a block or so in the other direction. I stop at a crosswalk with a dozen other pedestrians, some hunkered down with their faces in their phones, some sipping on hot chocolate or coffee. The aroma is pleasant, if not rewarding.

I watch the clock tick down in red numbers kitty corner to where I stand. A dog yaps at a stranger and then backs away into a red fire hydrant, where a broken slab of concrete stands lifted from the surface of the sidewalk several inches and is painted in yellow to indicate a pedestrian hazard. This would be the same corner where the pedestrian had been hit by the car, and it seems as though it has been eons.

I cross the street, letting the cold air whip into my face. Reveling in how pleasant it feels, as opposed to being stung with a piercing cold, I erupt in a short-lived smile, gaze at a woman walking toward me, and then round the corner to pass the bakery.

Between there and where Harley usually hangs out, a clothing store advertises the best deals on the most current fashions and touts the best selection of stylish accessories. A woman exits, wearing a tan, tweed sun hat with a floral ribbon, and a sleek, striped skirt. She carries a designer bag flung over her shoulder and totes a shopping bag full of new clothes. Fifty feet away, Harley is gawking at her. Standing next to him is a woman I can barely remember. Her hair seems to have grown darker, and definitely cleaner. She wears modest, modern clothes, as opposed to the tattered rags she was wearing when I dropped her off here.

She recognizes me on sight and offers a polite smile.

Approaching out of the shadows next to her I see Joaquin, grinning like he'd just led his troops to a resounding RPG victory. He gapes at my appearance. My clothes are damp and covered with mud and dirt, and my hair is so filthy with sweat and grime that it might take a week of showers to get me feeling clean again.

"Damn, you look like you got cleaned out by the Chiefs line," Quin shouts over the din of traffic.

I don't dare reward him with a smile.

"How'd you fare against the Elder Shade? I hear you battled one."

"It," I say, approaching. There was only the one, the prime servant of Erebus. "And fifty-foot-tall skeletons, chimeras, a vicious hydra, the Icarus, The Typhon and about a dozen clones of it, some guys with no eyes, thousands of Naiads—"

"Damn. I take it you didn't find your invisible girlfriend?"

"Oh, I did, and about a million other things that I'm slowly forgetting about already." Turning to snarl at Harley, I continue, "Which leads me to you."

"The hell is Vanessa?"

I don't wish to talk about it. Instead, I pulverize him with a dozen questions on why time seems to be so fickle and how so many monsters could be out to get me when all I was doing was trying to rescue a random girl from a random timeline. It all leads up to my biggest question yet.

"Why can you visit the same dimension twice and end up in completely different circumstances? That happened a few times."

He considers the question and strokes fingers through his salt and pepper stubble. "Uncertainty Principle, or perhaps a hidden aspect of the Butterfly Effect. Remember when I was explaining the behavior of electrons in an atom?"

"Couldn't you have told me about it beforehand? Couldn't you have warned me about bumping into my future wife and our ten-year-old son, in several different places? You're as informed as you are sensitive."

He narrows his eyes, and Quin raises his palms to opt out of the discussion.

"Shit. Thanks, I guess."

"So tell me about it. Why can two different dimensions exist in the same time frame, and how is it that I can remember both after going through a half dozen other realms?"

"Future wife? Wouldn't peg you as the type. But it appears the traveling ain't so random. I never claimed to know all there was to know; I just told you to be careful." Looking me over, he adds, "Advice you seem to have ignored.

"There was once a physicist called Heisenberg. He suggested that we can't know both the position and speed of a particle, and the more we know about the particle's speed, the less we know about its position."

"I thought you preferred layman's terms."

"You and I are made of particles. Protons, electrons, photons. And they're all moving, all the time. Pick one out in my body and tell me how fast it is moving, or exactly where it is. I'll wait."

"You're a sorry excuse for a human being," I say, accusingly.

"Says the man who abandoned a stranger here, left his future wife, and lost the one woman I've ever loved."

"You and Vanessa?" I frown. "She couldn't have picked you out of a lineup."

"Never been in one. But to answer your question, think back to the accident here the other day. Memory is fickle and subject to outside interpretation. I would guess that a different dimension can have that same effect."

"This is why you don't put money on the Jets," Quin jabs, possibly referring to the game we'd watched together.

I turn to him and eye him carefully. "Ran into you a couple of years ago. Came into your office with Vanessa to ask you a question."

"You and the woman with really long braids, olive skin? Attractive, but yeah. First time we'd met in Philly."

"You think so?" Of course it hadn't been, but I already know why he remembers it differently than I do. It's because we met up with him in that dimension possibly months before we both knew we lived in the city. Then again, it was my alternate dimension, so why would it have affected his memory?

"Yeah. What, did travelling across time warp your memory?"

"Now that you mention it—"

"Where's Vanessa?" Harley jabs. "Son of a bitch."

I frown and gaze at my feet. Offering a full explanation is not something I'm in the mood for. It still punishes my mind with dark emotions that I can hardly contain. To stop myself from weeping, I put on my most masculine face and try to pretend I'm a robot with no feelings whatsoever. If it shields me from the torment of losing her, it works for me, and Harley doesn't deserve it.

Still, he doesn't deserve the abuse, either. After all, he *did* warn me. And I didn't take the threats seriously enough, for which I have paid dearly.

Regret fills my soul as I search his face. The realization dawns on him from my reaction, and the dour look on my face. Defeat; it does deceptive things to a man's ego, and Harley is showing me his.

If he wanted to, he could punch me, and then when I'm rolling on the ground in pain, kick me in the groin. Instead, he allows himself a moment to ponder the news, offers a slow nod, and lets a tide of sorrow cover his face.

"You can still see her," I explain. "Every time you look up at night and see the Big Dipper, part of Ursa Major, the Great Bear. Otherwise known as a goddess called Callisto."

"Mighty fine imagination you have," he says somberly.

Instead of rearing back to hit me, he collapses into me and pulls me into an embrace so tight that I can barely breathe. Understanding the news has brought humanity to us both, and clearly Harley considers me to be a close friend.

"You found the girl," he said. "Gonna go off and marry her now, leave me alone on the street like I never existed? You're a good guy, after all."

He releases me and watches me shake my head pensively and shrug. "Don't know. I'm—you know.... Becky."

"Thought you said her name was Sarah."

"There was another woman," I say. "Didn't want to say goodbye, but I had to. It might take me a few years to get over it. I would guess hours, with the way memory from future dimensions treats me, but how can you forget a woman like that so easily? I just ... need time."

"Jeezus, Larry," Quin says, gawking. "Always the softie. How you got *two* girls to like you I'll never know."

"Three, I think," I say, trying to remember how Vanessa felt about me. With her gone, it is fading quickly.

Instead of filling him in on more info he doesn't need to know, I take the woman's hand, watch her grin at the glittering skyline, and feel her rest a palm on my wrist. "Ready to go home?"

She nods, as though she suddenly understands English.

"Let's go." I walk her slowly down the street with hope tingling on my fingers and my heart working in overdrive. The tourists begin to gather around a bearded man holding a guitar, and some are fishing dollar bills out of their wallets to toss into his case.

He strums on the strings to create a dreary yet harmonious tune, and then begins to sing in a clear, glorious voice that sounds like the dewdrops of morning in a meadow. The harmony melts into my heart, and the last thing I hear before I round the corner with the woman on my forearm, is Harley shouting my name above the solemn song.

"Hey, is she really a goddess?"

I nod humbly, and with more power than I know, offer a simple sentence I can barely hear over the strumming of the guitar. "And I'm a Titan."

32

Ashes of Gaia

(Five years later)

Harrisburg is a beautiful, historic city surrounded by green forests and rolling hills. I'm about ten minutes early, arriving at the church and reserving a pew near the back of the chapel all to myself. It offers a good view of the podium while being far enough away to avoid drawing too much attention to myself.

The Reverend Jeff L. Martin is promising an uplifting sermon, and while the topic of discussion is still a mystery, I have heard good things about his speaking style. Maybe the message is exactly what I need.

The reason for my trip is ostensibly a history tour, but hours ago an interesting feeling crept over me. I don't want to call it a voice in my head—I don't really get those anymore, at least not ones that are not constructs of my own brain—but an odd *intuition*.

When I'm done with this trip, I'll no doubt head back to Philadelphia an unchanged man, having just heard a good sermon that doesn't apply to me in any way. That's what usually happens at church in my experience. I'll have lunch with Harley downtown, and maybe help Joaquin create some characters for his regular game meetup. I'm not a fan of role-playing games myself, but the fables draw my attention, and Quin is a fantastic artist.

The parishioners arrive in spurts, quickly filling up the pews toward the middle of the chapel, while leaving vast, empty rows of cushioned seats along the front. Dozens of people arrive during the choir's melody, and I close my eyes reverently to hear the message the reverend will offer.

After he is introduced, a hush falls over the congregation; I cross my legs with impatience, fold my hands in my lap, and listen to the reverend talk about some of the many wonderful people he's met during his travels.

He goes on a little longer than feels comfortable, yet I listen anyway.

"Some years ago," the Reverend continues, "I had the pleasure of travelling to London during the winter for a meeting with various faith leaders. After spending the night in a comfortable hotel room, I decided to ponder on what I might learn by talking a brisk morning stroll.

"The fog was so dense that if I extended my arm, I could barely make out my fingers. Such an unnerving phenomenon; but the fog can teach us a lesson.

"Being new to London, I didn't know my way around. It didn't take me long to get lost in the mist but having a general idea of the location of my hotel based on my relative direction of travel, I could somewhat accurately guess the correct way to move. Still, without landmarks as a guide, I could not see where I needed to go.

"But walking is an exercise as much for the spirit as it is for the legs. I had stopped to try to find my bearings. Instead of panicking, I put one foot in front of the other and took a step, and then another. After some time, I had found my way back.

"Brothers and Sisters, the Lord works revelation through us in re-markable ways. He trusts you to take a single step into the fog, which will let you clearly see your next step, and then your next, and so on.

"Revelation isn't always earth-shaking. It's more often built upon precept. You'll understand your destination more fully if you do the work to keep on walking."

The reverend may or may not have a point that I can apply to my life, but his talk seems illuminating enough. It could perhaps be his engaging style, or the warm, fatherly expression he so often bears. I don't know why it seems so familiar or true, but it does.

I listen to the rest of the sermon and move to stand before the choir is even finished singing. A beautiful young woman is sitting with her back to me, about five rows from the pulpit near the center of a long, padded pew. I exit into the foyer, where a pair of well-dressed young men are waiting. One of them smiles at me and asks how I enjoyed the talk.

"It was pretty good," I say, sincerely, but hoping not to offend.

"Have you heard about the summer party in two weeks? We've got some fun games, good food, conversation, and dancing. We'd really love to see you there. Maybe you'll meet some new friends."

"I live in Philly," I admit, "but maybe I'll head out this way."

I don't mean what I say. Work at the construction site is ramping up and Bones Holdings is asking all subs to work overtime with as much manpower as possible to meet the project deadline, which they say is behind. In two weeks, I'm going to be up to my ears in work, with Jamal issuing new demands. We are building a health club in the suburbs, a state-of-the-art spa with two full size swimming pools and a childcare wing. Getting back to Harrisburg will be nearly impossible.

Driving to the city along winding country highways gives me ample opportunity to reflect on the pastor's words. Is revelation something that can work for me personally? I haven't been to church in so long that I don't remember any of the words to the Lord's Prayer, and I haven't been particularly interested in it for ages. Not since that time travel debacle a few years ago, most of which I don't remember.

If I'm lucky, Sarah will be in town to celebrate the coming holiday. I'll have to text her and ask. I still haven't found the courage to ask her out, but maybe that day will come eventually.

The party is being hosted in a red barn building reserved for special events, just outside of the Harrisburg city limits. The farm stretches for several acres beyond the barn, some of which has been converted into a bumpy, gravel parking area. I'm probably late, and may have missed the food already, but the games sounded fun.

I made it here by a miracle. Two days ago, the jobsite shut down over a dispute with the swimming pool contractor, who was refusing to proceed on work due to an expensive change order that Bones doesn't want to pay for. "It's clearly spelled out in the project specifications to follow the manufacturing standards," the project manager had said, "and as required by legislation, to meet all health code requirements, the original intent of the construction documents stands until further notice."

And they've got the lawyers involved already. The politics of jobsite construction can be contentious and infuriating, but when large sums of money are involved, the politics necessitate litigation.

At the last minute, I found the party invite in my car and decided to drive to Harrisburg on a whim, thinking it couldn't hurt to get out of Philly for a while.

When I arrive, loud music is playing, and I can see some people dancing through the open barn doors. The barn is painted a traditional red, with a sectioned gable roof overhanging a bank of broad windows designed to allow more sun to light up the interior. The exterior walls on the long sides are flanked by large shade trees, which filter the sun and wave gently in the afternoon breeze. I enter through the overhead door and find a seat at a round table, away from the bigger groups. I don't know anyone here. If I'm still alone in ten minutes, I tell myself, I'll get up and go find someone to chat with, just to break the ice.

A large group of women has assembled around a blue plastic water cooler to fill up paper drinking cups while giggling about something. One of them is wearing a long blue dress with a pattern of white chevrons, stretching from the hem to the modest neckline. She is of an average build, several inches shorter than me, and sports sleek black hair that she has curled to frame a gorgeous face.

I shift in my seat when she glances in my direction and pretend to watch a couple dancing to some odd cowboy-bop music that is frustratingly annoying, made all the worse when people start to clap along with the beat.

I am sitting alone at the round table, and the woman in the blue dress has left her group. She pulls out a chair next to me and politely asks if she can sit. I attempt to strike up a conversation on anything other than the music, which almost immediately meanders to our professions.

"I'm an administrative assistant in the Harrisburg school district," she says.

"How long have you been doing that?"

"About three years," she explains, "after I graduated college. It's really rewarding, and you don't have to work with kids as much. What do you do?"

I lean back in the chair and clasp my hands together at the stainless-steel band around the perimeter of the table. She offers a polite smile and reveals white teeth and a pleasant aura. "Assistant foreman and construction labor captain," I say, trying not to make it sound so formal.

"That sounds interesting. What does it entail?"

I smile. "I work just under the job foreman, who is the head boss on the jobsite for the subcontractor I work for. I oversee the people running tools back and forth, transporting plans, keeping the tool bins and supply inventory organized. Six laborers, and I'm the lead. Good money, but I hope to make PM one day."

"Sounds ambitious," she says in a sing-song sort of tone, when the music switches to a better tune. It is a slower song, and a growing number of people rise out of their seats and wander onto the dance floor, leaving behind plates of half-eaten food and empty water cups.

The woman I'm talking to leans forward, smiles at me again, and asks my name.

"I'm Kerry. But some people call me Larry."

"It's good to meet you, Kerry."

Her face seems to melt the ice in my soul. Suddenly she's the most beautiful woman in the barn, and I don't even want to bother meeting anyone else. If I do it right, I can get her number by the end of the night, but I'm so horrible at meeting people that I'm sure I'll destroy my chances if I stay too long. Still, an unknown force seems to be holding me to the spot.

"It's Susanne, but you can call me Becky."

It's going to be a great friendship. I swallow a mouthful of water, push my chair back, and hold out my hand. "Care to dance, Becky?"

She agrees and we sway comfortably to the music. At the end of the song, I retreat to the table, and she follows. We exchange phone numbers before I even think about asking. I'll text her in a week and ask her out. I don't know what we'll do, but I promise myself that it will be the best evening of my life.

For once, there's promise in the future.

Acknowledgements

About twenty years ago (it must have been around 2003) I outlined a short story called "Walking Thin" that would later become this novel. The outline described a woman who goes invisible, while the hero, a young construction worker, tries to figure out what happened to her. As he searches, he uncovers a web of corruption among the contractors that he must solve to find the lost young woman.

I wrote a page or two of the story, which has become lost to time, but the idea stayed with me all these years in unwritten form. While I don't remember where the next push of inspiration came from, the basics of the story gradually started coming to life inside my brain. Originally, the invisible woman had an unusual medical condition that caused her to temporarily disappear, but upon further exploring the plot, it became clear that she was being transported to an alternative dimension.

You may have noticed that this story is narrated in first person present tense. Fantasy novels often revolve around world-building, and in the early stages develop numerous important characters. Authors mostly prefer the past tense. To bring a more current and personal feel to this story, this style and tense became necessary. I often struggle reading in this perspective because of tense confusion, which I hope I have satisfactorily avoided.

I began this novel with heavy references to astronomy, which I found to accurately parallel aspects of Greek mythology. As it turns out, many of the constellations and star formations in our night sky are named after mythological figures. Naturally the two concepts intertwined, and so formed the plot.

As a loyal reader, you likely know that I mostly stick to private investigator thrillers, which I plan to continue. But sometimes a writer has other stories that need to be told.

I usually take a modified "seat of the pants" approach to novel writing, where I envision a concept, identify some major events, and build out from there. I did almost no outlining with this book, which has allowed the story to naturally evolve, almost as if independent from the author's brain. Once I really got into writing it, it took only about nine months to complete the rough draft.

The "seat of the pants" style always engenders some holes, which the writer hopes to fill during subsequent edits.

A large amount of research went into this book, and I must credit certain works that helped in that regard.

First, I referenced *Peterson Field Guides: Stars and Planets* by Jay M. Pasachoff, to gain a general understanding of star maps, and the legendary stories inspiring the names of certain bodies. Internet searches on some of these characters keyed in details and relationships to others.

I took artistic liberty with a few of these legends, especially as they relate to actual characters in this novel. For instance, Ariadne's special gift is my own invention, and there is no mythological reference indicating that Callisto could ever have been reincarnated.

I also identified a part of the plot that needed a religious perspective, which so happened to coincide with one of the overarching themes of the story, which became the title. Jeff L. Martin is not based on any one religious figure, but his message about walking in the fog to receive revelation was inspired by a portion of a video lecture by Church of Jesus Christ Elder David A. Bednar titled "Patterns of Light: The Spirit of Revelation."

I do not remember who first shared Elder Bednar's message with me, but if you know who you are, know that I appreciate the inspiration. Also, I thank Elder Bednar for so thoroughly explaining one method of revelation in simple terms. I've avoided quoting him directly, but his words helped shape this aspect of the plot.

One thing I think many Christians get wrong is the idea of fearing God. Fear is a negative emotion that often leads to dark attitudes, anger, and hate. But the Hebrew word translated to mean fear, actually refers to awe, wonder, and loving respect. In a variety of phrasing, the Bible tells us to "fear not" three hundred and sixty-five times. It is my opinion that God does not want us to *fear* him. Ariadne's gift of energy would not have worked without hope, which in many ways is the antithesis of fear.

Having hopefully just finished reading, you will know that this book is not about religion. Fear can be ascribed to many aspects of modern-day life from personal and professional struggles to religion, to mortality, and even to politics. This novel explores all these facets and more; to tell a complete story, it must.

Now that I have that out of the way, I have some special thanks for those either directly or indirectly involved in this project.

Special thanks go out to my friend and fellow author Bernard K. Finnigan, who graciously agreed to beta read for me in order to help identify first draft problems and offer constructive feedback. I thoroughly enjoyed Mr. Finnigan's most recent science fiction novels *The Human Sliver* and *The Kinder Green*.

Once again, I give credit to the wonderful talents of Jeanine Henning, who designed both stunning versions of the cover art.

I have also opted to again work with Tarryn Thomas, who ran through the third draft line by line to correct spelling, grammatical, and character errors. Her touch and attention to detail is critical to a polished finished product.

Thank you to my family and friends, who have helped me though trying times. Even if it is only supporting my mental health, it is a huge benefit.

Last, but not least, thank you, loyal reader, for your continued support. Without you, there are no books.

-bm

About the author

Brad Mathews bends genre rules by creating dynamic, unorthodox characters thrust into criminal investigations.

He is known to use abstract imagery to construct striking realities that build into suspenseful mystery tales.

Mathews is Certified in Plumbing design, and his extensive Building Information Modeling experience gives him a unique ability to detail mechanical and industrial settings in his novels.

Mathews resides in Boise, Idaho with his family.